MARY CONNEALY

Montana Rose

BARBOUR
PUBLISHING

ISBN 978-1-60260-142-0

All scripture quotations are taken from the King James version of the Bible.

This book is a work of fiction. Names, characters, places, and incidents are either products of the author's imagination or used fictitiously. Any similarity to actual people, organizations, and/or events is purely coincidental.

Cover design: Lookout Design, Inc.

Published by Barbour Publishing, Inc., P.O. Box 719, Uhrichsville, OH 44683, www.barbourbooks.com

Our mission is to publish and distribute inspirational products offering exceptional value and biblical encouragement to the masses.

 Member of the
Evangelical Christian
Publishers Association

Printed in the United States of America.

I wrote *Montana Rose* shortly after reading Janette Oke's beautiful, classic romance, *Love Comes Softly*. I wanted to explore that same basic premise, a widowed, pregnant young woman in desperate need of a husband who has no choice but to marry a virtual stranger. Of course, in *Montana Rose*, as in everything I write, there is mayhem, disaster, comedy, and gunfire. I can't seem to control myself. For all the years of wonderful reading pleasure, and with my sincerest apologies for daring to compare even a tiny part of my work to hers, I'm dedicating this book to Janette Oke, a great spiritual as well as literary inspiration.

CHAPTER 1

Montana Territory, 1875

Cassie wanted to scream, *Put down that shovel!*

As if yelling at the red-headed gravedigger would bring Griff back to life. A gust of wind blew Cassie Griffin's dark hair across her face, blinding her.

For one sightless moment it was as if the wind showed her perfectly what the future held for her.

Darkness.

Hovering in a wooded area, concealed behind a clump of quaking aspens that had gone yellow in the fall weather, she watched the hole grow as the man dug his way down into the rocky Montana earth.

Muriel, the kind storekeeper who had taken Cassie in, stood beside the ever-deepening grave. If Cassie started yelling, Muriel would start her motherly clucking again and force Cassie to return to town and go back to bed. She'd been so kind since Cassie had ridden in, shouting for help.

In a detached sort of way, Cassie knew Muriel had been caring for her, coddling Cassie to get her through the day. But Cassie had gone numb since Muriel's husband, Seth, had come back in with the news that Griff was dead. Cassie listened and answered and obeyed, but she hadn't been able to feel anything. Until now. Now she could feel rage aimed straight at that man preparing the hole for her beloved Griff.

"I'm sorry, little one." Cassie ran her hand over her rounded stomach. "You'll never know your daddy now." Her belly moved as if the baby heard Cassie and understood.

The fact that her husband was dead was Cassie's fault. She should have gone for the doctor sooner, but Griff ordered her not to. At first Griff had been worried about the cost. He'd shocked Cassie by telling her they couldn't afford to send for the doctor. Griff had scolded Cassie if she ever asked questions about money. So she'd learned it wasn't a wife's place. But she'd known her parents were wealthy. Cassie had brought all their wealth into the marriage. How could they not afford a few bits for a doctor? Even as he lay sick, she'd known better than to question him about it, though.

Later, Griff had been out of his head with fever. She stayed with him as he'd ordered, but she should have doctored Griff better. She should have saved him somehow. Instead she'd stood by and watched her husband die inch by inch while she did nothing.

Cassie stepped closer. Another few steps and she'd be in the open. She could stop them. She could make them stop digging. Refuse to allow such a travesty when it couldn't be true that Griff was dead.

Don't put him in the ground! Inside her head she was screaming, denying, terrified. She had to stop this.

Before she could move she heard Muriel.

"In the West, nothing'll get you killed faster'n stupid." Whipcord lean, with a weathered face from long years in the harsh Montana weather, Muriel plunked her fists on her nonexistent hips.

Seth, clean-shaven once a week and overdue, stood alongside his wife, watching the proceedings, his arms crossed over his paunchy stomach. "How 'bout lazy? In the West, lazy'll do you in faster'n stupid every time."

"Well, I reckon Lester Griffin was both, right enough." Muriel nodded her head.

Cassie understood the words *lazy* and *stupid*. They were talking about Griff? She was too shocked to take in their meaning.

"Now, Muriel." Red, the gravedigger, shoveled as he talked. "Don't speak ill of the dead."

On a day when Cassie didn't feel like she knew anything, she remembered the gravedigger's name because of his bright red hair.

One of the last coherent orders Griff had given her was, "Pay Red two bits to dig my grave, and not a penny more."

Griff had known he was dying. Mostly delirious with fever, his mind would clear occasionally and he'd give orders: about the funeral, what he was to be buried in, what Cassie was to wear, strict orders not to be her usual foolish self and overpay for the grave digging. And not to shame him with her public behavior.

"Well honestly, it's a wonder he wasn't dead long before this." Muriel crossed her arms and dared either man to disagree.

"It's not Christian to see the bad in others." Red dug relentlessly, the gritty slice of the shovel making a hole to swallow up Cassie's husband. "And especially not at a time like this."

It was just after noon on Sunday, and the funeral would be held as soon as the grave was dug.

Cassie looked down at her dress, her dark blue silk. It was a mess. She'd worn it all week, not giving herself a second to change while she cared for Griff. Then she'd left it on as she rode for town. She'd even slept in it last night. . .or rather she'd lain in bed with it on. She hadn't slept more than snatches in a week. Ever since Griff's fever started.

She needed to change to her black silk for the funeral.

Cassie wanted to hate Muriel for her words, but Muriel had mothered her, filling such a desperate void in Cassie that she couldn't bear to blame Muriel for this rage whipping inside of Cassie's head, pushing her to scream.

"Well, he was a poor excuse for a man, and no amount of Christian charity'll change that." Muriel clucked and shook her head. "He lived on the labor of others 'n' spent money he didn't have."

"It's that snooty, fancy-dressed wife of his who drove him to an early grave," Seth humphed. Cassie saw Seth's shoulders quiver as he chuckled. "Of course, many's the man who'd gladly die trying to keep that pretty little china doll happy."

Cassie heard Griff's nickname for her. She ran her hands down her blue silk that lay modestly loose over her round belly. Fancy-dressed was right. Cassie admitted that. But she hadn't needed all new dresses just because of the baby. Griff had insisted it was proper that the dresses be ordered. But however she'd come to dress so beautifully in silks and satins, there was no denying she dressed more expensively than anyone she'd met in Montana Territory. Not that she'd met many people.

But snooty? How could Seth say that? They were slandering her and, far worse, insulting Griff. She needed to defend her husband, but Griff hated emotional displays. How could she fight them without showing all the rage that boiled inside her? As the hole grew, something started to grow in Cassie that overcame her grief and fear.

Rage. Hate.

That shovel rose and fell. Dirt flew in a tidy pile and she hated Red for keeping to the task. She wanted to run at Red, screaming and clawing, and force him to give Griff back to her.

But she feared unleashing the anger roiling inside her. Griff had taught her to control all those childish impulses. Right now though, her control slipped.

⤪⤪

"A time or two I've seen someone who looks to be snooty who was really just shy. . .or scared," Muriel said.

Red kept digging, determined not to join in with this gossip. But not joining in wasn't enough. He needed to make them stop. Instead, he kept digging as he thought about poor Cassie. She'd already been tucked into Muriel's back room when he'd come to town yesterday, but he'd seen Seth bring Lester Griffin's body in. He couldn't imagine what that little woman had been through.

"When's the last time she came into our store?" Seth asked. "Most times she didn't even come to town. She was too good to soil her feet in Divide. And you can't argue about fancy-dressed. Griff ordered all her dresses ready-made, sent out from the East."

Everything about Cassie Griffin made Red think of the more civilized East. She never had a hair out of place or a speck of dirt under her fingernails. Red had seen their home, too. The fanciest building in Montana, some said. Board siding instead of logs. Three floors and so many frills and flourishes the building alone had made Lester Griffin a laughingstock. The Griffins came into the area with a fortune, but they'd gone through it fast.

"That's right," Muriel snipped. "*Griff* ordered them. A spoiled woman would pick out her own dresses and shoes and finery, not leave it to her man."

Seth shook his head. "I declare, Muriel, you could find the good in a rattlesnake."

Red's shovel slammed deep in the rocky soil. "Cassie isn't a

9

rattlesnake." He stood up straight and glared at Seth.

His reaction surprised him. Red didn't let much upset him. But calling Cassie a snake made Red mad to the bone. He glanced over and saw Muriel focusing on him as she brushed back wisps of gray hair that the wind had scattered from her usual tidy bun. She stared at him, taking a good, long look.

Seth, a tough old mule-skinner with a marshmallow heart, didn't seem to notice. "This funeral'll draw trouble. You just see if it don't. Every man in the territory'll come a-running to marry with such a pretty widow woman. Any woman would bring men down on her as hard and fast as a Montana blizzard, but one as pretty as Cassie Griffin?" Seth blew a tuneless whistle through his teeth. "There'll be a stampede for sure, and none of 'em are gonna wait no decent length of time to ask for her hand."

Red looked away from Muriel because he didn't like what was in her eyes. He was through the tough layer of sod and the hole was getting deep fast. He tried to sound casual even though he felt a sharp pang of regret—and not just a little bit of jealousy—when he said, "Doubt she'll still be single by the time the sun sets."

Muriel had a strange lilt to her voice when she said, "A woman is rare out here, but a young, beautiful woman like Cassie is a prize indeed."

Red looked up at her, trying to figure out why saying that made her so all-fired cheerful.

Seth slung his beefy arm around Muriel with rough affection. "I've seen the loneliness that drives these men to want a wife. It's a rugged life, Muriel. Having you with me makes all the difference."

Red understood the loneliness. He lived with it every day.

"She's a fragile little thing. Tiny even with Griff's child in her belly. She needs a man to take care of her." Muriel's concern sounded just the littlest bit false. Not that Muriel wasn't genuinely concerned. Just that there was a sly tone to it, aimed straight at Red.

Red thought of Cassie's flawless white skin and shining black hair. She had huge, remote brown eyes, with lashes long enough to wave in the breeze, and the sweetest pink lips that never curved in a smile nor opened to wish a man good day.

Red thought on what he'd say to draw a smile and a kind word from her. Such thoughts could keep a man lying awake at night. Red knew that for a fact. Oh yes, Cassie was a living, breathing test from the devil himself.

"China doll's the perfect name for her," Muriel added.

Red had heard that Griff called his wife china doll. Griff never said that in front of anyone. He always called her Mrs. Griffin, real proper and formal-like. But he'd been overheard speaking to her in private, and he'd called her china doll. The whole town had taken to calling her that.

Red had seen such a doll in a store window when he was a youngster in Indiana. That doll, even to a roughhousing little boy, was so beautiful it always earned a long, careful look. But the white glass face was cold and her expression serious, as if someone neglected giving the poor toy a painted-on smile. It was frighteningly fragile. Rather than being fun, Red thought a china doll would be a sad thing to own and, in the end, a burden to keep unbroken and clean. All of those things described Cassandra Griffin right down to the ground. Still, knowing all of that didn't stop him from wanting her.

Cassie got to him. She had ever since the first time he'd seen her nearly two years ago. And now she was available. Someone would have to marry her to keep her alive. Women didn't live without men in the unsettled West. Life was too hard. The only unattached women around worked above the Golden Butte Saloon and, although they survived, Red didn't consider their sad existence living.

"You're established on the ranch these days, Red. Your bank account's healthy." Muriel crouched down so she was eye level with Red, who was digging himself down fast. "Maybe it's time you took a wife."

Red froze and looked up at his friend. Muriel was a motherly woman, though she had no children. And like a mother, she seemed comfortable meddling in his life.

Red realized he was staring and went back to the grave, tempted to toss a shovelful of dirt on Muriel's wily face. He wouldn't throw it *hard*. He just wanted to distract her.

When he was sure his voice would work, he said, "Cassie isn't for me, Muriel. And it isn't because of what it would cost to keep her. If she was my wife, she'd live within my means and that would be that."

Red had already imagined—in his unruly mind—how stern he'd be when she asked for finery. *"You'll have to sew it yourself or go without."* He even pictured himself shaking a scolding finger right under her turned-up nose. She'd mind him.

He'd imagined it many times—many, many times. And long before Griff died, which was so improper Red felt shame. He'd tried to control his willful thoughts. But a man couldn't stop himself from thinking a thought until he'd started, now could he? So he'd *started* a thousand times and then he stopped himself. . .mostly. He'd be kind and patient but he wouldn't bend. He'd say, "Cass honey, you—"

Red jerked his thoughts away from the old, sinful daydream about another man's wife. Calmly, he answered Muriel, "She isn't for me because I would never marry a nonbeliever."

With a wry smile, Seth caught on and threw in on Muriel's side—the traitor. "A woman is a mighty scarce critter out here, Red. It don't make sense to put too many conditions on the ones there are."

"I know." Red talked to himself as much as to them. He

hung on to right and wrong. He clung to God's will. "But one point I'll never compromise on is marrying a woman who doesn't share my faith."

"Now, Red," Muriel chided, "you shouldn't judge that little girl like that. How do you know she's not a believer?"

"I'm not judging her, Muriel." Which Red realized was absolutely not true. "Okay, I don't know what faith she holds. But I do know that the Griffins have never darkened the doorstep of my church."

Neither Seth nor Muriel could argue with that, although Muriel had a mulish look that told him she wanted to.

"We'd best get back." Seth laid a beefy hand on Muriel's strong shoulder. "I think Mrs. Griffin is going to need some help getting ready for the funeral."

"She's in shock, I reckon," Muriel said. "She hasn't spoken more'n a dozen words since she rode in yesterday."

"She was clear enough on what dress I needed to fetch." Seth shook his head in disgust. "And she knew the reticule she wanted and the shoes and hairpins. I felt like a lady's maid."

"I've never seen a woman so shaken." Muriel's eyes softened. "The bridle was on wrong. She was riding bareback. It's a wonder she was able to stick on that horse."

Red didn't want to hear any more about how desperately in need of help Cassie was.

Muriel had been teasing him up until now, but suddenly she was dead serious. "You know what the men around here are like, Red. You know the kind of life she's got ahead of her. There are just some things a decent man can't let happen to a woman. Libby's boys are off hauling freight or I'd talk to them. They'd make good husbands."

Muriel was right, they would be good. Something burned hot and angry inside of Red when he thought of those decent, Christian men claiming Cassie.

It was even worse when Red thought of her marrying one of the rough-and-ready men who lived in the rugged mountains and valleys around the little town of Divide, which rested up against the great peaks of the Montana Rockies. It was almost more than he could stand to imagine her with one of them.

But he also knew a sin when he saw it tempting him, and he refused to let Muriel change his mind. She badgered him awhile longer but finally gave up.

He was glad when Seth and Muriel left him alone to finish his digging. Until he looked up and saw Cassie as if he'd conjured her with his daydreams.

But this was no sweet, fragile china doll. She charged straight toward him, her hands fisted, her eyes on fire.

"Uh. . .hi, Miz Griffin." He vaulted out of the shoulder-deep hole and faced her. The look on her face was enough to make him want to turn tail and run.

She swept toward him, a low sound coming from her throat that a wildcat might make just before it pounced.

She'd heard it. All of it.

God forgive me for being part of that gossip, hurting her when she's already so badly hurt.

Whatever she wanted to say, whatever pain she wanted to inflict, he vowed to God that he'd stand here and take it as his due. Her eyes were so alive with fury and focused right on him. How many times had his unruly mind conjured up the image of Cassie focusing on him? But this wasn't the look he'd imagined in his daydreams. In fact, a tremor of fear ran up his backbone.

His grip tightened on his shovel, not to use as a weapon to defend himself but to keep her from grabbing it and taking a swing.

"Stop it." Her fists were clenched as if to beat on him. "Stop saying those awful things." Red saw more life in her eyes than he ever had before. She was always quiet and reserved and distant. "Give him back. I want him back!" She moved so fast toward him that, just as she reached his side, she tripped over her skirt and fell. A terrified shriek cut off her irate words.

"Cassie!" Red dropped the shovel and caught her just as she'd have tumbled into the open grave.

She swung and landed a fist right on his chin.

His head snapped back. She had pretty good power behind her fists for a little thing. Figuring he deserved it, he held on, stepping well away from the hole in the ground. He pulled her against him as she pummeled and emitted short, sharp, frenzied screams of rage. Punching his shoulders, chest, face. He took his beating like a man. He'd earned this by causing her more pain when she'd already been dealt more than she could bear. Of course he'd tried to stop it. But he'd failed now, hadn't he?

"I'm sorry." He spoke low, hoping to penetrate her anger. He could barely hear himself over her shouting. "I'm so sorry about Griff, Cassie. And I'm sorry you heard us speaking ill. We were wrong. So wrong. I'm sorry. I'm sorry." His voice kept crooning as he held her, letting her wale away on him until her squeaks and her harmless blows slowed and then ceased, most likely from exhaustion, not because she'd quit hating him.

Her hands dropped suddenly. Her head fell against his chest. Her knees buckled, and Red swung her up into his arms.

He looked down at her, wondering if she'd fainted dead away.

In his arms, he held perfection.

She fit against him as if his body and his heart had been created just for her. A soul-deep ache nearly buckled his own knees as he looked at her now-closed eyes. Those lashes so long they'd tangle in a breeze rested on her ashen face, tinged with one bright spot of fury raised red on her cheeks.

"I'm so sorry I hurt you. Please forgive me." His words were both a prayer to God and a request to poor, sweet Cassie. He held her close, murmuring, apologizing.

At last her eyes fluttered open. The anger was there but not the violence. "Let me go!"

He slowly lowered her feet to the ground, keeping an arm around her waist until he was sure her legs would hold her. She stepped out of his arms as quickly as possible and gave him a look of such hatred it was more painful than the blows she'd landed. Far more painful.

"I'm so sorry for your loss, Cassie honey." Red wanted to kick himself. He shouldn't have called her such. It was improper.

She didn't seem to notice he was even alive. Instead, her gaze slid to that grave, that open rectangle waiting to receive her husband. . .or what was left of him. And the hatred faded to misery, agony, and worst of all, fear.

A suppressed cry of pain told Red, as if Cassie had spoken aloud, that she wished she could join her husband in that awful hole.

Her head hanging low, her shoulders slumped, both arms wrapped around her rounded belly, she turned and walked back the way she came. Each step seemed to take all her effort as if her feet weighed a hundred pounds each.

Wondering if he should accompany her back to Muriel's, instead he did nothing but watch. There was nothing really he could do. That worthless husband of hers was dead and he'd left his wife with one nasty mess to clean up. And Red couldn't be the one to step in and fix it. Not if he wanted to live the life God had planned for him.

She walked into the swaying stand of aspens. They were thin enough that if he moved a bit to the side, he could keep his eye on her. Stepping farther and farther sideways to look around the trees—because he was physically unable to take his eyes off her—he saw her get safely to the store.

Just then his foot slipped off the edge of the grave. He caught himself before he fell headlong into the six feet of missing earth.

Red heard the door of Bates General Store close with a sharp *bang*, and Cassie went inside and left him alone in the sun and wind with a deep hole to dig and too much time to think. He grabbed his shovel and jumped down, getting back at it.

He knew he was doing the right thing by refusing to marry Cassie Griffin.

A sudden gust caught a shovelful of dirt and blew it in Red's face. Along with the dirt that now coated him, he caught a strong whiff of the stable he'd cleaned last night. Cassie would think Red and the Western men he wanted to protect her from were one and the same. And she'd be right, up to a point. The dirt and the smell, the humble clothes, and the sod house—this was who he was, and he didn't apologize for that to any man. . . or any woman.

Red knew there was only one way for him to serve God in this matter. He had to keep clear of Cassie Griffin.

The china doll wasn't for him.

CHAPTER 2

"T he Lord is my shepherd; I shall not want.'" Parson
Bergstrom stood in the buffeting wind.

Red filled in Cassie's precious husband's grave while the
parson, with his black coat and flat-brimmed hat, stood in the
fall breeze, reading from his open Bible. The parson intoned
the Psalm, using it as a prayer for peace and strength.

Cassie had neither.

She looked down at Griff, and the wind whipped the
blanket away, exposing Griff's forever-closed eyes. One second
later, dirt landed, covering the still, white face.

Had Red done that on purpose, thrown dirt on Griff's face?
Her fists clenched. She wanted Red to get away from Griff. She
wanted to attack him and claw him until he bled as red as his
hair. Glaring at Red, who didn't seem to notice her, she saw that
he had a puffy lip and a slightly blackened eye. She'd done that
to him. The satisfaction of it was shocking. She wanted to shove
Muriel's arm off her shoulder. To think this woman considered
herself superior to Griff. All of that raged inside Cassie's head,
but outwardly she forced herself to remain calm.

Each time the shovel bit into the soil mounded beside Griff's grave, Cassie felt it cut her heart, scoop it out, and toss it in with Griff. Or it might as well have. She wouldn't have hurt anymore. The shoveling went on and on, obscuring the blanketed body of her dearly loved Griff.

" 'He maketh me to lie down in green pastures: He leadeth me beside the still waters,'" the parson continued.

She was aware, in an impassive way, of the people hovering around her: Muriel, Seth, Parson Bergstrom, Red. There were others but she didn't know them and had no interest in getting to know them.

The parson was a circuit rider, and he'd been passing through town when Griff died, or the town would have settled him underground with an awkward prayer and an off-key verse of "Amazing Grace."

" 'He restoreth my soul: He leadeth me in the paths of righteousness for His name's sake.'"

The shovel bit again, working until it was a steady beat, rhythmic, in time with the words, nearly setting Cassie's nightmare to music. The pace fixed, unstoppable, like a heartbeat. Cassie felt hers beating, and it told her she wasn't dead. But Griff was and she wondered if that might not be the same thing.

" 'Yea, though I walk through the valley of the shadow of death, I will fear no evil: for thou art with me; thy rod and thy staff they comfort me.'"

Besides Muriel, every one of the twenty or so mourners was a man. Divide, Montana, was a rugged place, tucked into the Rocky Mountains. And women didn't come here. Cassie and Muriel and a couple of others were the exceptions that proved the rule. Women were too soft, Griff said. Muriel said women were too smart.

Cassie didn't have an opinion. It wasn't a woman's place to

have an opinion. But Griff had told her often enough that time would change the lack of women, and the settlers who were here first would become barons over this vast, empty land.

Griff's dream of being a powerful cattle baron was being buried along with him.

" 'Thou preparest a table before me in the presence of mine enemies: thou anointest my head with oil; my cup runneth over.' "

The hole filled until it was running over. It happened so quickly Cassie wanted to scream at Red Dawson to stop. But she'd surely screamed enough for one day. Griff would be so ashamed of her if he could have seen the way she carried on earlier. But at least that had been with Red, in private. She would not carry on so in front of this crowd.

She stood, contained and serene, perfection in her demeanor, only marred by the tears dripping off her chin. But inside, she could still see herself striking Red, screaming at him, wanting the cruel words he'd spoken to disappear and the horrible grave to vanish. She nearly staggered back. He was dead. Griff was really dead.

" 'Surely goodness and mercy shall follow me all the days of my life: and I will dwell in the house of the Lord for ever.' "

There was no goodness without Griff. God had no mercy.

The hole mounded until Red tossed in the last shovelful of dirt. He turned and gave Cassie a compassionate look that locked their eyes together.

Cassie wanted to demand he give Griff back to her. She needed to take her rage out on someone and Red was here. He looked strong enough to take it, and she already knew he was kind enough to let her attack him without returning the pain.

"I'm so sorry for your loss, Mrs. Griffin." Red's quiet words were accompanied by eyes that seemed to speak to her, as if he understood her grief and rage. As if he cared.

The moment between them stretched too long. Red's blackened eyes dropped shut as if he had to stop looking but didn't have the will to turn his head. His chin tilted down and Cassie saw him open his eyes and stare at the grave. Then, without looking at her again, he swung his shovel up to rest on his shoulder and walked away.

She wanted to scream at him. Call him a coward. Tell him to get back here and let her rant and rave. Red's broad shoulders disappeared into the crowd of men, but even after he was gone, Cassie looked after him.

"Red's a good man, Cassie." Muriel patted Cassie's arm.

No, he wasn't. Cassie wanted to shout that in Muriel's face, but of course she didn't. A good man wouldn't have left her here.

" '*Yea, though I walk through the valley of the shadow of death.* . . .' " Those were the parson's words. Surely that's where Cassie stood now, in that valley of the shadow. It came to Cassie that the parson's words would come true soon and she could walk on through and then dwell in the house of the Lord forever, because without Griff she would surely die. The truth hit her, and instead of frightening her, it gave her peace.

How simple.

Griff was dead. She'd die, too.

Of course.

Without Griff to take care of her there was no way to go on. She clutched her hands around her stomach. Her baby. She'd never know this little one she loved so much. Would God judge her harshly because she hadn't protected her child?

Something fierce rose in Cassie that wanted to fight for her child. But how? Griff had told her so often that she was stupid and useless. And this moment proved Griff right, because she couldn't imagine how to live without her husband. So, she'd die and her precious baby would die with her. Through her grief and her overwhelming failure, she was almost relieved. Death—so simple.

"Let's get on with it, Parson." A rough voice broke through Cassie's grief and fear and roused her temper. Fine enough for her to decide to die, but no one had the right to tell her to get on with it.

Muriel stood on her right, supporting her. Now her arm tightened around Cassie's shoulder until it hurt. "This is not the time."

Time for what? Cassie wondered, slowly bringing her concentration to focus on the group around her.

The men surrounded the filled grave. Now they stepped nearer. She noticed the ones across the grave from her walked across the newly filled hole.

"The parson's here. We get it done," the same voice growled.

Cassie was watching this time. She saw an overweight man, with a full beard more gray than brown, shouldering his way to the front of the assembly. He came so close to Cassie she could see the line of tobacco that drooled from the corner of his mouth and stained his beard. She caught the hot, rancid odor of his breath and the stench of his unwashed body. She glimpsed his blackened teeth.

"Back off, Marley." The voice came from farther back in the crowd. "She hain'ta gonna choose you anyhow. You're old enough to be her pa and fat enough to be let out with her cows."

The crowd broke out into loud, coarse laughter.

"Miz Griffin likes 'em old, don't ya, sweetheart?" a third man shouted.

More laughter followed.

"Well then, you're it, you old coot." Someone shoved the old man aside and others jostled forward to take his place.

Cassie couldn't keep up with who was talking. She felt

Muriel's fingers tear loose from her shoulder and turned to see Muriel being jostled aside and pushed away until Cassie couldn't see her anymore. Seth was on her left, and the parson pushed up close to stand in the spot where Muriel had been. He and Seth were knocked into her until she thought she'd be crushed between them.

"Stay back!" Seth shouted.

"Give her time." The parson sounded like he was threatening the crowd, but they showed no affect from his words.

One man's beefy arm snaked past Seth and caught hold of the sleeve of Cassie's black silk dress. "Take care of your fussy dress, darlin'—you won't be gettin' no more. No matter who ya choose."

Seth shoved the man's hand away.

Choose? What were they talking about? She shrank away from the reaching, grasping hands but backed into someone, and a frantic look over her shoulder told her the men were behind her, too. Her heart started to pound in fear.

Through the milling crowd, she looked down the slope to town and caught a glimpse of Red walking toward the stable, his shovel resting on his shoulder. She saw Muriel rush up to Red and catch his arm and start talking rapidly, waving her arms and pointing at Cassie. Red looked at Cassie and shook his head.

Cassie thought of how she'd attacked the man and felt shame. She also felt some regret that she hadn't taken another swing at him.

Another man touched her, this time on her protruding stomach. "Iffen it's a boy, you kin call it after its pa if you choose me."

The parson shouted, "Please, gentlemen, can't you see she's in no emotional state to make this choice now? She needs time to grieve. Her husband is newly dead. Maybe in a week or two."

A week or two? Cassie tried to understand that. The parson expected her to be done with her mourning in a week or two? Cassie knew she'd be mourning Griff for the rest of her life, be it short or long.

"He's cold, Parson. That's all we need to know. You're a pretty li'l thing, china doll. I'd sure like you keepin' me warm through this next winter."

Cassie gasped. She'd overheard gossips on occasion call her china doll—not least of all Seth and Muriel this morning—but no one had ever called her that to her face except Griff. And he meant it warmly.

"Pick, li'l lady." A tall, thin man pressed forward from the right. "I've got chores to get to at home."

"See here, I won't stand for this." The parson stumbled and nearly fell, knocking into Cassie.

"You're leavin', Parson. We get it done now, today, or she'll be livin' with one of us for months 'til you come back. Griff's young 'un 'll be born and she'll be broodin' with a new one by then."

"She will if she don't marry an old codger like you."

An outburst of laughter sent Cassie stumbling backward. Her stomach heaved at the sickening things they were saying.

"It took Griff years to get a babe on her. Maybe it's her."

"I'd be willin' to keep trying were you to choose me, china doll." That brought the loudest outbreak of laughter yet.

She knew what they were talking about, but she kept turning her mind away from it. Without Griff, the only choice she could see before her was to die bravely. It was inevitable so she accepted it. It had never occurred to her to save herself by choosing another husband. She looked around the crowd, and more than ever death sounded like a better option.

"A barren woman's better than no woman at all."

"Choose, Miz Griffin. I'm young. I've got a good place, well started."

"You live in a soddy, Harv. Think she wants that after what she's livin' in now?"

The men bandied their crude jokes and shoved each other, trying to get close to her.

The parson fell to the ground beside her, and arms jerked him sideways until he disappeared in the crowd. Someone slid his arm around the girth of her protruding belly and pulled her hard against him.

Her head started to spin, and her knees threatened to give out. The mob pressed closer and more hands clung to her, touching her, sometimes improperly, but there were so many that each bit of contact was as much a violation as the next, regardless of where that touch occurred. She wished she could sink beneath the dirt that sheltered her husband.

"Miz Griffin will marry me," a voice thundered from the back of the crowd. The men turned at the harsh, tyrannical voice that overwhelmed even this rough assembly.

Cassie recognized that awful voice. Mort Sawyer had arrived.

A huge black horse pranced right up through the middle of the mob. Mort seemed unconcerned if he trampled anyone under iron-shod hooves, and the men seemed to know it. They snarled and grumbled in protest, but they fell back far enough to allow the man through, like wolves giving way before the leader of the pack.

Five other horses followed the black, driving the mob back farther. Cassie recognized several of the riders, particularly Wade Sawyer, the young, hungry-eyed son of the rancher. The younger man rode one pace off the lead horse. Wade studied her with piercing green eyes that sent a shudder of fear climbing like a scurrying insect up the back of her neck.

"Miz Griffin, I'm mighty sorry to hear of your loss." Mort tipped his black Stetson. He spoke like a man paying heed to a social nicety with no emotional interest in his words. And why not? He didn't really know her. She'd taken pains to never speak to him and to stay out of his sight. And the little Mort had to do with Griff had been unpleasant. Tense meetings over the natural spring just behind Griff's house, one of the few in the area that flowed freely even in the dry season. Mort Sawyer had the bad habit of turning his cattle out during the long summer months, so they could drink from that spring.

Mort dispensed with his hollow expression of sympathy and returned to his usual imperious tone. Mort's ability to dominate with that voice made Griff's endless chiding sound like playful schoolyard banter by comparison.

Mort Sawyer, the name Griff had spoken with his dying breath.

Most of what he'd said toward the end was incoherent, so if he was cruel, she didn't hold him to blame. If in his delirium he knocked her to the floor a few times, it wasn't his fault. He'd fallen into a stupor, occasionally rousing to swallow a few drops of water or rant at her for letting him get so sick.

Then, as Griff's breathing became shallow and his eyes fell shut, he found the strength to speak one last time. "Sawyer never got the spring while I lived."

Cassie remembered the triumph in Griff's voice, like his life had been a success and now he could die happy.

"I reckon Miz Griffin's comin' with me. Parson, let's get it over and done."

A howl of protest exploded from the other men and brought Cassie back to the present. The volume of the noise forced Cassie back a step. She ran into someone and turned to face the heavy, tobacco-chewing man and be assaulted by his breath again.

Mort Sawyer's son, Wade, pushed his mount past his father and reached for Cassie. He leaned down, grabbed her under her arms, and yanked her up onto the saddle to settle her in front of him. Her legs scraped painfully on the saddle horn.

Wade turned to his father. "I want her, Pa."

"She's mine, boy. We've had it out. The spring's gotta be in my hands."

Wade lifted Cassie's chin roughly until she looked straight into his eyes. She'd looked into those eyes before. Too many times.

Wade had the habit of dropping by her home when Griff was gone. He'd done it too often for it to be chance. Now he studied her with those weird, bright green eyes, the color of envy and rot. Wade Sawyer was responsible for one of the few true acts of defiance Cassie had to her name. She'd learned to shoot. Practicing when Griff was away. And she'd kept a gun close at hand all the time.

Of course, she didn't have it now when she needed it.

Wade sank his fingers painfully into her jaw and leaned his face so close that for a second Cassie thought he meant to kiss her. She jerked her head sideways to escape his grasping fingers and pushed at the hand that shackled her waist but couldn't dislodge Wade's grip.

He was amused by her struggles. Only inches from her, Cassie saw he had a black eye and a slightly swollen lip that seemed to underscore the violence in him. She thought of Red and the black eye she'd given him and wished she'd been responsible for Wade's.

He said loudly enough for the crowd to hear, "Well then, I guess you're gonna be my new mama." Then Wade kissed her until she felt bruised. Releasing her, he looked at her with greedy eyes that didn't match the humor in his voice. Dead serious eyes that claimed her in a way no marriage could.

Mort edged his horse next to Wade's and grabbed Cassie then hefted her into his lap. His beefy arms settled around her, even before Wade's had left her body.

The touch of the two men induced shudders so violent that she lost a battle with self-control, just as she had this morning with Red. She wrenched against Mort's grip and started shrieking like a madwoman.

She caught Mort Sawyer in the belly with her elbow, and his response was a mild grunt. He wrapped his arms more tightly around her fat middle and roared, "Where's the parson?"

She struggled more wildly, kicking at Mort's leg and making his horse prance sideways. She looked around at the men. They had all fallen back and seemed content now to watch the show.

She heard the parson say, "I'll not marry a woman to someone against her will, Sawyer. I won't stand before God and conduct such a travesty. This isn't something you can dictate. You let her go right this—"

Mort's horse charged forward under his master's skillful hand. Mort reached down and grabbed the parson by the front of his black suit. He lifted the man onto his tiptoes with one hand while he controlled Cassie with his other. "You'll marry us, Parson, or I'll take her home, and when she's broken in, maybe after she's given me a son or two, she'll agree nice enough."

Wade laughed, but it was a sickening, hollow sound. "I'm gonna have a baby brother."

Mort shoved the parson back and he fell to the ground. A man who would do that to a preacher would do unspeakable things to his wife.

Darkness spun in front of her.

A quiet voice behind her cut through the noise. "I'll marry Mrs. Griffin, if she'll have me."

Cassie's head cleared, and as she twisted around to locate the owner of that kind voice, her eyes focused on Red Dawson. The man she'd hated more than any other on this earth ten minutes ago.

"Beat it, Dawson. She's mine," Mort Sawyer said.

Cassie remembered Wade's eyes. Even though she had always been sheltered, she knew terrible things were in store for her if she was taken to the Sawyer ranch.

Mort marched the horse straight at Red.

Red stopped the horse by patting its nose. "Whoa, boy, easy there."

Then he looked at Cassie. With a voice as out of place as a breeze in the midst of a tornado, he asked, "Whattaya say, Cassie, will you marry me?"

"Parson, it's settled. We get it done now!" Mort roared.

Cassie heard the violence in Mort and recalled the foulness in Wade and smelled the filth in her nearest other suitors. . .and saw the decency in Red's eyes. She still hated Red Dawson, although less than she had a few minutes ago. Or more correctly, she now hated other people more.

Unless Griff's grave opened this minute and let her jump in, Cassie didn't see as she had much choice. A minute passed as the chaos went on around her and the trampled grave stayed closed, and as if someone else spoke out of her lips, she said, "Yes. . ."

She almost said, *Red*, before it occurred to her that Red must be a nickname. She didn't know the name of the man who proposed to her. It was humiliating to ask him.

Somehow it seemed less humiliating to just say, "Yes, I'll marry you."

CHAPTER 3

Cassie was a widow one day and a newlywed the next.

The wedding was held at the cemetery with a good share of the wedding guests standing on her dead husband's grave.

She didn't so much have wedding guests as she had a lynch mob. Twenty-five armed men wanted Red Dawson dead. Cassie thought that no doubt one of Red's murderers would then insist on marrying her. If the pattern continued, she'd be forty or fifty times a widow within the next few hours. At that rate, Divide would be a ghost town by the weekend.

Cassie Griffin's contribution to Montana.

Red had reached up to take Cassie off Mort's horse. Mort had spurred his horse away, but Red had caught the reins and soothed the animal while glaring at Mort.

"You will do the right thing, Mort Sawyer. Before God and all these witnesses, Cassie has refused your offer of marriage and accepted mine. Now let her down."

Cassie felt the hands on her body, not sure who all was touching her. But Red lowered her to the ground. She suspected that "all these witnesses" was a better incentive than "before

God." Considering his treatment of the parson, Mort didn't seem to be much interested in what God saw when He looked into Mort's black heart.

Red pulled Cassie to his side, looked down as if to check that she was in one piece, and then reached his hand down to assist Parson Bergstrom in standing.

"Let's get it done quick, Parson." Red slid his arm around Cassie, and Seth did some shoving to get to her side. The crowd grumbled, but even Mort Sawyer only made noise.

"Do you, Cassie Griffin, take Red Dawson to be your lawfully wedded husband?" The parson spoke the words so fast it was obvious he was scared to death.

To Cassie, that didn't speak well for the man's trust in eternal life. But maybe he believed well enough, he just didn't want to pass through those pearly gates into eternal life right now today.

Someone said, "I do." Cassie suspected it was she.

"Do you, Red Dawson. . ." The parson repeated the most abbreviated version of marriage vows Cassie had ever heard— though in truth she hadn't heard many. The parson used an economy of words, most likely planning his escape all the while.

The service took about two minutes, including the time it took for Red to get Cassie off Mort Sawyer's horse. How he managed it Cassie didn't really know. There was a relentlessness to the way Red moved. He seemed unconcerned with the hostile explosions surrounding him.

The only rational thought Cassie had about Red was if she'd blackened Griff's eye the way she'd done to Red, the punishment would have been severe and swift. She expected nothing less with her new husband. Hopefully Red would wait until they were alone to mete out her punishment.

Wade Sawyer was openly furious, but his father controlled him, maybe thinking the cold-blooded murder of an unarmed man in front of dozens of witnesses might be too much for even a Sawyer to walk away from.

Cassie was summarily married, and Red took her arm and led her away from the mob toward the stables. He stooped to pick up his shovel on the way.

Cassie remembered the argument she'd seen Muriel having with Red in the same spot where the shovel lay. "Muriel nagged you into marrying me, didn't she?" Cassie looked at Red fearfully. Now Cassie veered from grief and shock to humiliation.

"I did what I thought was right, I reckon." Red hurried her to the stable, whether because he had work to do or because he was looking for shelter from the horde, Cassie couldn't say.

Then she thought of the way Wade had looked at her and the tyrannical way Mort had taken her from the other men. Well, she'd made the best of a bad situation. She'd come up with a plan.

Death.

Marrying Red Dawson was her second choice, and it was a poor second. But, all things considered, she'd do it again.

They moved on toward the stables, her wedding guests prowling around behind them. Cassie had a moment to wonder if possibly Red lived in the stables. She really didn't know the man at all. She'd seen the red hair a time or two around town, and fortunately his nickname was easily recalled. But Red Dawson, along with almost every other person in Divide, was a stranger.

Red went into the stable and headed for a saddled buckskin that was half as tall and a quarter as pretty as the magnificent bay Cassie had ridden to town bareback when Griff died. The bay had been stabled here ever since.

Cassie looked over at the regal animal who stood eating in a stall. Seth had gone for Griff's body without taking Cassie along. He'd brought her dress and Griff's suit because she quoted

Griff's careful deathbed instructions. Seth had fed and watered the other bay, left out at the ranch. That one was a matched partner to the one she'd managed to bridle and climb onto after a long struggle. The two horses were the only livestock Griff had left when he died.

Red didn't even look at the bay. He hung the shovel on the back of his saddle, turned to stretch out his hand to her, and said, "I'll give you a leg up."

"I'll ride my own horse." She realized with a start those were not proper words for a wife to say to her husband.

His ordering her onto his horse, telling her what to do—that was something familiar. Her objecting—that was rude.

She clamped her mouth shut, determined to be as good a wife to Red as she'd been to Griff. But they really did have to take the horse.

"The horse belongs to the bank." Red held his hand out, waiting for her to come to him.

Cassie shook her head, trying to rattle the words around inside her head so they made sense. "B–Belongs to the bank? I don't understand."

"They're mortgaged, Cassie. Your place has a lien on it for the property, the livestock, and the contents of your home."

"Griff mentioned a loan. But surely the horses…we brought them west with us. They were from my parents' stable. I know they were paid for."

"They were paid for then…maybe."

Red's tone made Cassie wonder how much was known publicly about her finances. Obviously far more than Griff had ever told her. Griff had always told her a woman shouldn't concern her weak mind with money matters.

Red went on. "Now they're mortgaged. I can't afford to pay off your loans. I'd end up owning horses I don't need, a house miles away from my place, and fancy furniture that won't fit in my soddy. The bank can take 'em."

"How did you know about the loan?" Cassie struggled to keep up. Every word he spoke was news to her.

"It's a small town." Red shrugged. "And I work at the bank some, washing windows and such. I hear talk. Besides, it's no secret. Everyone knows." He reached for her, pulling back as he studied her stomach. He ran one finger over his puffy lip, glanced at her for a second, and then said, "I'll have to. . .to lift you onto Buck. Excuse my. . .my *familiar*. . .uh. . .touch." He very carefully, looking alarmed, put his hands under her arms and lifted her so she sat facing sideways on his saddle. He settled her gently.

"Uh. . .try hooking your leg over the horn."

Cassie shook her head, confused at what he was asking her to do. "I. . .I don't ride. . ."

"I don't have a sidesaddle. You'll just have to learn to ride Buck like this or straddle the horse. Except, if you do that, your skirts'll. . .um. . .they'll. . .well. . ." Red's face turned a color that matched his hair. "You'd best just figure on sittin' sideways."

With another nervous glance that met her eyes, he gingerly took hold of her right leg and swung it around the saddle horn. Again he was gentle and Cassie thought of the sharp scrape of Wade Sawyer's saddle horn when he'd slammed her onto it. She grabbed at the saddle horn through the layers of her gown.

Red untied Buck and swung himself up behind the saddle with a single graceful leap. He pressed against her back as he shifted the reins from one hand to the other. He brushed her arms and sides. He looked around her and his chin nudged her hair.

When he got so close, touching her, close enough to smell the earthy scent of dirt and sweat, Cassie realized what she'd done by marrying him. She thought of a husband's manly needs. Her stomach quivered at the humiliation that lay ahead of her. If only he wasn't as demanding as Griff had been. He'd left her alone at first, because he said she was too young. But for the last year, scarcely a season had gone by that Griff hadn't come to her bed. Griff had explained that it was her duty so she'd endured it.

Then she remembered what else Griff had said. A woman was unclean when she was with child and he wouldn't be with her until after the child was born. She barely suppressed a sigh of relief. Surely she had time before Red claimed his rights. Maybe by the time the baby was born he'd forget what his rights were.

Red shifted his weight and made a clucking sound to start his horse moving. She shifted forward so he wouldn't be so close, but he caught her. "Hold still. I can't see when you lean that way."

Cassie obeyed quickly, hoping she hadn't annoyed him.

"It might be a good idea to stop at the bank and talk this out with Norm. He'll move to claim the property, but I don't want him to think we're not willing. It'll ease his mind some if we tell him we expect it."

Red steered Buck around to the back door of the bank. Red slid off, reached up, lifted Cassie down, and led her into the bank through the back door. "It being Sunday, the bank isn't open, but that Norm always has something that can't wait until Monday."

She'd never been inside the bank. She'd always either stayed home or remained in the carriage when Griff had bank business. A door was ajar next to the safe and Red walked toward it, but Cassie hung back.

"Norm, I can always trust you to be working on the Lord's Day."

"Now, Red, don't start," a deep voice replied. "I never catch up."

"Can I talk to you a minute?" Red asked.

"Come on in my office."

Red rounded the counter then leaned back to look at her. "Come on, Cass. I'm in a hurry. I've got chores."

As always, Cassie obeyed because a woman must always obey her husband, but she couldn't imagine why she needed to hear this.

"Hey, Norm. Cassie Griffin and I just got married." Red reached across the desk and shook hands with the formally dressed older man who rose from his chair.

Red was dressed in coarse brown pants and a shirt made crudely from flour sacks. He was liberally coated with dirt from his grave digging. But he greeted Norman York like they were close friends. Griff had always called him Mr. York.

"Congratulations, Red. Congratulations, Miz Griffin, um, Miz Dawson, that is."

For the first time, Cassie realized she had a new name.

"Sit down." Mr. York gestured to the pair of heavy wooden chairs that faced his desk.

"No thanks, Norm. We're in a hurry. Stock's waiting." Red got right down to business. "Now, we've heard about the mortgage. The one bay is in the stable and the other un's out at Griff's place. Seth fed him enough for a couple of days. We're turning over ownership now. I'm not going that direction, so you'll have to bring him in yourself. Reckon the whole place is yours now, so handle things any way you want."

"Griff's furniture. . ." Cassie began to protest.

"I'm sorry, Mrs. Dawson." Norman York became very formal. His grammar improved along with his posture. "Your husband mortgaged everything—the house and its contents. I really can't allow you to take anything out of it. Of course the dress you're wearing is yours to keep. Although I think there's a bill at Seth's to settle up on it."

"But, there are personal things, my great-grandmother's pearls. . ."

"Those are included in the mortgage, Miz Dawson."

"I. . .I inherited them. They have been in my family four generations. Griff wouldn't mortgage them!"

Mr. York went to a cabinet and pulled a file drawer out. He sorted through papers until he found what he was looking for. He handed it to Cassie.

She read it with ever-increasing shock. "My mother's cameo? And the. . .the *frames* my grandparents' portraits are in? But the portraits, surely I can have them?" Cassie looked up from Mr. York to Red, humiliated. She struggled to gain control of herself. It didn't matter. Her heirlooms were all just foolish vanity. Surely that is what Griff thought.

She glanced back at the note one last time and lost her composure. "My Bible?" She looked up at Mr. York. "No, a Bible has no monetary worth. But it's been passed down for generations in my family. It's precious to me. No one else would ever want to buy it."

Mr. York fiddled with his string tie for just a second as if it had been pulled a bit too tight. "The thing is, Miz Dawson, that Bible came from Germany a long time ago. I told your husband the same thing, that no one wants an old Bible except the folks who have their names written in it, but Griff knew that huge old book was a New Testament of something called a Gutenberg Bible. It's worth quite a bit. I will have to ship it back East to sell it, but it alone is mortgaged for over two hundred dollars."

"Two hundred dollars?" Red exclaimed. "For an old Bible?"

"I know it's crazy for any book to be so valuable." Mr. York nodded. "Your husband—uh, that is, your former husband— tried to convince me it was worth far more than the amount I agreed to. We could build a church with that. A big, beautiful church. If things settle up right, the Bible is the first thing I'll save back for you. But you can see that I can't just give it back. I will get the photographs for you but not the frames."

"My family Bible is mine. Griff had no right—"

"The fact is, Miz Dawson," Mr. York cut her off with considerable force, "a woman's possessions become her husband's on the day they marry. Now you may not understand that, but it's the law. Griff had every right to mortgage that Bible. And if you didn't want him to, you could have lived without your silk dresses."

"Norm, that's enough," Red said.

Mr. York quit glaring at her and turned to Red. A look passed between the two men, but she couldn't gather her wits enough to analyze its meaning. She was struck speechless by the venom in Mr. York's voice. He blamed her for her fancy clothes. He probably blamed her for every beautiful thing Griff had bought. Her whole world shifted at that moment as she realized that the cutting comments she'd overheard about the china doll and the rather stiff way Muriel had always treated her came down to the perception that she was the one who demanded everything be so fine. Mr. York clearly believed that. Did Red?

This was a fight she should never have started. She swallowed hard and felt doubly stupid for having argued with the man while she was so ignorant of the law and of a man's rights. Finally, she folded her hands, searched deeply for the china doll, and regained her self-control. She spoke demurely, her eyes lowered. "When you get the Bible, would it be all right for me to copy the names out onto a piece of paper? I'd like to keep a record of my ancestors."

When Mr. York spoke, his voice had none of the unkindness that it had before. "That'll be fine, Miz Dawson. I'll have the Bible here when Red comes to town next week. He can bring it out to you, and when you've finished with it, send it back."

Red looked at her. "It's time to go. I'll take care of the bill at Seth's now. I know there's a bill at the lumber mill and one at Harv's. Anywhere else in town?"

Mr. York said, "The doc, the stable. . .check the blacksmith."

Cassie listened to the list and felt the weight of all she owed press down on her shoulders. She swayed slightly and held herself upright by sheer force of will.

Red nodded. "I'll take care of it."

"It's not your responsibility, Red. No one expects you to stand good for her fancy. . .that is. . .for Griff's bills."

"I pay what I owe, Norm." The tone of Red's voice pulled Cassie back from the edge of a faint. There was something cold in Red's voice.

"I didn't mean to imply you don't pay your bills, Red." Mr. York pulled a kerchief out of his breast pocket and mopped his brow.

"Good, I'm glad to hear you know better'n to say different. When I married Cassie, I reckon I married her bills. I knew that going in."

Married her bills? Cassie couldn't quite make sense out of that. Married her bills?

"I know, Red." Norman York held both hands in front of him. "If I come out ahead on the mortgage, you have my word I'll put it to his other debts. But I don't think there's gonna be much."

"Mort'll take the spring," Red warned. "You'll have to be careful or he won't pay for it. Too bad there's not a second bidder."

"Maybe Linscott will come in on it." Mr. York watched Red closely as if afraid of him. "He's got adjoining land."

Cassie would do well to remember that Red was a man people feared.

"Yeah, but it's too rugged between Tom Linscott's land and

that spring. He couldn't use it."

"Probably not." Mr. York sounded thoughtful. "But he surely does hate the Sawyers. More importantly, Tom's not afraid of Mort."

"Throw in that Tom would usually rather fight than get along." Red nodded.

Cassie thought the name Tom Linscott was vaguely familiar. She had a mental image of a huge, dangerous black stallion and a fairly young man with overly long white hair who'd struggled to control the beast and nearly run Cassie down in the street one day as she'd followed a few paces behind Griff. Linscott had apologized and seemed genuinely sorry and worried at her fright. Then Griff had lit into him and all of Mr. Linscott's kind concern deserted him as the two had exchanged unpleasant words. It was one of the last times Cassie had been allowed to come to town with Griff.

"Yep, making Mort pay through the nose for that spring will suit him. I'll see him before I talk to Mort."

"Mort's probably moving his cattle in on it already. And he wanted Cass, so he's mad."

"He really wanted the spring, not me," Cassie said faintly.

Mr. York nodded. "I'll watch him."

"Wade wanted me." Shuddering, she wasn't aware of saying it out loud.

Red turned to her and laid one hand gently on her shoulder. "I know, Cassie. I saw. That's why I stepped in. No decent woman would be safe around him."

Cassie remembered the evil in Wade's green eyes and recoiled from the memory. She forced herself to focus on the banker. "If my dress is not paid for, Mr. York, perhaps I could return it."

She turned to Red. "It's not useful for every day, and if I'm to have only one dress. . ."

"We can check with Seth. You're a little thing, but with the waist let out. . ." Red shrugged and shook his head. "I doubt Muriel will fit in that thing, and no woman in town wears silk anyway."

"Maybe one of the girls at the Golden Butte—" Mr. York stopped talking when Red turned toward him. Cassie couldn't see Red's expression, but Mr. York mopped his brow again.

Cassie wondered who or what the Golden Butte was.

"Let's go, Cass. We've got a few more stops."

Cassie followed behind Red. He strode out the back of the bank with Cassie trailing along.

CHAPTER 4

Wade shoved past Anthony Santoni as he emerged from the Golden Butte. Santoni was just going in. Wade sneered at the worthless man who lived off his wife and openly betrayed her in the Golden Butte.

Across the street, Wade saw Red and the china doll walk past the alley that opened between the bank and the general store. Swallowing hard, Wade's hands trembled as he wished for the guts to reach for his gun and separate the china doll from her new husband. She'd been in Wade's hands. He looked down at his shaking fingers, which flexed and burned with the memory of holding her. And having her torn away.

At least his father had failed. That was one bright spot in this mess. Red had thwarted that fat old man today, and Wade couldn't help but enjoy that. Except his father's failure had been his own because now the china doll was beyond his reach.

Wade touched the tender bruises on his face. His father's plan had been sickening, but at least she would have been at the ranch. Now she'd be with Dawson instead.

Thinking of his china doll with that dirty odd-job man,

living in his decrepit house on his poor excuse for a ranch, made Wade want to hurt someone. His hand went to his Colt revolver.

Tom Linscott chose that moment to ride that brute of a stallion down Divide's main street. Linscott rode up the street toward the doctor's office. Wade had heard one of Linscott's hands had broken a leg, falling off a bronc. Linscott must be coming in to visit.

The tall Swede cut in front of Wade in a way that prevented Wade from looking down that alley. The china doll was long gone, but it was easy to switch his anger to Linscott. The man had never given Wade the respect due him as son of the area's largest rancher, and that rubbed Wade wrong. Especially since Linscott wasn't that much older than Wade.

Wade strode down the street to block Linscott's way. Linscott wasn't one for the Golden Butte, neither the girls nor the whiskey. The man had a hair-trigger temper and seemed like he was born looking for a fight, but he didn't have the vices Wade enjoyed.

Linscott was heading into the doctor's office without watching where he was going much, and Wade made a point to step right in Linscott's path and slam his shoulder into the man. Linscott was a couple of inches taller than Wade and twenty pounds heavier, all hard muscle. A part of Wade wanted to hurt somebody, and hurt him bad. Another part expected to be given a beating. It seemed like the physical pain canceled out the pain in his heart to think of the china doll married again.

Linscott stumbled back then lifted his gaze to Wade and scowled. "You looking for a fight, Sawyer? Because you'll find one with me. I don't step aside for a little man just because he's got a big old brute of a daddy."

Wade wanted to put a notch in his gun. He'd been hungry to claim he'd killed a man for a long time.

Linscott shook his head in disgust. "You're such a fool,

Sawyer. Get out of my way."

Wade's fingers itched and they flexed near his six-gun.

Laughing contemptuously, Linscott said, "You haven't got the guts to pull that gun, and if you did, I'd beat you to the draw and put you down like a rabid skunk."

Wade took a wild swing and landed a blow to Linscott's chin, mainly because the man wasn't taking any of this seriously.

Linscott staggered back, and his head knocked into a post supporting the overhang on the doctor's office. Then Linscott's famous temper ignited. He cocked his arm and hammered Wade in the face.

Wade hit the wooden sidewalk with a thud.

Two hands from the Sawyer ranch came out of the Golden Butte, and Wade landed at their feet. They both pulled their guns in the flash of an eye and aimed them at Linscott.

Wade looked with smug satisfaction at Linscott. He'd bought into a fight with the wrong man.

Linscott took two steps back, rubbing his chin, looking with cool eyes between Wade and his cowhands. Still, Wade saw no fear on Linscott's face. Wade envied the man his guts and hated him at the same time.

"I'm not fighting your whole ranch, you yellow coward. You want to come at me, you come alone." Linscott shook his head in contempt then turned as if the guns weren't of any concern to him at all. Somehow that dismissal made Wade's feelings of failure deepen.

One of the men standing over him said, "Pick a fight with someone you can beat next time, you young pup. Maybe a little girl-child." Both men laughed and holstered their guns as they stepped over Wade to head for their horses.

Burning with shame, Wade hated everyone until the fire of it nearly burned a hole in his soul. That hate reminded him of the one person he didn't hate.

The china doll.

She was only out of his reach as long as Red Dawson was alive.

He could accomplish two things at once. Kill a man and have his china doll.

Wade finally thought he could do it. He could kill. True, he'd never been able to before and he'd had his chances to draw and ducked them. But he'd never felt this kind of rage. He wanted this enough.

He pictured it.

Red dead.

The china doll his.

He'd be saving her, rescuing her. For that, Wade could kill.

Red and Cassie walked down the dirt walkway that ran behind the bank and led to the back doors of four other stores. All closed for Sunday.

Cassie stayed a step behind Red and didn't speak when he went to the back door of the first one and knocked.

One by one, they were invited into the family living quarters. Each had a bill with Lester Griffin's name on it. Red talked quietly. Cassie remained several paces behind, embarrassed by the business being conducted in front of her.

Griff had always told her a woman had no head for figures and it was not her place to buy and sell. Now Cassie felt as if she was watching something unseemly, and her cheeks warmed until she feared she blushed crimson. She got some scowling glances from the people with whom Red conducted his business, but he seemed to be ignoring her. That was a situation she hoped continued.

Before they were done, they'd been on both sides of the street and stopped in nearly every store in Divide.

They left the general store for last.

"Cassie needs a better work dress, Red." Muriel gave Cassie a sympathetic look as if the expensive black silk she wore was something to be ashamed of.

Red and Muriel debated about her dress for a while. Cassie did her best to behave herself and not listen.

Then Muriel led Cassie into the back room. "I've got one that I hope will fit. It's not cut for a woman who's expecting, but it's several sizes too big for you so I think it'll work." Muriel patted Cassie on the arm.

Cassie looked up at Muriel. "I'm sure it will be fine."

"Red told me that you overheard what we said about Griff and you, honey." Muriel didn't look like a woman given to tears. She was tough and weathered and she'd seen too much, but Cassie thought the older woman's eyes watered a bit and there was definite regret in her expression. "I apologize for that. It was gossip and it was sinful. I'm ashamed of myself. I hope you can forgive me." Muriel extended a thin blue calico dress to Cassie.

"I forgive you." Cassie didn't really see it as her place to give or withhold forgiveness. She'd come to expect criticism for her incompetence in all things and accept it. Her fury had been all to defend Griff and she'd burned that off long ago. Red had the black eye to prove it. The events of the day had left her too exhausted to hold much anger.

"Thank you. I know I talk too much. I plan to study my Bible again tonight. Red reminded me of the verse, from Luke. Part of it says, 'That which ye have spoken in the ear in closets shall be proclaimed upon the housetops.' I certainly learned that lesson today. My words were a sin and I hurt you with my sinning. I am sorry." Muriel gave Cassie an awkward hug.

"I've never heard that one before." Cassie wondered if what *she* thought in private would be proclaimed from the housetops. If that was so, God was going to be very hard on her on Judgment Day, because Cassie's thoughts were sinful beyond redemption. She usually kept them to herself, but she'd shouted at Red and hit him. Her stomach twisted when she thought of how he'd retaliate later. . .in private. It took a terrible effort to keep from breaking into tears.

"Do you need help changing?" Muriel looked doubtfully at Cassie's heavy silk dress, the skirts held wide with petticoats and a bustle. At least the row of tiny buttons ran up the front, or Cassie most likely couldn't have dressed alone.

"I can manage, thank you." Cassie blushed to think of Muriel or anyone being near her while she was in her under-things. Griff was always chastising her if he caught so much as a glimpse of her throat or ankles. To her knowledge, Griff had never—day or night—seen even a bit of Cassie's skin except her face and hands. He'd stressed the decency of that, and Cassie had learned to never flaunt herself.

Muriel pressed a brown paper–wrapped package into Cassie's hands. "This is a wedding present. I know the bank is takin' everything. So you'll need this. Red'll be good to you, Cassie. He's a good man. Leave the silk behind. I'll get enough for it to settle Griff's bill. This calico is better for life out here anyway."

After Muriel left, Cassie missed the motherly lady. Except for the gossiping at the grave site, Muriel had been nice to her since Griff had died. She exhibited none of the cool politeness that had always been between them. Griff said Muriel and Seth were common and beneath them, so although Griff had to do business with them, Cassie kept her distance. But Cassie had leaned on Muriel since she'd come to town for help. She'd stayed in her rooms above the store, and what bit of food she'd eaten, Muriel had prepared and served.

Remembering those shocking words out at the grave site,

Cassie realized that Muriel and Seth actually looked down on Griff. It was such a shift in Cassie's world that she turned her thoughts away from it.

Without Muriel, Cassie had a long struggle to get changed. It had taken forever to get the black silk dress on earlier today. Cassie didn't see the dark blue silk she'd worn to town. Most likely it was mortgaged, too.

Finally she donned the blue calico. It took only minutes. It was far too big, but that was a good thing or it wouldn't have fit over her stomach.

Cassie left behind her stylish black hat, the reticule, and her lace handkerchief. She had several heavy petticoats. She left them, too, keeping only her shoes and her chemise and stockings. The stockings were silk, but they were the only ones she had, and modesty required she keep them. Then Cassie remembered the solid silver pins in her hair. She removed them and left them for Muriel, letting her heavy dark hair drop into a plain braid down the center of her back.

When she emerged from the back room, pounds lighter in the simple dress, Red and Seth were debating something heatedly. Red saw her come out and fell silent for a moment as he looked at her. Then he shook his head sharply, spoke again to Seth, and turned to her. "Let's head out."

Before they could start toward the back door, the bell over the front door rang and drew their attention.

A woman walked in whom Cassie had never seen before. A strange woman, wearing a riding skirt and a flat-topped black hat with a silver band. She pulled her gloves off as her boots clunked on the wooden floors. Spurs jingled with every step. A woman wearing spurs?

"Howdy, Belle." Seth moved to stand behind the counter. "I'm mostly done with your list."

"Thanks, Seth. The wagon's out front. Sorry to bother you

on a Sunday. I appreciate you opening up for me." Belle tucked her gloves behind her belt buckle.

That action drew Cassie's gaze, and she realized that the woman was with child. Not as round as Cassie but definitely expecting.

The woman, Belle, looked up, and her gaze froze on Cassie, moved to her belly, and then their eyes met.

Muriel had been standing in the hallway to her living quarters, behind Cassie and Red. Now she squeezed past Cassie and went to Belle. "This is Cassie Dawson. She and Red got married today."

Belle's eyes slid between Red and Cassie, and Cassie had the strangest urge to throw herself into Belle's arms. She had no idea why. The woman was a bit older than she, but not that much. Still, the woman had the look of a mother, a warrior mother.

"Today?" Belle asked Muriel, but her eyes stayed on Cassie, flickering to her obviously round stomach again.

"Her husband died, just yesterday. Lester Griffin?"

Belle snorted and Cassie caught way too much meaning from that sound. Here was another person who thought ill of Griff.

Red shifted a bit closer to Cassie as if she needed protection. But there was no danger to Cassie from this woman.

Belle walked straight for Cassie then, spurs ringing.

Muriel gave way like dust in the wind, and Cassie had a shocking urge to smile.

Red held his ground, but Belle ignored him and spoke past his shoulder straight to Cassie, "Was this your choosing? This marriage?"

Cassie was speechless. Her choosing? What did that have to do with anything? "Wh–What do you mean?"

"Belle, it's done." Red leaned as if to block Belle from Cassie, but she glared at him so hard he straightened, shifting so they stood in a circle in the hallway of the store.

This woman had made a man move aside with a single look. Cassie's heart started pounding. She'd never heard of a woman who could do that.

Belle turned to Red. "Yes, it's always *done*, isn't it? Done to a woman. No one gives us a *choice*. Look at her. She doesn't even know what I mean by 'choosing.'"

Muriel came up behind Belle. "It's all right, Belle. She had to pick a man. You know that."

Belle rested her hand on her belly. "I don't know any such thing." Her jaw tightened, but kindness was there, along with anger. "You can come home with me."

Red shook his head. "She's a married woman."

"She belongs with her husband, Belle," Muriel said.

Belle ignored them both and spoke to Cassie. "You can come home with me if you want. I've got a husband who spends most of his time hiding from work and three daughters who would love a big sister. When that baby comes, I'll have one more. We'll pray it's a girl. And I'll help you; you'll help me. We'll get by. What do you say?"

Cassie almost launched herself at Belle, grabbed her, and clung to her.

Some of that must have shown in her eyes, because Red stepped close and slid his arm around her shoulders. "We were married before God and man, this very day. My wife stays with me."

Muriel's eyes snapped with satisfaction. Cassie didn't understand that.

Cassie nearly shook as she realized she'd bound herself to a man she didn't know. A man she'd have to obey. Tears burned her eyes. This was a way out. She knew if she said the word, Belle could make it happen. Just as Red was strong enough to snatch her out of Mort Sawyer's arms, Belle was strong enough to settle things her way. Cassie marveled at the woman, her strength, her confidence. Muriel had a glimmer of it, but this woman looked like she'd stand toe-to-toe with any man and come out the winner.

"Let me talk to her, Red."

So Red and Belle knew each other? Why had Cassie never seen this woman before? There weren't that many women. Surely Cassie wouldn't have forgotten one.

"You can talk to her, Belle, but she stays with me." Red's shoulders relaxed. "If it helps any, maybe you should know Cassie gave me this black eye."

Belle's head whipped around to stare for long moments at the purple bruise. "Well, maybe she will be all right."

Muriel snickered.

Red let Belle come close. Belle rested a work-roughened hand on Cassie's shoulder. Cassie felt the calluses through her dress. The hand was scarred and brown and so strong, Cassie wondered what Belle could hold on to with that hand.

"I know you took vows," Belle said quietly, "but just tell me, if there'd been a choice, would you have married again today, a day after. . ." Belle fell silent, shaking her head. "Lester Griffin, worthless excuse for a man. Dead now. No surprise. How old were you when you married him?"

"F–Fifteen."

"I was fifteen when I first married."

"First?"

"William was my first husband. I'm on my third. I tend to marry stupid and they all tend to die, although Anthony seems to be hanging around so far."

"She might have married fast, Belle, but she didn't marry stupid." Red settled his Stetson on his head and his voice sounded warm. Considering how tough Belle was, that warmth didn't make sense to Cassie. It was almost as if he. . .pitied this woman.

Belle snorted. "I've decided *married* and *stupid* are the same words. I'll bet if we had a dictionary, one would define the other."

Muriel coughed and covered her mouth.

Cassie was shocked and almost smiled at the nerve. What would she give to have the courage to speak so to a man. . .to anyone?

"What's done is done. I'll take care of her. And you should have known better than to marry Anthony anyway."

Belle jabbed her thumb over her shoulder at Muriel. "Except I had people like Muriel saying a woman has to have a man."

"Well, she does, Belle."

Belle turned around and glared at Muriel. "I didn't."

"Cassie does."

Belle, her back to Cassie now, stood solid, staring at Muriel.

Finally, Belle gave a harsh jerk of her chin as if it was decided. Belle turned back. "I reckon she's right that you needed someone to take care of you, and I live a long way out. No one would have thought to come for me." Belle's brows formed a straight line, with deep furrows between. "But I'd have taken you in, Cassie. No woman has to have a man. But I reckon you needed someone. If you ever need a place to run, come to me. I live in a mountain valley through the gap worn by Skull Creek."

Cassie realized she believed this woman. If Cassie needed a place, Belle would take her in. Tears burned her eyes as she nodded. "Thank you."

Belle turned her eyes on Red. "You treat her decent. I'll come and check, and I'd better like what I see." With a deep sigh, she shook her head. "Seth, you got my order ready?"

"I'll be at it awhile, Belle."

"I'll leave the wagon out front. I need to talk to the blacksmith, then I'll stop by Herschel's and see if they'd feed me on a Sunday." Belle turned to Red and shot him a look that could have nailed a two-by-four to a fence. "I *will* stop by. Do you hear me?"

A smile bloomed on Red's face. "I hear you."

Belle's expression softened. "You're right. I never should have married Anthony. What was I thinking?"

Red tugged on the brim of his hat. Belle turned and weaved her way around Muriel. Seth handed her a wooden box full of supplies and followed her out, carrying another one. At the door, Belle froze. Seth almost ran into her from behind.

Cassie saw Belle staring out the front window of the general store at a building at the far end of Divide's modest Main Street. Cassie saw the words GOLDEN BUTTE painted over the swinging doors to the building. The banker had said something about Cassie's silk dress being worn by the ladies of the Golden Butte and then he'd looked nervous.

A dark-haired man had stepped out of that building on the arm of a woman dressed in a shocking red dress, starchy with frills and lace, cut up to nearly her knees in front.

Seth said, "I'm sorry Anthony stepped out just now."

Belle turned her head with a hard jerk as if she had to physically tear her eyes away from the sight. "He's in town more than he's home, Seth. I'm used to my husband shaming me. I don't care anymore."

But Cassie saw the downward turn of Belle's mouth and knew Belle did care. This hurt, and Cassie knew all about being hurt.

"What was I thinking?" Belle shoved the door and stepped out.

Cassie watched as the dark-haired man noticed her. The woman in red stepped out of his arms and flounced back into the building. The man—it had to be Belle's husband, Anthony—turned and walked quickly in the opposite direction.

Belle went to her wagon as if nothing had happened and set her box inside. Then she walked directly away from Anthony with the thud of boots and the *clink* of spurs.

Red and Muriel exchanged long glances. Cassie remembered the pity she'd sensed in Red and knew Belle's husband with another woman on his arm was a usual occurrence.

Settling his hat more firmly, Red rested his hand on Cassie's back. "Let's head out."

Confused by that rare, frightening look at a woman who would stare a man straight in the eye and say her piece and feeling awkward about witnessing Belle's shame, Cassie did as she was told and headed out, following Red. The way a woman was meant to behave.

She remembered the way Belle had looked at her, straight out along that hat brim. Eyes direct, speaking her mind, issuing orders that sounded like threats. Cassie felt like a huge world yawned at her feet. A world she might have entered if she'd had the nerve to go with Belle. But did that bold gaze and her strong words cause Belle's husband to disgrace her?

Cassie would never follow Belle's example. Instead, she obeyed. It was her place.

Muriel hurried and got the wrapped package Cassie had forgotten in the back room and handed it to Red. He walked beside Cassie to where Buck stood at the back door. He stored the gift in his saddlebag and slipped his hands under her arms and hoisted her gently onto the horse just as he had the first time. He hooked her knee around the saddle horn again, and she clung to it through the layers of calico. She had a much better grip without the silk and petticoats.

He jumped on behind, and as he did, Cassie dared a glance at his face. His jaw was set and his eyes flashed with anger.

Had it angered him that she'd listened to Belle? Was it the bills Red had paid? Was he remembering that she'd attacked him at the graveyard? It looked as if he'd wait and make her pay for misbehavior when they got home. She was grateful her humiliation would be, at least, in private.

She shuddered to think of the times Griff had been this upset with her. He hadn't done it for a long time, but she well remembered the heavy belt he'd used almost daily when they were newlyweds, before she learned a woman's place. Fear climbed inside her at what was to come until she could learn to please Red Dawson. Burning tears cut her eyes. Knowing men hated tears, she swallowed hard and stared at the horizon to keep them from falling.

They rode out of town in the opposite direction of Griff's holding. Then Red leaned forward. She braced herself for his angry words.

"Buck is strong and you weigh next to nothing. I always run him flat out the whole way home, but we won't be able to do that riding double. We'll push hard for a while, though. I asked Doc and he said a gallop wouldn't hurt the babe if you didn't take a fall. But Doc said I shouldn't trot, so we'll take off fast. It's a far piece to my land."

She was so shocked at his concern for the baby she didn't answer him. He rested one hand on her rounded waist to steady her and clucked at the horse. The short-legged horse shifted smoothly to a ground-eating gallop. No more talk was possible.

Although Cassie would have loved to enjoy the wild ride, she couldn't relax until she'd received her punishment and made amends in whatever way Red demanded. She just held on and tried to make herself as small as possible.

It was the same thing she'd been doing since the day her mother died when she was twelve. Griff had become her guardian, and he'd helped her understand how much she had to learn. And though it was a terrible burden to him, he'd been left with the chore of being her teacher and wouldn't shirk it.

CHAPTER 5

Cassie woke with a start to feel strong arms carrying her.

Still groggy with the first deep sleep she'd had in too long, she rubbed her cheek against warm, coarse cloth and used her arms to hold herself steady.

She almost went back to sleep, when she heard a deep voice say, "Are you awake, Cass? I've got to set you down. I can't do the door one-handed."

Cassie's eyes flickered open and she looked into Red Dawson's face. They stood on the ground, beside his horse, and he had her cradled in his strong arms. In a split second it all came back to her. Griff, the funeral, her wedding, all those bills, Red's anger. And here she lay with her arms wrapped around his neck. She pulled quickly away from him and he set her down. She carefully folded her hands, fixed her eyes on the ground, and waited for him to mete out the punishment she had coming.

It took her a second to realize Red was gone. He had walked on without her and was wrestling with a wooden door in the side of a hill. He got it open and said, "This is home, such as it is."

Cassie stood, transfixed, staring at the door, wondering where her punishment was.

Red waved her forward. "Let me show you what little there is to see, then I've gotta do chores."

Cassie obeyed. He waved her in and she flinched when his hand got too close, but she quickly controlled herself. Griff had hated that and punished her more severely for it.

She walked into a cave.

Red stepped briskly in behind her and brushed past where she stood frozen near the door. "The front part's a soddy." He pointed to an opening on the far wall. "I built it onto the mouth of a cave. The cave is my. . .our. . .uh. . .*your* bedroom."

"That one"—he pointed to another much smaller opening with a buffalo hide hanging over it—"is a smaller cave. It's real cool because a spring comes out of the rock right there. We don't have to haul water, and it keeps milk and butter chilled. I was real lucky to find this spot.

"The big cave has a second way out that I'll show you later. It winds through the mountain some," Red said. "What you need for food is in the cooler. That's what I call the little cave, and what you need for cooking is here." He walked across the room to a dry sink and a huge stone fireplace. He turned toward her. "You cook, don't you, Cass? I can do it. I always have for myself. But. . .well. . .that is. . ."

Cassie nodded silently while he fumbled around asking. Then she forced herself to speak. "Yes, I'll cook." She'd been good at it at one time, but Griff had very special tastes and he had never been satisfied with her efforts.

She would have to learn all Red's personal preferences in food now. If only she could feed him this once tonight without shaming him. For now he seemed to have forgotten his anger, although she knew a man never forgot for long.

Red moved to a wood box near the fireplace. "I'll get a fire started then." He hurried through the chore.

Cassie compared Red's fireplace to Griff's stove. Griff's had been a huge rectangular monster with water wells and two baking chambers. It had levers to adjust the heat and keep the food cooking at just the right speed. Griff had been disgusted with her for running it so poorly.

Cassie had cooked over an open fire on the trip out West. She'd been better over a fire than she'd ever been with that intimidating cast-iron cookstove.

Red finished lighting the fire. "I'll get a bucket of water so you can wash and have some for cooking. Then I've got chores."

Red disappeared into the little cave and returned with a large tin bucket. "I'll be late. If you're tired and want to go to bed, it's through there." He pointed to the larger door. "I'll sleep in the. . ." Red faltered. "I—I want you to know—I won't b–bother you none, Cassie. Just take the bedroom. I'll find a place out here."

"What would you like for supper?" She didn't recognize her voice. She didn't recognize anything about her life. She was still too confused by the changes of the last day.

"Anything's fine." He shrugged and plucked a battered hat off a nail by the front door, hanging his nicer Stetson on the same nail. He was very close to her, studying his broken-down hat intently.

"I know it's not what you're used to, Cass." He glanced up and away quickly. "I know it's not fancy. When you. . .when Mort was grabbing you, I knew I had no business asking a lady like you to come out here. But I. . .there was no one else to. . .I had to step in."

He was embarrassed. Cassie almost smiled when she realized it. The impulse shocked her. Griff hated frivolity. She couldn't remember the last time she'd smiled. Red was worried that she didn't like his home. Something eased inside her, and she laid her hand over his to make him stop torturing his hat.

He looked up at her and she saw the pure blue of his eyes. "It's a fine home, Red. And I know what was ahead of me with Mort." She couldn't stop herself from squeezing his hand tight. "Thank you. You don't have to sleep out here. We're married and I understand what that means."

Offering him that assurance almost made her sick, but she knew her duty. Red had his rights. Except she was unclean. But Red would know that. If he didn't, she'd be glad to remind him.

"Now tell me what to make you for supper. I'd like the first night to be something you really like, and I don't know your preferences."

Red smiled. "Anything I don't have to cook myself would be a treat, Cass. There's a ham back there if you'd like to fry a couple of slices of that. Anything, and only if you're feeling up to it. I. . .I haven't told you how sorry I am about Griff."

He had. He'd told her more nicely than anyone else. And to repay him she'd given him that black eye. But she didn't correct him.

"I know this has been hard for you. Now your man is gone and a baby is on the way. Even. . .even if I share the bedroom, I'll. . .I'll keep a respectful distance. You'll have your time to heal, Cass."

He looked at her a moment longer, and for a while Cassie forgot everything but Red and his pure blue eyes.

Then he looked abruptly down at his hat again. "Gotta go." He almost ran out the door, leaving it open to the fall breeze.

Belle slammed the bridles down on the support beam. She whipped the wall as she hung the traces on the nail, not caring that she missed and the leather and metal slid to the floor with a *clank*. She turned to the wagon full of supplies and fought the temptation to start throwing bags and cans.

"Ma, what happened?"

Belle turned to see Lindsay staring wide-eyed. Belle closed her eyes and pulled in a long, slow breath, fighting to control her temper. The only trouble with that was if she quit being mad she was afraid she might cry.

Well, she wasn't going to do that. That was weak. She'd just stay furious.

She'd always been honest with her daughters, so she saw no reason to be less than that now. She paced the length of the barn toward Lindsay. "I saw something in town today that's just got me all churned up." And no, she wasn't going to talk about Anthony. She was blunt with her girls, but they didn't need to understand this.

She got close to her thirteen-year-old and realized Lindsay was only two years younger than Cassie Griffin Dawson had been when she'd married that no-account Lester Griffin. And now at eighteen, Cassie had just been forced into another marriage. It was too much like Belle's life.

"Who, Ma? We don't hardly know no one in town."

It was Belle's life all over again, except Belle had been able to take care of herself. Cassie Griffin was helpless. Belle caught Lindsay by both shoulders. Lindsay, to her credit, didn't flinch, despite Belle's blazing temper.

"I've done my best, Lindsay, to make sure you're never helpless. You understand that it's about more than me needing hands on this ranch. You know how much I love you girls and want to protect you."

Lindsay shrugged under Belle's grip. "I know you need help. I know husbands are worthless."

Belle flinched internally. Not all men were worthless. She knew that. Her pa had worked hard and had been a good rancher. He'd treated her wrong in the end, once he'd been blessed with a son to inherit the ranch after years of grooming Belle to run it. But mostly her pa was a decent man.

Seth at the general store stood at Muriel's side and did his full share and more. Red Dawson owned a fair piece of land and ran a good, solid operation. That's the only reason she hadn't hauled Cassie out of there at gunpoint. That and knowing she'd probably end up arrested, and her worthless husband, Anthony, would have a free hand to break the unusual agreement she'd made him sign before they were married, leaving her sole owner of the Tanner Ranch. Plus the idiot would let her girls starve to death.

She didn't correct Lindsay, though. Best to believe all men were worthless and prepare yourself to manage alone. Then, if she failed her girls and let them end up married, they'd be able to fend for themselves.

"There was a woman in town. . .a girl. . .eighteen, not that much older'n you. Her name's Cassie Griffin."

"Eighteen's a lot older'n thirteen, Ma."

"But she married today for the second time. She first got hitched when she was fifteen. That's only a little over two years from your age."

"Well, I'm not ever getting married so don't worry about it. And remember you promised not to either."

Belle nodded. "I remember. Once Anthony dies, I promise. No more husbands." Belle laid her hand on her belly and spent five seconds in hard, concentrated prayer.

Please, please, a girl, Lord God. Let it be a girl.

How could she possibly raise a boy up to be anything other than worthless? Any male seemed to have a powerful inclination toward that result.

Lindsay interrupted Belle's prayer. "I've heard of Griffin's house. Big, shiny mansion of a place."

Her girls had almost never been to town. Belle had to travel several hours fast and hard to get there, stock up supplies, and get home, which was slow with a loaded wagon. She only made the trip once or twice a year, and she never took the girls.

Emma rode into the barn from the corral door. She rode a green, broke filly that had lines Belle wanted in her saddle stock. The horse was behaving perfectly.

"You've got her settling in nice." Belle admired her second-born's hand with the horses. Emma had a rare knack.

"She's a little beauty, Ma. We did some cutting today and she really got onto it. She'll give us some good foals." Emma patted the bay's shoulders, already strong and broad as a two-year-old.

Her two oldest daughters were a matched pair. Flyaway white blond hair, eyelashes and brows just as white, shining blue eyes so pale they were almost gray, they were the image of their pa, William Svendson. Her third daughter, Sarah, was a redhead with a thousand freckles and emerald green eyes. Her pa, Gerald O'Rourke, used to say Sarah's eyes were as green as Ireland when the whiskey was on him. . .which was most of the time.

Belle, with her straight brown hair and light brown eyes, didn't seem able to pass on a single physical trait to her girls. She had no doubt the baby she carried now would have black curls and snapping black eyes like Anthony Santoni, worthless husband number three. But if they didn't carry Belle's looks, they carried her strength. She could still teach 'em what they needed to survive.

"Put your horse up and come listen while I tell Lindsay what happened."

Emma made short work of her unsaddling. The eleven-year-old was better at handling a horse than Belle or Lindsay, and that was saying something.

"What is it, Ma?" Emma pulled her leather gloves off as she walked toward Belle. No spurs. Belle had a gentle hand with the stock, but she knew a spur came in handy on rare occasion. She couldn't convince Emma they were necessary.

She repeated to Emma what she'd told Lindsay about Cassie Griffin. "I just want you girls to know that you never have to get married if you don't want to."

Emma and Lindsay exchanged long looks.

Lindsay spoke first. "We don't plan on getting married, Ma. We've learned our lesson from watching you."

"Good." Belle nodded. "I should hope so. Husbands bring you children, of course." Belle rested her work-scarred hand on her round belly. "A nuisance being with child, of course. Slows me down some. But you girls, well, I reckon my life is only worth living because I've got you."

"So, you mean you've changed your mind and you think we *should* get married?" Emma asked fearfully.

"No, no. Of course not. I'm just saying some good can come out of the whole mess. I'm trying to lay the whole truth out for you is all."

Her girls nodded, their expressions grim.

"I just want you to know that you don't have to make a choice like that because people tell you a woman *has* to have a man. You can make it on your own. As long as I'm alive you'll have a home with me. We run this ranch smooth and easy."

"Well, Ma, we work from can see to can't see." Emma slapped her gloves against her hand. "We bust broncs and brand steers and dig dams and cut and stack hay. So *easy* ain't 'zactly right."

"I mean easy except for the backbreaking work. By *easy* I mean we do it right. The ranch runs easy. . .without a hitch. Don't interrupt me while I'm explaining things to you."

"Sorry, Ma." Emma tucked her gloves behind her belt buckle.

"This is an important point. That little woman today. . ." Belle considered Cassie little more than a child. Both in age and in temperament. The woman was being led along by that meddling Muriel and Red Dawson. Truth be told, Belle wasn't yet thirty, but she felt as old as the hills that surrounded her beautiful mountain valley.

"That woman, Cassie, wasn't given a choice today. I don't know much about the man they forced on her. There's such a thing as a decent man, I've heard. Seen little sign of it, but that's not my point." Belle wondered if Sarah had supper going in the house yet. Most likely. A dependable child, her Sarah.

"What is your point, Ma? I've got chores left." Lindsay looked bored.

Belle suspected she'd told her girls all of this before. . .a thousand times or more. But seeing Cassie today, quiet, obedient, being told what to do and who to marry and most likely how to breathe, had scared Belle to death. Belle was ten times as strong as Cassie Dawson, and *she'd* fallen into the same a-woman-had-to-have-a-man trap as Cassie.

Belle had to save her girls from such a fate. "You don't have to marry some man just because you're of marrying age. A woman can get by on her own. I am raising you girls to work and work hard. The strength of your back and the sense in your head will carry you through life without having to drag some worthless husband along with you. Might as well just tie an anchor to your leg and tow that."

Belle took a couple of steps toward the barn door so she could see the house. "Has Anthony come around?"

"He's not on the roof?" Lindsay came up beside her.

"No. And I saw him in town today, but I had a lot of errands and figured he headed home before me. And riding horseback he'd've made good time. I suppose he'll come back. Free food."

Emma pointed toward the Husband Tree. "He's there."

Belle squinted. Sure enough, Anthony was sitting on his backside. . .as usual. But instead of climbing on the roof, which he was partial to—somehow that must make him think he was beyond Belle's reach, as if Belle would ever *want* to reach him— he was sitting, his back propped up by the Husband Tree.

"Does he know he's sitting on one of the other husbands?" Lindsay asked.

Belle shrugged. "Don't know. You can't tell there are graves there anymore. I didn't waste time markin' 'em. But I'm sure that's the side your pa is on. I wanted him to face the ranch. I don't remember if I buried Gerald on the left or right side. I didn't give it much thought. And I sure didn't care if *he* could see the ranch layout. Better he should face the Golden Butte in Divide." Gerald had liked the Golden for its liquid pleasures, while Anthony was more interested in the sweeter enticements of the place. William had never gone there, she'd give him that. He'd just grumbled and griped and taken long walks.

"Well, Anthony's still alive and kicking so far." Lindsay turned to look at the chicken coop. Belle was proud of the girl for being more interested in chores than the problems of being yoked to a slug of a man.

Belle sighed. She'd been a long time in town, and then she'd had the heavy buckboard to pull home. "He could live a long time, I reckon, although he's stupid, and stupid'll get you killed in the West."

"Are you done telling us *again* we don't have to get married, Ma? 'Cuz I got chores." Emma pulled her gloves free and started tugging them on.

"I'm done for now." Belle wasn't really. She didn't think she'd said enough. "I just. . . Today, hearing about that young girl passed around like she was a box of groceries, it just hit me hard."

She looked from Lindsay to Emma and back. "I want to save you from husbands if I possibly can."

The three of them looked at Anthony. The way he sat, his

head leaned back, he looked like he was catching a nap. Resting up for bedtime, no doubt. It didn't matter if he was rested or not, he had his own bed. Belle slept with her cast-iron skillet these days.

"We hear you, Ma." Emma headed for the hog pen.

"Loud and clear." Lindsay went to saddle her horse.

Belle watched them walk away. Her pride in them. . .well, she was back to holding on to her temper to keep the tears away. She laid her hand on her baby, due in early spring.

Be a girl. God, let her be a girl.

She went in to have the same heart-to-heart talk with Sarah. Even at eight, the child wasn't too young to learn her lesson. Belle ignored the pain of Anthony's betrayal. It was an old pain. Instead, she nursed her fury over the fate of that poor, sweet, helpless Cassie Griffin Dawson.

It was, quite possibly, the sweetest moment of Cassie's life, at least the sweetest in the years since her mother had died. Cassie stood, stunned at Red's kind speech about Griff and her baby and keeping his distance.

For the first time, Cassie realized that Red was very young. He carried himself with such ease, and he was treated with deference by a lot of men and as an equal by the others. For some reason she'd been thinking he was Griff's age. But the twisted hat and the stuttered speech made her think differently. Now she wondered if he wasn't about *her* age. He had to be twenty-one to file a homestead. But if he'd been here two years like Griff and her, Red could be twenty-three, a barely grown boy striking out on his own in the West. She wished she had the nerve to ask him his age. That wouldn't be too forward a question for a wife to ask. Or would it? She wished Griff was here to tell her.

She explored the cave she now lived in, and somehow the combination of realizing her husband was hardly more than a boy and finding out she lived in a cave made her feel young and adventurous. She'd gotten to thinking of herself as the same generation as Griff, but she was only eighteen.

The bedroom was large and very dark. There was a good-sized bed. Only one. Not two smaller ones like Griff said was appropriate for a married couple. In fact, at Griff's house she'd had her own room. She felt heat rush into her face as she realized what she'd been offering when she told Red he could join her in the bedroom. If he suggested staying in the front room again, she'd agree.

She found the little notch in the back of the room. The passage winding away into the heart of the mountain caught her imagination and she was sorely tempted to explore. She stepped away from it. She had to ask Red first. She didn't want to start her marriage by being disobedient.

She left the bedroom and went into the cooler. She was amazed at the drop in temperature. She followed the pleasant trickle of water, careful not to trip over anything. She was clumsy and she'd gotten worse with the baby on the way. Griff had rebuked her for it many times.

She found a brisk little spate of water pouring out of a crack in the rock. It landed in an overflowing pail on the floor and disappeared into the ground. She touched the water and shivered from the frigid temperature. Cold water. What if it stayed cold in summer? What a luxury that would be.

Her eyes had adjusted to the dim light and she saw food piled everywhere. Hams hanging over her head. Eggs! Cassie hadn't eaten an egg since she came west. It was all she could do not to grab one and take it directly to the stove to cook.

Red must have chickens and pigs. There was butter, and a pail of milk hung on a nail on one wall. A milk cow, too? She found potatoes, carrots, onions, and beets. There was flour, salt, sugar—both brown and white—honey, and cakes of yeast. She couldn't begin to search through all of the crates and barrels packed in that room.

She had lived in a beautiful home with Griff, but food had sometimes been a problem. There was the spring near their home and he'd had good luck fishing. But they'd eaten a lot of trout. Griff wouldn't let Cassie help in the garden, although as a child she'd enjoyed working by her mother's side. Griff had helped her understand how crude her mother had been to do man's work. She wondered how long Red had been here to be so established. Then she realized how much time she'd spent dreaming over the food and hurried to work on supper.

The main room of Red's home was small. The fire blazed cheerfully now and cut the chill in the kitchen. The sink was simply a hollowed-out log split in half, with a hole in the center of the bottom and a bucket under the hole to catch draining water. A small but well-built table with two sturdy chairs sat near enough to the fireplace to make a meal cozy even on a cold night.

The floor was dirt and a handmade broom stood in one corner. Cassie wasn't sure how she'd know when she was done when she swept a dirt floor. She looked around the room and realized that except for a few pots and pans, there was nothing in the house that wasn't handmade. Red had created this strange house with nothing but his bare hands. Cassie wondered at the pride a man would have if he could care for himself like Red did.

She started a rising of bread. They would have fresh-baked bread for breakfast. She warmed the ham in a cast-iron skillet and hung it from a hook in the fireplace. She pared potatoes, careful to waste as little white flesh as possible, put them in the covered pot full of water, and tucked the pot into the corner of the fireplace. She made biscuits. The heat was uneven and she feared things would burn, so she kept a careful eye on everything. Ham, potatoes, and biscuits. If she could get a good gravy from the ham, it would be a simple but tasty meal. She wished she could figure out an excuse to fry eggs with the meal. She'd do it for breakfast, she promised herself.

The bread had risen. She'd punched it down and shaped loaves which were rising again. The table was set with one tin plate and one chipped china plate, the only plates she could find. The food was done. Even the mashed potatoes were whipped high with butter and milk and set in a pan of warm water, waiting for when Red came back.

The door swung inward and Red entered, looked at her, and smiled rather abruptly.

Cassie had the impression he'd forgotten he was married.

CHAPTER 6

Red hadn't been able to think about anything all day except that he was married.

Married!

He'd left here yesterday a single man with too many chores and too many goals and not a second to spare for anything else. Now there was a woman in his house. He looked at Cassie and saw the most beautiful woman on earth.

She turned from his fireplace in his kitchen, and he thought back to how he'd held her in his arms all the way from town. He'd loved every minute of it.

"H–Hi, Cassie. I see you're cooking." He felt like some kind of monster to marry a woman standing on the freshly dug grave of her husband. But he'd seen no way out of the marriage. The crowd wasn't even going to allow them to move out of the cemetery.

Cassie nodded and didn't speak. Which gave Red a moment to remember why he'd married her—to save her. And why he shouldn't have—because she wasn't a believer.

Marrying Cassie was a sin, the greatest sin of his life.

But he'd had to help her.

But he could have thought of *something* short of marrying her.

Except he couldn't think of *anything*.

But he should have tried *harder*.

But he'd tried *hard*!

The events had chased themselves through his head over and over while he did his chores until he'd wanted to crack his head into a rock a few times, hoping the pain and a big knot on his head would give him something else to think about.

It was just that at the time Muriel had been nagging him to save the poor little thing. That overbearing Mort Sawyer had been ignoring Cassie's pleas and demanding to the parson that they "get it done." Then Cassie'd started screaming to raise the dead, which considering they were standing on her dead husband at the time, she might have been trying to do exactly that. Throw in Wade looking on all hungry and evil and it had all forced his hand.

Except that wasn't really the whole exact truth. Yes, it was part of the truth but not all of it. Red figured the only fool bigger than a man who tried to lie to himself was a man who lied to God. Both were just a pure waste of time. Red supposed he was seven kinds of a fool, but at least he was an honest fool. And the plain honest truth was he *wanted* to marry Cassie. He wanted to marry her almost desperately. In his own way he was just as bad as all those ruffians who were fighting over her.

Red couldn't shake the idea that somewhere God had spent a lifetime preparing a perfect mate just for him, a woman who was a believer above all else, and Red had just gone and tossed God's plan back in His face by marrying the wrong woman. Cassie Griffin. Cassie Dawson. *God, forgive me,* he thought. *I do like the idea of her having my name.*

Red had done his chores thoroughly, but it was a good thing

he'd done them a thousand times before because his mind was not on his tasks. Even though Rosie was going be hurting bad by the time he milked her, he left the cow until last because he didn't want to go back to the house to leave the milk. He almost dropped everything ten times and ran back to the soddy to see if Cassie needed help finding supplies, or lifting a bucket, or squashing a bug, or crossing a mud puddle....

Oh, no doubt about it, he had it bad. He wanted that woman, that overindulged, beautiful, non-Christian woman desperately. He sat down to Rosie and she thanked him for his prolonged neglect by kicking him soundly on his backside. He figured it was just what he needed.

And now here his wife was, smiling at him, a sweet, shy smile, and he thought about how he'd finished with Rosie and grabbed the bucket of eggs and forced himself not to run to the house.

He'd been twenty feet away when he smelled the cooking. He'd assumed she wouldn't cook. He knew she was pampered. A person only had to look at her beautiful clothes to know that. And everyone said Griff was broke because of Cassie's greed. Red didn't listen to gossip, and he held that a man had free will; and no one, even a wife as pretty and perfect as a china doll— which is what everyone called her—could make a man spend money if he didn't want to. And Red had known Griff enough to know the man was stiff-necked and arrogant all on his own. No one could blame Cassie for that. But whether Cassie was spoiled by Griff's wish or her own, Red had never known. He did know he hadn't expected the cosseted china doll to cook. Yet there she stood, holding a heavy pot in her hands.

Red had seen the Griffin place and he knew Cassie didn't lift a finger outside. He'd seen Griff working in the garden and hauling water, and everyone knew she bought all her dresses ready-made, so she didn't sew. Those were all chores that most women would do, especially when there was so much work on a ranch and Griff didn't hire any hands.

But Cassie refused. Why even on trips to town, on the rare occasion that Cassie would lower herself to appear, she rarely left the carriage, sitting alone, ignoring all and sundry. Yes, there was no doubt Cassie was spoiled.

But she'd cooked. He wondered how a man could unspoil a woman. He'd better figure it out, because however Cassie Griffin was, Cassie Dawson was going to have to rough it. There'd be no more silk dresses. Yup, Cassie was going to have to learn, and if it had to be the hard way, so be it.

He felt all strict and manly standing there with the milk and eggs. He was thinking that milking cows and collecting eggs were woman's work and she'd better start carrying her weight around here with the stock, too. Then he asked God for an extra-large dose of wisdom and went inside to the wonderful smell of warm food and the even more wonderful sight of a beautiful woman.

She looked at him with that perfect china doll face. She blinked her huge brown eyes at him, and he thought maybe he could see why Griff would die trying to keep her happy.

Red stepped inside, setting the eggs down to swing the door shut without taking his eyes off his brand-new, beautiful, perfect wife.

His last thought as the door thudded shut was that he'd have to be careful, or he'd end up dying trying to keep her happy himself.

"Red Dawson, you're gonna die." Wade Sawyer lowered his rifle and rolled onto his back with a deep grunt of self-contempt. "I should've done it. I should've killed him where he stood."

He'd had Dawson in his sights. One shot and the china doll

would be his. He'd take her away and not bring her back until she had accepted Wade as her husband. Not even his pa would have a chance at her.

He rested against the cool rocks on the overhang near Dawson's poor excuse for a house. "No one would have known. And even if anyone wondered, who would challenge a Sawyer's word?"

Something quick and hard twisted in his stomach as he watched the dusk settle in through the branches of an overhanging pine. The china doll was nowhere in sight. A stray bullet could have hit her. Wade tried to convince himself that he'd held off with the shot because of that. But it wasn't true. The truth was he was a coward. He should have killed Dawson. He should have proved to himself that he was man enough to take what he wanted.

He'd never had the guts to kill a man. He'd had his chances. Drunken cowpokes looking for trouble. Rustlers. A cardsharp once who had cheated him. His father's men were always around, backing him up, like they'd done today with Tom Linscott. And some of Pa's hands were salty enough that they'd step in eagerly to do any shooting without Wade having to show his yellow streak.

"I'm a coward. I should have killed him, but I'm too yellow." Wade stared up at the sky and hated himself for being weak. Losing the china doll today was the final proof of it. He should have stood up to his pa. He should have told that old tyrant that he'd have to kill his own son in order to claim that beautiful woman.

When they'd heard about Griff, he'd told Pa he wanted her.

His pa had said, "Let's share her, boy."

It made Wade sick to think it now, and to stop his head from working, he sat up and fished his pint of whiskey out of his saddlebag and took a deep pull on it, trying to drown out the sound of his father's filthy suggestion. His pa had gotten in the habit of thinking himself above the law. And that included the laws of God. Once a man started thinking that way, everything he wanted to do was right.

Surely even his father's arrogance didn't extend so far that he meant share the china doll. . . . Wade's mind veered away from the thoughts and swallowed more of the rotgut. What Pa had *meant* was he'd take the land and Wade could have the woman. But that wasn't what Pa *said*. And even if Pa intended to leave Cassie to Wade, Pa would still be her husband and Wade wouldn't be able to marry her and treat her honorably. Even the hint of something so foul happening to the china doll drove Wade into a rage.

When Pa had said those words, "Let's share her," Wade had lunged.

Mort, in his seventies and half crippled from arthritis, had backhanded Wade so hard he'd been knocked to the floor. Then he'd kicked Wade in the ribs until Wade had cried and begged him to stop.

Mort had grabbed his hair and jerked his head back and roared, "You come at me, you'd better be ready to win, you whinin' pup. You're eighteen years old but you're lyin' on your belly crying like a baby girl. Now I expect you to back me up today."

Wade should have crawled out of the room and come back with a gun. Instead he'd followed his father's orders and humiliated his china doll. He'd mocked her in front of that crowd. He'd played the fool because he always did.

He thought about how much he hated his father. How often he'd dreamed of having the strength to beat him into the dirt. How often he'd had nightmares that ended in his own death at his father's hands. But his other favorite dream ended when he killed his father. He woke up half crazy from all those nightmares, and only whiskey would quiet the torment.

Now Wade drew deep on his brown bottle, then lay on his back and nurtured his anger and fed his hatred, focusing it on Red Dawson.

The rage boiled in Wade's stomach, a killing fury stirred in him, and he rolled back over, picked up his rifle, and took a bead on Dawson's door. If Dawson stepped outside at that instant, he'd die.

Wade was ready. He was finally ready. He was finally man enough to kill.

He waited and watched and wanted and hated.

Cassie had been rehearsing what she'd say when Red returned. She was determined to talk at least a little, since she'd been mostly mute the whole time they'd been together. Griff had wanted an intelligent conversation with dinner. He'd always said she couldn't hold up her end because she was so uneducated. Which was true. She'd quit school at fifteen when she got married. And he'd pointed out that her mind was naturally childlike, as was the case with most women. She thought that was true, too, because inside her head she spent a lot of time screaming and complaining and making sharp, crude remarks—very childish.

But Griff needed to be allowed to discuss his day. He said a man couldn't relax properly without that. She had learned to smile politely and nod and make encouraging comments to keep him talking. She would try to talk enough to let Red tell her about his day but not so much as to annoy him.

"Everything's ready. If you want to wash up, we can eat right now." She hoped she wasn't being bossy.

Red smiled wide. "It smells great. To walk in and have a meal set down in front of you is a real nice thing, Cassie. It makes me feel like a king. Thank you very much for this."

Cassie was dishing the ham onto Red's plate and she almost dropped it. Making dinner was her duty. The notion that Red would thank her for that almost knocked her over. She nodded and almost smiled, but she controlled the silly impulse. "There's water warming in the fireplace. I could ladle it for you." She set the ham down and moved toward the fireplace where she'd settled a pot of water to warm.

"No, I'll get it. You've done enough." Red waved her away and hurried to scoop water into a basin. He set the basin in the sink, rolled up his sleeves, and washed his hands all the way to his elbows. Then he washed his face and ran his hands into his hair, finger-combing it. He took the bowl outside and tossed the water and came to the table.

While he washed, Cassie spooned a plateful of potatoes, gravy, ham, and biscuit for each of them and hung a coffeepot over the flames to be ready when dinner was done.

As Red pulled out his chair, Cassie sat quietly, ready to memorize any critical word he said about the potatoes she'd whipped so smooth or the gravy she'd fussed over to rid it of the tiniest lumps. She needed to confess her use of yeast on the biscuits because he would no doubt disapprove of extravagance. And she was afraid she'd made too much of everything and it would go to waste. Or too little of everything and Red would go hungry. She took small servings herself, even though the wonderful smell of ham had been torturing her for an hour. She would take more later if there was any left.

She picked up her fork and lifted the first bite of the luscious meat to her lips, when Red said, "We say the blessing first, Cass."

She almost dropped her fork. Those were words her mother had always said to her as a child. *"Before we eat, we ask God to bless the food, Cassandra."*

Griff said it was a meaningless ritual.

Cassie laid down her fork and folded her hands in her lap. She nodded at Red then bowed her head.

There was a long silence and it took all of Cassie's willpower not to peek at Red and see if he'd prayed silently and was now eating without her while she sat, eyes closed, waiting. When Red finally spoke, it wasn't like the sweet, memorized prayer her mother had always said. Red just talked to God.

"Father, Cass and I got married today. You were there, Lord, I felt You there. Bless this marriage we began today and bless the soul of Lester Griffin. And take care of the babe, Lord. It's a big responsibility. I need You to give Cass and me the wisdom to be good parents. Thank You for this wonderful meal Cassie made. Let us use the strength we get from this good food to do Your work on this earth. In Jesus' name. Amen."

Cassie lifted her head and said, "That was a nice prayer, R—uh. . .uh. . ." Cassie was struck speechless. She pressed her fingers over her lips as she realized that she didn't know her husband's name and found she couldn't call him Red.

"What, Cass? Is something wrong?" Red looked worried and she saw him take a quick glance at her stomach.

Cassie dropped her eyes to her lap and whispered, "I. . .Red isn't. . ." She glanced up at him, afraid he'd be angry at her stupid question, but she had to ask. She whispered, "Should I know your real name?"

He looked dumbfounded for about two seconds, then he grinned so widely that she lifted her fingers away from her lips and smiled back.

"I reckon a wife oughta know her husband's name," Red announced and started laughing. Cassie was amazed to hear the sound of laughter come from her own lips. It was a sound she hadn't heard for three years. She slipped her fingers back over her mouth to stop herself.

She remembered the moment, the circumstances of the last time she'd laughed. Griff had asked her to marry him and she'd yelled, "Yes!" and laughed and flung her arms around his neck. He'd pulled her arms away from him roughly and shook her so hard her head had snapped back and forth and tears had come to her eyes. He'd told her she was making a fool of herself and to please try and moderate her voice and not flaunt herself.

Griff had corrected her from the very beginning, even before her mother died when he'd cared for the family accounts. Then, when he'd been put in charge of Cassie's inheritance, he'd been even more strict. She accepted that because he was so much older and wiser. But Griff had always been kind, carefully explaining things to her and with incredible patience telling her he didn't expect much from her until she'd had the chance at proper training.

But that day, he had shaken her so violently her neck stung and she could feel the bruises forming on her arms. She'd immediately apologized, and she'd begun the hard work of growing up so she could be worthy of a man as fine as Griff. She'd never, never shouted again and she hadn't laughed out loud in three years.

Now Red was laughing, and she had laughed back. He didn't seem upset at all. Cassie decided in that moment that it wasn't what the rules were that was important. It was finding them out and obeying them. She would have to learn a whole new set of rules, but she could do it. She could be the wife that Red deserved.

"My name is Fitzgerald O'Neill Dawson. My mother was born in Ireland and she landed all her love for the Old Country right smack on my head with a single name."

"Fitzgerald O'Neill Dawson?"

"It's a mouthful." Red turned to his ham and started cutting.

"It's a fine name. Do you want me to call you Red?" She'd

always called Griff by his nickname because he had dictated that she should. Now she waited for Red to make his wishes known. Cassie carefully imitated Red's motions, picking up her fork and knife seconds after he did.

"Red's okay. I doubt if I'd know to answer if anyone called me Fitzgerald of all things. Even my ma called me Red."

"Tell me about your parents, Red," Cassie asked politely. She was suddenly excited about the wealth of questions she could ask of a man she didn't know at all. She could keep him talking for months.

"Well, let's see. My pa was a parson. Ma had hair as red as mine, and there were ten children in all."

"Ten children!" Cassie gasped.

"Yeah, I was the youngest. Six of the kids died of one thing and another, mostly before I was born. So, there are four of us grown. Let's see. . .of the six that died, we lost one in the War Between the States. Another fought and got home okay, but scarlet fever went through and killed him. Another brother, the one that was next older than me, and the two sisters next older than him died of yellow fever before I was born. And I had a sister who died having her first babe. I was old enough to remember that."

A somber expression crossed Red's face as he recited this litany of death, but he didn't dwell on it. Cassie didn't expect him to. Death was a part of living and it made no sense to rail against it.

Red continued. "I'm a straggler anyway. Then losing those three that were next older, there's a long spread of years between me and the rest of the family. Pa did his preaching on Sundays and owned a feed store besides. Ma and all us kids helped out. The whole bunch of them settled down young and started right in raising families. Last count I had five nieces and eight nephews. I guess I'm the maverick of the family, but there was always something that called me to ranching. Ma said it was the Irishman's love of the land. Pa said I was a dreamer. When they opened Montana for homesteading, I jumped at the chance. They were old when I was born, near fifty, and they've both passed on now."

"If you're a rancher, why do you dig graves?" Cassie asked.

"I turn my hand to a dozen jobs in town to make this place pay. The general store lets me work off my bill. The blacksmith keeps my horses shod. I bought a horse at the stable in town, and I'm paying that off with a pitchfork. Whatever it takes to get done what needs doing."

"And how did you decide to live in this cave?"

Red grinned and shrugged. "I've got a better home for my chickens and pigs than I do for myself."

"Oh, no! This is a wonderful home," Cassie protested.

"Do you really like it? Because I didn't want to build a house for a few more years."

"If you do build a house, whenever you do it, could we just add it on to this one?" Cassie asked. "I'd never want to give up that cold spring."

"Yeah, sure, that's what I've always had planned. It may be awhile."

Cassie heard the note of warning in his voice. She said, "I like it just the way it is. When a house gets too big, it's next to impossible to keep it warm. This is so cozy with only the fireplace burning."

Cassie went back to her meal while Red talked. Asking questions was the perfect way to pass the rest of her life.

"Now tell me about your folks, Cass. You and Griff came from New York, right?"

Cassie was struck dumb. She had a mouthful of mashed potatoes, and she had to force herself to swallow them. She hadn't been asked to offer much to a conversation in years.

Suddenly words wanted to rush out. She had so many things she wanted to say, the words jammed behind each other like piled-up logs at a narrow spot on a river.

She just looked at Red and shrugged silently, acting just as stupid as Griff had always said she was.

CHAPTER 7

Do you have brothers and sisters?" Red scooped himself a big bite of potatoes.

Cass found she could answer a direct question. "No, I am an only child."

Red looked up from his plate. "That sounds lonely. Although I was so much younger than my brothers and sisters, in some ways, I was almost an only child, I reckon."

Red ate his potatoes, then casually sliced a generous piece off his ham steak and laid it on Cassie's plate. "I've got too much here."

She didn't know if handing her food counted as a criticism or not. She didn't have time to decide.

"So what does your father do for a livin'? Or has he passed on?" Red attacked his meal with relish.

Cassie realized that as long as he talked, he couldn't eat. Maybe he thought it was rude of her to question him when he was hungry. She inhaled slowly and decided she had to talk so he could finish his meal.

"My father worked for the railroad. First in an office in

New York City, but before I was born, they'd moved to Illinois, to Chicago. Mother was Spanish, but several generations ago."

Red smiled. "The pearls from the Spanish countess."

Cassie nodded and resumed talking. "She was four generations away from the Spanish countess, and our family these days is more German and English than Spanish. But my mother was still as proud of being Spanish as your mother was of being Irish."

Red was eating with relish now, and Cassie's heart lightened at his enjoyment. "Father died when I was very young. I just barely remember him. He left us quite well fixed, though. Mother and I lived alone from then on in a large house in Chicago. Mother died six years ago. I was twelve."

Red stopped eating and his forehead wrinkled. "That's really hard to lose your parents when you're still a child. Who took care of you?"

"Griff did."

"What?" Lowering his fork, Red stared at her.

He looked so shocked, Cassie hurried to explain. "There was no other family, and Griff was an assistant my mother hired to see over our affairs after Father died. He had fallen out with his father and been disinherited, so he had no start in the world. He became less of an employee over the years and more of a family friend. When my mother died, she'd left the management of my estate to him and named him my guardian. We were married when I was fifteen."

"Wow, that's young for marriage." Red slathered butter on his biscuit.

Cassie found that watching his hands and the melting butter was easier than looking him in the eye. "One day, when we'd been married about a month, I overheard some gossip between a storekeeper and our cook about Griff marrying me when he was closer to my mother's age than mine. Griff was furious at me for listening to gossip, especially because I had gone out to the shops without gaining his permission. He fired the cook at once, of course, and I was forbidden from leaving the house alone again." Cassie rubbed the side of her face, still remembering the stinging slap she'd earned for her childish defiance. It wasn't the first time Griff had punished her, but it was the first time he'd left marks where they'd be visible to others. She'd been banished to her room for two weeks, allowed to see no one but Griff until the bruises faded. She'd been so badly behaved back then.

"My pa didn't forbid my ma to do much. She wasn't one to take orders a bit good." Red took another bite of biscuit and chewed slowly, watching her so carefully she wished she could end her story.

"I convinced him to forgive me, but he was still very upset about it. To avoid the talk, Griff decided to come west. He had dreams about being a cattle baron and proving himself to the world. With my inheritance, it seemed like Griff's dreams could come true. But it takes a lot to get started in the West."

"Not if you live off the land like I do." Red had quit eating.

"Griff wanted a home for us like the one we'd left behind, and of course, things Griff wanted to make our home pleasant were so costly out here." Cassie sighed. Things Mr. York and probably others thought she'd demanded.

"Then Griff was cheated when he bought cattle. They never gained weight well and most of the calf crop was lost. The grass on our property was never as lush as we had hoped. And the property was heavily wooded and mountainous rather than grassland, not what had been represented to us at all. It was just one thing after another. We'd have made it, I'm sure, if Griff hadn't died."

Cassie noticed Red's plate was nearly cleared. "Do you want more? There are more potatoes and biscuits."

Red shook his head, leaned back in his chair, and rested a hand on his stomach. "I am stuffed. I can't remember when I've enjoyed a meal more. The food was delicious, and I did like havin' a beautiful woman talk to me while I ate. I'd drink a cup of coffee, though."

Cassie stood, but Red waved her back. "Let me get it, Cass. You've had a rough day." Red moved to the fireplace and picked up the heavy coffeepot with a towel to protect his hand. He poured them each a fragrant cup of the boiled coffee and, with a *clank* of metal on metal, returned the pot to the hook.

He moved gracefully, at home in the kitchen handling women's work. Griff had never lowered himself to do anything like that, but somehow, when Red did it, it didn't seem like he was less a man. Cassie added a new rule to her collection. Man's work and woman's work wasn't the same in every family. Instead, like all rules, they were set by the man to be how he wanted.

Red slid a cup of coffee in front of Cassie. She cradled the tin coffee cup in both hands, absorbing the warmth even though it wasn't a cold night.

"When is the baby due, Cass?" Red settled back in his chair.

Shocked, she lifted her head from her contemplation of the new rules. She'd never dreamed Red would ask such personal things about the baby. Griff had avoided the whole subject, saying it was inappropriate to discuss such things. She felt her cheeks heat up as she floundered for something to say.

"I didn't mean to embarrass you." Red sat up straight in his chair, looking as uncomfortable as she felt.

That made Cassie feel even worse. The only reason he would have mentioned her embarrassment was if the heat in her cheeks meant she was blushing. She set down her cup and clapped both hands over her cheeks to cover the red. "I didn't think you'd want to talk about it."

"If you're uncomfortable talkin' about it with me, I understand. I just want to know when it's due. We may need to have the doctor out, and as winter comes on, that gets harder, so I was wonderin' if it's very soon." Red shrugged and lapsed into an awkward silence.

"I. . .I don't exactly know. How can a woman know such things as when it's coming?" She wanted to tell him what he needed to know.

"You mean you don't know how long you've been expectin'?"

"Um. . .I know that. Griff thought it was unseemly to discuss fe—female things. . . ." Cassie fell silent, exhausted from forcing such personal words past her lips.

"Oh." Red nodded for a second. Then Cassie was amazed to see him smile. "I don't really think of having babies as a female thing, Cass. Well, in a way it's probably the most female thing there ever was, but there's got to be a father somewhere and it looks like I'm it. So, that makes it a male thing, too. So, tell me how long."

"I. . .I knew I was. . .that is, my time. . .my lady's time. . . didn't. . .wasn't there. . .in March last. I told Griff about it a couple of months ago and he said I was most likely bearing a child, and we weren't to discuss it or be. . .be close until after, because a woman was unclean when she was bearing. . ." Cassie gave up again, humiliated. She propped her elbows on the table and rested her burning face in her hands.

Red caught one of her wrists in his hand. "Cassandra Dawson?"

Cassie looked up and saw Red smiling kindly at her. "Yes?"

"We aren't going to have things we don't talk about in this house. Having a baby does *not* make a woman unclean. I reckon I'm the head of this house, and I say that's the way it is. Now, if you need to blush over this, that's okay, but we're still gonna talk about it. If you missed your. . .um. . .time in March, that means. . ." Red sat silently for a few seconds and Cassie saw him ticking off his fingers. "That means you're seven months along. A woman takes nine months to grow a child inside her, so you'll be having this baby in December. We've got two months."

"Nine months. . .are you sure?"

"Cass, didn't anybody ever tell you these things? Didn't your ma have a talk with you, or wasn't there a woman friend?"

"Mother died when I was twelve. I can't remember her saying anything about it except what to do about my. . .my. . ."

"Your monthly lady's time?" Red asked gently.

Cassie's cheeks heated up again. She nodded, hoping they could move on from this topic. "I've got to clean up the dishes." She reached for the plate in front of Red.

Red had never released her wrist. He tightened his grip and held her still. "So you have no idea what to expect when the baby comes?"

Cassie shook her head, keeping her eyes on the table.

Red tapped her on the chin, and she looked up at him. His eyes were as warm as a Montana summer and he smiled at her even as, with his calming touch, he held her in her seat and made her look at him. "There is nothing wrong or unclean or embarrassing about having a baby, Cass. It's the most natural thing God ever created. Birth is the foundation of the world. Every plant has a seed, every animal recreates in its own kind. God put people on the earth and told them to be fruitful and multiply." Red let go of her wrist and slid his chair out from the table so he could lay one hand on her stomach. "This baby is a gift from God."

Cassie flinched away from the unfamiliar touch. Griff never touched her, never held her hand except for a moment when she would step out of a carriage perhaps, never hugged or kissed her. Except for the brief and infrequent coming together in the dark, nothing physical ever passed between them.

Red didn't let her move away from him, and after the first

shock, she found she liked his touch. It was like a part of her uncurled and grew, nurtured by the human contact. She didn't tell him all that, but she forgot herself enough to lay her hand over Red's and press it against her stomach.

"Cassie, I want you to take pleasure in this gift and understand the glorious work you are doing to bring a new life into the world. This baby will be a blessing to both of us."

Red's voice was so solemn Cassie felt as if they were exchanging wedding vows a second time.

"I'll try, with God's help, to be a good husband to you, Cassandra Dawson, and a good father to the baby. We took vows before God today, and I want you to know I intend to keep them. I don't think we know each other well enough to promise to love like a romantic love. That will take time. But for now, I love you because God calls us to love others as we love ourselves, and I can promise to keep doing that. I'll honor you. That means I want to know what will make you happy. I'm not talking about things. I can't give you nice things like Griff did, but I want to give you what you need for your heart and your soul. I'll give you all of that as part of honoring you."

Cassie nodded, unable to look away from Red's kindness.

"And I'll cherish you. That means love, too, but to me it means more than that. It means enjoying all that is special about you and making sure you know I do."

Cassie listened, wide-eyed. She'd never heard such talk from a man before.

He went on. "And the vows say a woman has to obey her husband, but I want you to know I'll never ask you to do something that sets wrong with your conscience, and I won't be issuing a bunch of orders and demanding you obey them. We'll talk things through and make decisions together. If the day comes when we just can't decide something, really disagree over what is right and wrong, I may pull out the marriage vows and try to insist you obey me, but I don't make a very good dictator. I had too many bossy older brothers and sisters.

"Getting married like we did was a crazy thing to do, I reckon, but we've done it and now we're going to build a life together, doing our best to love and honor and cherish and obey. So don't be embarrassed about anything, Cass. There shouldn't be anything a wife can't say to her husband, okay?"

Cassie nodded, and the heat of tears burned behind her eyes. She had the strange sensation of the china doll Cassie and the screaming, childish Cassie drawing together until they were nearly one. She pressed her hand more firmly over Red's, which still touched her stomach, and wanted to say something as nice to him as he had said to her. Maybe that she liked him to touch her and she'd be glad to obey him—he didn't need to worry about that.

At that moment the baby kicked. Red pulled away with a gasp, then he stared at her stomach. "It moved!" He laid his hand on her again.

After a second, Cassie pressed both of her hands over his. "Try over here." She guided him to where there was more movement. The baby kicked harder this time.

He looked up from staring at her stomach. "Does it do that all the time?"

Cassie nodded and couldn't stop herself from smiling. Until this moment she'd thought Red must know everything about babies. But she remembered that he'd started this off by asking her questions. Now, with that little kick, she realized she knew lots of things he didn't. Eagerly, she said, "The baby kicks a lot. Sometimes I can't get to sleep at night for the kicking and rolling around it does."

"Rolling?" Red asked, his eyebrows arching to near his hairline.

Cassie nodded. "It sometimes feels like she's trying to beat her way out. Sometimes the whole top of my stomach stretches back and forth and I can picture the baby's head bunting me. Or over here."

She moved Red's hands slightly to her right side, at waist level. "I'm sure that is her feet." Cassie looked up at him. "The movement is littler but harder, if that makes any sense."

"Her, huh? You think it's a girl?"

Cassie hadn't realized she'd said "her." Imagining the baby to be a little girl was something private she wouldn't have admitted to if she'd been thinking. "Men want boys, I guess," she said, feeling her cheeks heat up.

The baby kicked again and Red moved his hand to find the source of this activity. "Is it exciting to think about a little person living in there?"

Cassie had never thought about it that way because Griff didn't want her behaving like a giddy girl, so excitement was something she controlled. But now that Red put it like that, she decided it was very exciting. "It's strange isn't it, to think that he—"

"Or she," Red interrupted.

Cassie smiled. She wanted it to be a baby girl so badly. "That he or she is in there, alive and waiting to get out. Nine months—no one ever told me that. That's only two more months. I'll have a baby by Christmas."

Red had both hands on her stomach now. He moved them around, searching for more movement. He looked up at her and lifted one hand to lay it on her cheek. "*We'll* have a baby by Christmas, Cass. We're in this together from now on."

Cassie's eyes burned with tears again, and she had the strange sensation of feeling safe. She'd never been safe with Griff, because she was always waiting for him to find fault with her and punish her. Now, at the surge of safety, hot tears spilled onto her cheeks.

Red wiped them away with his thumb. "Don't cry, Cass honey. I know you miss your husband and—"

Cassie kissed him. She leaned forward, only really thinking about making him stop talking because she was so ashamed at her disloyal thoughts about her newly dead husband. Her hands were full holding Red's on her stomach, so all she had left was to bump her mouth into his.

The kiss was over before it started, but it had the desired effect. Red quit talking.

Cassie jumped to her feet when she realized what she'd done. She knocked the chair over behind her as she backed away and might have fallen if Red hadn't caught her arm.

"It's okay, Cass. I know it's. . .I understand you're still in mourning." Red pulled her close and wrapped his arms around her. She stiffened against him, but he didn't do anything but hold her and smooth her hair. It felt so wonderful that she slowly relaxed against him. But relaxing was a mistake because the minute she did, she started to cry.

Red's arms tightened. The first tears were for Griff, and those tears flowed faster when she thought of her cowardly decision this afternoon to die, denying her baby life. The tears deepened into sobs over her fear of Mort and Wade Sawyer and all the men who had touched her. She wept over her terror of Red's anger about her bills. Then her body shuddered from the relief that he hadn't punished her for them, even though she knew he and every other person in town blamed her for Griff's financial straits.

She cried until she wasn't aware enough anymore to know why she was crying.

And always Red was there. He rubbed her back and brushed her hair off her forehead and crooned sweet words into her ear, surrounding her with strength and kindness.

The storm started to wane at last, and she became aware

that she was sitting on Red's lap. Her cheek was pressed against his coarsely woven shirt and her arms were around his neck as if he was the only steady thing in a reeling universe.

She pulled her arms away from him, ashamed of the closeness between them. Slipping sideways, she tried to stand.

Red didn't let her go. "Just rest another minute, Cass. You needed to cry those tears. You've been through a terrible time. Just let me hold you." There was an extended silence while she relaxed back into his arms, ashamed of herself for using his strength when she should have her own.

At last the trembling weakness receded. "I need to clean the kitchen, R–Red." She stumbled over his name again. Odd that she was having trouble saying it.

Red tilted her chin up with one finger. "You're going to sleep, little mother. I'll clean up in here."

Cass said, "This is my job. I'll do the—"

"Do you know how to milk a cow?"

The question struck her as so strange she didn't answer.

He smiled. "Would you be willing to learn? And I'd like you to gather the eggs, too. There are a few things left in the garden, some beets to dig and a few pumpkins that I left, hoping the frost would hold off and they'd ripen. I'd be obliged to you if you'd tend to those things, and most of the time, I'll be thrilled if you clean up after meals. But I'm used to doing for myself, and when you've had a hard day, I'm willing to pitch in."

Cassie was amazed that Red had framed his offer to help so perfectly. It was as if he knew she'd want to do her part, and he was reassuring her that accepting his assistance this once didn't mean she couldn't contribute. The words could have come from her own mind. They were possibly the only words that would have made her leave the kitchen to Red.

"I'll be proud to help with the milking, Red. I've never done it. We didn't have a milk cow, but I'd try real hard to learn. I'll help wherever you need me. I want to be however you want me to be, Red. Just tell me what to do."

"Right now, I'm telling you to go to bed. We can start worrying about chores tomorrow."

Cassie nodded and eased herself off Red's lap.

"Oh, I almost forgot." Red went to the saddlebags he'd brought into the house with him when they'd first come home. "Muriel said you'd need this tonight."

Cassie looked at the brown paper package and vaguely remembered Muriel saying it was a wedding present. She unwrapped it and found a snow white nightgown. It was embroidered around the neck and made from the softest flannel Cassie had ever touched. She thought it was more beautiful than the finest silk.

She remembered it was not an appropriate piece of apparel to look at in front of Red and blushed as she folded it quickly and held it against her chest. She looked nervously at him and expected him to say something about immodesty as Griff would have. But he was smiling at her as if he were reading her mind and found her embarrassment at looking at a nightgown in front of her husband funny. Another one of those new rules she needed to learn.

"I'll go on to bed then," Cassie murmured.

Red nodded. "Good night, Cass. Sleep as late as you need to in the morning."

Cassie hung her only dress on a nail in the bedroom and donned her nightgown quickly in case Red would come in. She crawled into bed. Her muscles ached as if she had been beaten. Her eyes were as scratchy as sandpaper from all her tears. The white nightgown wrapped around her, touching her almost as warmly, not quite but almost, as Red's hands.

Her husband had been buried today. She'd been married today. Already her new husband was superseding thoughts of the old, and she supposed that made her as stupid and childish as Griff had always said she was.

The day was finally over, but she was afraid the guilt and confusion would last the rest of her life. This had to be the worst day of her life, but she had survived it. Tomorrow would have to get better. Tomorrow Red was going to let her help him. It was something she had longed for with Griff, but he'd never given her the chance to prove herself.

She fell asleep planning a wonderful new life where all her dreams would come true.

CHAPTER 8

Red's life was a nightmare. And he was never going to wake up.

"Cassie! Don't open that. . ."

Cassie started screaming and flapping at the escaping chickens.

". . .gate!"

Cassie screamed and started yelling, "Shoo, no, stop! Shoo, chickens!" and frantically waving her skirt at the escaping hens. Her noise and flapping skirts only served to make the chickens run out of the coop faster.

It bothered Buck, too. It was just pure bad luck that when Buck started crow hopping, Red was on one of the chancier spots on the steep path down to the spring where his animals watered.

Red was watching Cassie instead of minding his horse. So he was unseated—and slid over the edge of the cliff. The drop-off wasn't sheer, and there was some brush growing. He grabbed it and dangled for just a few seconds before he clawed his way back from the brink. There were lots of stunted evergreens on the slope, all the way down, so Red figured if he'd missed the first bushes, he'd have caught the later ones.

As he dragged himself back onto the trail, he saw Buck run off, kicking his heels. Once he'd landed himself on the level ground, slightly panicked at the close call, he admitted he hadn't been *that* close to death. The last drop-off, which was thirty feet straight down to jagged rocks, was still quite a ways away when he'd stopped sliding.

Cassie, as near as Red could tell, hadn't noticed him fall, because she was busy jumping and screaming and flapping her skirts to try and stop the chickens from flying the coop.

He rushed over to calm her down. "Cass, honey, calm down."

She whirled to face him, looking terrified. She didn't seem to register his dirty jeans and torn shirt or his scratched-up arms and face. Or the fact that his hat now had a horse's hoof-print stomped straight into the crown.

"Red, I'm so sorry. I—I didn't mean to let them go." Cassie turned to him with fear in her eyes.

He had scolding words pressing to get out, but he couldn't say them. How could he yell at her when she looked so scared? Instead of shouting, which had been his natural inclination, he said, "Don't worry, Cass. They get out from time to time. They used to do it to me."

That was the truth, strictly speaking. They'd gotten out just this same way when he'd gathered eggs for his mother.

He was five at the time.

He'd learned his lesson then, and he reckoned Cassie had just learned hers, so there really wasn't any point in talking about it.

"Don't worry, Cass. Just remember to always close this outer gate before you open the inner gate. Then close the inner gate while you're inside, and on your way out, make sure all the chickens are in the inner yard before you open this outer one."

She'd left both of the gates wide open. "Yes, Red. I'll never leave them open again." She pressed her hands to her chest, and he could have drowned in those big, scared eyes.

"Most of them will come home to roost come nightfall." He patted her arm to get her to calm down. "I let them out to scratch most days in the spring and summer."

In the spring and summer when there were weeds to pick at and bugs to chase. In the fall they'd wander far afield looking for food, then they'd roost wherever was handy. Red didn't tell Cassie all that.

"Gather the eggs and go on back in and start breakfast. I'll milk Rosie and bring in the bucket."

Cassie still looked nervous. She said with an almost pathetic eagerness, "Didn't you say last night that you wanted me to milk the cow?"

Red's stomach sank at the thought of what Cassie might do to his precious Rosie. Rosie, a big-boned black and white Holstein, had followed him out here from Indiana, tied behind his covered wagon. He'd raised her from a calf. Rosie was one of the gifts Red's pa had given him when he'd first gone out on his own. It was one of the last things his pa had done before he died. In short, Red had known Rosie a lot longer than he'd known his wife.

"Sure, I want you to learn." Red propped both gates wide open and scattered cracked corn around the inner yard, hoping some of the chickens would come around scratching for food. "But I'll be done by the time you've hunted up all the eggs, so I'll take care of her this morning."

Cassie nodded and entered the little chicken yard. "Ugh!"

He turned from his hurried trip to the barn to get Rosie milked before Cassie could help. She had a sickened expression on her face as she scraped her foot. Red wondered what kind of person didn't know to watch her step in a chicken coop.

Turned back to the barn and his milking, Red noticed Buck loitering around the corral, still loose. The horse looked eager to enter his pen but turned contrary when Red tried to catch him.

"Get back here, you old galoot." Red hustled after the stubborn critter and finally cornered the beast.

By the time he got to Rosie, she was overdue for milking and kicked him a couple of times to remind him to keep to a better schedule.

"Do you want me to try?" Cassie had leaned down over his shoulder.

He jumped. Rosie, startled, kicked over the nearly full bucket of milk. The bucket skittered across the barn floor and slammed into the hay bale where the lantern sat. Kerosene spilled across the hay.

"Cassie, fire! Get out of the barn." Red raced toward the burning hay with a feed sack.

Cassie didn't get out. She charged the haystack with her bare hands. Her skirt caught on fire.

Red grabbed her and pulled her to the barn floor. "Roll, Cassie. That'll put the fire out." He swatted at her skirt until the flames were gone, and then he turned back to the crackling barn.

Red had dropped his burlap bag. He retrieved it and dunked it in the spilled milk and doused the flames.

Red turned to ask Cassie what in heaven's name she'd been doing with a lantern in the barn in the full daylight. She stood behind him, tears streaming down her face.

Red's anger fizzled away as surely as the fire. "Now don't cry, honey." Red went and slung an arm around her trembling shoulders. "We're fine. The fire's out."

He glanced down at her charred skirt. Her one and only dress. He shuddered to think of how badly she could have been burned. He tipped her chin up to look at him.

"Everything's fine now, Cassie. I want you to stop that crying, okay? The important thing is that you weren't burned. There's no damage except to a little bit of hay, and I have plenty. It was pure clumsiness on my part to let Rosie knock that bucket of milk over. I'll be more careful next time."

Cassie pulled herself together and squared her shoulders. "It's my fault. I shouldn't have startled you. I shouldn't have brought the lantern in with me. I was trying to learn to light it and I wanted to ask you if I needed to turn the wick down. I'll never bring a lit lantern into the barn again. That hay catches fire too easily."

"That's a right good idea. I think we oughta make that a rule. I'll never bring one in here either." Red wanted to say, "Only an idiot brings a lantern into a barn full of hay and leaves it sitting close behind a cow like that." But he figured she'd learned everything his yelling would teach her. And besides, he wasn't much of a yeller.

Red smiled down at her pretty, sad face. "It was my fault and you're sweet to try and take the blame, but I won't have it. Just go on back to the house now and start breakfast."

Please, dear Lord, let her go back to cooking. She has a knack for that.

Cassie sniffled for another second and the terror faded from her eyes. She nodded and headed out of the barn.

With a sigh of relief, Red turned to untie Rosie. Just as he let Rosie out into her corral, a piglet squealed, Cassie screamed, and it was all drowned out by the bloodcurdling roar of an angry mama sow.

Red raced out of the barn, took in the situation in a glance, and dived between Cassie and the furiously protective mother. "Drop the pig, Cassie," he roared.

Harriet slammed, with slashing teeth, into Red's leg. He rolled and dodged her, kicking at her gaping fangs.

Cassie dropped the piglet, and it ran toward the pen. Harriet whirled away from trying to kill Red and chased after her baby.

Red scrambled to his feet and rushed to the gate Cassie had so casually left open. Apparently the woman had decided she wanted to cuddle a cute but unwilling piglet. He glanced down and saw two long slits in his pant leg. Before he could check for bites, he needed to make sure the gate was secure. When he had it tightly wired shut, he turned, his temper simmering, to brace Cassie about being so reckless. He took one step toward her, and his ankle, still sore from his fall off the horse, almost gave out on him. He caught the gate to keep from falling, then decided to turn his attention to his ankle until he quit wanting to holler at his wife.

Harriet was still woofing, but she was focused on her babies.

Red bent to look for bites. He found several deep scratches on his leg but was relieved to find Harriet hadn't drawn blood. Animal bites could turn septic, and Red had heard of many a man dying from a bite that wasn't very serious.

This time he'd have to say something. Cassie couldn't touch anything on his ranch, ever again. Red turned to look at her and saw her face had gone pure white. His heart clutched and his anger vanished. Could this much fear hurt the baby? He hurried as best he could over to her side, doing his best to hide his limp.

"Are you all right, Cass honey?" Red reached for her face, to study her pallor, then hesitated and wiped his hands on his pants, still filthy from being thrown off Buck, never cleaned after he fought the fire, and now worse from being rolled on the ground by Harriet. Red had a second to think of what could have happened to Cassie if Harriet had gotten to her instead of him.

"Red, Red, I'm sorry—" Her voice broke.

Red didn't give her another second to talk. He scooped her up in his arms and carried her to the house, his leg only a distant, nagging ache. He got through the stubborn, heavy door with her still in his arms and settled her in a kitchen chair. He knelt down in front of her. "You're okay, Cassie." All he could think of was calming her down before something awful happened. He jumped up and got a dish towel and plunged it into the bucket of water he'd hauled from the cooler this morning. He wrung out the cold water, then dropped back to his knees and bathed her chalky skin.

"You're fine, Cass. No harm done. I'm sorry I didn't warn you about Harriet. She's fierce about her babies. No one would ever know a mama pig could be such a dangerous animal." He felt the worst of the tension drain out of her. Her eyes, fixed wide with horror, dropped closed, and she sagged against him until her head rested on his shoulder.

They stayed like that for long minutes. Her trembling gradually eased and he felt some strength return to her muscles. She slowly raised her head.

Red sighed with relief. Her color was better. He pressed the cool cloth on her cheeks and forehead again. "Are you all right? Do you need to lie down?"

"No, I'm better now." Cassie shook her head and straightened her spine.

He had to admire that. A mama pig could take the starch out of a mighty steely spine. "You just rest here. Let me go finish the chores. Then I'll come back and get us some breakfast."

"No, you shouldn't have to do that."

Red shuddered. Then he thought of last night's supper. Yes, she could cook. If only she'd just agree to do nothing else.

He said, with a calm that took a Herculean effort, "So what's for breakfast?"

"I'll fry some eggs if that suits you."

Red nodded. "Eggs sounds fine. Let me add some wood to the fireplace for you."

"Thank you," she said so breathlessly, he felt like he'd offered to slay a dragon.

"I won't be gone long." He patted her knee, rose from the floor, stoked the fire, and made it out the door without limping.

He didn't bother to hide his limp once he was alone. He hobbled around finishing his chores, double-checking the gate as he always did.

He checked the hay pile a dozen times for any smoldering embers. Then he got to thinking about how close she'd snuggled up to him in the night last night. They'd started the night with a solid two feet of space between them, but in the morning he woke with her arms wrapped around his waist as if she craved his warmth. He thought of how her soft hair had fallen out of its braid and spread over his arm and across his chest.

He was far gone thinking about Cassie when he tripped over the basket of eggs Cassie had left sitting by the front door. He fell down and hurt his ankle a little worse.

She rushed to the door to see what the racket was. "Oh Red, I should never have left that basket sitting there. I was almost in the house when I noticed the pigs and went to look at them."

Red could blame her for everything else that happened this morning, but this one was all his fault. He reassured her he was daydreaming. Not for one second did he consider telling her what he was daydreaming about.

She lost that look she got, like she was afraid of him. She seemed to believe him when he took responsibility for this latest mess, a trifling matter compared to what had gone on earlier. He picked up what was left of the eggs and limped inside with them.

The sun was just fully up and already she'd about ruined him. He'd never survive the week. If he did, it wouldn't matter. All his animals would be dead, his buildings burned to the ground, and she'd probably find a way to lose all his ranch land and dry up his creek while she was at it.

He tossed split wood on the embers of the fire, determined to take charge of all fire-related chores from this moment forward.

"How did your shirt get torn, Red?"

He looked down. He was more of a wreck than even he'd realized. "I reckon they're just old and have been torn for a while." Red was an honest man, but *a while* could be weeks or it could be minutes, and the fact that one of the two outfits of clothing he owned was now halfway to rags, even though it'd been fine when he'd put it on this morning, didn't mean it hadn't been "a while."

"I'll mend your clothes if you take them off and leave them with me."

"How about I just wear 'em for the rest of the day, and you can do them tomorrow?" He thought if she had anymore hijinks in mind, maybe he'd better stick to the clothes that were already ruined.

"My clothes from yesterday are still dirty. I'll wash them up today and wear them tomorrow. You can mend these then."

She smiled timidly, as if she was out of practice. "I'll wash your clothes, Red."

"Thanks, Cass. If you have time." Red tried to think of the possible disasters involved in swishing pants around in water.

She'd smiled bigger, and he couldn't think of a thing that could go wrong.

She turned to the fireplace, her charred skirt swaying. Cracking eggs into a pan, she hummed as she worked.

She was his wife. She was the most beautiful woman Red

had ever seen. She was feeding him and sewing for him and doing his laundry and she'd just asked him to take his clothes off. Red decided if she wanted to kill him, he'd just sit back and thank God for every second of his life until he died.

And just in case there was a chance he wasn't going to die, he'd make sure she forgot all about his asking her to help outside and stayed strictly in the house.

CHAPTER 9

Cassie spent every minute of every day outside helping.

She was determined to learn everything as fast as she could. When Red didn't offer to show her what to do, she struggled to figure things out herself. She'd never leave a gate open again. She stayed out of reach of the terrifying mama pig. But she watched, and she did her best to make sense of the mysterious business of ranching.

The first evening as Red came in for dinner, Cassie met him at the door and pointed to the little building built with slender saplings. "Look at how many chickens came back. You were right that they'd come home." The chickens had wandered in a few at a time all day. Cassie had been careful not to go near them while they moseyed along, scratching for food.

Red pulled his hat off the peg after supper. "I'll wander the woods some and see if I can find any roosting." Red was complimentary about the beef steak she'd cooked over the open fire and didn't complain a bit when he went out around sunset, leaving her alone.

She carefully stayed outside, on watch for his return. She

guarded the closed gate to the coop so she could open it for him. He came walking in from the wooded area behind their home with his hands full of chickens. The chickens hung down at his sides. As he drew near her, they all started flapping their wings and squawking violently. Cassie used every ounce of her courage to stay on guard.

He made a lot of trips that evening, working long after dark until he'd gathered quite a few more.

"We got a lot of them back, didn't we?" She carefully closed the inner gate before she opened the outer one.

Red passed through the gate and locked it for her with a smile. "About half."

"Already?" That seemed like a good start to her.

"A great start," he agreed.

They walked side by side into their cave house, and Cassie marveled that Red had never once let his temper loose on her.

She gathered the eggs the next morning with Red right at her side the whole time. She enjoyed his company. "I only got four, Red." She waited, afraid he'd be angry. This was all her fault.

"They laid them in the woods this once. We'll get more tomorrow. It's no great loss, just a day's gathering."

She stepped close to him, the four eggs clutched in her hands. "It'll never happen again. I promise."

Red stayed close to the house all day. He said he didn't need to check his herd of cattle too often. Cassie accepted that because Griff, explaining to her that they foraged for food and needed little handling, hadn't checked his often either. Sometimes not for weeks at a time.

When he did go out riding, he made her promise faithfully to stay inside.

Red's house was so small and easy to keep tidy, the time hung heavy on her hands if she stayed inside.

One day, when he came back from checking the herd, she was sitting at the kitchen table fidgeting.

As if he read her mind, he asked, "Would you like to explore the cave off the bedroom?"

"Oh, yes. I've wondered about it, but I didn't want to go in without permission."

Red looked at her a little oddly, and then he shrugged. "Let's go."

"There are dead ends down this way." Red held her hand as they passed through the dark opening in the back bedroom. When the ground was especially uneven, he'd stay close to her side in the narrow passage, with one hand resting on her shoulder. "This part here is really steep. If being so big with the baby makes you feel off balance at all, you'd better not cross this section alone."

"I'll never step foot in here without you. I promise." Cassie thought the tunnel was spooky but found she enjoyed the little thrill of fear she got from walking through it. The tunnel descended quite a ways over its length, and it opened into the rocks right near the creek where Red took Buck and Rosie to water.

Red showed her a deeper spot in the creek where he took baths. The water was bitterly cold and Cassie preferred to warm a basin in the kitchen. But Red promised that if she wanted to bathe, he'd walk her through the tunnel and leave her in privacy to brave the chill.

"See this crack, down low here?" Red knelt and passed his hand into the crevice. "Feel how cold it is. It must have water in the back of it, same as our cooler. We could store cold things in here if the cooler didn't have enough room."

Cassie shivered with cold and excitement to know the little

details about Red's cave. She'd have liked to explore some more but didn't want to impose on Red's time.

She wasn't much help around the farmyard, because Red politely but steadfastly refused to give her a chance with milking. She chafed with the memory of Red saying she'd have to help. She knew that's what he wanted and she was determined to abide by his wishes. He no longer urged her to help outside, but she knew he was just being kind. Whenever she did start a chore, Red would jump in and do it for her. She thought it was sweet of him, but she was determined to learn. She tried her hand at milking a few times when Red had gone off to ride herd and nearly got her head kicked off. But she could tell Rosie just kicked out of cantankerousness. There wasn't any real meanness in it. By the end of the week she still couldn't get milk out of Rosie, but she felt like the little cow liked her.

Most of the chickens were back. Red had quit hunting for them at night. The mama sow had. . .well, Harriet still wanted her dead. And Cassie decided she wanted to learn to ride Buck.

She hadn't worked up the nerve to tell Red that she'd never been on a horse. With the exception of the terrifying trip to town on her bay to tell Seth and Muriel that Griff had died, and the ride she'd slept through with Red after their wedding, she'd always ridden in carriages. Griff had said it was unseemly for a woman to ride, even sidesaddle.

She was surprised to find out Red had a nervous streak. She didn't really know him, of course, but he'd seemed like a calm man. She found out he was prone to clumsiness. He'd hurt his ankle in a fall and he'd scared Rosie that first morning. When he offered her help with some job, he'd talk a little too fast and stumble over his words, and he seemed to spend time fixing things around the farm that had seemed fine when she'd been working with them.

She was serving him his noon meal on Saturday when she started to ask about riding the horse. Before she could gather her courage, Red announced they were heading for town as soon as dinner dishes were done.

"Town? Why?" Cassie's stomach fluttered with excitement. She loved going to town, although she'd gotten so she avoided it whenever possible with Griff. He made her sit quietly in the carriage while he conducted his business. She wasn't to speak to anyone or even smile or make eye contact. Griff said it was familiar and indecent behavior for a married woman, and Cassie had done her best to please him.

"I've got several jobs I do in town on a Saturday afternoon. To raise money and barter for supplies. And I've got to preach tomorrow morning at Seth's. I've considered it awhile and I've decided we'll stay in the hotel. Grant has always offered me a room. But sleeping on the ground has suited me. The nights are getting sharp, though, and I think you need a bed."

"Can I help with your jobs, Red?" Cassie began cleaning up after the noon meal, hurrying so Red wouldn't have to wait when he was ready to go.

"Most of it is heavy work. That's why they hire me." Red carried his own plate to the sink.

Cassie was still amazed when he did woman's work.

"You could spend the afternoon with Muriel if you want," Red suggested.

"Why do you do all that work, Red? You have everything you need here. You grow your own food and you seem to have a fair-sized herd of cattle. Why do you do all those chores in town?"

Red began drying the dishes Cassie washed. He was silent as he considered her question. Cassie realized that the way he talked to her, not as if she was stupid but as if the questions she asked were interesting, was the thing she liked best about her new husband. She also liked that he never yelled and the way he savored every bite of the food she made. It was amazing to her that he'd complimented her on the food. She'd never thought a man would bother with such a thing. Why, she even found his nervousness endearing.

Now, he stood there helping her and thought about her question as if the answer were important. Which meant the question was important and somehow that made Cassie important. It was wonderful.

"When I first moved here, I had nothing. I got out here a year before they opened this area for settlers because I reasoned that this would be next. I scouted until I found this place, the creek, the grasslands, the mountain valleys that could feed so many cattle but would be worthless without the creek. I'd even found this cave and had the beginnings of my home built. I was working odd jobs around Divide to earn enough money to buy a few cattle. I staked out a few good water holes and bought them up nice and legal as soon as I could scrape together the money. I bought ten head of cattle from a herd passing from Montana to the rail yards in Kansas City. I had the cows and the land, but I still needed money."

Red kept wiping until the few dishes were done, then poured them both another cup of coffee and settled at the table. "I had my eye on the forty acres next to me which had never been claimed, so I worked like crazy, afraid someone would beat me to it. As soon as I got the money together, I bought it."

Cassie sat down across from him.

"Doing odd jobs in town turned into bartering my labor at nearly every store where I did business. I almost never pay cash for anything, and if I get ahead, they pay me or they keep an account open for me. Like at the general store last week, I was able to have Griff's bills taken off what I had in my account, and they traded the value of your dress. So that bill is all settled.

Quite a few of them are."

"You are paying all of Griff's bills with your labor?" Cassie sipped carefully at the burning hot brew.

"Sure. Labor is how you get money. How else do you think I could do it? If I paid cash—I do have some money in the bank these days—that money is all labor, too. It's the same."

"But. . .then why didn't Griff work for them when he owed so much?" Cassie's voice faded away. She knew why. Griff would have found working for Seth beneath him. Even now Cassie could feel a twist of embarrassment to picture Red doing all that menial labor for the town shopkeepers.

"Griff had his way. I have mine. I've managed to add another 160 acres to my holdings as other settlers gave up. Because I have good water, I control several thousand more acres. I'm buying it all up as fast as I can because I don't want there to be any question about the title.

"I worked at the lumbermill to pay for the barns and corrals. I traded work with a farmer to get the chickens. I traded one of Rosie's calves for Harriet. I'm up to nearly five hundred head of cattle now, with last spring's calf crop. There's a lot of money to be made in cattle drives back East, but I take a little less and sell my cows in Divide because I don't want to be gone from my place for the whole summer. I don't hire a lot of hands like a lot of ranchers do."

"Five hundred cattle? You built that up from ten cattle in only. . .how many years?"

"I've been out here four years now, counting the year before I homesteaded. I've spent hundreds of hours hunting the hills for cows that have gone maverick. I've bought cattle cheap that weren't ready for market from settlers who were folding up. I've sold off the steers only once. I had a few three-year-olds ready to sell last spring, but I've held on to all the mama cows so they could build the herd. It's a lot of work to build something from nothing, but God gave us a bountiful world. He put gold under the ground in California and He put gold in the ground here in the form of rich soil and plentiful grass and water."

"I'd be proud to help you in town if you needed me to, Red. I'd like to be part of what you're building."

"We'll see. Like I said, a lot of it's hard labor and heavy lifting. But I'll think on it."

"Didn't you say you haul groceries from Seth's to Libby's Diner? I could carry that back and forth, just take a lot less each trip than you do. Please, Red, you've been so good about letting me help. Oh, I want to say again how sorry I am about knocking you out of the hayloft in the barn earlier. I was trying to lift the bucket of corn up there so I could pour Harriet's food into her trough from overhead. She gets so upset whenever she sees me. And now that the colder weather has forced you to move the feeder away from the fence to keep it out of the wind, I can't reach it to pour in her ears of corn. I thought you saw me raising that bucket up to the loft."

"I did see you, Cass. I just thought you looked like you didn't have a very good foothold. I shouldn't have grabbed you like that. It's all my fault. I was just afraid if I said your name to warn you I was there, you might be startled and fall. That straw can be slippery. I guess I proved that by slipping on it." Red smiled.

"Thank heavens you landed on the haystack. You could have really been hurt."

Red's cheeks got pink and his jaw tightened, and she thought it was sweet he was embarrassed at his clumsiness. His sweetness reminded her of the way he snuggled up to her every night, even though they were careful to fall asleep with a respectable space between them. This morning she felt him rubbing his chin on top of her head when he was still asleep. It had almost felt like his mouth instead of his chin, but despite his assurances that a woman expecting a baby wasn't unclean, she could tell he didn't want to kiss her.

She remembered that awkward kiss the first night they'd been together. She was the one who had kissed him. He'd never followed with a kiss of his own, so she knew he didn't like kissing. But she liked to pretend he kissed her while she slept.

"The haystack was lucky all right." Red finished his coffee in one last, long gulp. "Let's not feed Harriet that way again. I'd be glad to do that chore. She's a cantankerous old monster."

"I suppose the haymow wasn't a good idea. But I'm sure to find a way I can keep feeding her."

"Yes, well, yes. . .you're sure to find a way. Let me wash these two last cups."

"No, you must have chores to do if we're staying away overnight. I'll get things straightened in here and come help you as soon as I can."

Red nodded. "I'd better get going then." He practically ran out of the house.

"He's always in a hurry," Cassie murmured to herself. "I wish I could help him more." She cleared the last bit of the kitchen quickly so she could get to her outside chores.

CHAPTER 10

I'll get a horse saddled for you, Cass honey." Red tried to saddle Buck for her, planning to ride another horse himself, but she'd approached Buck then backed away with one excuse or another until she'd practically been dancing around the horse. Then Buck had started acting spooky.

"Uh. . .would it b–be all right if I just rode with you, like we did last week?" Cassie gave him a look of such longing, like the idea of sitting so near him really appealed to her. Buck had held up well being ridden double home from town last week. But Red was worried about working the horse too hard.

If Red didn't share with her, she'd have to ride Buck, because he was the best-trained horse Red owned, but truth was, Buck hadn't ever calmed down much after Cassie and the chickens had scared him. Red was afraid he was permanently spooked now and would never be as good a mount. Red had a remuda with a dozen horses, but they were green broke—rough horses born on Red's ranch or rounded up from the wild, well suited to cutting cattle when guided by a firm hand but not saddle ponies for an unskilled woman. The buckskin had come with him from Indiana, just like Rosie, and was almost as much a pet as Rosie. But he'd taken a skittish turn since he'd met Cassie, and Red was worried about Cassie riding him alone. Riding double solved that problem.

It took him a full hour to figure out Cassie had never ridden a horse before, or at least not much. She was terrified but doing her best not to let him see that.

He thought about hitching Buck up to the wagon. It was slower but it would have been okay. Unfortunately, he figured out about Cassie's fear when they were a long way down the road to Divide. It was too late to go back.

Cassie had started out sitting sideways on the saddle while Red rode behind the cantle. But that proved to be not only uncomfortable for them both, but Buck didn't like Red sitting back so far and proved it by bucking every few feet. Cassie had nearly fallen off a few times. Red fixed that by moving into the saddle and holding her firmly on his lap just as she had been after their wedding. Red found this arrangement to be no hardship.

Even after Red moved, Buck was fractious.

"Is this how it usually is to ride a horse, Red?" Cassie tried to sound calm, but Buck wasn't cooperating. Now Cassie's flapping skirts and her constant squirming around on Red's lap weren't making his horse a bit happy.

Red was happy. . .just not his horse.

"Buck's a little jumpier than usual, I reckon. He'll calm down once we've ridden a ways." Red hoped.

Cassie's constant nervous fluttering wasn't bothering Red at all. He liked the feel of her against him, and every time she moved, he realized that being married was a wonderful thing. But Buck wasn't married to Cassie, and he probably didn't think she was heart-stoppingly beautiful, what with Buck having his own standards of beauty that included four legs and gigantic teeth. So Buck didn't like her one bit.

They'd been on the trail a far piece when Cassie said, "I'd like to learn to ride a horse, Red."

"Learn to ride? What's to learn? You're doin' it."

"This is only the third time I've been on a horse in my life. I should know how to do it if I'm going to be a rancher's wife. Shouldn't I?"

Red's stomach sank at the thought of what lay in store for him if Cassie got her mind set on the death-defying task of riding a horse. Then under the fear, he registered what she'd said. "Only the third time? How did you live in Montana for two years and come across the prairie in a covered wagon without riding a horse?"

"We had the carriage and Griff said riding was not ladylike. So I never. . ."

Red felt a little stir of his temper. It usually wasn't too much trouble, but sometimes he had a little problem with it. "Cassie, Griff told you not to ride. Griff told you not to talk about the baby to the point you don't know a thing about what's to come. Griff told you a woman was unclean when she was carryin' a child. Griff mortgaged all your family heirlooms without telling you so you could have a useless new silk dress every year. Excuse me for speakin' ill of the dead, Cass, but your husband wasn't very smart, was he?"

All Cassie's fluttering and squirming stopped. She sat frozen in his arms.

Red tensed up when he realized he'd gravely insulted his new wife's dead husband. It wasn't a good way to endear himself in her eyes. He started to apologize, but he wanted to see her face first to judge just how hurt and angry she was.

Before he could get a peek at her she said, "Do you really think Griff was wrong about all those things?"

"Now, Cass honey, I shouldn't have said that. I know you loved him and you. . ."

"Answer me!" All the softness was gone. She sounded almost frantic.

"Well, don't you?"

Another silence, longer than the first, stretched between them. "You mean I get to decide if I think he was smart or not? Surely that's not a woman's place."

"I don't rightly know if Griff was *smart* or not. I just said he did some things and told you some things that weren't smart. No one can know everything. I'm sure Griff was real smart about lots of things, but he was wrong about some things, too. He shouldn't have said you were unclean. But maybe that's somethin' he was raised with. Some people have funny notions. And he should never have mortgaged your things. I know all about the law and how it treats property between a husband and wife, so legally those things were his. But there's right and wrong, too, Cass. Morally those things were yours. Maybe you would have agreed to mortgage them, but I'm bettin' you'd have said, 'I want my family Bible more than I want a new dress.' Now isn't that right? Isn't that what you'd've said?"

It took a long time, with Cassie staring at her hands, before she answered. "I'd have parted with the Bible for food, for something we really needed. Well, maybe not. No, not the Bible. I wouldn't have parted with that ever. That book was something my mother treasured. I'd have gone hungry before I parted with that big old book. . . ."

Her voice faded and Red was afraid he'd made her cry. He felt like a brute to have reminded her of her precious belongings. He'd hurt her with his words when she was the most precious thing in the world to him.

"But the pearls and the portrait frames, I would have held on to them if I could, but I would have let him have those if it was for something that was important to the ranch. But I'd have never mortgaged them for a dress. I had two other black silk dresses. Griff wanted me to always have new things. He said we needed to keep up the right appearance."

Red tried to distract her from her keepsakes. "And as far as not thinkin' a lady should ride a horse, why honey, I've never known a lady in Montana who *didn't* ride a horse. Even in Indiana most ladies rode. Surely Illinois isn't much different. Griff was just plain wrong about that."

"When he was dying, Griff kept insisting I not go for help." Cassie looked up at Red, her eyes brimming with tears. "I didn't know how to catch the horse, so it was easy for me to mind him. Then I waited too long. When I finally did catch one, I couldn't make the horse obey me. It went back to the house at least six times before I got it going toward town. But it didn't matter by then anyway; Griff was dead. I stood by and let my husband die rather than ride for help. I didn't do a thing to save him because I was a coward. A stupid, cowardly child. That was one thing Griff was right about." The tears overflowed and Cassie looked as if she hated herself for failing that idiot Lester Griffin. Like she still wished he was alive so she could be married to him.

Red knew all the stories about redheads having fiery tempers. And he knew, in his own life, that there was some truth in that. He didn't get angry very often, but on occasion he really blew up. Listening to Cassie say Griff called her a stupid, cowardly child set him off like dynamite detonated inside him. He clamped his jaw tightly shut and didn't let the words escape that were roaring around inside him. He'd already insulted her husband once today. He knew he didn't dare do it again. He'd remember her tears of grief for Lester Griffin if he lived to be a thousand.

Red prayed for restraint. He'd wrestled with his temper all his life, and the grace of God had helped him gain pretty good control of it. He froze his jaw solid and prayed and tried not to let his fury spread to his body for fear he'd squeeze Cassie so tight she'd squeak. And he asked God to forgive him because he was sorely afraid that if Lester Griffin had been standing in front of him right now, he'd have beaten him to within an inch of his worthless life.

Cassie seemed to be lost in her guilt about letting that no-account husband of hers die, so Red was free to struggle with his temper. He finally felt controlled enough to say through clenched teeth, "You're not stupid, and you're not a coward, and no woman who's gonna have a child any minute counts as a child herself. So Griff was wrong about that, too. Now, hold on 'cuz Buck is rested and we're gonna gallop."

He kicked Buck in the sides before she could respond to him, because he was very much afraid that if she called herself stupid and Griff smart again he was going to say something he'd regret. Buck broke into a ground-eating gallop. Red felt his horse's enjoyment of the hard run in the way Buck relaxed between Red's legs. Buck forgot about the fidgety woman who had been annoying him for the last week.

Red wasn't so lucky.

He had the jolting realization that he'd just fallen completely in love with his wife. His wife, who was still in love with the village idiot.

With murder in his heart, Wade watched Dawson and the china doll ride away.

He'd learned the woodlands around the Dawson place so well he could come within a hundred feet of the house without being seen. He didn't have his rifle today. Today he had other plans.

He saw the way Dawson held Cassie. Wade pulled the flask out of his hip pocket and tried to soothe the inferno of jealousy with the bitter whiskey. He touched the pearl handle of his six gun. He wasn't after Dawson today. He walked up to the front door of Dawson's decrepit shack and went inside.

He'd loved walking around inside the Griffin place. He'd loved to run his hands through the china doll's silks. He'd touched her combs and jewelry and kept strands of her hair until he'd gathered enough to make a little braid of it to keep in his pocket.

Now he needed more of her. It had been too long since he'd had her alone, as he sometimes did at Griffin's when her foolish husband went to town. Wade knew the fear he sensed in her was fear of her attraction to him. Any decent, married woman would be afraid of such stirrings. If he had just had his chance and the china doll wasn't bound to someone else, she would have turned to him.

He wandered through the house looking for signs of her. He didn't find a single dress. There was no silk or satin anywhere. She had no mirror or hair combs that he could find. He gathered several strands of hair from her pillow, but there was nothing else.

"You've come down in the world, china doll. First you were married to a man who hurt you. Now you're married to a man who can't give you nice things." Wade took a long pull on his flask and savored how eager she would be to come to him.

"And maybe Red Dawson hurts you, too." Wade thought of Red putting his hands on the china doll and fury burned in his gut. "I want to rescue you from this."

He reached into his pocket and pulled a handkerchief out. It was so delicate that his calloused fingers snagged it when he rubbed it between them. He thought of leaving it for her. But he knew better than to let Dawson know he was around. And besides, he didn't want to give up this latest memento he'd claimed from the Griffin house. Most of the things had been taken out and sold to pay off the bills that no-account Lester

Griffin had run up. There wouldn't be any more pieces of Cassie to collect. Wade rubbed the handkerchief and smelled the beautiful scent on it and pitied her.

Drinking deep of the whiskey fueled his anger, and he wanted to lash out and destroy this ugly home she'd been imprisoned in against her will. He raised his fist to smash the lantern, shouting, "Red Dawson stands in our way!"

Something almost echoed in the decrepit excuse for a house and Wade paused without wrecking the lantern. He listened again. The echo he'd heard wasn't his own voice. It was something else, something far away and quiet and small, but it seemed to burrow into him deeply. It was all wrong. He knew the way he was acting wasn't reasonable. But he couldn't stop thinking about the china doll. It ate at his gut to think of her trapped here, like Wade was trapped with his father. Wade wanted to run off, start a new life without Pa telling him every breath to take. But he couldn't leave the china doll. He had to save her. Then they'd run together.

Whatever that echo, it calmed him enough that he didn't smash the house to pieces and burn it to the ground. But he didn't stay and listen for it again either.

Instead he took a long pull from his whiskey bottle and stormed out before he did something stupid.

He needed to plan.

He needed to set her free.

CHAPTER 11

W here's Anthony, Ma?"

Lindsay lightly touched her roan's neck with the reins and used her knees to steer the horse close with its travois on the back, then swung down to help with the harvesting. Blond and pencil slim, thirteen-year-old Lindsay was as tough and competent as a seasoned cowhand.

Breathing a prayer of thanksgiving that none of her girls took after their pas, except in looks, Belle looked up from where she plucked a pumpkin off the vine. "I haven't seen him since the noon meal."

She set the pumpkin on the growing pile. The last of her fall garden was nearly stripped clean. She straightened and rested one hand on her back. Good thing the baby would come by spring. She didn't want to do branding while she was expecting. Her belly got in her way.

"What do you need him for?"

"These pumpkins are heavy, but it's not like it's really *hard* work. I thought maybe he'd pitch in." Lindsay pulled her pumpkin free with a *snap* of the crisp, dead vine.

Belle chuckled. "Well, you are a dreamer, youngster. I suppose you can hope, but it's not likely to happen."

"I saw him." Sarah came walking up from the derelict cabin they lived in. "He was sitting under the Husband Tree again. Did you ever tell him he was sitting on one of the husbands' graves?"

Belle straightened and looked up the long slope to the bluff that towered over her house. A lone oak where she'd buried William and Gerald. "Too bad he doesn't die up there and save me the work of hauling him up."

"He might live, Ma. Just because you've chosen men who proved to be rickety in the past doesn't mean Anthony won't last."

Belle knew that to be the absolute truth, but she could hope. The only good thing about being married to Anthony was it kept other men from coming around the place.

She settled her eyes on the oak tree, its branches swaying in the brisk fall breeze. Winter came early up this high. The first snow could come any time.

"And he doesn't get drunk near as often as my pa did." Sarah was too young to remember her pa, but Belle made sure Sarah heard all about him.

"And Anthony's never come after you with his fists." Lindsay picked up another pumpkin and set it in the heavily laden travois.

The horse snorted and shook its head, jangling the traces. But the animal stood still, trained well by Belle and Lindsay and Emma.

"I think he's just too plumb lazy to get after anyone." Belle grabbed the heavy orange pumpkin, remembering how heavy Gerald's fists could be. But he hadn't landed many blows. A well-placed frying pan had proven to calm him considerably. And once he knew she'd use it, he'd quit with the fists anyway, unless he was powerful drunk. And then he was easy to best.

"I like him up there better than on the roof." Lindsay stared at the man barely visible, leaning back against the tree trunk. "It gives me the creeps the way he sits up there like a turkey buzzard."

"Where's Emma?" Belle looked around, not alarmed, just curious. Her girls were completely competent around the ranch. She didn't spend too much time fussing after them.

"She's dragging windfall limbs out of the spreader dam. She wants to clear the water paths before they freeze."

"I've a mind to ride over to see the Dawson place one of these days."

"You're still worried about that woman they forced into marriage." Sarah straightened with a pumpkin nearly her own weight in her arms.

Belle smiled. Her girls knew how to *work*! "I just. . .well, honestly it's bothering me day and night. That little girl looked so trapped and scared." Belle shook her head, wishing she could dislodge the image. But even her dreams were haunted by Cassie. What if Red Dawson used his fists? Belle could protect herself, but Cassie wouldn't know how.

"You can get away once the fall garden is cleared."

"No, I've got three herds left to bring down from the high pasture. And the snow will close us in before you know it. What if I rode out and the snow came before I got back? I could be shut out until spring." The thought terrified Belle. Her girls stuck in here alone all winter. Oh, they'd survive. They were tough as all get-out. But it would be a hard, cold winter for them.

"How far is it? You could watch the weather. And the cattle, well, just because a snow closes the pass doesn't mean you can't still bring in cattle. It stays nicer in the valley than it does up on the gap."

"I think I'll do it." Belle rested her hand on her stomach

and thought of the long, hard ride up to her high pasture. She wished she'd dared to skip it this year. She'd have to be out overnight, and the ground seemed to be harder than when she was younger. Smiling at herself, she decided maybe she would wait until spring to ride up. If the cattle up there got hungry, they'd come down closer to the ranch. They knew where the hay was stacked.

"Maybe I'll ride over there in the next few days. There's one pasture that closes up early, and if I don't bring those cattle down, they'll have to spend months up there and the grass might not hold out. But most likely the cows will be all right. I don't think many cattle went up that high. And it'll bother me all winter if I don't go check on Cassie." Belle straightened and rested both hands on her back. Carrying pumpkins when she was round as a pumpkin herself was hard work. "And girls, I'll warn you right now. If I don't like what I see, I might just grab that girl and bring her back with me."

Lindsay brightened. "That'd be great, Ma. I'd like another sister."

Belle smiled. She'd seen the possessive look on Red's face. He wouldn't give up his property without a fight. But maybe she could check on the girl, and if she didn't like what she saw, she could pretend to leave, then watch the ranch, and when Red left, snatch Cassie and bring her home. The mountain gap would snow shut, and by spring maybe Belle could teach the girl how to handle herself. Give her a frying pan of her own. Belle had a spare.

Satisfied with her plan, she said, "I think I'll do it. We most likely have a few weeks before the first big snow, so I'll put off fetching down that one herd. . .maybe until spring. I'll make sure it's a fine day then just run over to the Dawson place and back."

"You rescue her if you've a mind to, Ma. It'd be fun to not be the oldest for a change."

Belle felt as righteous as a fire-and-brimstone preacher as she bent to pick up another bright orange pumpkin, thinking of the misery she could spare that poor little Cassie Dawson.

Cassie had never had so much fun in her life.

She laughed as the buckskin ran full out into the cool fall afternoon. What a wonder. Her husband *liked* her to laugh.

Red held on to her so tightly that she didn't think the baby had been bounced around much at all. He'd ridden straight to the general store, which surprised her. She expected him to go to the stable first and see to Buck. He'd jumped off the horse and lifted her down without a word. Then he'd caught her by the hand and dragged her into the store and found Muriel.

"Cassie needs somewhere to spend the afternoon," he snapped at Muriel.

Cassie turned to look at him, wondering where that angry voice had come from.

"She doesn't know the first thing about having a baby either. Could you talk to her?"

Cassie felt her cheeks grow so hot with embarrassment she half expected her head to ignite. She dipped her chin down so no one could see her red face.

"Hmm..." Muriel said no words, but the sound, well, Cassie glanced up at the woman and saw some strange kind of satisfaction on Muriel's face as she looked between her and Red.

A smile lurked behind Muriel's understanding nod. Cassie didn't have time to beg Red not to leave her because he must have taken that noise to be agreement on Muriel's part. After his abrupt request, he took off like the building was afire.

Cassie looked after him, worried that it was something she'd said. "Maybe I should—"

"He's a man. Ignore him." Muriel caught Cassie's hand and

pulled her toward a table full of gingham. "We'll just have a nice chat. I don't get to visit with womenfolk much."

"He's a man. Ignore him"? Cassie thought those words might well qualify as blasphemy before God. Griff would have certainly said they did.

"I just got a shipment of dress goods in on the noon freight wagon. Can you help me stack them on this shelf over here, Cassie?"

Cassie was relieved to be asked to help rather than be given a lecture on the details of something so personal as childbirth. "I'd be glad to help."

Long before Red came back, Cassie and Muriel were fast friends. Cassie couldn't believe this nice lady had lived so close to her for two years and they'd never spoken beyond polite niceties.

Libby Jeffreys came over to put in her usual weekly order and pick up a few necessities that couldn't wait until Red delivered the supplies. Seth came in and out of the store, filling Libby's order, and left the women alone.

Muriel poured coffee, and Libby stayed for over an hour, drinking coffee and laughing over the comings and goings of Divide. Leota Pickett came just as Libby was leaving, and Libby settled back into the rocking chair, one of four Muriel had by her potbellied stove, and accepted another cup of coffee.

Cassie realized all of them were hungry for talk with another woman. She'd never known it before today, but she was hungry for it, too.

They all gave her polite words of sympathy for Griff and asked avidly how life was with Red. Somehow, without her noticing, they started talking about babies. Libby had two sons, grown and on their own, both bachelors living nearby. Leota Pickett had five young'uns at home, the littlest still in diapers. Muriel surprised Cassie when she talked about two children she'd lost in a diphtheria outbreak just before they moved west. There were never any more children for her and Seth. Muriel's grief was old, and Cassie had the impression it was almost a comfort to her because it was all she had left of the two toddlers she'd lost.

The ladies started talking about how they brought the children into the world, giving shockingly specific details, then laughing wildly over things they'd said and done during their laboring. Cassie was only vaguely aware that she was learning dozens of things she needed to know about delivering a baby. And Muriel promised she'd come and help bring the baby, saying she'd done it many times, including for Leota's youngest. All Cassie had to do was send word. Cassie wasn't sure how she'd do that, but Muriel mentioned that there was a ranch owned by a family of bachelors only a thirty-minute ride from Red's holding. Red would have plenty of time to ride to the Jessups' and one of the Jessup hands could come to town.

They had everything settled, and Muriel had even come up with a swatch of cloth that matched Cassie's singed dress. After Libby left, Muriel and Leota sewed on a patch while Cassie was still in the dress. She sat and watched them.

The two older ladies had dozens of suggestions for house-keeping that were a revelation to Cassie. And with a little encouragement, she told them about her week, including the array of mishaps that had befallen Red.

The ladies laughed hysterically until they couldn't keep stitching. Cassie didn't understand their wild laughter at Red's expense, but they wouldn't let her feelings remain wounded. They teased her until she was laughing with them and told her little ideas for handling livestock and gardens and lanterns. Cassie absorbed every word.

Leota overstayed the time she should be away from her children. She explained to Cassie about Red taking over some

of the stable chores so Maynard could come in from work early on Saturday, and how Leota cherished her few minutes at the general store with Muriel and her long evening with her husband at hand for a change. Then Leota hurried off.

Muriel propped a sign on the counter that said customers should holler for help. She took Cassie into the back to start supper. Cassie was able to help Muriel, but Muriel had lots of little tips for preparing dishes. Cassie remembered working beside her mother in the kitchen occasionally when she was a child, but her mother had employed a cook, so preparing meals was a special event. Her mother's advice returned to her some because Muriel had the same patient way of talking.

The general store had a busy time later in the afternoon, and Muriel couldn't visit with her anymore.

"I think I'll start delivering Libby's supplies to the diner," Cassie said.

Muriel shook her head as she filled an order. "You just leave that for Red, now, Cassie. I'm not allowing you to tote bags and boxes."

"But I want to help," Cassie insisted. "I feel guilty letting Red pay all our bills. Red told me work and money are the same thing, so it'll be like I'm paying for my dresses myself."

"You're a sweet girl to want to help, but—" The bell rang and another customer came in. Muriel didn't have time to talk. "Go ahead then. Libby's things are stacked by the back door. But just take small things, and promise me the minute you get tired, you'll stop. Any little thing you take will lighten the load for Red later."

"I'll be sure to quit when I get tired." Cassie hurried to the back door, feeling like she was really contributing to the ranch at last. Then she saw the mountain of food Seth had set aside for Libby. Cassie's inclination was to forget about helping, but she'd made too big a deal about it, and remembering Muriel's

words that even a little bit would help, Cassie decided she'd just carry one thing at a time.

Cassie appeared in Libby's Diner with a fifty-pound bag of flour in her arms. "Where do you want this?"

"What in the world are you doing carrying that heavy thing?" Libby rushed to lift it out of her arms. "You're in a delicate condition. Red would have my head if I let you deliver my groceries."

Cassie didn't want Libby to get in trouble. "I'll just carry lighter things from now on. I'll leave the big loads for Red. I promise."

She hurried away before Libby could forbid her to help. She crossed Main Street, went through the alley to the back of the general store, and went in. The door didn't close behind her, and she turned to see a crowd of men. Each of them scraped their feet a bit and apologized for following her and picked up a case of this or a crate of that. They delivered Libby's groceries in one trip.

Cassie followed them back, carrying a small basket of eggs. She sheepishly offered them to Libby. "Does this ruin Red's job? Neither of us did the work. We shouldn't get paid for it."

Libby just laughed. "You are a natural, honey."

"A natural what?" Cassie didn't know what she meant.

Libby laughed harder.

All the men had quietly returned to their seats and were eating at the meals they'd deserted.

Cassie gathered every ounce of courage she had, plus manufactured a little from out of thin air, and said, "Thank you all so much for your help. I appreciate it more than you can ever know."

Every man stared at her as if she'd spoken some foreign tongue. Then all jumbled together they said, "You're welcome, Miz Dawson," or, "Glad to help, ma'am," or something like that.

Cassie thought she heard someone say, "Red's a lucky man." It occurred to her that any of these men might have asked her to marry him a week ago.

Cassie went back to Muriel's.

Muriel was bustling back and forth, filling one order after another. Finally Cassie, who was sitting in rather nervous silence at the heating stove, gathered her wits about her enough to start helping. She really thought she did help this time. The crowd dispersed quickly after her efforts doubled the speed with which the customers, all men, were waited on. She acknowledged all their kind remarks and asked their names. Griff's words about them being riffraff echoed in her ears.

Muriel heaved a sigh of relief when the store finally emptied. She turned to Cassie and said, "If Red is going to keep coming in here and doing his odd jobs every Saturday, why don't I hire you to work with me here. Saturday afternoon is my busiest time. I'd love the help as well as the company. Once the baby comes, we'll set up a cradle, and any time the baby needs you to nurse him or change his diapers, you'll be able to take a break in the back room."

"It sounds just fine, Muriel. I'd be glad to help. Would you let me work off Griff's bill and then use what I earn toward the supplies Red and I need?"

Muriel said, "Griff's bill is taken care of, but you can swap for supplies."

"I'd need to ask Red first. But if it's okay with him, I'd be most grateful for the chance. Do you think I dare to make all the men in town deliver Libby's groceries every week?"

"What?"

Cassie told her how she'd managed to deliver that mountain of supplies.

Muriel laughed until she had to wipe her eyes on her calico dress.

So Cassie, who'd become the china doll for her last husband, became an odd-job girl for her next one. She thought it was an improvement.

CHAPTER 12

"Cass, wake up."

She had the odd sensation of being a baby back in her mother's arms. Being rocked gently back and forth. She fell back asleep. The rocking continued.

"Cass honey, wake up. We gotta go."

The gentle voice kept pestering her. She was disoriented for a few seconds.

Red crouched in front of her; his hand rocked her shoulder and he spoke in hushed tones. "I'm sorry it got so late. I had more to do than usual. And thanks for delivering the groceries. Libby told me all about it."

Cassie realized she was asleep on Muriel's couch in the dim light of early evening.

The first thing she thought of was how she'd ruined his job at the diner. She whispered because he was whispering. "I'm sorry, did Libby still pay you? I didn't mean—" She stopped her mumbled apology when Red smiled at her.

"Don't worry about it. Libby said if they volunteer to help you when you're doing my work and the job gets done, it's

135

all the same to her."

Cassie pushed against the couch, her stomach a bit unwieldy in her groggy state. Red slipped his arms under her shoulders and knees and lifted her into his arms. She was fat with the baby, but he lifted her as if he didn't notice her weight.

He continued speaking softly. "Muriel said you'd eaten with her and Seth. Then we decided to let you sleep while she fed me and told me about the job she offered you."

"Is that okay with you, Red? She was really busy. I just pitched in to help her. It was only after we were done that she suggested paying me."

"It's fine for now, but I told her when the baby got closer it might be too much for you. We don't want you to be exhausted now, do we?" He hefted her up and down a few times in his arms as if to remind her that she was indeed very tired or she wouldn't be cradled in his arms this way.

"I'll be careful, Red. Muriel will know what I can and can't do." Cassie leaned closer to him to share her wonderful discovery. "Muriel knows everything about babies. She and Libby and Leota told me so much today. I feel smarter already. Except then later I thought of a lot of questions, so I want to talk to them again. And the way they just talked and talked about having babies and caring for them, like it was the most natural thing in the world to do, it made me feel better about everything. And, I. . .I shouldn't have done it because it was disloyal to Griff, but I said about an expectant mother being unclean and. . .oh, Red, the things they said about Griff. It wasn't right at all and I made them stop, but maybe there are more ways than just his of seeing things." Cassie laid her heavy head on his shoulder, exhausted and a little shocked at the way she was chattering and saying such a horrible thing about Griff. She'd have never admitted that if she wasn't still half asleep.

"I got us a room at Grant's. 'Bye, Seth, Muriel, and thanks."

Only then, as Red carried her out of the room, did Cassie realize Seth and Muriel had been standing just behind him the whole time. She felt her cheeks heat up at the thought that they'd seen Red hold her so close. She thought about the whispered conversation she and Red just had and realized she'd been unconsciously keeping quiet because she'd thought everyone else in the house was asleep. Next she wasn't sure if she'd said critical words to Red about the ladies for being upset at Griff. She peeked around Red and said, "Good-bye."

Seth waved and Muriel had a satisfied smile similar to the one she'd had this afternoon when Red had left Cassie in her care.

Cassie worried the whole way to Grant's Hotel. Then she realized Red had carried her the entire distance, right down Main Street, and she worried about that. It was quiet and all the businesses were closed. The only thing lit up was the Golden Butte, and tinny music came out of the swinging saloon doors.

She was still consumed with her doubts when Red set her down in their room. Letting him carry her the whole way was so rude. "Is it very late, Red? It gets dark early this time of year, but it's not full dark. We don't have to go to bed yet if you don't want to."

"I have preachin' tomorrow 'cuz Parson Bergstrom is out of town. I've already thought of what I want to say, but I want to spend a little time studyin' on it, so if it's all right with you, I'll sit up for a while with the lantern on. If it doesn't disturb you, that is. I think you should sleep, Cass. You've had a big day. If my reading bothers you, Lars will let me use his dining room."

"I'm sure you won't bother me," Cassie said politely. She felt anxious at the idea of his leaving her alone in this unfamiliar room.

"Okay then, I'll read in here. I'll give you a few minutes of privacy to get ready for bed." Red politely left the room while she hurried around to find her nightgown.

She changed, and when she was ready, she cracked the door open an inch and peeked out. He was leaning patiently against the wall straight across from her door, reading a Bible.

"I'm ready now," she said shyly. "You can come back."

She ducked behind the door and crawled into bed quickly before Red came in.

Red sat in a rocker, reading his big black Bible by lantern light.

She thought it was the most comforting sight in the world. "What are you reading?"

"I'm going to talk about marriage tomorrow morning. That's all I ever do, talk about what I've done during the week and how God has been with me. I don't exactly preach a regular sermon. I'm studying with the parson to be a licensed minister. He's helping me get approved through his mission society so I can take over in Divide and he can serve other towns."

"Is that hard, to get licensed?"

Red shrugged and she saw his strong shoulders rise. He carried a lot of weight on them, with no complaint. "It's a lot of Bible study, but I like doing that anyway, so no, I wouldn't call it hard."

She compared Red's tattered Bible with the massive elegant book her family had handed down. No one had ever read it because it was printed in German. It was only for recording family history and for show. Her mother had often told her it was a gift to royalty, given to Cassie's countess great-grandmother back in Spain. She ached to think of giving it up, but it couldn't be helped now.

On a soft sigh, she relaxed as she watched Red's competent hands silently turn the tissue-thin page. She decided she liked Red's Bible better.

She fell asleep almost instantly.

Red always got to sleep late on Sunday.

It was something he'd been doing ever since he'd taken over the preaching at Divide, as if his body had a clock of its own and it knew he was miles from his stock and his morning chores. Usually he was outside on the hard ground, something he enjoyed. Although in the winter, it got a little rugged. Muriel had been known to let him sleep on the floor inside, since they held the church services in the general store. But this morning he woke in a soft feather bed. One he'd turned and beaten himself just yesterday. He could still smell the fresh outdoors on it from when he'd let it lie in the sunlight for a while.

He didn't think much about the smell and the fluffed-up feathers. They were just a little slice of pleasure added to how Cassie felt in his arms. She was hanging on him just like every morning. Red took a long time praying his thanks to God for how nice she felt. He marveled at how wonderful heaven must be if it was better than how he was feeling right now.

He had plenty of time before he needed to get up for services. They didn't hold them until real late, nine o'clock, so people could get their morning chores done and get in from out of town.

The time at church was Red's favorite time of the week. He wasn't a man who believed you had to go to church to talk to God. He carried God with him in his heart all the time, but he loved the joy that rose up in his soul when he talked and sang with other believers. Sharing his faith as a preacher inspired him to study his Bible and pray to God a dozen times a day. He found something exciting every time he read, and God touched his life in a hundred ways during the week that he wanted to tell people about.

He didn't run a church service in a very normal way. He

didn't exactly preach a sermon like Parson Bergstrom did. He'd just start talking about something he'd read and how he'd reacted to it. He'd ask the people who were there what they thought about his impressions, and they'd all end up talking long and hard about the Bible verse he'd selected that week.

He was especially looking forward to this Sunday morning. Being married had given him a new angle on a lot of the Bible. He was viewing love from a husband's perspective now, and that had given a depth to several Bible stories that he'd never thought of quite the same way.

He kept coming back to Ephesians and the directive from Paul for wives to submit themselves to their husbands. There were three verses that talked about wives, and Red figured that was where the wedding vows got the word *obey* for wives but not for husbands. Then for the next ten or so verses it told husbands all they had to do for their wives. Care for her as he would his own body. Love her as Christ loved the church. Die for her if need be just as Christ died for everyone. The Bible made far more demands on the husband than it did on the wife. And Red reckoned that if a man held up his end of the bargain, no wife in the world would have trouble obeying a man that decent.

He hugged Cassie a little tighter and smiled to himself. Cassie didn't obey worth a hoot. But then Red didn't exactly order her around either. It just wasn't in his nature to be bossy. His main goal in life was to protect her from one brush with death after another without hurting her feelings any.

He kissed the top of her head as he did every morning and admitted she was getting a little better. She never made the same mistake twice. It was just that she kept coming up with new ways to kill herself and him with her. He thought if they could just live out the next couple of weeks, she might turn into about the best little wife a man ever had.

He got kicked in the side, and Red almost trembled from

the stunning sensation of a little life growing inside Cassie. The tiny assault drew him from his satisfying musing about marriage to a more personal inspection of his lawfully wedded wife.

Cassie's head nestled on his left shoulder. Her black hair had been braided when she went to bed, but as it did most nights, it escaped her ribbons. It was spread across his chest and her back all the way to her waist. Her left leg was hooked over his. Her warm belly rested between their bodies, and maybe the little feller was saying it was too tight a squeeze because he seemed to be trying to knock himself a little more space.

Red's arm rested across the top of Cassie's stomach, and he didn't resist the temptation to brush her hair aside, smoothing it over and over. Once in a while the babe moved so vigorously that Red thought he must be doing a somersault. He laughed silently at the energetic tyke and longed for the day he'd come on out and join the family.

Red knew he ought to just slip out of bed as he did most mornings at home, but this was Sunday and they had a good hour to dress and eat breakfast before services. He had no excuse to tear himself away. So he smoothed her hair and held her close and decided Sunday, already his favorite day, had just become about a hundredfold better.

Cassie's breathing became slightly less regular, and he knew she was waking up. He watched her face closely, eager to memorize every nuance of her expression when she realized how she was clinging to him. Like the mornings when he hadn't slipped away quickly enough, he expected her to pull back in alarm and put about a foot of space between them. He didn't mind, not too much. He thought her trust in him and her desire to be close to him when she was sleeping was a good sign because her actions weren't all clouded up with grief and embarrassment. She honestly liked to be held in her sleep, and he thought with time that would spread into the daytime. And he'd be glad to be the one to hold her for the rest of her life.

She rubbed her cheek against the bristly hair that peeked through the top of his nightshirt, even turning a bit to lightly scratch her nose. She muttered a bit and the babe kicked again. Cassie's hand glided slowly across Red's waist to rest on her stomach. Her eyes fluttered open and she stared straight at Red.

Quickly before she could pull away, Red ran one finger down the curve of her cheek and said, "I like feelin' the babe move this way. Thank you for lying close to me like this."

Red felt her control that little jump of embarrassment that accompanied waking every morning. Instead, she let her hand rest on the baby, and Red's hand joined hers and they stared at the visibly moving white flannel on her belly and just incidentally went on holding each other.

After her muscles had relaxed against him, Red said, "Tell me what all Muriel and Libby and Leota said about babies yesterday."

Cassie surprised him by laughing. He thought that meant she was comfortable hugged up against him and that made him happy.

"Oh Red, the things they said right out loud. Private things I'd never before heard anyone say."

Red tilted her chin up. "Now Cass, just because you've never heard it before doesn't mean no one else has. You've been mighty sheltered, with your mama dying when you were so young and Griff being uncomfortable talking about such things. I want you to talk to me about this. I'm telling you right now, nothing is too personal for a wife to say to her husband."

Cassie nodded. "You're right. It just seemed so. . .sort of wicked, I guess. But they aren't wicked ladies. I know that. So I decided to listen and learn and we ended up laughing at the whole business of delivering a baby into the world. Muriel asked me terribly personal questions and I answered all I could. She. . . she wanted to know how evenly my l—lady's time was spaced. When I told her sometimes months apart, she wanted to know how long before I missed my. . .time had I been. . .been. . ." Cassie stopped talking.

Red rubbed one finger down the length of her nose. "Say it, Cass."

"She wanted to know when Griff and I had. . .had seen to his. . ." Cassie had buried her face more and more in his chest. "His husbandly. . .prerogatives." She glanced at him when she was finished and her face was blazing red.

Red wanted to blush, too. When he'd said they could talk about anything, he hadn't expected this. He wanted to yell at her that he didn't want to hear about her and Griff, but he stayed calm because he'd be taking back all he'd said about them talking about anything. "And what did you say?"

"I said I wasn't sure exactly but it was the one in the winter."

"The one in the. . ." Red choked his startled question.

Cassie looked at him uncertainly and he struggled valiantly to keep a straight face.

She looked back at his chest. "Yes, and very often the one in the winter was toward the end, so early to mid-March. Then, when I said that, for some reason they all three started laughing like crazy and they wouldn't tell me why. I guess it's because I don't know anything and that struck them funny, but they didn't want to hurt my feelings by saying so. Then Muriel said the baby would come in mid-December. That's six weeks. And she told me how to know the laboring had started and that you're to send word to the neighbors and one of the Jessup hands would come for her. Is that all right?"

Red heaved a sigh of relief at the suggestion. He'd been terrified that he'd have to deliver the baby on his own. He'd seen a lot of baby animals born and even aided a few cattle that were having trouble, but he'd been having nightmares about being alone and letting Cassie and the baby die because of some stupid mistake. "Yes, that's a good idea. The Jessups will be perfect. They're good friends of mine."

Cassie revealed details about having babies that Red found extremely embarrassing. He realized she'd taken his order to talk about everything to heart. For a while he wondered if he'd started something he was going to regret because he didn't want to know some of this stuff, but he'd made the rule. He couldn't quite believe Cassie was telling him all of these amazingly indelicate things.

Then with dawning delight, it occurred to him that Cassie had obeyed him. The more he thought about it, the more he remembered dozens of times when she'd quietly obeyed him in the last week. He'd just been lying here thinking that she didn't obey worth a hoot, but that wasn't true.

She wasn't disobedient. She was incompetent.

Her attempts to help around the ranch were well-meant efforts to obey his pronouncement the first day that he'd like her to milk and garden and gather eggs. He hugged her a little closer and controlled a shudder at the graphic things she was saying to him. He wondered if women talked like this all the time or had Muriel taken his gruff edict that Cassie didn't know anything about having a baby seriously and swallowed her own embarrassment.

He did his best to ignore what Cassie was saying and decided the next week was going to be different. He wasn't going to resist her attempts to help anymore. He was going to teach her, just like Muriel had done.

Cassie took a break from her gory tales of blood and screaming women, tales that didn't seem to be upsetting her at all, and Red said, "We have to get up and go to church now."

"Yes, Red." She rolled away from him, got up, and began collecting her clothes.

Red's heart expanded at how instantly she'd submitted to him. It made him feel like a king. He wasn't sure it was Christian to feel like a king, so he tried not to enjoy it too much.

CHAPTER 13

Cassie was surprised when Red went to the back door of Bates General Store and went in without bothering to knock.

He went through the hallway that passed the living quarters without making his presence known to anyone and started moving things around in the store, clearing a space for people to gather around the stove.

Cassie started to help, but Red said, "Not the pickle barrel, Cass. I'll get that. It's too heavy for you and it spills easy. If you want to help, pull the lighter barrels to one side, the crackers, and those crates of apples."

Cassie did as he directed but wished she was more sure of what all needed to be moved. Red never was one to give very good orders, leaving it to her to figure it out alone. She much preferred being told specifically what to do.

She took everything light, which was a goodly share of the stacks of supplies in the store, and he took everything heavy. After just a few minutes, Red called a halt, saying there was room enough for everyone to gather.

Muriel came in about then and stopped short. "I would

have lent a hand, Red. I was poky this morning."

"Nah, we were fast. Cass did most of it." Red smiled over at her and her heated cheeks told her she was blushing.

Muriel went to the front door, picking her way carefully through the jumbled merchandise. She unlocked the door. "Cassie's a worker, all right. She saved the day yesterday. I declare I would still be here filling orders if she hadn't taken a hand."

Cassie thought her head would explode from the effort to contain her pride. *"Cassie's a worker."* She'd never heard it said about her before.

Libby came in just in time to hear the last of Muriel's comment. Her husband was just behind her and several more people were with them. "You should have seen her bring my supplies, Red. She carried a fifty-pound bag of flour in her arms like a baby and asked as sweet as you please where she should set it and that she'd be back with the rest. Every man in the place stood up from his chair as if they had springs in their backsides and just followed her back to Muriel 'n Seth's."

Libby's husband, Ralph Jeffreys, laughed, and Cassie looked at Red again, uncertain if she robbed him of his honest pay.

Ralph said, "I was there when she came back, carrying, what was it, Cassie, a can of peaches or a. . ."

"It was eggs," a man just entering the store said. "We weren't about to let this pretty li'l lady, with a baby on the way to boot, carry five hundred pounds of groceries for you. I'm right ashamed of you for asking her to, Libby Jeffreys."

Libby turned in outrage. "I never asked her to carry five hundred. . ." Libby saw who was talking, gasped out loud, and chuckled. "Sam, you scalawag! I didn't know you were back from hauling."

The newcomer came and lifted Libby into a bear hug, laughing. "Howdy, Ma. Just teasin'."

He tipped his hat to Cassie, who had backed a little away

from the growing crowd until she was standing pressed against Red. Red rested his hand on her waist and anchored her to his side.

In the next ten minutes, the general store became crowded with people, friendly and happy to see each other. Red greeted each of them by name and shook hands. He introduced Cassie to them and she said, "Hello," trying to put names and faces together. She recognized quite a few of them from yesterday in the store, and although she continued to greet them by name once they'd been introduced, she soon gave up any hope of remembering all these men, overwhelmed by the sea of strangers.

She did know Norman York, and she tried to remember Leota Pickett's husband and the little Pickett children. Children were a rarity in Divide and they were enchanting to her. She was sure she'd never forget their names.

Then as quickly as the people began crowding in, everyone settled into silence, and Red left her side and stood close to the heating stove. He said, "Let's start with a prayer."

Cassie found herself startled to have her husband in charge. Of course she'd known he was leading the service. He'd said so often enough. But somehow she hadn't really thought what that meant. It had just seemed like another of his many jobs. Now a strong surge of pride in her handsome husband swelled in her chest as he took charge of this large group.

She remembered the fire-and-brimstone preaching she'd grown up with in Illinois, and she waited for that kind of intensity to come out of Red. But Red just stayed his sweet, quiet self. He prayed in front of all these people with the same casual, loving manner he'd used before their meals.

Halfway through his prayer—Cassie expected it was only halfway because she'd heard a lot of praying as a child and knew it was a lengthy proceeding—Red said, "Many petitions in prayer are pleasing to the Lord. Would anyone like some concern of his heart lifted up to God?" A deep voice behind her spoke to God about his brother's broken leg healing straight and strong. Another asked for his ailing mother in St. Louis to be remembered. And so it went. There were many needs in the West and many worries.

She could sense burdens lifting as they all put their worries before God and prayed together. She didn't speak out loud, but for the first time in a long time, she prayed, too. She prayed for her baby's health and for Red's safety and for more of the chickens to come back. Then Red surprised her by resting his hand on her shoulder. He'd moved away from her when he'd started talking, but he had moved closer to her during the prayer. He prayed for Griff, for God to shelter his immortal soul. Then Red thanked God for her.

Cassie couldn't contain a tiny gasp of pleasure. Red didn't ask God to make her less clumsy and stupid. He didn't pray for childlike Cassie Griffin Dawson to quit shaming him and grow up. He thanked God so kindly for making her his wife that she couldn't help but believe he meant it. And he prayed for the baby and prayed quite fervently for Muriel to get there in plenty of time to help deliver it. That made everyone laugh, which Cassie didn't understand, but the laughter, laced with the sweet prayer and Red's kindhearted thanks for her, had lifted her spirits so that she laughed a little herself with the pure pleasure of the day.

Then Red said his, "Amen," and moved back to where he'd stood in front of everyone and started talking about marriage. He didn't preach a sermon like any she'd heard before, and the congregation seemed to feel free to interrupt him as often as they liked. One man said marriage was a bad subject since so few of them were married.

Red said, "Leave your cattle to the wolves and go find a wife. It's worth it."

Everyone laughed and Cassie was so pleased with Red she was sorely tempted to cry.

He talked about a wife obeying her husband and how all the burden lay with the husband, because he is called to love her more than his own body and to never do anything to harm her soul, so a man must never ask a woman to obey anything that is against her own ideas of right and wrong.

Seth told him to change the subject before Muriel got the bit in her teeth.

Muriel said, "When have I ever obeyed you anyway, old man?"

All in all it was the oddest and most wonderful church service Cassie had ever attended. It didn't escape Cassie's notice that Red very quietly kept things from straying from the basic subject of his selected Bible verse.

A spirited debate bounced back and forth between people of goodwill with lots of laughter and a warm display of genuine love between the three married couples: the Bates, the Jeffreys, and the Picketts. It dawned on Cassie after a bit that she hadn't included the Dawsons in that count of married people.

And as she thought of the questions Red had asked and how they applied to her, she thought, *I'll be proud to obey you, Red.*

The whole room turned to face her and it took her a second to realize she must have spoken her thoughts aloud. She wasn't sure if she blushed or not. She'd done so much of it lately it was getting harder and harder to humiliate herself. It didn't matter. They wouldn't have stared at her any harder if she'd grown a second head.

Red moved from his spot at the front of the group and stood beside her.

Cassie wasn't sure if her outspoken comment had shamed him or not, and despite everything she'd learned about Red this week, she couldn't control the surge of fear that he would punish her for talking out loud in public like that.

"Cass, I am a lucky man. I reckon you will obey me, 'cuz you're such a sweet thing, you'd just naturally do your best to make me happy. But I want you to know I won't ask you to go against your conscience, and I'll listen if you disagree with me. And if you are ever upset with me, it'll be as much my doing as yours, so you can speak right out and never be afraid of me."

Cassie remembered her first wedding to Griff, with her wild desire to die along with him and her terror of the Sawyers and the surly mob keeping her ears deaf to what was being said. Now they stood before believers and Cassie looked into Red's eyes. "I'm lucky, too. Thank you for marrying me. I know you didn't want to."

Red smiled. "I didn't think I should, but that's a long way from not wanting to. I wanted to marry you something fierce, Cass honey."

He leaned down, and Cassie thought he was going to kiss her. They hadn't kissed since their wedding night, and that had been her doing. Although she'd dreamed that he'd kissed her hair several times while she'd slept beside him and the dreams had been nice. Now maybe he was going to do it for real.

Wade Sawyer chose that minute to slam the door open. "I got an order here, Seth. I need it right now!"

Wade's belligerence broke into the pleasant church service and garnered everybody's attention.

Muriel slammed her fists on her hips and stepped in front of Wade. "See here, Wade. We're closed on the Lord's Day and well you know it."

Wade swaggered up to Seth, who had stepped to Muriel's side. He ignored Muriel as if she were nothing more than a buzzing mosquito to be brushed aside as a nuisance. "I've ridden all the way into town and you're here doin' nothin'. I'm not goin' back without my order. You've done enough Bible thumpin' for the week."

Seth said quietly, "We've been over this before, Wade. There's someone in from the Sawyer outfit nearly every day of the week. I know for a fact you were in town yesterday."

"Don't tell me you won't fill my order." Wade stepped forward, looking hard into Seth's eyes. "I saw Belle Tanner loading a wagon just last week. If you'll do it for that woman, you'll do it for me and like it."

"Belle had to make a special trip and she almost never comes to town from clear out where she lives. Of course I was willing to help her out. The Sawyer place is right outside of town. Leave the order. We'll have it ready first thing tomorrow, and when someone from your ranch is in town, he can pick it up."

Wade's eyes narrowed, then they shifted past the Bates and found Cassie.

Dread twisted in her gut like it always did when Wade was too near. She saw in his greedy green eyes that awful hunger, that fixated look that was only for her. He hadn't come in here to get supplies. He'd come in because he'd known she was here.

That sounded like her pride talking, thinking Wade was interested in her. But for whatever reason, it was true. She knew it. Wade's eyes reminded her that she knew how to shoot a gun—she was quick and accurate, and just maybe, with those mean eyes on her, she could even find the courage to pull the trigger. Of course this was the second time in a week that she'd come face-to-face with Wade and didn't have her gun handy.

She took a step back and bumped into Red. He put his arm around her waist. Red's hand was an anchor in a sea of fear. She grabbed his hand with both of hers and held it firmly around her.

"Miz Griffin." Wade tipped his hat.

"It's Dawson now," Red corrected him in a mild tone.

"Oh, yeah. The widow lady remarried. I seem to remember she was so anxious for a man that she stood plumb on the fresh-turned dirt of her dead husband to take her vows."

Several people in the crowd gasped. Cassie didn't know if it was because of her and the location of her marriage or Wade's callous words.

"Wherever she took her vows, Wade, she took 'em." Red sounded so quiet, but Cassie heard the strength behind his words and hung on to him even harder.

Wade reached one hand into his pocket and several men tensed as his hand moved near the gun that hung low on his hip.

Cassie remembered again that she'd learned to shoot, but now she didn't even have a gun anymore. It had been lost when her home had been taken for the mortgage.

Wade pulled something from his pocket. "Me and Pa are runnin' your old place, china doll. The bank took everything you and your worthless husband had left. We found some things left behind. It's trash but you might want it." Wade unfolded what he was holding and very deliberately pulled his knife and slashed it in half, then slashed it again. He wadded up the pieces into a tight ball and tossed them at Cassie.

Cassie flinched away, but Red's hand came up and deftly caught them. Cassie reached for them, but Red whispered, "Later, Cass. Not in front of Wade."

Wade said, "We'll use your house for a line shack. It's a fool's house. Too big to heat and too far from our ranch for any use. Maybe we can store hay in it."

Cassie was surprised that his insults toward her house didn't upset her. The fact that she didn't care about the house gave her the strength to face Wade straight on and wave her hand carelessly. "If the house is yours, then do with it what you will. It's nothing to me."

"Even after the floors rot and the rats move in it'll be better than the hole you're livin' in now with Dawson."

Cassie gasped indignantly. Odd how the slur against Griff's house left her unmoved but his insults to Red's house were fighting words. She met Wade's eyes but she couldn't hold the look. Wade's eyes burned with something that had always scared her. She still had the china doll inside her, and she said placidly, "Red's got a wonderful home. We have everything we need."

Wade's face contorted into rage. "So then you must have Dawson bowin' and scrapin' for you just like you had Griffin."

Cassie saw Wade's weasel eyes shift to Red. "I often wondered what she did for Griff that he'd let her walk all over him like that. Tell me, Dawson. Does she earn your favors like a real flesh-and-blood woman? Or is she as cold as the china doll she seems to be?"

Red suddenly moved, and Cassie felt his anger at Wade's crudity. She caught him with a quick backward move of her hands.

She said clearly, so clearly that it was possible Mort Sawyer could have heard her out at the ranch, "Remember we're in church, Red. And remember the man who won has to be big enough to stand a few temper tantrums from the loser." She looked over her shoulder and smiled sweetly at Red.

He glared down at her for a second, obviously frustrated, then he relaxed. "Only 'cuz we're in church, Cass. The 'temper tantrum' comment from you wouldn't have saved him any other time."

"Saved me?" Wade blustered. "The day a man can hide behind a woman's skirts and that'll stop. . ."

"Enough, Sawyer. We're in the middle of church." This was from Norm York. "Your pa wanted Cassie's spring and he paid a fair price for it. You Sawyers got what you wanted. You've no call to come in here insulting a fine woman and threatening Red. You're standing in front of dozens of witnesses to your actions, and you can't get away with starting anything. And if something happens to them any other time, you're the first one we'll come looking for. So you'd better pray they don't even accidentally get hurt. If you want to stay and hear the preaching, we welcome you."

Suddenly Mr. York's voice became very sincere. "We do, Wade. Forget all this anger and stay. We have God here with us, and you need to hear about Him. There is always room for anyone who wants to worship the Lord. But the store is closed on Sunday and always has been, as you well know. We need to get back to services."

Cassie noticed that every man in the place squared off against Wade, some moving to place themselves between Wade and her until she couldn't see him anymore. Even though anyone from out of town would have a rifle on his horse because of the dangers along the trail, none of them brought a gun into church. Wade was the only one armed.

Seconds stretched to a minute.

Cassie leaned sideways to see Wade. His eyes, burning with anger, shifted from one man to another. He flexed his fingers as if fighting the urge to destroy anyone who thwarted him. His eyes connected with Cassie and they held. Under the anger and hunger, Cassie saw something else. Some deep longing that told her Wade wasn't just fighting because he was a troublemaker. Wade's desperate yearning aimed straight at her made her shudder deep inside.

With a sneer, Wade's hand dropped away from his gun. "This isn't over, Dawson. You got what's mine and I aim to get it back."

She couldn't see him anymore, and she stayed behind Red, not wanting Wade's eyes on her. But she heard the obsession in his voice, and icy fingers of fear crawled up her spine and grabbed at her throat.

She saw him again as he turned and wrenched the door open, slamming it behind him so hard the glass rattled.

The congregation stood silently for a moment. Cassie saw

fear on many of the men's faces. She knew the ruthless Sawyer bunch had made dreadful enemies.

Finally Red broke the silence. "Let's bow our heads and pray for Wade and his father."

Several people turned sharply to face Red, their faces revealing they were not ready to let go of their anger or fear. Most nodded soberly.

"He's so lost," Muriel said.

Cassie couldn't believe the gentle murmur of agreement. Not a minute ago a fight brewed that might end in the deaths of some of the people in this room. Now they were praying for a man they so obviously feared.

She thought of her practice with Griff's gun and her own desperate plans to protect herself. Never for a second had she considered praying for Wade. This was a kind of Christianity that Cassie didn't understand.

A peace settled over her as Red's comforting voice started talking to God in a way that made it seem God was a personal friend.

Cassie prayed that God would be her friend, too.

CHAPTER 14

Cassie wondered about the papers in Red's pocket as the church service wound down, the general store was put back to rights, and she and Red prepared to head for home.

He lifted her onto his horse, and she decided to get settled into Buck's gallop before she asked.

She awoke when he swung off the horse in front of their house. He was still holding her.

She insisted she could walk.

He just nodded. "I know you can, Cass honey." He carried her inside and set her on a chair.

"Thank you, Red." She didn't admit it, because it made her feel like a burden, but she was secretly glad she hadn't needed to use her shaky legs.

She sat on the chair, letting her head clear for a few seconds. And then she remembered Wade. "What was it Wade tore up?"

"Let's see." Red pulled the wad of paper out of his pocket and smoothed it.

Cassie recognized it. "My family portraits and the painting of the countess."

Tears burned sharply across her eyes. She forced herself to say what Griff would have wanted to hear. "It's. . .it's only portraits. It's all frivolity."

Red lay the mangled pieces of paper and canvas side by side on the table. "They're not frivolous. We'll fix 'em. They won't be nice like before, but we'll remember what your family looked like, and that's the real point of portraits, right?"

Cassie thought of how lovingly she'd cared for those paintings all of her life and her mother before her, so there was never any damage to the canvas and no sun faded the color. But what Red said about remembering lifted the dark sorrow from her heart. Griff's voice, accusing her of childish longing for unimportant things, faded.

"You're exactly right. The portraits are important." She smiled up at him as he bent near her shoulder, arranging the portraits. Red knew *why* they were important, and that reason wasn't lost because of wrinkled paper, nor was it frivolous. She felt immensely better and began helping him put the pieces together like a jigsaw puzzle.

Red produced another paper from his pocket and bent over her shoulder to smooth it out on the table. They had copied all her ancestors' names out of her old family Bible. As they worked on the torn portraits, Red asked, "Did you mean it about the Bible, Cass? You weren't just being brave? It's a beautiful old book. I've never seen one so big and grand. If you want to keep it, we can think of something."

"It's not even in a language we can read." Cassie shook her head. "Of all the things we might save from my past, I think the Bible is the least important. And Mr. York seems to think he might get more from it than even the mortgage price. I like your Bible better. Maybe there's a place in it for my family's names."

Red glanced sideways at her and smiled. "There is. I got

this Bible new so I've never written in the pages set aside for that kind of thing."

The smile warmed Cassie's heart as their gazes held for a long moment. Then Red turned back to the tabletop. The portraits began to take shape in front of them. "These folks are your mother's grandparents, right, Cass? And the oil painting is the countess?"

"Yes, my grandfather was one of the original executives who began building the railroad." Cassie pointed to a stern-looking man with a slight twinkle in his eye. "My grandmother was one of the finest hostesses in New York. Mother always said I looked just like her and she looked like the countess. I just barely remember them. They came to visit us in Illinois several times, but Grandfather died the year after my father, and Grandmother just a few years after that."

"Do you know stories of your ancestors, Cass?"

Cass looked up from her scraps. She'd been enjoying making her grandparents emerge from the mess. "Oh, yes. Mother talked about them all the time."

"I can see our children putting these portraits together just like this and you telling them about their heritage. We'll do it as often as we can. We can tell them about my ma and pa and my brothers and sisters, and your great-grandma, the countess, too. We'll hand down more than portraits to them, Cass. We'll make sure they know where they came from."

"They?" Cass said, her voice faint.

"Sure. I want to have a big family. Don't. . ." Red's voice faltered as he looked away from the work he was doing. "D–Don't you?"

They looked at each other before Red straightened away from her, his cheeks turning as red as his hair.

Cassie knew what a big family meant. It meant she was going to have to really be married to Red. Her first reaction was dismay, but after she had a second to think about it, she knew she'd agreed to a real marriage when she took her vows. And she remembered how he'd almost kissed her just before Wade barged into the church service, and how much she'd wanted him to. Yes, she'd be willing to have a big family if it would make Red happy.

All she said was, "I hope they all have red hair."

Red smiled and rested one hand on her shoulder. "That's fine for the boys, but I hope the girls are all as beautiful as you. I'd like to stay and help you get the portraits finished, but I've got chores waiting."

"Oh, let me help, Red. I want to share the work with you."

Red hesitated, and Cassie guessed he was thinking how tired she was. It made her feel like such a burden to him. He was always making excuses why she didn't have to help.

"I've been thinking, Cass. I want you to help, but I haven't been taking the time to teach you. Now I want you to milk Rosie today and feed the chickens and Harriet, but I don't want you to start without me. I know you've been trying to do these things to save me time, but at first it's gonna take *more* time because learning always does. Now, I've got to water Buck and Rosie before anything else. Don't start without me." He shook his finger in her face. "Promise me. Not even with the chickens. There're a couple of things I want to show you about them I didn't get to before."

"I'll wait, Red." She thought taking direct orders was the safest thing in the world. She longed for Red to tell her just what to do.

"And don't start a fire in here yet. I don't have time to do it, but it's tricky. I'll teach you how to do that, too. It'll be chilly for a while, but we'll just have to wait for a fire even if that makes dinner late."

She nodded, elated to be obedient. "I promise I'll sit and

work on these portraits until you're ready for me."

"Good, yes, that's a good idea." Red bent quickly down to his Bible and opened it to a paged lined but with no writing. "And put your family names in here while you're waiting. I'll hurry. I should be ready to milk Rosie in fifteen minutes. I'll call out when I'm back from the stream."

Cassie smiled at him, her heart soaring.

Red grabbed his hat from a nail beside the door. He glanced back to see her still smiling at him. His hand faltered as it reached for the wooden peg that latched the door shut. Something passed over Red's face that transfixed Cassie. He stood there frozen for a long minute.

Suddenly, he jammed his hat crookedly on his head, took two broad paces toward her, and lifted her out of her chair by her shoulders. He kissed her hard and quick, then set her back in the chair and left without looking back.

Cassie sat dazed, feeling his strong hands on her shoulders and his warm mouth on hers. It was over so fast that she hadn't really felt anything while he was kissing her. But after he left, she started tingling until her whole body was buzzing with the pleasure of Red's abrupt kiss. She forgot all about her grandparents' portraits and her ancestors' names and sat daydreaming. She wanted him to do it again. They'd have a lot of children, because Muriel had explained what caused babies, and she knew kissing led to that cause, and she'd liked his kissing very much.

Cassie almost hummed she was so happy thinking of the future and all the kissing she and Red were going to do.

He was wrong to kiss her like that, and it wasn't going to happen again! Not until he was sure Cassie wasn't doing it out of a need to be submissive.

Red rode the buckskin to the spring, berating himself for his rough treatment of his sweet, kindhearted Cassie. He pegged Buck there and went back for Rosie, who was her usual cranky "you're-late-milking-me" self. Rosie didn't like not being milked until the afternoon on Sundays.

He tied Rosie so she could drink, led Buck home, and went back for Rosie.

Rosie was cranky about being dragged home. "I know I'm hurryin' you, girl, but I'm afraid Cassie will forget her promise and start helping in some dangerous way or other."

Rosie jerked her head and almost pulled Red over backward. He turned and thought he saw skepticism on her long face. "Okay, the truth is I just want to get back to her. I want to hold her again, gently this time, not like the ham-handed ox I was earlier."

Rosie mooed loudly and Red realized what he'd said. "Well, I didn't mean any offense to oxen, of course. That's your family, I know. But I'm not supposed to act like one. And anyway, I can't kiss her again."

Red glanced back as if maybe Rosie could give him some advice. "I can't. It's too soon for her."

He wanted a real marriage in every way with Cassie. Almost like watching a flower unfold from its bud, he could see Cassie blooming. It was as if she'd hidden her real self to be a perfect wife for Griff.

Cassie didn't even realize how Griff had used her. Griff had abused his position of trust to marry her. Then he'd squandered her wealth and left her at the not-so-tender mercies of the men in Divide. The things she'd said about Griff calling her unclean and the money Griff had spent on foolishness made Red so mad he wished Lester Griffin were here so he could beat some sense into him.

But if Griff were here, then Red wouldn't be married to Cassie. His breath caught on the delight of having her waiting for him in the house.

Red had even put aside his worry about Cassie's faith. She bowed her head with him at every meal and she'd seemed content to attend services with him. Red had the sudden unsettling thought that maybe Cassie was trying to turn herself into a perfect wife for Red Dawson, just like she'd turned herself into a perfect china doll for Lester Griffin.

Red's heart panged at the thought and he froze in mid-step. Rosie plowed into him and shoved him along until he was walking again.

Cassie had agreed so sweetly to wait for him to do the chores. Red had told her to sit in that chair, and suddenly he was sure that she wouldn't even stand up the whole time he was gone. She'd said, "I'll be proud to obey you, Red," right out loud at the church service. He didn't want Cassie to twist and turn herself around trying to become whatever Red wanted her to be. That made him no better than Lester Griffin. He wanted Cassie to feel safe enough to be herself.

She'd been living by someone else's wishes since she was fifteen. No, since she was twelve, because that's when Griff had first gotten charge over her.

Red remembered seeing Cassie sitting perfectly still in the carriage waiting for Griff. He thought of the times he'd seen her, her hands folded in her lap, the unnatural look of composure on her face. She had been out there because Griff had insisted she stay, like a trained dog, confined to that carriage as surely as the horses had been tied to the hitching post.

With a flash of insight, Red knew no one learned to be so submissive without a harsh taskmaster administering the lesson. He thought of the fear that flashed in Cassie's eyes every time she thought she might have displeased him. Once she'd even flinched away from him.

Sickened by the direction of his thoughts, Red knew that

there'd been more than scolding and insults involved in Griff's discipline. It took a hard hand to wring that kind of fearful obedience out of anyone—man, woman, or child.

At that moment Lester Griffin was fortunate to be dead and beyond Red's reach.

Red contrasted Cassie's detached serenity in her Mrs. Griffin days with the girl who had pitched in and helped Muriel yesterday. Was that what Cassie wanted to do, or was she just following Red's example?

Red knew then that teaching her all of the ranch chores would be easy, and he knew he could have the perfect little ranch wife, hurrying to do his bidding. And he could kiss her as often as he liked and have a dozen children if he wished. And he'd never know if any of it was what Cassie wanted.

He also realized he couldn't know if Cassie's faith was real. Red the husband could fumble around and do his best with Cassie, but Red the preacher couldn't settle for letting Cassie's soul be neglected.

Red decided to start out teaching her because she really did need to learn, but what he wanted was for her to defy him. He wanted Cassie to look him in the eye and say, "I'm doing enough around here. Do it yourself."

He tied Rosie up in her stall and started for the house. He thought ruefully that at least he no longer wanted to grab her and kiss her senseless. She'd just go along with that, too.

As he reached his soddy, he realized that his mind had led him in a big circle that took him right back to where he started.

Until he was sure what her wishes were, he was never going to kiss her again.

❧

Wade scuffed his foot against the bedding of pine needles as he waited impatiently for Dawson to go into the house. He was learning their schedule.

Morning chores. Ride out to check the cattle. Noon break. Ride out for slightly longer to check the cattle. Evening chores. Supper. Dawson always stayed inside after supper. Always hurrying, always working.

Wade knew better than to leave much sign of his passing. Although Dawson never scouted around the highlands behind his cave, he did move like a man who had lived in wild country. He would study the landscape. Take time to look at the sky. Pay attention to any ruckus set up by his horse or his stock. Wade wondered if that was how Dawson always acted or if he was suspicious for some reason.

Wade knew his pa was suspicious. Pa had never paid much attention to what Wade did. There were plenty of hands to take care of things. But Wade had taken to leaving before first light almost every day and riding for over an hour to set up his lookout of the Dawson ranch, and Pa had noticed. So far Wade had defied his father's curt questions about Wade's comings and goings. The defiance felt good and added to the visceral pleasure he got from watching the china doll.

Wade waited hungrily for a sight of her. She came out and helped with chores a lot, and Wade could hardly keep himself from charging down to that pitiful ranch and grabbing her. Oh, she'd fight him. She was a respectable woman, after all, and she was married. But inside she'd be glad he took her. She'd even be glad if her husband was dead so she'd no longer be bound to him.

Wade remembered how he used to watch the Griffin place until her fool husband rode off to town. As soon as Griffin was gone, he'd ride up to the house. He'd come up on the porch and hammer on the door until she opened it. Then he'd deliberately stand too close to her. He thought of her fear. Because his love for her was hopeless, he'd been furious. He'd wanted her to be afraid. But now he understood. She wasn't afraid of Wade. She was afraid of what he made her feel.

The anger surged upward again, and he grabbed for his whiskey flask to wash the anger back down before it choked him. He thought about Dawson inside that house with the china doll for the night, and suddenly something snapped inside him. He wanted to kill Dawson, then drag the china doll off and marry her before his father knew anything about it. And if his father objected, Wade would kill him, too. Wade's hand itched to pull his revolver and go down to that house and have it out once and for all.

Wade's eyes traveled over the Dawson place, and he noticed the cattle moving slowly toward a water hole Dawson had dammed up across his creek. Wade's eyes narrowed as he thought of how he'd always pulled back from killing. He took a long pull on his whiskey, let the burn stoke the fire of his rage, and thought of a way to strike a blow against Dawson.

This he did have the guts to do, and maybe it would make the next time, the time Dawson died, easier. Wade drank until his conscience was silenced then he planned. Soon he left his lookout and rode home to get what he needed to strike before morning.

CHAPTER 15

Belle rode out before first light.

She'd told the girls she was going, and they were already hard at work before dawn anyway. The three of them would stay outside until breakfast time. Anthony would be awake by then. . .maybe.

The weather looked fair, and she pushed her mount hard to eat up the ground.

Still, it was midmorning before the Dawson place came into sight. She'd never been here before and she noticed the way the soddy was built up against the canyon wall. Smart. She wished she'd have thought of that. She had a lot of skills but she'd never had the knack for building a sound structure, and there was no one to teach her. Her house and barn showed it.

She rode straight up to the soddy, noting the solid barn and the tight corrals. Even the sod house was square and solid looking. She tied her horse to the hitching post and strode to the front door, pounding on it.

It took a long time, but finally the heavy door, hinged with leather straps, scraped open and Cassie looked outside.

Belle thought she looked about the same age as Lindsay, and it made her mother's heart turn over to think of this woman on her second marriage, having a baby she had probably never asked for. It made Belle want to go to war to protect her.

"Uh...you're...Belle? Right? Belle Santoni?"

"Most folks call me Belle Tanner. They can't keep up with the different husbands." Belle nodded. "Just stopping in to visit if that's okay."

Cassie nodded and swung the door wide. "I've got coffee on. Red usually comes in for a cup about now. There's plenty and I've fried some doughnuts."

Belle could smell the grease and sugar and the savory hot coffee. The house smelled wonderful and Cassie smiled as she let Belle pass.

Belle felt awkward. She'd expected to find the girl in terrible straits. And perhaps she was. But it was hard to tell from the smile on her face.

Looking around, Belle noticed the cave entrance. "He built this in front of a cave?"

"Come and look. The cave is our bedroom, and over there"—Cassie pointed to a circle of buffalo hide hanging on the wall—"is a cave with a cold spring running through it we call the cooler."

Instead of rescuing the girl, Belle was struck dumb with envy. She got a full tour then settled in at the table with coffee and sweets.

"When's your baby due?" Cassie laid her hand on her stomach.

"Spring or thereabouts."

Cassie's eyes grew round. "Don't you know for sure either?"

"*Either?*" Feeling her brow furrow, Belle tried to answer in a way that would keep Cassie talking. Didn't the woman know when her child was coming? "Well, it's never exact. But I can guess pretty close. When is yours?"

Cassie began talking like a woman who was starved for another woman. Belle knew she'd be half mad with loneliness if her girls weren't always at hand.

"Muriel told you what?" Belle gasped at the amazing amount of detail Muriel had dumped on Cassie. Belle considered setting the poor thing straight but worried she'd just upset Cassie more with conflicting information.

"And then her mother-in-law had her bite on a stick so. . ."

Belle had never considered biting on a stick. The idea had merit. Belle listened more closely. When the girl ran down, Belle said, "I've had my young'uns pretty much by myself, without knowing overly much about what to expect. They just go ahead and be born no matter what you do. Not much sense learning a bunch of rules about 'em 'cuz my three were all different."

Cassie's eyes grew wide. "They're different? What do you mean?"

"Well, different lengths of time that the laboring goes on. Different feeling to each time, one'll be harder, the next easier. Not much rhyme or reason to it."

"Leota Pickett has five, and she said hers were all mostly the very same."

Shrugging, Belle changed the subject. "So, how do you like married life?"

"It's wonderful but kind of sad, too."

"What's sad about it?" Belle knew good and well what was sad about married life. The list was so long. . .well, there wasn't enough paper and ink in the world.

Blushing, Cassie leaned close and whispered, "Red won't kiss me."

Belle jerked upright in her chair. "He won't?" Belle never had that problem.

Cassie shook her head, her cheeks blazing pink. "You've been married three times. Could you get any of them to kiss you?"

Because she couldn't collect an intelligent thought in her head, Belle poured her coffee down her throat even though it was still nearly burning hot and held out her cup. "Can I have some more?"

Cassie hurried to get the pot and pour while Belle tried to gather her thoughts.

By the time Cassie settled in, Belle said, "So you must like having a husband, then?"

Cassie nodded.

"Did you like your other one?"

Cassie froze, her eyes wide as a startled deer. "Of. . .of course."

Belle shook her head. "I didn't figure you did. Worthless man. My husbands have all been pretty much worthless. Made more work for me."

"Well, I'm trying to work, but Red won't let me do much, and he hovers. Can I ask you a question?" Cassie had a look like she was scared to death of the next words she planned to say.

"Sure." Belle braced herself. This was going to be more overly personal details about having a baby. The girl was just full of questions and strange information.

"The way you talked to Red, and Muriel and Seth for that matter, how. . .how did you work. . .work up the courage to speak so boldly? I've never known a woman to be so. . .so. . ."

"Cranky?" Belle fought a smile.

"No, well, yes, a little I guess, but I wish. . .I mean, do your husbands like it? Did they tell you to act that way?"

Belle set her tin coffee cup down with a *click* and rested her arms on the table. She bent closer to Cassie. "No man tells me how to act. I act as I like, and he can put up with it and keep his mouth shut or get out."

Cassie's eyes got wide, and Belle wondered if the girl was

going to tell Belle to get out. But those eyes studied her. Quiet, watchful.

"What are you thinking?" Belle had spent most of the last fourteen years shut up in her mountain valley. Truth be told, she hadn't been around women much. . .nor men. . .save her children and the husbands.

"I'm just trying to remember the way you look straight into my eyes. The way you speak as if you don't give one tiny fig if I like it or not. That's. . .that's. . ."

"Arrogant? Rude? Stupid?" Belle arched one brow.

"Wonderful." The word was breathed quietly. "Did your mother act like this or did one of your husbands ask it of you?"

Belle was torn between snarling and smiling. The thought that one of her husbands would order her to be so contemptuous of him was really pretty funny. "My mother was a perfect Southern lady. My husbands have been content to let me be however I want to be as long there's plenty of hot food and I let them slink off and hide come chore time."

"Griff said a woman's place was in the home and it was shameful to do men's work."

Belle didn't respond but just stared straight into Cassie's eyes, wondering if the girl would realize that she'd just insulted Belle mightily.

"But I think it's wonderful. I wish I was more like you."

And just like that, Belle had a sister. Not a child like her girls, but a woman who didn't look down on her. Even admired her. Belle wanted to take Cassie home now more than ever.

The door opened fast and Red came in, breathing hard.

Belle suspected he'd recognized her horse and figured she was here to kidnap his wife. Well, Belle knew for a fact Cassie wouldn't want to be kidnapped, and it made Belle so curious it was killing her. How could Cassie be *happy*? Was Red an actual *good man* or was Cassie just that gullible?

Belle had to admit the ways of God were a pure mystery.

The little pang of jealousy surprised Belle as she studied Red. His eyes were sharp. His chest heaving as if he'd sprinted. But he didn't say a word except to greet her.

"Belle, you've come for a visit. Good to see you. You should have brought the girls."

Belle had tried to be casual with Cassie, but because she didn't know how to be much else than blunt on the normal course of things, she said, "I came to check if she was all right."

"I'm glad you did. And you can see, she's fine."

Belle turned back to Cassie, who was busy staring at Red as if she were trying to think of a way to trick him into kissing her.

"It defies reason, but she does seem to be fine."

Red laughed as he poured himself coffee then settled onto the floor by the fireplace before Belle even realized there were only two chairs in the house. "I spent the morning trying to help a critter bent on killing me even though I was trying to save his life." Red was off telling them both about a rambunctious steer that had gotten its horns hung up when it was trying to climb into a really tight clump of aspen trees. When Red tried to get him, the steer had fought as if Red were planning on turning him into a steak dinner.

Red was obviously here to watch out for his wife. But he wasn't rude about it. In fact, he was so kind and friendly, and had so obviously been working hard all morning, that Belle was nearly unable to believe Red's story.

A sudden flash of insight told Belle that *all* men weren't worthless. And didn't that mean that the problem was really with *her* because she picked such a poor lot? It was a sad thing to admit.

Belle stared into her cup of coffee while Red told his story, Cassie hanging on every word, laughing given half a chance.

Red made the story alive and funny with his arm movements

and exaggerated tones. Belle realized she'd never had this long a conversation with one of her husbands. Oh, she'd talked at them and they'd talked at her, but they didn't interact. She expected nothing of them and they gave her exactly that. Would Anthony be different if *she* were different? Maybe. Belle had never considered it before.

When Red finished his tale, Belle decided since she had a chance at talking to a man who might have some sense, she'd see if she could learn anything. "How'd you build this sod house? How do you make it weathertight?"

Red leaned forward. "Is your house giving you trouble? Maybe Cassie and I could come up for a day and give you a hand. I don't suppose Anthony—"

"Anthony is nothing." Belle wondered now if that was completely fair. "And you can't come because the pass is getting ready to blow shut. You might find yourself trapped in there for the winter."

"So why are you out here? Aren't you afraid of getting snowed out?" Red looked straight into her eyes.

Belle had dealt with too many weasel men in her life. She wasn't used to this kind of straight talk and respect. She could give Red nothing less than the truth. "I just needed to make sure about Cassie."

"I'm all right, but thank you for worrying."

Belle turned to Cassie. "I—I haven't been able to stop worrying about you. You remind me of myself when I was younger. Married to a man who wasn't much use. Then alone and forced to marry again. It was hard. I felt like I could protect you from that life."

"I don't need protection from Red." Cassie's cheeks pinked up again.

Belle realized that what Cassie needed was a husband who would kiss her. Well, Belle could give her no advice or guidance that didn't include a skillet. She saw the way the man looked at Cassie and the way Cassie looked back and suspected Red would figure everything out on his own and soon enough. She'd be switched if she'd give advice on that. And anyway, she'd never tried to get a man to do such a thing in her life. Avoiding a husband was the trick she'd perfected. She laid her hand on her belly. Nearly perfected.

"You're going through the winter with a house that isn't tight?" Red sounded worried, as if he were considering following her home and helping out.

"We'll be fine."

"Do you know how to drive straw into the chinks to stop the wind?"

Belle shook her head.

"Come on outside and I'll show you what I do. It makes a big difference. And I use mud to plug up holes, too." Red stood without a single grunt or groan, no whining that Belle was making work for him or nagging him.

"Can I come, too?" Cassie asked.

Red smiled at her, a private kind of smile that made Belle's heart ache in a way it never had before. She didn't even know why it hurt.

"Sure. Come along, Cass honey. Get your coat, though. It's sharp out today." He even helped Cassie on with her coat.

Red insisted on telling her about how to chink the cracks in her house.

Belle had never had a man. . .outside of someone from the Bates' store, do anything to help her. Belle went home alone, no kidnapping necessary, riding hard in case of a sudden storm, confused by Red's kindness and Cassie's longing for her husband to kiss her.

The gap hadn't closed, but a storm was brewing in the west, and Belle's heart pounded to think she'd have been trapped away from her children all winter. She did a ragged job of tarring the house and chinked the holes with hands full of straw, showing her girls how to help her.

Anthony had gone back to sitting on the roof, but their activity so close seemed to disturb him, and he climbed down and walked up to the Husband Tree to find peace. She watched him go, trying to imagine wanting him to kiss her. She put up with what she had to because a man had his rights, but she avoided it whenever she could. As he strode away, Belle considered all she'd learned today. Mainly, if all husbands weren't no-account, then she'd either picked in ignorance or deliberately married bums. And either way it added up to her being an idiot.

And a tiny, guilty part of herself wondered if she hadn't been so bossy and rude, if maybe William or Gerald or Anthony might have stepped up.

Looking up, she saw Anthony planting his backside down to sit and lean against the Husband Tree. She decided she'd give the man a chance to be a man.

"You like me, don't you, girl?" Cassie leaned her head into Rosie's flank.

The ornery cow slowed her kicking if Cassie wedged her head in the exact spot Red had shown her. Rosie kept chewing on her manger full of hay, but her tail quit twitching for an instant and Cassie took that for a yes.

Rosie liked her. And miracle of miracles, Harriet seemed to be beginning to like her. It wasn't that the sow wasn't fully prepared to kill Cassie at the drop of the hat. That was a given considering a mama sow's temperament. But Cassie was slopping Harriet every day and staying well away from the little pink piglets, and as her part of keeping the peace, Harriet had quit rushing the fence, woofing and snarling with her jaws gaping.

It was a start.

The chickens didn't seem to care about her one way or the other, but Cassie had learned chickens were close to the dumbest creatures God had ever put forth upon the earth. Red said they were only close to the dumbest because he'd worked with sheep before. He said sheep were just waiting, watching for any possible opportunity to kill themselves with their stupidity, which was the reason he didn't have any—they'd all died.

Even Buck was starting to like her. Sort of.

Red had given her riding lessons every morning that week, and she was learning that there was no great trick to riding a calm, well-broken horse. A horse was a living creature, though, with a mind of its own, and Buck had boosted Cassie out of the saddle once. When she'd fallen, Red had almost had a heart attack, and he'd declared no more riding until after the baby was born. But Cassie had wanted to continue, and in the end he let her ride, but he insisted on leading Buck every step of the way. She was now riding him twice a day down to the creek when Red took him for water.

She was also leading Rosie down, which Red let her do completely alone, and she had taken over the milking and most of the barnyard chores so Red was free to ride herd on his cattle. Red acted like Cassie was his dream come true because she was helping him so much.

Cassie had also found a barn cat that had the temperament of a rat rather than a pet. The cat slinked around the edges of the farm, only showing itself by accident. Cassie started putting out milk for it, but Red said not to bother. It lived on mice and that was how it should be. Cassie sneaked and put milk out anyway. The tiny defiance made her almost giddy. The milk was now gone every morning, but the cat still wasn't a lick friendly.

Rosie chose that moment to kick the bucket of milk right into Cassie's face. Dodging the hooves, Cassie fell backward onto her seat.

Red was just entering the barn. He rushed over to her side and stepped between her and Rosie. "Maybe it's time for you to give up some of your outside chores, Cass. Now that the babe's getting closer, you oughta be more careful. I think—"

Covered with milk, Cassie wailed, "You think I'm too stupid to learn anything."

Cassie clamped her mouth shut on the criticism of her husband. How had she dared to speak to him like that? She thought of Belle and her straight talk. Belle would certainly criticize if she thought it was deserved. But she certainly wouldn't whine.

"Now, Cass honey." Red slid his hands under her arms and lifted her to her feet. "Stupid's got nothing to do with it. Think how long it'd take me to teach the chickens to milk Rosie."

Cassie was on the verge of tears, but the image Red drew made her giggle instead.

"You're much better at this than our hens would be." He pulled a handkerchief out of his back pocket and swiped at the milk dripping off her head. "It's all in who you compare yourself to. From now on, if you're feeling like you're bad at something, pick the chickens to compare yourself to, 'cuz you'll come out of that contest feeling brilliant."

"So you'll let me keep doing it?"

Red hesitated. "For a fact, my ma milked the cows up to the day I was born, or so I've been told."

"Then it must be all right."

Red shrugged. "I s'pect. I just don't want you to get hurt."

Red's eyes got an intent look that made Cassie think back to the day he'd kissed her. His gaze went to her lips for an instant and Cassie wondered if there was still milk on her face. But if her face was dirty, she didn't want him noticing. Besides, she had to focus on her real goal—protecting one of her beloved chores.

Turning quickly back to Rosie before Red changed his mind, she crouched down and wedged her head into Rosie's flank. Locking her knees tight around the bucket, Cassie went back to work and got a few more cups of milk out of the little cow.

Red stayed nearby. Then, when Cassie was done, he went to let Rosie out in the pasture and Cassie went back to the house.

Yes, Rosie and Buck and Harriet liked her. But none of that mattered a bit because Red didn't like her. Oh, he was nice as could be to her. But he'd never come close to grabbing her and kissing her again like he had last Sunday.

Cassie didn't know what she'd done.

Saturday at noon, Red prayed with an unusual fervency over the dinner, asking for God's leading about whether they should go to town or not.

Cassie decided he must have gotten an answer because he got up from the table as soon as he was done eating. "I want to check the cattle. Then I'll do evening chores early while you clean up in here."

"Let me see to Rosie and the other livestock, Red. I did it fine for the last two days, didn't I?"

She could see Red waffling. He was so sweet to her, always wanting to be right on hand in case she needed help. He was letting her do nearly every chore she considered hers now, but the man did like to hover. She was surprised when he gave a quick jerk of his head in agreement.

"Milk Rosie, feed Harriet and the chickens. There might be a few eggs by now. Don't water anything. I don't want you lifting those heavy pails. And you can't go to the stream yet with Rosie. Leave that for me."

"I'll handle it."

"C–a–s–s?" Red drew her name out until it was nearly three full syllables. "Promise me."

Cass almost smiled even though she was pretty frustrated. He was getting to know she had a knack for not lying while she let him believe something that wasn't quite true. That had worked well on Griff. "All right. I promise."

"I'll be back before you're done with everything anyway. And Cass. . ." He waited until he had her full attention.

"Yes, Red?"

"Be careful of Harriet."

"Yes, Red."

He headed for the door then stopped and turned around. "And don't let Rosie kick you. Remember if you push hard. . ."

"With my head against her flank," Cassie talked over the top of his familiar instructions, "she can't get any force behind her kick." Cassie nodded. "Yes, Red. I'll remember."

Red gave one approving jerk of his head, reached for his hat, and put it on his head. "And don't leave any gates open. None. Remember the inner and outer gate for the chickens, and for heaven's sake, don't open Harriet's—"

"No gates," Cassie interrupted, then realized how rude she'd been to cut him off like that. "I won't forget, Red."

Red hesitated.

Cassie knew he was thinking up something new to be worried about.

He reached for the door latch then dropped his hand away. "And if anything goes wrong, or something comes up that we haven't talked about, don't try and figure out what you should do. Just wait. . ."

Cassie stood beside the table with her hands folded in front of her and tried to reassure him. "I'll just quit. I'll leave anything I'm not sure about to you."

This time Red got the door open, but he turned back and his face was really grim.

Cassie had a feeling this warning was more important than the others and maybe it was the cause of all the others.

"If anyone should ride up. . .well, it's always a good idea to be careful."

"Anyone? You mean like Belle might come over again?" Cassie had enjoyed her visit with the strange woman.

"I was thinking. . .Wade. . ." Red's voice died away.

Cassie could tell he'd been recollecting Wade and his threats and wasn't sure if he should worry her about it. She'd been thinking about Wade, too, and not wanting to worry Red about it. "Wade? You think he'll come?"

"I don't know, Cass." Then Red said gravely, "I think he might. Sometime."

She hadn't wanted to tell Red this because he already watched over her so, but almost against her will she said, "He used to show up at Griff's house when Griff went to town. I—he never did anything but talk, but I knew it was deliberate, him coming out when I was alone the way he did. He must have been watching. Except Griff had a routine, so maybe Wade just knew Griff went to town every Wednesday."

Red's brow furrowed and he dragged his hat off his head and clutched the brim.

Cassie didn't like to be the one to start putting worry lines in Red's face.

She liked his face very much just the way it was.

CHAPTER 16

Red knew that dead coyote hadn't been an accident. "If he ever shows up here, I want you to go into our bedroom and go into the tunnel."

If a man would poison an animal, he'd hurt a woman. He tossed his hat at the peg, not even bothering to check if he'd hung it up, and grabbed her by the wrist. "Let's find a good hiding place for you."

Red didn't tell Cassie somebody had poisoned his water hole. But maybe he should.

He hated to scare her. But if Wade had bothered her when she was married to Griff, then she was scared already and rightly so.

He'd found two dead coyotes and a dead grouse in one of the water holes he'd built. And there were no buts about that. Those animals had been poisoned and Red could read signs. Wade's horse's hooves were around that pond.

He started dragging her into the tunnel, but she pulled hard enough to stop him. "Red," Cassie interrupted his musing, "let's think it over while we're in town. Wade won't come if you're close by. At least he never did at Griff's. And if he does, well, I'll find a spot to hide." Cassie looked over her shoulder at the crevice in the back of the bedroom. "I've explored it and I could duck into a couple of little nooks. He'd never find me. We'll pick out a good spot together when we're back from town."

Red looked from the door to Cassie to the dark slit in their wall that led into the bowels of the earth. Cassie's plan was full of holes. Wade could find her if he took a lantern from the kitchen or if Cassie made a noise at the wrong time.

She walked over to Red and laid her hand on his chest. "You take good care of me, Red. The tunnel will work if need be. And anyway, you never go off and leave me, not for long. It's not like it was at Griff's."

"You always call it Griff's."

"What?"

"Your old home. You call it Griff's. You call everything Griff's. Doesn't it strike you as odd that you say Griff's carriage, Griff's horses, Griff's house?"

"Well, it was all Griff's. It doesn't seem so unusual to say that." Cassie kept looking at the tunnel.

Red wanted her to hear what he was saying. In frustration he took hold of her elbow and turned her to face him.

Her forehead furrowed and she tried to answer him again. "It doesn't mean anything. They were Griff's, mine, both of ours. What difference does it make what word I use?"

"I think it does make a difference. This is your home, Cass. I don't want you to say, 'Red's house' or 'Red's cow.' It's all *ours*. I want you to think of it that way. I wonder if you really thought of the house you shared with Griff as yours."

Red could see the protest forming on Cassie's tongue. Before she could speak, he said, "In a way, since it was all your money, inherited from your ma and pa, that house and everything in it was more yours than his. But you never thought of it that way.

Why do you suppose that is?"

"I guess it was because Griff knew just what he wanted, and I didn't care that much. He had such a clear idea of how our home should be built, how our furniture should be, how we should dress and conduct ourselves. He was a fine man to step in and take care of me like he did. And I. . .well, I was so grateful to him, taking me. . .all young and stupid and clumsy, and helping me grow into a woman who was worthy of him."

"Worthy of. . ." Red almost shouted the words, then he cut them off.

"What is it, Red? I'm grateful to you, too. I didn't mean I still want to be how Griff wanted. I want to be just how you want now. I'm trying to learn your ways."

Red grabbed her by her shoulders and pulled her up to within an inch of his face. A chill of fear flash across Cassie's face and it made him sick to think of how she'd learned to fear a man's anger.

"Red, I'm sorry. I didn't mean to. . ."

She quit talking. Red watched the huge internal effort she made to keep her feelings from showing on her face. She battled with herself until a deep serene expression emerged from the turmoil. Griff had trained her well. He'd taught her that she could only be loved when she'd achieved that appearance of tranquility that made her look as perfect as a china doll.

She had hold of her composure now. "I will remember what you said and refer to this house as ours, Red. I can see why you wish it that way. I'll try to call Griff's. . .um, I mean my old house mine from now on. It was just a bad habit to say it the way I did. It won't happen again."

"Cass. . ." Red pulled her roughly into his arms and held her very close.

She began to apologize again. Then she slipped her hand between them and rested her fingers over her mouth.

Red looked at her hand then back at her eyes. He could see that she was fully prepared to stand here until he'd said his piece. He glanced back at her fingers, and some of his irritation faded as he watched those fingers touch her pink lips. For just a few seconds he forgot what they were talking about. At last he tore his eyes away from her mouth. "If you disagree with me, you can say so. I want you to speak your mind."

"Yes, Red," she said from behind her fingertips.

"And you don't always have to say, 'Yes, Red.'"

"Yes, Red. . .I mean, I'm glad to mind you. It's a woman's place, after all."

Red clenched his jaw tight until he saw a shiver of fear pass through her. Red relaxed his hold on her shoulders and rubbed her arms, trying to reassure her that she was safe with him. No matter what he said, she just agreed so pleasantly, it could turn a man's head if he wasn't careful. But he didn't want an obedient, frightened china doll. He wanted a flesh-and-blood woman. "Ah, Cass, can't you hear me?"

"I hear you fine. You just said—"

"Don't you get my meaning, though? I don't want you to ever be afraid to speak up. I—I wouldn't ever hurt you, Cass. I mean. . .I'd never raise my hand to you."

"If you wanted to do that, if I'd done wrong, well, a man has a right—"

"No man has a right to hit a woman," Red roared.

She stepped back a pace before she found that blasted composure and stood her ground, obviously awaiting whatever resulted from Red's anger.

"Stop doing that." Red grabbed her and shook her again, but not hard, considering how furious he was.

"Doing what, Red? Just tell me what I'm doing wrong and I'll stop."

"Stop that. Stop agreeing with me all the time. If I yell

at you, it's because I lose my temper. That's *my* sin, *not* yours. I would never strike you, and if Griff did, then he was *wrong*. There's no excuse for a man treating a woman like that."

Cassie clung to the appearance of serenity.

Red inhaled and took a step back from her. He rubbed his hand across the back of his neck several times and stared at the floor. Finally he looked up at her. "Okay, you want to obey me? Then here's the rule. I order you to tell me what you're thinking. Every time I say something, I want the truth from you, even if the truth is, 'Red, I think you're as dumb as a post and as smelly as a polecat.' I want you to start telling me what you want. I want you to say at least once a day, 'Do it yourself,' or, 'Quit bossing me around,' or, 'Eat it or throw it out to Harriet, but I'm not making you something else.'"

Cassie's eyes widened at the horrible things Red was ordering her to say. "I could never do that."

"Oh, so you're disobeying me then?" Red crossed his arms and glared at her. "I thought it was a wife's place to *obey*. And I like a *mouthy*, *rude* woman with her own ideas and her own emotions. I want you to have a coat as prickly as a porcupine and a hide as thick as a buffalo and a spine as solid as the Rocky Mountains. I don't want you doing a single thing you don't want to do. I can't be happily married to a woman who doesn't nag me a little. All this polite, 'Yes, Red,' and 'Whatever you say, Red,' is making me *crazy*. You work on it and I'll tell you when you're finally doing it enough."

She clamped her hand harder over her mouth.

Red grabbed her hand and pulled it away. "You can't sass me when you're holding your mouth closed."

"I. . .I. . ." A tiny giggle escaped Cassie's lips.

The sound eased some of Red's frustrated anger, but he continued in the same domineering tone. "And I like laughing, too. Big, loud belly laughs. I'm an unhappily married man if you don't laugh every time you take a notion to."

"You want me to call you a polecat?" Cassie giggled a little louder.

"It's an order." Red said it sternly, but he didn't try to keep the pleasure from shining out of his eyes when he heard her laugh.

"I don't think I can do it right now. Um. . .call you a. . .a polecat. I'll have to work up to it." Cassie giggled again.

Red smiled at her then sobered. "I don't know what things were like between you and Griff, but I'm not like him. I want a woman to stand beside me, not trail along behind. That was Griff's way, but it was wrong. I don't want you to be afraid of me. And maybe if you sass me a little, even if I get mad, you'll see that you can trust me to never hurt you. I promise it before you and before God. I want you to believe me."

The fear returned to Cassie's expression, but this time Red didn't think she was afraid of him. He thought she was afraid of the whole idea that Griff was wrong to control her so completely.

"Red, if you don't want to step in and tell me what to do, now that Griff's gone. . ." Cassie's voice grew so weak he could barely hear her. "Then who is going to?"

The last of Red's anger died away, replaced with a deep compassion unlike any he'd ever known. "I reckon you're a woman grown." He laid his hand on her belly. "You've got a babe on the way who's gonna need a ma correcting him and teaching him right from wrong. I saw you reading Norm's mortgage note at the bank. Do you know how few of the men out here can read? You're smart, Cass. And God gave you a conscience like anyone else. You can just take over the job and tell yourself what to do."

"I don't have much practice at that," she whispered.

"Well, it's time to start getting some, Cass honey. Now I have to go do chores and check the herd. We're gonna be late to town as it is. We can talk on the way, unless you fall over asleep again."

Red saw a war taking place within her. He saw the fear and excitement battle for control. He didn't think it was a battle he could fight for her.

Finally, fear overcame the first meager surge of self-rule. She went back to the meek little Cassie he'd wanted to banish. "I've been getting better with Buck. Do—do you want me to ride him by myself this time, or will we still ride double?"

Red hesitated, dissatisfied with the results of their talk. But he didn't know what to say and he didn't have time to say it if he did. And he was afraid if he opened his mouth again he might just blurt out something like, "I'm completely in love with you."

Finally he plunked his hat on his head and said, "One hour. And don't forget what I said about Wade." He ran like a yellow-bellied coward out the door.

Cassie watched him go, thinking how much different he was than Griff.

She'd controlled herself because Griff had never spared her a punishment because of apologies or tears or pleading. In fact, his rebukes were more stinging if she carried on. But in the last year especially, if she could become the china doll, if she could face him calmly and let him do his scolding until he was finished speaking his mind, he'd often "spare the rod" as he put it. She'd forgotten for a bit those hard-taught lessons of Griff's. She knew if she'd only be a good enough wife, Red would call her sweet names again. She vowed in her heart to try harder to please him, to learn faster, to take more of the burden from his shoulders.

Cassie thought she had him figured out now. She might even

try just a little to sass him once in a while, because although she could tell he'd been joking, Red was a man who liked to laugh, and if she did it just right, she thought he'd like a little more show of just the right kind of spirit from her.

And Red respected work. She had to work harder. It was all going to be fine. She was sure of it. She'd keep listening and learning and working hard, and after a time, maybe she could work her way straight into Red's heart.

CHAPTER 17

This time Libby and Leota and Muriel were ready for her.

Cassie woke as Red lowered her to the ground. Leota came hurrying up to the front door of Bates General Store before Red had completed his brief hellos to Muriel and Libby and rushed off to work.

Cassie said, still half asleep, "I can stock shelves if there aren't any customers."

Muriel laughed. "I'll work you like a mule later, Cassie. I've got a pot of coffee on the stove and I've pulled up four chairs. Sit."

She waved all the ladies toward her heating stove, and Cassie welcomed the warmth. The fall weather had lingered more than usual this year but the wind bit as if to warn them winter was coming. The cold didn't keep Cassie from sleeping. In fact, she seemed to need a nap most afternoons. It was one of the things she'd wanted to ask the ladies about. It was actually one of the few questions that she had the nerve to ask outright. She hoped to slip the other, more embarrassing questions in later. She held her hands out to the stove until some of the chill left then headed for the rocking chair the other ladies had left vacant.

Libby pulled yarn out of a cloth bag she was carrying, and Leota began stitching on quilt blocks, each only an inch square. Muriel had a basket sitting beside her chair and lifted a half-darned sock out of it. "I should have some handwork to do, too," Cassie said awkwardly.

Muriel smiled up at her. "You just sit there, young lady. You're growing a baby. That's work enough."

Cassie sighed as she sat, still slightly groggy and bemused from her long rest in Red's arms. "I declare, I take an afternoon nap just like a child. It doesn't mean I'm sick, does it? Or could something be wrong with the baby?"

Muriel laughed. It was such a pleasant sound. Cassie hadn't heard much laughter in her life. At least not for a long time.

"Seth's mother was such a sweet lady." Muriel sighed, and her eyes were looking at far-off memories that no one else could see. "I remember once, before I knew my eldest was coming, I was at her house helping her with threshers. Ten starving men and they ate like mules as much and with as many manners. It was right after the noon meal. The men were gone back out and we'd cleaned the kitchen. I sat down at the table to visit with her and I fell asleep. I didn't even know it."

"Four hours later, Seth was there, waking me up to take me home. I'd spent the entire afternoon with my head lying on my arms at the table. My mother-in-law must have tiptoed around that whole time but she let me sleep. I tried to apologize for it and she smiled so kindly at me and said, 'A baby takes a lot out of a woman.' And I said, 'What baby?'"

Leota and Libby laughed and Muriel joined in. Cassie's heart eased some when she realized she wasn't the only woman who'd had to be told she was with child. "I didn't know there was a baby coming until July."

"That's four months. You must have been feeling some movement." Leota laid two little squares together and began a row of tiny, neat stitches.

Cassie said, "I remember some now that I'm feeling it a lot, but back then I didn't recognize it as anything but muscles twitching."

Libby's needles clicked efficiently. "That's just what it feels like at first."

"I only found out in July when I mentioned it to Griff because I was worried about my. . .my time not coming for several months. I might not have said anything then except he was. . .he wanted to. . ." Cassie didn't know how she ended up going down such personal paths. Muriel had told everyone about finding out she was expecting without having to refer to marital intimacy.

"It was time for the one in the summer?" Libby asked lightly without looking up from the dark red yarn in her hands.

Cassie nodded.

All three women started laughing.

Cassie felt she had to explain. "It's just that, at first Griff said I was too young."

"Too young for what?" Leota asked blankly.

"Hush, Leota," Muriel said with her lips quivering suspiciously. "Too young to be. . .umm. . .together as man and wife, right, Cassie?"

Leota looked at Muriel then quickly returned to her sewing.

Cassie said so softly her voice almost squeaked, "That's right. I was fifteen when we married. Griff said that was too young. So, it's only been the last year he's. . ."

Muriel said, "Decided you were old enough?"

"Yes," Cassie said with a sigh of relief. "And then he wasn't. . . that is, I wasn't. . ." Cassie was suddenly exhausted and wanted the whole conversation to end.

Muriel set aside her darning and got to her feet to pour coffee. "You weren't old enough very often?"

Cassie nodded and the ladies started laughing again. Muriel had to lean on her chair until she got control of herself.

Cassie's cheeks warmed. She'd embarrassed herself again but she wasn't sure how. Just the reference to such a personal topic, she imagined. "I thought he should know before. . .before. . . lest there be anything wrong with me. And it was a good thing, because a man isn't to. . ."

Leota lowered her quilt blocks and exchanged a quick glance with Muriel and Libby that somehow left Cassie out. "He said you were unclean." The ladies all sobered.

Cassie remembered their reaction to that last Saturday and hurried to change the subject before they began to once again berate Griff.

"Red taught me how to milk his cow this week, and I'm caring for the chickens and our sow and her piglets."

"A mama pig is a fierce critter," Muriel said. "Take care around her."

"She attacked Red once." At the ladies' urging, she told about Harriet and Red's accident, and the struggles she'd had trying to feed the grouchy mother pig. They seemed delighted with her stories of life with Red, so she talked more than she could ever remember talking in her life.

On occasion, Muriel would have to get up and help a customer, but she hurried them through ruthlessly and came back to the stove.

Leota finally slipped her needle securely into her growing quilt and got to her feet. "My husband will be hauling the children on his back through town, screaming my name, if I don't get home."

Libby rolled the scarf around the ball of yarn and pinned the whole thing together with the two long knitting needles.

"I have baking to see to before suppertime."

"I don't think I'd better carry anything over to your diner, Libby. I don't feel right about the help I got last week."

Libby said, "Carryin' for you last Saturday and hearin' your sweet thank you was the highlight of those men's lives. You shouldn't deprive them of the pleasure."

Cassie laughed and she wished she could do this job for Red, but she didn't haul the groceries.

The general store got busy as the afternoon wore on. Muriel said menfolk didn't buy anything ahead. They just noticed they needed something when they ran out, so right before suppertime every night she had a crowd.

Red appeared briefly out of the back room and said, "Hi." He hurried away with a wooden box of supplies for Libby.

After that, Cassie was aware of every movement from the back of the store, but Red never came up front again.

Mort Sawyer came in with an order and seemed surprised to see Cassie folding a bolt of cloth in front of the counter. He said hello gruffly.

Cassie inhaled slowly and said, "I heard you bought the spring, Mr. Sawyer. I know you wanted it. I'm glad it worked out."

Mort studied her with narrow eyes, and she knew somehow he'd taken her comment as offensive. She opened her mouth to apologize for she knew not what, but Red came from the back at that moment. He'd come to lend support. She smiled gratefully at him.

"Afternoon, Mort." Red stood beside Cassie, with one hand resting on her lower back.

Mort had been annoyed with her, but surrounded with people like she was, Cassie hadn't really been afraid of him. When Red showed up, Mort seemed content to refocus his temper on Red.

"Your interference cost me over a thousand dollars. There were two other bidders on that worthless spring, and it should have been mine along with her." Mort tipped his head at Cassie like she was nothing except a part of the bargain.

"You know that's not true, Mort," Red answered mildly. "Cassie no more belonged to you than that spring. And a thousand dollars is a fair price for a good water source like that. And you can afford it. Plus you got the house—"

"That house is worthless and you know it! No one can live in it back in there!" Mort said gruffly.

"Rip it apart for the wood then." Red shrugged casually. He tightened his hold on Cassie's back just a little as if to apologize for Mort's dismissal of her beautiful house. Cassie stood calmly beside Red, determined to make him proud of her. She didn't even flinch when he suggested tearing down Griff's house.

Wade stepped into the store at that second and came to stand beside his father. Standing side by side like that, Cassie thought Mort had the look of an aging wolf. Some of his strength was gone, but he'd replaced it with a lifetime of brutal lessons. Wade looked like a fox, with shifting eyes and a mind that turned to slyness. He had none of his father's strength of character. Even though Mort used his iron will to solidify power at the expense of others, no one could deny that Mort had what it took to conquer this unforgiving land. Wade would have never made it out West without his father's wealth and power to ease the way.

In a moment of insight, Cassie knew that Mort was the cattle baron Griff had always wanted to be. She had an urge to smile as she thought how far from Mort's vicious ruthlessness Griff had been. Griff had been more fox than wolf, too, but without Wade's sadistic streak. Then Cassie thought of the times Griff had raised his hand harshly against her and wondered if Griff didn't have more in common with Wade than she wanted to admit.

Then she wondered about Red. He'd said he had five hundred head of cattle. Did that make him a cattle baron, too? "How many head of cattle do you have, Mort?" Every person in the place turned to look at her before she realized she'd spoken aloud.

Mort wouldn't probably have deigned to answer her question except it gave him a moment to boast in front of all Muriel's customers. "Over ten thousand head."

"And how much land?"

Mort said, "With my water claims, I control forty thousand acres. It's the biggest spread in western Montana."

Cassie shook her head from side to side. Mort and Wade watched her, curious about her question. She even thought she saw a gleam in Wade's eye like maybe he thought she was considering whether she'd chosen right to marry Red when she could have had a Sawyer. "If you're so well-to-do, then surely a thousand dollars isn't that much to you. Why are you so upset about spending it?"

"I can afford twenty times that amount if I want to!" Mort roared at her.

Two weeks ago, Cassie would have fainted dead away in the face of all that male anger, but Red was beside her, and he'd even been angry with her before and it hadn't been so bad. Somehow Mort had lost a lot of his power to intimidate, and it was easy for her to stand face-to-face with the two of them. "And why do you need me for a wife?"

She turned to Wade. "Or you? With all your land and cattle and the nice place you live, can't you go find a wife somewhere who *wants* to marry you? I know women are in short supply, but get away from here for a few months. Denver is a big city. Go spend the winter in Denver and bring yourself a wife back. Chasing after me the way you've been isn't necessary for a rich man like you."

Cassie didn't think she was being rude. It just seemed like common sense. Of course a man ranching alone couldn't abandon his place and go wife hunting. But with all the hands on the Sawyer place, Wade didn't have to be alone if he didn't choose to be.

She didn't expect Wade to lash out at her like a striking snake. He grabbed her arm and yanked her forward until she was so close to him their noses touched. "No little snip of a woman is gonna tell me..." Wade's eyes flickered with a stunned look and he loosened his hold on Cassie. He sank to his knees in front of her.

As his face left her vision, she saw Red's arm around Wade's neck, choking him so tight that Wade lost consciousness within seconds of Red's getting ahold of him. Red grabbed Wade by the collar to stop him from falling on his face.

Muriel stepped to Cassie's side and pulled her back as Cassie babbled, "I didn't mean to be insulting. I—I just thought— It's just common sense that he'd—"

"Let up on him, Red," Mort said quietly.

Red stepped back, grim lines etched around his mouth. He still spoke calmly, but there was iron in his voice. "He's not gonna lay his hands on Cassie. Get him under control, Mort, before he comes to a bad end. You've raised yourself a poor excuse for a man. He's been prowling around my place, and he poisoned my water hole this week. I'm letting it pass because none of my stock died, but I'm watching for him now. He won't get off so easy next time."

"You can't prove nothin', Dawson." Wade dragged in a deep breath of air. His voice was hoarse.

"I can read signs, and every man here knows it. Your horse steps high and takes a long pace, and your boots leave a mark as good as a signature. There's law out here, Wade, even for a Sawyer. And if you ever touch Cassie again, you'd better hope

I remember I'm a Christian man, because that's the only thing that will protect you."

Cassie was standing well back from Wade. Red was right behind him. She was watching Wade struggle to his feet until she glanced at Red. He wasn't looking at Wade. He was focused on Mort.

Right before Cassie's eyes, that hard, old tyrant shrank to something far more human, and Cassie could see that Red was Mort's equal. Red was as tall. He wasn't as broad, but that was because Mort had gone more and more to fat over the years. Red had broad shoulders and corded muscles in his arms. But the thing that really made Red a man to respect was the force of his will. He held Mort's eyes and spoke with a confidence that no one could deny. There was no threat in Red's voice, only promise.

Wade staggered sideways as he stood and knocked into his father, breaking the stare down between Red and Mort. Mort looked at his son and disgust crossed his face.

For a second Cassie felt sorry for Wade. Wade had grown up weak because his will had been broken by his father.

Cassie knew in that instant that Mort might respect Red and leave him alone, because Mort was the kind of man who would face anyone head-on. But Wade would turn to deviousness—like poisoning a water hole or manhandling a woman or shooting someone in the back. Mort couldn't promise anything for Wade and Cassie knew it. She hoped Red did, too.

"It's over, Red." Mort turned to Wade. "You hear that, boy? There'll be no feudin' with the Dawsons. You stay off his land and keep away from the china doll. She ain't for you. Not anymore."

"I hear you, old man." Wade sneered and started for the door. "I hear you bawlin' 'cuz you're afraid of the preacher here."

Mort snapped at his son. "Remember what I said, Wade. It's over."

Wade jerked the door open and left the store, slamming the door much as he had the Sunday before.

Mort turned to the gathering of people around him, and stepping past them like they were stray dogs beneath his notice, he went up to Seth. "I'll be back for my order in an hour, Bates. Have it ready." Mort thrust a piece of paper at Seth and left the building.

The second he left, Cassie rushed to Red's side. "I'm sorry, I didn't mean to start all that. I didn't mean to be so bad-mannered. I'm the cause of—"

Red leaned down and kissed her. He didn't kiss her for long, but she quit talking to try and catch up with the kissing. He pulled away and said flatly, "Don't go anywhere alone, Cassie." He looked up and said to Seth, "You see she minds me, Seth. You have to watch her every second. She's a wily little thing."

Several people laughed, and some of the tension in the room fell away.

Red looked back at her. "And don't you dare take the blame for Mort and Wade Sawyer. There's not another man in this place, maybe in the whole *territory*, who would grab you like that even if you spit on him and told him his lacy pantaloons were showing under his skirts. Why, most of us would thank you for the insult and keep the spit for a memento of having a moment of your attention."

Several men surrounded them and they all added their agreement to Red's statement.

One of them said, "I'd be much obliged for you to spit on me, ma'am," and the crowd laughed.

"No decent man hurts a woman, Cass." The way Red was looking at her, she knew he was talking about Wade, but he was thinking of Griff, too. And these crude, uncivilized men who had always been beneath Griff's notice felt the same way.

There was silence between her and Red for a second until she nodded slightly.

Red rubbed her arms as he did sometimes, as if she were chilled and he wanted to warm her. "The Sawyers were pestering the people around here long before you or I came, and a sweet little thing like you can't make 'em better and you can't make 'em worse, so don't bother to try."

Red's tone lightened and his smile took on a teasing quality. "Anyway, even if it's all your fault, it doesn't make any difference."

"Why not?" Cassie asked suspiciously.

Red leaned so close his lips brushed against her ear. " 'Cuz, I knew when I married you, you were gonna be trouble."

Cassie pulled away slightly, trying to conceal her hurt.

Red caught her chin with two fingers and leaned in close and spoke so nobody could hear. "Now's when you're supposed to say, 'Red, you low-down, worthless excuse for a man, I'm not trouble. You are. And if I am any trouble, I'm worth every minute of it.'"

Cassie could feel her cheeks turning pink at the very thought of speaking so to her husband. She whispered something completely different than what he'd ordered her to say. "Red, I think you're about the finest excuse for a man I've ever known."

Red's eyes looked deep into hers. For a long moment Cassie felt joined to another human being in a way she never before had. Then he seemed to remember himself because he shook his head a little. "You are one disobedient woman. All this niceness is a big disappointment to a man who likes sass."

"I promise I'll try to be meaner," Cassie said demurely.

Red laughed and tapped her on the tip of her nose. "You do that."

Cassie had a sobering thought. "Mort can't control him, Red," she warned softly.

"I know. But I had to give him a chance to try. I've never killed a man, and I never want to. I don't want it to come to that. It's about more than wanting something like that on my conscience. I don't think it's too judgmental of me to suspect that if Wade died now, he'd never make it to the Pearly gates. In some ways it would be better for *me* to die than him because of what he's facing in the afterlife. I don't know if I'd have the courage to die to save the life of a man like Wade Sawyer, but it would be the right thing to do, I reckon. But I have you and the babe to consider. I have to protect the two of you. Maybe Mort can do something. Maybe he'll send him to Denver like you said."

"Oh, but the poor woman who'll end up married to him."

Red smiled. "Maybe he'll marry someone like Belle Tanner. She could handle him."

Cassie arched both brows. Belle *could* handle Wade. "But Belle's already married."

"True, but her husbands don't seem to be permanent, exactly." Red looked out the door as if seriously considering introducing Wade to Belle. Then he shrugged. "Let's don't worry about the imaginary woman he marries now. I've got food to deliver and the windows to wash at Grant's and a few more things to do before I can quit for the day."

"I wish I could help you with the food, Red."

Muriel interrupted. "I can't spare you, Cassie. Red's gonna have to do it alone."

A look passed between Muriel and Red, and Cassie knew Muriel had special instructions to not let Cassie overdo. Cassie's heart warmed to think people were taking care of her.

Red headed to the back of the store, and, to Cassie's surprise, a dozen men who had gathered to get supplies while Mort and Wade made their fuss filed past her, each tipping his hat. They followed Red back and each hefted an armload of the goods that were sitting there, gathered to fill Libby's order. Cassie hurried to the hallway to watch and saw the men follow Red across the street.

Red was ahead and didn't notice them until he was opening Libby's door. He turned enough to see he was leading a parade, and he started laughing. Cassie smiled to see Red's shining white teeth and generous smile. Then, although he had two fifty-pound bags of flour on his shoulder, he held the door for the whole long line of men.

The men filed straight back out and came to be waited on at the store. Cassie made sure to thank each of them personally and did her best to call each by name.

CHAPTER 18

Mort knocked Wade into the wall. His head cracked against the rough native stones of the fireplace in the huge Sawyer dining room and he sank, stunned, to his knees.

His father drew back his fist. "I'm not telling you again, boy!"

That huge club of a hand hammered Wade's jaw. Wade flew sideways, landing with a *thud*, stretched out flat on his belly. His head reeled.

"You leave that woman alone!" Mort's boot slugged Wade's chest, flipping Wade to his back. "I'm sick of you sniffing around her!"

Another kick made the room go dark. Wade struggled to remain conscious. Through blurred eyes he saw a smear on the floor where blood dripped from his nose.

He was a man. Eighteen just last summer. Wade lay there and wished his father dead. He hated himself for not having the guts to kill him.

He struggled for air. In his muddled brain he heard the china doll cry for help. She'd been done wrong, too. Wade had seen the marks Griff left on her porcelain white skin. Now Dawson had her. Wade's head spun and he clearly saw Dawson raising his fist to poor Cassie. She'd told Wade to go to Denver. Now he heard the real meaning.

Go to Denver and take me with you.

"Get up! Stand up here and take it like a man!" Mort taunted.

Wade didn't move. He knew his father in a mood like this, and only abject submission would make him stop.

Wade swore it was the last time.

"You're a little coward. How'd a man like me raise such a weakling?" Mort leaned down and grabbed the front of Wade's shirt and lifted him until his feet dangled above the ground. "The hands laugh at you to your face."

Mort threw Wade against a table. He crashed to the floor. A broken pitcher slashed his skin.

"They sneer at you right in front of me and I can't even call them on it because they're right." Mort kicked him in the stomach. "I'm ashamed to call you my son."

Wade coughed and spit up blood. He didn't move. His vision blurred and the blood seemed to be doubled and tripled. He lay there, trampled into the floor like dirt and knew every word his father said was the sheer truth.

He was weak. He didn't have the nerve to pull his gun. If he could kill a man, his father would respect him. Maybe even fear him. And maybe, if Wade ever found the backbone to use his weapon, his father *should* fear him.

Mort finished his tirade and stormed out, slamming doors. Wade laid there, a whipped pup.

The cowhands, when Wade had been knocked down by Tom Linscott, had called him a pup.

Gertie, their housekeeper from the time Wade's mother had died, came in as soon as the door slammed and sank to her knees beside Wade. She already had a wet towel to wipe away the blood. "I'm so sorry, Wade. Poor baby," Gertie crooned as she bathed his face, bathed his face like an infant that had made a mess eating his food.

"Poor baby," Gertie called him.

"Ashamed to call you my son," his father said.

"A poor excuse for a man." That's what Red had said in front of nearly the whole town.

He couldn't fight his father or the cowhands, and Gertie meant no harm. And anyway, all he wanted was to get away from them. They had nothing he wanted.

But that wasn't true of Red Dawson. Red Dawson had Wade's woman. His china doll. Wade needed to save her from a life like the one Wade lived. She'd asked him today to take her with him and go to Denver.

And there was only one way the china doll would be free to go with Wade.

Red Dawson needed to die.

Cassie kept getting better at the chores, and Red was less afraid she was going to kill herself. Or him.

He let her do more without supervision. As winter closed in around them, Red brought all the cattle down from the rugged high pastures to the grasslands that opened up in front of his home. He'd saved back the lush prairie hay that grew there and let it cure on the stem. It simplified his chores in the bitter cold and kept the cattle fat and contented through the winter.

Red scouted more carefully around his holding than usual and found a dozen spots where Wade had stood for long stretches of time and watched the house. He never caught Wade lurking around and he didn't see any new tracks—which would have been impossible to hide in the almost daily dusting of snow. Red stayed as close as possible to the cabin, but he made a quick check of his cattle every day and no more water was poisoned.

He kept up his guard until the next Sunday, when on their ride home from the church service, Cassie said, "Muriel saw Wade get on the stage for Denver. He's gone for the winter, the Sawyer hands all said. Maybe for good."

Cassie turned to look at Red, holding her on his lap like always. Red had offered to take the buckboard, but it doubled the time it took to reach Divide, and Cassie found it no hardship to be held in Red's arms. "Muriel said he was so battered she could barely recognize him. He'd taken a terrible beating."

Red closed his eyes and breathed in slowly. "Mort. I know Mort raises his hand to Wade. I've heard talk." Red's eyes flickered open. "Can we say a prayer for him, Cass honey? I know he's a bad man, Wade, but I—I shouldn't have turned Mort against him that way. That's my fault. What is wrong with a man that he could do that to his son?"

"Mort's a strong man, Red." Cassie rested a hand on her husband's cheek. She'd made herself some bright red mittens, taught by Muriel, and the yarn earned with her own work. She loved them, but the joy went out of her when she thought of Mort turning those huge hands on his son.

"Everyone thinks of Mort as strong, but he's not. He's a weakling." Red looked angry and troubled.

"No he's not. How can you say someone with his wealth and power is weak?"

Red leaned down and kissed Cassie on the forehead. "It's pure weakness to hurt someone smaller than you. It's a weakness of the mind and the soul. It has no bearing on how strong his back is."

They rode silently for a moment, then Red looked down at her. "Let's pray. I know we're scared of Wade, and I'm glad he's gone, but it's right to pray for your enemy. It's right to bless those who curse you."

Cassie lifted her shoulders a bit. "Sometimes the Bible doesn't make much sense."

Red's grim expression lifted and he managed a small smile. "That's when I like it best, honey. When it makes no sense, that's when it's telling us something really important."

Cassie frowned. "Well, that makes no sense either. But I'll be glad to pray along with you." It was the least an obedient wife could do.

Despite his compassion for Wade, knowing the man had left the back country was a relief. Red finally began to relax.

Wade had taken Cassie's hint and left for Denver, or that's what he told everyone. Truth was, he'd climbed off the stage at the first stop, untied his horse from the back of the stage, bought a pack horse and a winter's worth of supplies with the money he'd saved up, and rode back to Divide.

He settled in with a spyglass high above the Dawsons' place. Dawson had increased his vigilance for a while, and Wade had stayed far into the back country. He'd even found a line shack not too many miles from the china doll and set himself up for the winter.

Wade watched carefully and he could tell when Dawson finally relaxed and began staying away from the ranch for longer stretches of time.

The occasional glimpses of the china doll were like drips of water to a man dying of thirst, and the day came when Wade couldn't stand it anymore. He took a long draw on his whiskey to try and quench that thirst and reached into his pocket to stroke the handkerchief he'd stolen from the Griffin place. He longed for it to be her he touched.

Wade had gotten his hands on the china doll in town for just a few seconds before Dawson had humiliated him. His fingers still burned from that touch. The need to feel her again was a fever in his blood.

She'd never agree to come away with him. The enormity of leaving her husband would stop any respectable woman. He would make the decision for both of them. After awhile she'd thank him.

Often enough he'd watched from a hill near the Griffin place. He knew plenty about how the china doll had suffered under Lester Griffin. Just as Wade had suffered under his father's brutal hands.

Wade had found a way out. He'd get her out, too. She'd thank him when Dawson was dead.

Wade emptied the flask down his burning throat then switched to drinking straight from the bottle as he waited for Dawson to ride away after the noon meal. He'd be gone for at least an hour. Wade watched the china doll stand at her door, then she turned and seemed to stare right at him. Wade gasped, jerked the spyglass away from his eye, and dropped behind a rock, breathing hard. But then he realized she'd known he was here. She was saying, "Come for me."

He lifted himself up, looked through his spyglass, and saw she'd gone inside. But he knew it was time.

Wade didn't hesitate.

"Can I speak with you, Anthony?" Belle had been working up the courage to talk with her husband for quite a while.

It went contrary to everything she knew about husbands to try and speak honestly with the man. But she felt goaded into trying by what she'd seen between Cassie and Red Dawson.

Anthony looked up from where he sat, morose and sulking,

under the Husband Tree. "My back hurts, Belle. Don't start in nagging about chores. That's all I ever hear—"

"I'm sorry you've got a bad back." Belle swung down from her horse and tied the animal to a low branch of the Husband Tree.

She was pretty sure her bay was standing on top of Gerald.

She sank down onto the cold ground, wondering how Anthony could endure it up here for hours. Surely working would keep him warm.

"I didn't come up here to nag you."

Anthony arched his brows in surprise.

Belle didn't blame him. She'd never gotten this close to him before by choice. Even now she didn't touch him. She didn't even consider wanting him to kiss her like that strange Cassie had spoken of.

"Well, what else would you ever have to say to me, Belle?"

Belle looked sideways at him. He was a beautiful man. The curls were out of control on his head and shining black in the cold sunlight. His eyes were a gleaming blackish brown, his nose strong and straight. Belle had seen a picture of a statue chiseled by some ancient Italian artist once, and Anthony, true to his Italian heritage, looked like that carved stone. *David*, that had been the name of the statue. King David from the Bible.

God, why did I marry him? Not because he's so handsome. Please, dear heavenly Father, don't let it have been for something so shallow.

After Gerald died and the men had come a-courtin', she'd balked and said no and done her level best to discourage the stream of suitors. Then one day she'd been tired of it all, worn out from running the men off. And Anthony, who'd been persistent, had come along, and she'd said yes just to make them all stay away. She'd married Anthony because he'd been the first to come along that day.

She rested her hand on her growing baby and knew this child—*please, God, let it be a girl*—would be beautiful. "I came up here because I want us to try and figure out a way to get along."

Anthony wrinkled his perfect brow. "Since when?"

Belle shrugged. "I've never given you much of a chance. I know that. But I quit even pretending to care when I caught you coming out of the Golden Butte stinking of perfume."

Anthony picked up a stick and began poking at the hard ground. He sat with his knees pulled up to his chest, scowling, refusing to look at her. The very picture of a sulking child. "I told you that was your fault."

"Yes, you did. And I told you we were done. I meant it. I won't be with a man if he's not faithful to me. So we live here, and I do as I please, and I don't care what you do."

"So why are you up here?"

Belle sighed. Why indeed? Because of Cassie Dawson wanting advice on how to get her husband to kiss her. Because Red Dawson acted so worried that Belle's house might be cold in the winter. That visit left Belle with the terrible knowledge she was missing out. She couldn't be a true wife to Anthony, not when he'd betrayed their vows. But was Anthony right that it had been her fault? She'd only met his manly needs grudgingly and infrequently, she knew that. She didn't like that part of marriage. Had she driven him to unfaithfulness?

Ultimately it didn't matter. She'd done what she'd done and Anthony had done what he'd done, and now they were left with the third wreck of a marriage in Belle's life.

She didn't trust him for good reason, and she had no intention of starting. But they could be civil. She could try to make their marriage some tiny bit normal. Having him lurk up on the roof or on that hill like a huge bird of prey was unsettling.

"Come on down and join the family. We won't make you do anything that'll hurt your back." Belle had to fight to keep her voice sounding sincere. Anthony's back had started hurting the day after their wedding and he'd never done a lick of work since. "Maybe you could just talk with us, even ride out with the herd with us."

"Riding hurts."

Belle didn't mention that the man managed to ride hours to the Golden Butte at least once a week. She also knew they were snowed in now. He wouldn't get out again all winter. She wished fervently he'd have been snowed on the wrong side of the gap.

"Fine, no riding. But Anthony, I'd like a chance to make our marriage better."

He finally looked up. Something flared in his eyes and he reached for her hand. She flinched away.

Anthony's hand clenched into a fist. "I thought you said you wanted to make things better."

"There are other ways things can be better. As far as. . ." Belle rested her hand on her baby and held his gaze. She was used to looking a man in the eye, and it didn't come natural to be submissive or act demurely. She only knew how to take charge and speak her mind. And those skills weren't of interest to most husbands.

"I get it." Anthony's hand lifted to rub his head. "The skillet stays beside you."

Belle nodded. "But come on down anyway. Let's try and do something to make this marriage a happier one."

Anthony picked up his stick again and poked the hard ground. "I'll be down in a little while."

Which Belle knew meant. . .in time for dinner. She nodded and stood awkwardly, her growing stomach making everything harder.

She swung onto her horse and rode down the long, long hill from the Husband Tree, wondering what in the world could possess Cassie Dawson to *want* her husband to kiss her.

CHAPTER 19

Cassie sighed as Red left the house without kissing her again.

She knew better than to hope he would. But knowing better didn't stop her.

She stood in the doorway and watched him ride away, and she smiled to think of how totally he'd come to trust her with the chores. He let her do everything now but ride herd with him, and considering her advanced pregnancy, she didn't even ask about it. Someday, though.

She turned back to go inside and tidy her kitchen, but as she moved, something bright glittered in the corner of her vision. She stopped and looked up at the nearby mountain peak, but she didn't see the flash of light again. A shudder of fear shook her and she didn't question it. She had stood here many times over the last few weeks. She had never seen a reflection before.

She grabbed the rifle off the rack above the front door and headed for the tunnel. She dashed into the opening and knew exactly where she was going to hide. She entered the narrow passage, using one hand braced against the stone wall to balance.

She didn't go far. In the pitch darkness, she found the first side tunnel. She had to get down on her hands and knees to crawl in, and with her girth from the baby and her long dress and the rifle, she barely slipped inside. She struggled through the narrow entrance for only a yard before it narrowed to only a foot high beside a trickle of water.

Cassie had pictured the spring that ran through their cooler, dripping into this little cavern for as long as there had been mountains. It had eaten away at the rock until it had dropped low enough to change directions and began running into the cooler.

Or maybe God had put it here for Cassie. For this moment.

There was no place that was completely dry. The ceiling was so low she had to rest on her side in the dank, cold crevice. The frigid water seeped through her dress. She shivered against the cold stone and called herself a coward to hide like this. She almost climbed out, but she couldn't shake off the fear that clutched at her heart. She was a coward, scurrying into a hole in the ground like a scared rabbit.

Time stretched and Cassie prayed for warmth and safety and Red. The cold chewed at her skin like a hungry rat until she shuddered with it, and the black mountain pressed down on her soul. She railed against her cowardice and almost crawled out a dozen times, but there was an almost supernatural strength to her fear and she couldn't overcome it.

Then she heard something that chilled her more deeply than the water ever could.

"China doll?"

Wade.

He spoke softly, coaxing as if she were a timid animal in need of taming. "Where are you, girl? I've come for you." His voice got stronger then faded as he moved around their cabin.

"Where are you, doll?"

There was a long silence.

She curled her body around the baby to try and keep her little one warm. As she lay there, she prayed for Red. If God could give Cassie a feeling of fear, then He could give one to Red, too. Then she thought of Wade's guns and feared Red *would* come. If only Wade wouldn't find her. If only he'd give up and go away.

"Are you in here, china doll?" Cassie jumped and scraped the gun against the cave floor. Wade had found the tunnel. He was close. Close enough to hear the slightest sound. She was cornered if Wade found her hiding place. The weight of the mountain surrounded her. She was trapped, and fear sucked the air out of the cave.

The wheedling left Wade's voice. "My woman doesn't hide from me!" He was standing directly in front of the opening now. He had a lantern and wouldn't have to lean down much to light up the fissure and see her.

Cassie felt the panic rising. She forced herself to remain still and hoped the frantic pounding of her heart wasn't audible.

"Where are you?" Cassie heard Wade's fists slam against the cave. He stepped farther into the cave, past the fissure where she hid, and called out again, more furiously. "I've come to save you. I'll take you away from here. Where are you?"

He moved on, ranting as he went. "I'll never stop hunting for you. Never!"

Cassie didn't dare move. Between the frigid water and her fear, she shivered violently. She buried her face in her drawn-up knees to cover the sound of her teeth chattering.

Wade's voice faded away, but she remained in hiding. She could feel him, crouching in the dark, waiting for her to move so he could pounce.

She moved beyond cold to pain, and only sheer terror kept her from leaving her hiding place. Then the shivering stopped and the cold didn't bother her so much. She began to feel drowsy and relaxed.

She hugged her baby close and laid her head on her drawn-up knees, against her soaked, frigid skirt and prayed.

Lord, keep Red safe. Protect my baby.

She remembered the compassion of the church members and Red's worry about Wade being hurt by his father and managed to send up a prayer for Wade. Then she remembered the lesson Red had taught last week. She couldn't think of all of it. The only words that she knew were, *"The Lord is my light and my salvation; whom shall I fear?"*

She understood that verse so clearly now.

"Whom shall I fear?"

No one.

In her soul—the only place that really counted—Cassie was safe.

"Whom shall I fear?"

The safety that verse gave her was almost like a voice telling her it was all right to come out now. She believed it. Wade was gone, and if he wasn't, he couldn't really hurt her. God was with her in life and death.

Again that voice inside her said, *"Come out. It's safe to come out now."*

She tried, but it was so much effort to move. She'd rest just a few seconds more.

In perfect peace, with no fear in her heart, she fell asleep.

The cabin door was wide open to the cold winter wind.

"Cassie!" Red dug his heels into Buck's side. He started praying before Buck took his first galloping stride.

"Cassie!" He saw hoofprints that had trampled down the new snow around the door.

Wade.

And he'd been here a long time and been gone a long time. Red charged into the cabin yelling, "Cassie! Cassie, are you here?"

He was greeted with dead silence. He saw the overturned table and the pans knocked onto the floor and felt Wade's fury.

Red ran toward the tunnel. He stepped inside. "Cassie!"

His voice echoed off the stone walls, mocking him. She wasn't here. Wade had taken her. Red ran for the door and leaped onto Buck's back.

He stopped after just a few dozen yards. There was something wrong with the tracks. Red swung down off Buck and tried to push his panic aside long enough to think.

God, where is she? Help me find her. Keep her safe.

Red crouched beside Wade's tracks and knew immediately what the problem was. The tracks were the same depth as when Wade rode in. The horse wasn't carrying two riders.

Red rushed back to the cabin. Could she be inside that tunnel, hurt too badly to answer? Or dead?

He stepped into the blackness of the tunnel then turned back to go for the bedroom lantern. It was gone. Wade must have found the tunnel and hunted through it, using the bedroom lantern. The one in the kitchen lay smashed on the floor, useless.

Red didn't have time to rig up a torch. He stepped into the tunnel, thinking of all the nooks and crannies where a scared little woman might hide. He felt his way along in the pitch-black corridor, calling for her, his hope faltering with every step.

Then he tripped. He fell heavily to the ground, which was strange, because he had been moving slowly and hanging on to the wall. And when he fell, his hand slid on the wet stone and he felt fabric.

Cassie's skirt. He remembered this cold little crevice.

"Cassie!" His voice wavered and cracked.

She didn't respond. Didn't move. He followed the wet fabric and found a leg. She was wedged into a fissure in the rocks so small Red had never gone into it.

He eased her out of the icy little hole, his heart clutching at her stillness. When he had her all the way out, he laid his ear against her chest and heard a heartbeat, weak but steady. She was so cold, so utterly still.

Red lifted her carefully in his arms, cradling her against his chest. He carried her out into the dim light of the bedroom. Her dress was so wet it dripped. He stripped her out of her soaked clothing, pulled her nightgown over her head, and laid her on the bed.

He saw no bleeding. He lifted her eyelids and her eyes flickered back and forth, and she moved slightly as if in protest.

He ran his hands over her body looking for bumps or broken bones and found only cold. Her lips were pinched and blue. Her fingernails were pure white. He had lived in Montana long enough to know what cold could do. And he knew how to combat it.

He kicked his boots off and shucked his pants and shirt, and wearing only his union suit, climbed into bed beside her, pulling the blankets over both of them. He held her close in his arms, cocooning the babe between them. He massaged her back and legs, wiped his tears on his sleeve, and asked God for a miracle.

For long moments he rubbed her arms, trying to warm her chilled skin. There was no response, no movement, her breathing shallow, her heartbeat faint.

Red's prayers were broken by fear as he held her and tried to share his heat. "Please, God, don't take my Cassie away from me. Protect her, Lord. Please." Red sent his petitions to God with such fervency that they generated their own heat.

Moments passed. Red could feel Cassie slipping away from him as if she were being drawn back into the mean, hard cold of the stones. The door to the outside was still open. He'd been running when he came in and let it swing wide. He needed to go out there, close the door, and stoke the fire to warm the cabin up, but he was afraid to leave her, even for those few minutes.

"Please, God, please. Protect her, Lord. I love her." Red kissed her cold, blue lips and rested his face against hers, shuddering from the lifeless, waxy cold.

Then her teeth chattered.

Red pulled back when he heard that bit of sound. She lay motionless, but he knew she'd responded. He continued caressing her, praying for her, calling her back to him.

The shivering started small and lasted only a minute before it stopped and she lay quiet for a while. Then it came again. This time it hit her hard, shaking her violently.

Red held her through it, rubbing her arms and back, moving his legs against hers and tucking her icy feet on top of his. Her teeth rattled until he was afraid they might break. Her body vibrated wildly. He massaged her and called softly. After turbulent minutes that seemed to stretch out for hours, the shivering eased. Red looked down at his precious wife and saw her brown eyes flicker open. He wasn't sure if she was awake or not. Her eyelids closed heavily.

"Wake up, honey," Red crooned. "C'mon, Cass. Come all the way back to me."

She shifted against him and her arms went around his waist. Her fingers were like icicles on his back and he pulled her hands around and tucked them between their bodies. He pressed her head into the crook of his shoulder, and her nose was so cold he couldn't control a little jump. He prayed aloud, hoping she could hear and draw comfort from his words.

The shivering started again. It lasted longer this time. The wracking seemed like it would tear her apart. How much could Cassie or the baby take? When this bout passed, Red looked down, hoping for another glimpse of her eyes. She was awake and staring at him.

"I'm here, Cass. I'm so sorry I wasn't here sooner. But I'm here now. You're going to be okay." Red prayed it was true.

"Wade came. I hid from him."

"You did good." Red hugged her close. "He didn't find you."

Cassie slid her hands down to lie on her stomach. "I tried to take care of her." Her voice broke and tears filled her eyes. "I tried."

"Did he hurt you, Cass honey?" Red didn't think Wade had gotten his hands on Cassie. If he had, she wouldn't be here.

Cassie shook her head. "No. No, he never found me. I was so afraid. But then. . .I wasn't afraid anymore, just tired. 'The Lord is my light and my salvation; whom shall I fear?'"

The shivering resumed. This time it wasn't as hard or long.

Red cradled her and praised her and stroked her cold body back to warmth. She tried to fall asleep, but Red didn't let up on her until he was sure she was warm again.

When the shivers receded for good, he finally let her sleep. He left her to warm the cabin up then lay back down beside her, pulled her into his arms, and held her, so relieved he couldn't stop the tears. So in love with her he was afraid to feel the force of it.

Then he thought of Wade, and the anger slammed into him like a freight train.

Red recognized that temper that went with his red hair. He controlled it pretty well, but at that moment he was overcome. He held his wife and his babe and he wanted to stay this close to both of them forever. But, almost as much, he wanted to get his hands on Wade Sawyer and tear him apart.

The fury consumed him as he lay beside Cassie's limp, sleeping body. He imagined himself hunting Wade down and thrashing him to within an inch of his life. He savored the vision. He reveled in the power of his hate. Ideas for Wade's slow, lingering death paraded across his mind, and carefully avoiding thoughts of God, he planned how he'd make Wade pay.

Just as he was mentally meting out Wade's final punishment with his bare hands, Red got a message from God he couldn't ignore. He got kicked in the stomach.

With a jolt, Red realized it was the first time he'd felt the babe move since he'd found Cassie in that icy little cave. He'd been so worried about both of them, but Cassie had taken precedence. The little kick told him his child was all right, too. It was as if his rational mind returned to him.

Red had a sense then of Satan sitting on his shoulder, suggesting ways to hurt Wade. Urging vengeance. Calling it justice when it really was hate. Red knew the devil well enough. He'd had temptations before. One of them was lying asleep in his arms right now. Red also knew his Master's voice, even when it came in the form of a swift kick.

He banished Satan by replacing him with love. Pulling back from Cassie just a bit, he laid one big hand over the little tyke and got kicked again. Red smiled down at Cassie's oversized belly. The babe was stirring so vigorously Red could see Cassie's flannel nightgown move. Red got the message.

He whispered, "I'm sorry, little one. You don't need a pa with a mean temper, do you?"

The babe kicked him squarely in the middle of his hand, and Red took that for a no.

"But what are we going to do? How am I going to protect you and your ma from him?" Red asked it of the babe, but the answer came from God.

"The Lord is my light and my salvation; whom shall I fear?"

Who indeed. Not Wade Sawyer.

Easy to say.

"Greater is he that is in you, than he that is in the world."

Wade was in the world, and today, although it had been a close thing, God had protected Cassie. They were safe.

"If God be for us, who can be against us?"

Well, Wade was definitely against them. But who was Wade compared to God? Red almost sat up in bed when he remembered falling practically on top of Cassie. Thinking about it now, he wasn't sure why he'd stumbled. He'd been walking carefully, holding on to the wall. Yet he'd fallen and his hand had landed on the tiny bit of Cassie's skirt sticking out of the hole.

Red smiled. God was definitely for them.

Then he thought, *"Love thy neighbour as thyself."*

That one stuck in Red's throat and his smile faded.

The babe kicked him.

Red hesitated and Satan whispered about justice and hate.

The babe kicked him again.

"Okay, little one," Red whispered so Cassie wouldn't be disturbed. "But Wade doesn't make it easy."

The babe booted him hard.

Red had to forgive Wade. It grated on him something fierce, but he knew he had to. He pulled Cassie back into his arms, and the babe seemed to do a somersault of approval. Red grinned, and Cassie shifted against him and moaned sweetly in her sleep.

Forgiving didn't mean trusting someone who wasn't re-pentant. But Wade was in worse trouble than the Dawsons. Red closed his eyes.

Thank You, God, for the miracle of life I'm holding in my arms. The miracle of two lives. Bless Wade. Bring light to the darkness that surrounds him. I love him, Lord. I do. He is Your creation. And I forgive him. But I hope You'll forgive me, Lord, if it's a sin that I'm not going to trust him.

He caught himself just as he dozed off. He had left Buck bridled and saddled, running loose. His home had been trashed and he still had evening chores to do.

With a quick check of Cassie's fingers and toes, which looked pink and plump now, Red got up and did his chores at a run. Then he quickly straightened the house, built up the fire, and hung Cassie's wet things to dry. When he got back to Cassie, she had rolled all the way to his side of the bed as if she were hunting for him to snuggle up against. He shucked his clothes again and crawled right back into bed with her.

Cassie had said, "The Lord is my light and my salvation." Did she mean it? Had Cassie really made her own commitment to the Lord?

Red prayed she'd moved beyond just saying what he wanted to hear. He prayed for her and thanked God for her every second he had. . .until he fell asleep.

CHAPTER 20

Cassie's eyes fluttered open and she rubbed her hand over Red's chest and savored the warmth.

Warmth!

She jerked to a sitting position in bed with a cry of fear and fell back because she was anchored by Red's arm.

"Don't be afraid, Cass. You're okay." Red untangled her hair from around his arm and behind his head.

Cassie looked at Red and started to remember what had happened after she'd gone into that dark little hole to hide from Wade. She looked into his kind, worried eyes, and with a little cry of anguish, she threw herself back into his arms.

He cradled her and crooned and stroked her arms.

She remembered this from last night. It was so fuzzy she wasn't sure what had happened and what she had dreamed. "You came for me. You saved me." She clung to him and shuddered from fear.

"You're okay," he murmured. "We got through it."

Red brushed her hair back off her forehead and chucked her under the chin so she'd lift her head from where it was burrowed against his chest. "You were so smart, Cass honey. So brave and strong. You saved yourself. I'm so proud of you."

Confusion warred with doubt. She shook her head slightly. "No. I was so afraid. I was such a coward. Running and hiding like a stupid—"

"Cass honey," Red interrupted softly.

"Yes, Red?" Her eyes flickered to his lips and back to his eyes.

"Shut up." Red kissed her.

It worked. She shut up.

Then he pulled away from her. His lips were moist from her kisses. She knew because she couldn't quit glancing at them to see if he might be going to kiss her again.

He rested his hands on her shoulders and firmly moved her back from him. He had to unwind her arms from around his neck, and while he did, Cassie sneaked in another kiss and he put up with it for a while. Quite a while. Then after a minute or two...or three, he went back to holding her away.

"Now, listen, young lady..."

He sounded like a scolding father, and because that was so unlike Red, whom she didn't think of as a father at all, she smiled. He tapped her under her chin again, and she realized she was looking at his lips. He seemed to want her to stop that. She really tried.

"I'm listening," she said demurely, trying to follow whatever order he was obviously getting ready to give.

"You were *not* stupid and you were *not* a coward," he said sternly.

"But I was, Red. You don't know. I was so afraid."

"Being afraid doesn't make you a coward, Cass. In this case, being afraid is just plain good sense."

"But I ran. I hid like some wild animal in a hole in the ground. I should have...have shot him or something."

"Well, the only trouble with shooting someone is that once you've done it. . ." Red hesitated.

"What?" Cassie asked.

"Once you've shot someone, then. . .well, the thing is. . .then you've. . .you've *shot* someone, if you get what I mean."

Cassie shook her head, feeling stupid again.

"It's not something you can take back."

Cassie stared at him and slowly nodded her head. She was glad she wasn't living with that on her conscience. But she'd still been so helpless. She'd been alone in that black hole with her terror, so completely at Wade's mercy. She'd felt so weak and pathetic.

There'd been so many times in her life she'd wanted to fight back, not just against Wade, and she always was left cowering in fear. Red had said she was smart and strong and brave. She was none of those things. But a husband's word was law, so she let herself enjoy the thought.

"What are we going to do, Red?"

"I don't know, Cass honey. I've been thinking about it ever since I found you. I can't ride off and leave you here alone again, not for even a minute."

"Could I ride with you to check the cattle?"

Red was silent for a moment.

Cassie hastened to embroider details on her plan. "I could ride with you on Buck. When you find a herd you need to work with, you could set me down somewhere out of the way but where we could see each other."

"It's so cold," Red said doubtfully.

"It's cold for you, too."

"I'm not carrying a growing babe."

"I've got a good coat."

"It could work. It's better than the plan I came up with."

"What was that?" Cassie was prepared to do whatever he said.

"Well, I had this picture in my head of building a corral around the cabin and turning Harriet loose in it."

"A guard pig?"

Cassie looked at him for a long moment, and then he grinned at her and she started to giggle. She buried her head against his chest and he held her close, and they laughed until the baby kicked them into getting up.

"You can come with me for today. We'll try it a day at a time," Red said as he grabbed Cassie's dry clothes for her then proceeded to get dressed.

"Yes, Red." Red had his back politely turned, so Cassie quickly slipped out of her nightgown and into her chemise, then grabbed for her dress.

"And I'll show you a better cranny to hide in that's not so cold, and we'll put the buffalo robe in it if I ever go off even for a second."

"Yes, Red."

He glanced over his shoulder to give her a disgruntled look, and she wondered what she'd done. She thought with the tiniest spark of annoyance that she really could hardly be any more obedient.

Red's expression cleared. "How did you sneak into the passage without Wade catching you?"

"I saw a flash of light high up on the hill. It scared me. I just grabbed the rifle and went straight in. I'd been in there quite a while before he came."

Red was silent for a long while. "I think you were scared because God was warning you."

"You do?" Cassie asked in wonder. If God had talked to her, it was her very own miracle.

"I came in early from checking the cattle because I couldn't shake off worrying about you. I think God was speaking to me, too," Red said with calm assurance.

"He took care of us," Cassie whispered. She knew it was true, because the fear she'd felt at that little flash of light went beyond a normal reaction.

Red said quietly, "Let's remember to always trust our instincts. God is watching over us, and if we're open to His leading, I think we'll be safe."

"Yes, Red. I will, Red," she said fervently.

Red looked annoyed again and she stood quietly waiting for him to reprimand her, but he never did.

Red shook his head as if to clear it. "I think the babe talked to me last night."

"The baby and God? All in one day?" Cassie said with what she hoped was well-concealed teasing.

"Yep." Red slung his arm around her and led her out to the kitchen. "It was quite a day."

"So what did she say?" Cassie noticed they'd gotten dressed in the same room at the same time. They'd never done that before.

"Well, first off, she said she's a he."

"She did not!" Cassie protested.

Red told her a silly story about being scolded with a series of kicks and twists while they made breakfast and did the morning chores together.

"Instead of checking the herd this afternoon, I want to ride to town and tell the sheriff about this." Red ate his steak at noon, but his stomach did back flips when he thought about Cassie so cold, so near death.

"Yes, Red. That's a good idea."

Red hated that obedient tone. But they were going to town regardless of her tone, so it would be stupid to growl about it.

"I doubt the law will step in, but I want a formal complaint so if Wade comes around again, we'll have some proof that he's been a problem before."

Cassie began cleaning as if he'd shouted at her to hurry.

Red shook his head at his submissive little wife then hurried to do a few chores. They rode to town, and though the town marshal didn't sound like he planned to pursue the matter, Red insisted on going through the motions.

Since it wasn't a Saturday, they went to pick up a few things at the general store, planning to rush home.

Muriel insisted on hearing the whole story of Cassie's plight. "Humph. That marshal is bought and paid for by the Sawyers. He won't do a thing."

"Well, there's not much he can do, really. All Wade did was walk around in our house a might clumsily, broke a few things. And no one saw his face, though Cassie identified his voice. If Wade could be found and forced to admit he was there, he'd just say Cassie should have come on out. He had no idea of harming her." Red's chest hurt when he thought of the way his cabin had looked. The violence in the damage. The strength of the fear God had placed on Cassie's heart.

Muriel snorted.

A group of Sawyer hands came into the store just then.

"You know Wade was out at the Dawson place today?" Muriel asked.

The closest man, Red knew he was the Sawyer foreman, shook his head. "He's quit the country. I saw him get on the stage to Denver myself."

"He's not in Denver." Red stepped in front of Muriel, not wanting the feisty woman to draw down the ire of the Sawyer bunch on her. "I recognized his tracks and Cassie heard him. She hid because she knew he was up to no good. Where is he?"

The burly cowhand scratched his grizzled chin. "We haven't seen him for a while or more. Him and his pa had it out, and Wade took off. The boy had a pair of black eyes and a split lip when he left. His pa don't put up with mouth offa his kid, and Wade had used up all his chances."

Red inhaled slowly as he thought of a father who'd hurt his son like that. He stared at the man, looking for shifty eyes. But the man seemed to believe what he'd said about Wade being gone. All that meant was Wade had lied to them, too.

"As far as we know, Wade is still in Denver."

Red and Cassie headed for home in the fading light of Montana's early evening. This time Red knew he'd never relax his guard.

CHAPTER 21

"I need to warn you girls what I've done." Belle waved her girls closer.

It wasn't hard to catch them without Anthony around. Being not around was the usual state of things.

Lindsay, Emma, and Sarah drew close, the whispered words drawing them in. They were in the barn shortly before it was time to eat dinner.

"I've decided it's a sin the way I treat Anthony."

Emma's brow puckered. "You mean feeding him and washing his clothes and picking up after him and giving him money to go to town twice a week? That's a sin?"

What Anthony did in town was most definitely a sin. But Belle had caught him stealing a few times, and when he was cornered, the man had a dangerous look in his eyes that made Belle want her skillet handy. Even though it sickened her to think what Anthony did with that dollar, she'd taken to giving him a dollar about twice a week, which seemed to be enough to keep him calm. Besides, she liked having him gone from the ranch, so it was like she was paying to have a couple of days without his brooding presence. Money well spent.

"No, it's a sin that I've treated him badly."

"How, Ma?" Sarah asked, her face worried as if her mother's confessing to sin scared her.

"Well, I've. . .I've been bossy and unkind and hostile. He says his back hurts, and instead of feeling bad for him, I've treated him like a liar, and a lazy one at that."

"He is a liar, Ma." Lindsay scowled.

Belle knew they'd all seen Anthony ride away on his horse, as fit as could be. His back only hurt where there were chores. The man *was* a liar, and no Christian charity could change that simple fact.

"Yes, I agree." Except that wasn't what Belle wanted to do. She needed to encourage her children to give the man the benefit of the doubt. "I mean, it's not for us to judge him." Belle pulled her flat-crowned hat off her head in frustration. "What I really mean is Anthony's sin is between him and God. We are still called to treat him with kindness and"—she wasn't sure she could choke out the word—"l–love."

All three girls inhaled sharply and straightened away from the little circle they'd formed.

"You're saying you're in love with him, Ma?" Lindsay shook her head. "I think that's a bad idea."

"No, for the love of heaven, I'm not saying that!" Belle felt sickened by the very thought. "I'm saying God called us to love our neighbor as ourselves. I'm saying I learned something when I went and visited Cassie Dawson."

"Who?" Sarah twisted her mouth as if the conversation was a nuisance, which it was. Sarah had supper to get and Belle knew it.

"She used to be Cassie Griffin. I told you how they forced her into a marriage. You remember that, right, girls?"

"So you're saying it's okay to let someone force us into

marriage?" Emma started wringing her hands.

"No! Now listen to me. Don't you *ever* let someone force you into marriage." Belle whipped her hat against her leg, wondering why she'd ever started this. "I'm saying I'm going to try and love Anthony as a neighbor. As a child of God. No, good heavens to Betsy, I don't love the wretched man."

That probably wasn't the thing to say if she was going to try and be a better Christian when it came to Anthony. "What I mean is, Anthony's lies, Anthony's laziness, those are between him and his Maker. And our behavior is between us and God. That's all we can control. I've been sinning by being unpleasant to the man, and I'm going to try and change. You know, I worry for Anthony's soul, though it's wrong to judge."

Belle had judged him as belonging to the netherworld before she'd been married to the man for two weeks, but that was her own sin. No sense spreading that to her children. Although she had to admit that realization had come a bit late.

God forgive me.

"I'm saying maybe we can. . .reform him. Show him how Christians are supposed to act. That's part of being a good Christian. Being a good example and behaving in a way that draws others to our faith. And I've been less than a good Christian to Anthony, and worse, I've been a poor example to you girls. I don't know if he'll come, but I told Anthony I wanted him to join the family. Even if he doesn't work, he can be with us, talk to us, join in with things besides meals. And I just wanted to warn you girls because I'll no doubt be saying things to him you don't understand. You might even find them shocking."

"What kind of things, Ma?" Sarah shifted her weight.

"My plan is to be. . .to be. . ." Belle shuddered and she knew the girls could see it, but she soldiered on. "Nice to the lazy coot."

All three girls gasped in shock.

Belle nodded. "I knew you wouldn't understand. That's why I had to warn you. And if you can possibly do it, try and be nice, too."

Lindsay shook her head, not in disobedience but rather as if she couldn't imagine a single nice thing she could say to her stepfather.

Belle patted her on the shoulder. "Just try. I know it goes against the grain."

All three girls nodded as if Belle had just ordered them into a war zone. . .unarmed.

She decided to arm them somewhat. "There's a Bible verse I heard once that said being kind to people who are bad to you is like heaping hot coals on their heads. So maybe it'll help to imagine you're doing that while you be nice."

Emma shrugged. "That might work."

"It's worth a try." Lindsay started pulling her gloves on.

"I'll do it." Sarah squared her shoulders and stuck out her chin. "But they're gonna be red-hot coals."

"Whatever it takes. Now go get supper on while we finish the chores."

"Will Anthony be coming in to help us with the chores?" Lindsay was being sarcastic.

Belle recognized the attitude. It came straight from her. "I doubt it. I saw him coming down from the Husband Tree and climbing up on the roof." Belle shook her head in disgust and tugged her hat back onto her head, pulling the flat black brim low over her eyes. "I'm going to go see if I can talk the idiot into coming down so I can get started being nice."

"She's turning somersaults again." Cassie rested her hand on her stomach as she settled into bed.

Red grinned and laid his hands beside hers. "He's still talking to me, just like that day you got cold."

"*She* can't talk yet." Cassie shoved at his hands, but Red held on.

"Be still, woman, so my *son* can tell me how he's doing." Red loved feeling the baby move and telling Cassie there was a little boy growing in her. It was closest she'd come to sassing him.

He quit letting her lie apart from him when she came to bed. He'd always pulled her close after she'd fallen asleep, but now he pulled her into his arms the minute she lay down. Better still, she came without protest.

Checking the cattle together worked better than Red had hoped. Occasionally there was an injured longhorn that needed doctoring, and after scouting around to make sure Wade wasn't in the vicinity, Red would find a sheltered spot and set Cassie down to watch from a safe distance while he roped and hogtied the beast and tended it. Every day there were a few head of cattle that needed something special. If possible, Red drove them back to the ranch and worked with them while Cassie did her outside chores.

That worked until the day Red came into the house and Cassie wouldn't face him. She always turned around from where she was working on supper to smile hello. Red hadn't thought much about it until she didn't do it. She stayed hovering over the fire with her back turned to him. He surely did miss her cheerful greetings.

"Hi, Cass. Supper ready?" He waited expectantly for her to warm his life with her hello.

She said, without turning around, "Hi. Meal's almost ready. Go ahead and sit down."

Red couldn't say a thing was wrong with the way she was stirring at the pot of stew she'd made, but he kept a sharp eye on her. She had the plates beside her on the sink, and she reached over for one with her back still turned. She started scooping up a plate of stew, and when he went beside her to wash from the basin of hot water on the sink, she turned away from him and set the plate on the table. He washed as she fussed with setting the plate just so. Then he went to the table and she turned back to the fire and got the other plate.

He waited for her to sit down until she said in an overly casual voice, "I think I'd better just tend this stew a bit more. Go ahead and eat without me."

Red surged up out of his chair and grabbed her arm. She cried out in pain and he let go immediately. "I'm sorry. I didn't mean to be so rough." Then Red thought about what he was saying. He hadn't been rough!

He said sternly, "What's going on here, Cassie Dawson?"

There was a long silence as he stood behind her and she faced the fire. Finally, with tortuous slowness, she turned around.

"What happened to your face?" Red reached to touch her then pulled back. She had a scrape across the whole side of her cheek and down her neck. He thought about the pain he'd caused her when he took her arm. "Let me see the rest of it."

Cassie started shaking her head. "Red, it's not as bad as it looks. It's just a scrape!"

"I want to see your arm. Right now!" Red stepped so he was behind her and started unbuttoning her dress. As he did he noticed a dozen slits in her sleeve that had been carefully mended.

"Red, please! You're overreacting!" Cassie turned to look over her shoulder at him in alarm as he clumsily undid the buttons down the back of her dress.

"What happened to you? How did you. . ." Red quit talking and gasped as he pulled her sleeve down. The scrape went down her neck, over her shoulder, and the length of her arm.

"Cassie," Red whispered in dismay. "Was it Wade? Did he hurt you?"

Cassie clutched the dress to her front. "No, I haven't seen Wade at all. I. . .I just fell."

"Fell where?" Red said in alarm. "I was around the place all afternoon. I never saw you fall."

Cassie didn't answer.

Red, unaccustomed to anything but complete obedience from his little wife, looked away from the nasty damage to her arm and neck and saw a stubborn expression on her face. "Ca–a–assie," he said gravely. "Tell me."

"You'll be upset." Cassie turned to face him, pulling her dress back into place. "It was my fault. I don't want you to. . ."

"*Now, Cassandra Dawson.* Tell me *exactly* what happened and *do it right now!*" Red thought he sounded just like his father used to when Red was naughty. But Red didn't want to treat his wife like a naughty child.

That stubborn look settled more deeply on her face. Red had the feeling that Cassie was saying some unpleasant things to him inside her head. He almost smiled. He'd wanted her to stand up to him. The trouble was, now that she was thinking about doing it, he didn't want it at all. What if Wade *had* come and somehow scared Cassie into keeping it a secret? What if he'd snuck up on the house somehow and gotten to her when Red was—

"I fell watering Buck!" Cassie said with a scowl after she'd finished fastening her buttons. "I just slipped is all, and I don't want you saying I can't. . ."

"I saw you take him down to the creek. He was walking ahead of you like always." Red let go of his worst fears as he thought about his cantankerous horse.

"He's getting better, Red. I'll be more careful."

Buck had never forgiven Cassie for flapping her skirts the

first morning she'd lived here. And he *wasn't* getting better. If anything, he had learned he could bully Cassie and was worse than ever.

"That horse has taken to dragging you along behind him," Red said. "You're too long on belly and too short on legs to make him mind."

"It's not Buck's fault I fell." Cassie crossed her arms and glowered.

"Yes it is. You shouldn't be watering him." Red felt a cold sweat break out on his forehead, picturing Cassie falling on that steep slope to the creek.

"Now, Red, don't say that." Cassie raised her hands in front of her as if asking Red to stop. "Please don't say I can't do it. It's not his fault. My hand just got twisted in the lead rope and I ended up sliding a ways. He didn't—"

"How far?" Red interrupted.

"How far what?" Cassie said, twisting her hands together.

Red knew she was ducking the question. He said through clenched teeth, "How far did he drag you after you fell?"

Cassie's jaw firmed and her lips clamped together. Red thought she was going to tell him to go soak his head. He had another quiver of humor go through him, but then he thought about Buck dragging her.

"*You tell me right now, wife, and that's an order!* When did you fall? And how far did he. . ."

"I fell right over the crest," she almost shouted.

"How far?" Red stormed at her.

"The rest of the way to the creek," she snapped back.

Dead silence reigned for just a second while Red contemplated his beloved Cassie being dragged down that treacherous path.

Speaking barely above a whisper through a throat nearly swollen shut with fear, Red asked, "And you thought you could hide this from me because you're worried about losing one of your precious chores. Right?"

Cassie's stubborn expression faded, and she looked like the worried, obedient little wife he was used to. She nodded.

Red leaned down so his nose almost touched hers and bellowed, *"You should be worried! You're losing all of them! You are going to mind me, woman!"*

He watched her fight to keep her temper from overflowing. She opened her mouth to speak a dozen times, but each time she stopped.

He wanted to goad her into fighting because it would do her good to stand up for herself. But this wasn't the time. He wasn't going to give on this. And maybe she was just too submissive to argue, or maybe she could see the stubbornness on his face just like he could see it on hers.

In the end she just said through clenched teeth, "Yes, Red."

CHAPTER 22

Wade heard the shouting.

He normally didn't come this close, but the raised voice carried up the draw to the hilltop where he watched, and he'd come down a long way toward the house, afraid Dawson was hurting his china doll right now. If only Dawson would go away, leave poor china doll for just a few minutes.

There was no window in that nasty little dirt structure, but the snow was trampled enough around the place that Wade dared to approach close enough to listen through the door. Wade had abandoned the line shack he'd found and moved into a cave a bit farther from the Dawson place. He was now a long way up the mountain, barely able to see the goings-on with his spyglass. But today for the first time, voices carried and Wade had set out at a run to save Cassie.

Dawson seemed like an easygoing dolt with his odd jobs and his work as a preacher. But Wade had learned that Dawson's eyes were sharp and he could read signs like an Indian scout. Wade had moved his campsite farther back four times now as Dawson's snooping had brought the man close to Wade's hideout.

Wade rested his hand on the butt of his holstered gun, longing to rush in, finish Dawson, and clear out with the china doll in tow. But he couldn't charge in with guns blazing. He couldn't risk hitting the china doll with a stray bullet.

And there was more to it than that. Wade rested against the sod wall abutting the door. He tilted his head back and stared at the sky, sparkling with a thousand pinpoints of light. What if he went in and couldn't pull the trigger?

Please give me the courage to save her.

Wade closed his eyes and came the closest to praying he'd ever done in his life. . .at least for a long time. He needed the courage to save his china doll.

Wade waited and hoped, but that courage didn't come. He was a coward. His father was ashamed to call Wade his son. He was a poor excuse for a man.

His mother had put herself between Wade and his father many times. His mother had taken the same kind of cruelty as the china doll. Except Wade's mother had died bringing a second baby. She'd called Wade in, knowing she was dying. Now, as Wade stood in the frigid cold, shut out of the love he knew the china doll held for him, he was transported to that horrible room, six years old, listening again to his mother's sobbing apologies for dying, for leaving him alone.

And she'd been right to apologize, because Wade had soon learned just how much his mother had sheltered him. With that shelter gone, Wade had taken the full brunt of his father's anger.

Now Wade wished he could be that shelter for the china doll. He could protect her, save her.

Red's voice came though the wall again.

Was he hitting her even now? With a coward nearby who was too weak to protect her. The china doll was taking that same treatment from her second husband.

Red yelled, *"You are going to mind me, woman!"*

And the china doll answered in a sweet, scared voice, "Yes, Red."

Words Wade had learned to say to his father, quickly, with just that same obedient tone. And yet, even knowing that, Wade stayed outside. A coward.

Had Red beaten that tone out of the china doll?

"Yes, Red."

The words echoed in Wade's mind as if they were repeated over and over. And still Wade-the-Coward stayed outside.

Wade sank to his knees in the bitter Montana November and hated Red Dawson.

Hated his father.

Hated himself.

All the outside chores were strictly Red's now.

November gave way to December, and winter came down around them so hard that Red didn't attempt the trip to Divide anymore.

Red held a simple church service for the two of them those days and gained some confidence in Cassie's faith, although he always wondered if it was real or if she was just following his dictate. In the end, he couldn't even decide if it mattered.

If she believed, for whatever reason, it was good enough. Except he worried that if something happened to him and she got a new husband, her new husband might not share her faith, and it would die as easily as it had been born. That in turn meant the only way to make sure Cassie got into heaven was to outlive her. Red couldn't exactly fit that notion with any scripture he'd ever read.

Because he couldn't rightly decide what to believe, he also called a halt to the kissing after that one sweet night. He just couldn't stand the thought of her accepting his touch without thinking she had a choice. She'd tried to kiss him a couple of times and Red said no. It was the closest she came to being annoyed with him. Well, fine. It would do his obedient little wife some good to get mad.

The baby was due anytime, so Red took to staying even closer to the house. He'd found definite signs that Wade was in the area until the last few weeks. No footprints or horse tracks had shown up lately. Red reluctantly left her alone in the cabin if the weather was too bad, but he was never gone for long.

He went out to ride herd on his cattle one particularly bitterly cold day with snow sleeting down, turning the whole world into an icy, slippery nightmare. He stayed away from Cassie as long as he thought he dared. Then in a wind that had picked up to near-blizzard strength, he made his way back to the house. He found Cassie coming out of the chicken coop.

While he was still at a distance, he saw her walk slowly over the glaze, carrying a bucket of eggs. She was in the house before he could get to her, so he put Buck away with a fine fury riding him and marched into the house to have it out with his contrary wife.

He shut the door with an unnecessarily loud *crack*.

Cassie whirled to face him with her usual welcoming smile.

"You're supposed to stay inside. You know Wade could be around, and even if he isn't, it's a sheet of ice out there. You could have *broken your fool neck!*"

Cassie's smile quickly faded to fear.

Red stormed up to her.

"B—But, Red, Wade wouldn't be out in this weather. And you're working so hard. I thought just this once it would really save you—"

"You," Red cut her off, "don't save me *ten minutes* with your blasted help. But I'd spend the rest of the winter working double-time if you broke your leg. If you don't have the sense to be afraid of Wade, you could at least have a little consideration for me!"

Cassie flinched away from him.

That made Red madder. She had a lot of nerve being scared of him when he'd been so patient. . .except maybe for right now.

"But Red, I can at least feed the chickens and gather the eggs. It's not like the chickens can drag me along on the ground."

"Don't argue with me." Red felt his temper flare white hot when she referred to the way Buck had bullied her. Her scrapes had barely healed from that episode. "It's icy outside. You could fall on your way to the chicken coop."

Cassie nodded, and her meek obedience blew the top off what little restraint was left on Red's temper. He bent over her so she had to lean back to look him in the eye. "Say it," Red demanded.

"Say what?"

"You know."

"No, I don't know what you're talking about, Red." Cassie furrowed her brow. He knew she was trying desperately to think what he wanted from her. Trying to be the obedient wife. Trying to be everything he wanted before he had to ask. But he didn't want that. He wanted her mad. "Say that nasty, awful thing you're thinking. Mind me, wife."

Cassie's eyes widened, and Red knew she really had been thinking something awful. He almost smiled.

"Why Red, I wasn't thinking anything nasty about you," she said sweetly.

"And I say you're a liar," Red announced with soft menace.

Cassie's eyes flashed.

Somewhere buried inside his meek little wife was a volcano under intense pressure and threatening to erupt. He couldn't stop himself from goading her. "A liar, and a poor one at that.

And a coward who won't speak her mind."

"Red Dawson, I am not. . ." Cassie's fingers flew to her mouth.

Red pulled her hand away. "What did you just say to me? Did you contradict me, woman? No wife of mine is gonna say anything to me but—" Red spoke in a wavery falsetto, a terrible mockery of a woman's voice, " 'Yes, Red. Yes, sir. I'll do whatever you say, and I'll do it right quick.' "

Cassie made the same instinctive movement she always made with her fingers, but this time she pressed her fingers against Red's mouth. He fell silent. Then from behind her fingers, he said softly, "Say it, Cass."

Her cheeks turned the most amazing shade of pink, and she sucked in a deep breath but didn't speak.

Red caught her hand and lifted it from his mouth and held it gently. "Say, 'You're a polecat, Red Dawson.' Tell me I'm a mangy, growly old bear. Tell me I'm a sneakin', low-down coyote. Tell me I'm as mean as a rattler and as cantankerous as Buck and as stubborn as an ox. Say it or admit you're a liar and a coward, Mrs. Dawson. Tell me I'm a—"

"All those animals," Cassie interrupted, "are put here by God for the exact purpose they serve." Rather sharply she added, "*You're* the problem."

Cassie seemed to realize what she'd said, and she pulled back a step. She'd have covered her mouth again if Red hadn't held tight to her hand.

Red grinned for a second. Then he tipped his head back and laughed out loud. It was a full belly laugh, and when he looked back at her, his eyes were damp from laughing and he had to wipe them. "Why, Cassandra Dawson, I do believe you just insulted me."

"Oh, Red, I'm sorry."

Red pulled her into his arms and kissed her. He kissed her

until he felt the starch go out of her knees. Then he swept her, big belly and all, into his arms, strode to a chair, and settled her on his lap so he could surround her completely.

Cassie pulled back, bewildered. "Red, does this mean you'll kiss me when I'm rude to you?"

"I reckon it does, Cass honey."

"I. . .I've been wanting you to kiss me, Red. I just never dreamed the way to get you to was to—"

Red kissed her again just for saying she wanted him to.

Cassie wrapped her arms around his neck, then slid her hands to his face and lifted herself away from him. "If you wanted me to be sassy, you should have told me you'd do this."

Red laughed again but not for long. He started kissing her again, exploring her face with his lips. He had been tormented by how sweet she smelled when she lay next to him and the tiny sounds she made as she slept. He'd dreamed of tracing the outline of her perfect, silken cheekbones with his lips.

He was so busy satisfying his curiosity that it took him awhile to notice Cassie wasn't being a shy little creature now. She had her arms tight around his neck, and she made little gasps and sighs of pleasure that were driving him crazy even before he was conscious of them.

Then suddenly she let out a gasp that was different from the others. She went rigid in his arms, so tense and distressed he pulled back, ashamed at his lack of restraint. He didn't get a chance to apologize.

Cassie snatched her arms away from his neck and grabbed at her stomach. "Something's wrong."

Red looked from her belly to her face to her belly to her face about fifteen times before he got his eyes under control. "Is it the babe? Do you think the babe's coming?"

Cassie's attention had been riveted on her stomach. When Red asked about the baby, she looked up at him frantically. "I can't have the baby yet!"

"But I thought you said it was due the middle of December. That's now, Cass. Why can't you have it yet?" Red tried to think of every possible thing that could be going wrong that made it dangerous for Cassie to have the baby right now.

Tears filled Cassie's eyes as she looked to him to fix whatever was wrong. She wailed, "Because I'm too young to be a mother!"

Red had seen her cry a few times, silent tears with an occasional genteel sob. Her mouth hadn't twisted, her skin had been pure, flawless white. She had cried more beautifully than any woman Red had ever seen. And with a bunch of big sisters, he'd seen a few.

This was nothing like that. Cassie opened her mouth and made a terrible ruckus with her sobs. Her skin got all blotchy, tears turned her eyes red, her nose ran, and her hair started sticking to her face wherever she was soggy.

Red rubbed her back. "There, there." It was all he knew about birthing babies. Although he'd made Muriel tell him a few things.

Birthing babies? Muriel! Red thought of the vicious sleet pounding down more fiercely every minute. No one was going to make it out here to help bring this babe.

"Ouch!" Cassie shouted through her tears.

"What? What's happening?" Red asked desperately.

"You're crushing me!"

Red was sitting, thinking about what was in store for them, and he'd been strangling her. He relaxed his hold.

"Go for help, Red," Cassie whispered. Her voice caught. She gasped raggedly for a second, then she choked out, "Go to Jessups' and send for Muriel."

Red was struck speechless. He wasn't going ten feet in this weather. He was going to have to do it alone. Cassie was too young to have a babe, and Red realized with a sickening twist of his gut that he was, too.

An urgent desire to do something, anything, made Red stand with Cassie still in his arms. "Let's get you to bed." He carried her into the bedroom.

By the time Red had her in the back room, she started pushing at his shoulders. "Let me down. I'm not going to bed."

Then she glared at him. "Muriel can't come out in this weather. Don't you dare go for her!" Cassie sounded calm and confident, not the frightened little girl she'd been two minutes ago and not the shy, submissive wife she was the rest of the time.

Red was having a little trouble adjusting. "No, I mean, yes, I mean, what do you want me to do?"

"Let me down this instant!" Cassie shoved at his shoulders again.

He lowered her to the floor, never letting go of her in case she sank into a heap on the ground or started moaning again or burst into flames. . .or whatever women in labor did.

"That took me by surprise, but now that I'm ready for it, it won't be so bad next time." Cassie looked around the bedroom ceiling as if she were searching for cobwebs and considering knocking them down. She gave a nod of her head and dusted her hands together and left the room.

Red trailed behind her.

Cassie headed for the cooler and ducked inside.

"What are you doing? What do you need in there?" Red joined her in the cramped room. She was slicing the ham.

Red grabbed the knife from her. "We don't need to eat now."

Cassie turned to him. "I don't believe I'll eat, no. But it's near your noon mealtime. You'll be wanting something."

The mere thought of food made Red want to choke. "Don't you think you should lie down?" Red asked, hacking at the ham just for something to do.

"Muriel says I should stay up for as long as possible. She said I'll be so sick of lying in bed by the end that I'll want these first few hours back."

"Hours?" Red stopped slicing and looked sideways at her. "How many hours?"

"Muriel said her first child made his appearance about twenty-four hours after the first pains."

"Twenty-four hours!" Red yelled.

Cassie patted him on the arms as if he were the one facing a full day of pains.

"Yes, but Libby said her first was only four hours and Leota said ten, so I guess we can't know for sure." Cassie took the slice of ham and didn't mention the fact the Red had hacked it into four pieces. She left the cooler.

Red hurried to catch up.

Cassie turned into a woman Red had never met before. She was utterly calm, totally competent, and almost maniacally busy.

She cooked him a noon meal even though it was only about half past ten. He didn't mention that fact, and she didn't seem to care. She peeled potatoes and mixed a batch of biscuits. She started a new rising of bread for tomorrow and wiped every inch of the kitchen.

And she talked. She talked more words in the following half hour than Red had heard her say since they'd gotten married.

"I never gave eggs much thought back East. Then when we got out here and there were no chickens, Griff had some sent from St. Louis. The cost of those chickens! And none of them lived out the first week we had them. We had a pig that died, and a milk cow that never gave us so much as a swallow of milk. Griff told me coyotes got the chickens and..."

Cassie bustled around the kitchen at about twice her normal speed, chattering about chickens and how much she liked eggs. She occasionally asked his opinion about something, and it took Red about five minutes to catch on that he'd better have an answer right quick, but it'd better be a short one. Her eyebrows would furrow, and she'd look nervously at him if he didn't hold up his end of the conversation. But if he answered more than, "Yes," or, "No," or, "Whatever you say," she'd start talking right over top of him. She was listening to him for the sound but she wasn't really *hearing* anything he said. He just humored her because he didn't have any idea what else to do.

He took anything the least bit heavy out of her hands and moved it to wherever she had in mind. He stayed out of her way as best he could, while she whirled from the table to the sink to the fireplace, preparing him a dinner he didn't think he could begin to eat.

Red had been hovering nearby for nearly half an hour, watching her for the first sign of impending disaster—which Red assumed was inevitable—when she stopped in her monologue to stiffen and hold her stomach.

The exact moment she started breathing hard, he stepped away from her because she'd been heading for the cooler with a bucket. He'd taken it from her, almost resulting in a tug-of-war before she let it go. He headed to the cooler to refill it. He glanced back at her and saw her gripping the back of a chair with whitened knuckles and staring blankly into space. He dropped the bucket and dashed to her side and held her.

"Don't touch me," Cassie snarled.

Red jumped back as surely as if a rattler had attacked him.

Then her voice deepened almost to a growl. "Get your filthy hands off me."

It was a voice he'd never heard come out of his submissive little wife before.

The minute he backed away, Cassie turned to him and

grabbed him around the waist. She buried her face against his chest. "Hold me, please, Red."

His head spinning, he cautiously wrapped his arms around her. He kissed her silken hair softly, like he did when they slept side by side. He rubbed her rigid shoulders. She moaned as if the touch were comforting. He felt her stomach grow hard between them, and his heart ached as Cassie whimpered with distress and burrowed closer to him. Since she seemed to like her shoulders rubbed, he slid one hand down her back and around to massage her taut belly.

"What are you doing?" She shrieked like he'd tried to push her off a cliff. "Get your hands off me." She shoved hard at his arm.

Pulling away from her, he stammered, "I'm. . .I'm sorry. I won't touch you if you. . ."

A loud wail broke off his wretched apology. "You think I'm fat and ugly." Cassie buried her face in both hands and sobbed as if she'd lost her best friend in the world.

"Cassie, no." He stepped away from her. "I think you're—"

"Red!" She hurled herself back into his arms. "Don't let me go. No matter what, never let me go."

Red held his hands carefully out at his sides, afraid to touch her as she snuggled up against him. He slowly lowered his hands, ready to snatch them back at the first sign of trouble. When his hands settled lightly around her waist, she whispered, "Thank you. Thank you so much."

He held her closer, careful to avoid her stomach, thinking that might have been the problem. Gingerly he moved with her to a chair and sat in it with her, as he had during her first pain. He rubbed her back and made meaningless noises of comfort to her, and thought, *Thirty minutes down, twenty-three and a half hours to go.*

The worst-case example was Muriel's daylong laboring.

Red didn't see any reason to hope for the best. He held her and rocked back and forth and prayed for divine intervention.

Suddenly, she shoved his arms away from her and stood briskly. "What are you thinking? I've got dinner to get on." She hurried back to the fireplace.

He wondered whether his twisting stomach could hold down a single swallow. And would he make her angry if he refused to eat? Worse yet, would she start crying again?

She started humming softly while she worked.

It occurred to Red that she had been yelling at him and demanding that he do her bidding and do it right now. With a sudden melting in his heart he thought, *I'm finally meeting the real Cassie. . .except insane.*

He knew it was true. This was Cassie with all of her conditioned behavior stripped away. Sassy and demanding and efficient and filling his home with music. He'd been half in love with her since the first time he'd laid eyes on her, and his heart had softened to her right from the beginning of their marriage, but now he knew that hadn't been love because now he knew what the real thing was.

Love, fierce like a lion defending its cubs, roared through him. This Cassie was who he wanted, and he wasn't going to settle for anyone else. He wished fervently that after the babe was born she'd stay like she was right now, but he knew there was little chance. It would take time, but they had all the time in the world. He'd dig this woman out of her shell if it took him the rest of his life.

Cassie grabbed at the heavy skillet she had hanging on a peg on the wall, and Red rushed to lift it for her. She whacked at his hands with a wooden spoon. "Don't you have any chores to do outside?"

"I'm carrying this frying pan for you." Red pried her fingers off it. "Now tell me where you want it."

Montana Rose

She fussed and scolded at him as she shooed him toward the fireplace.

Red thought, *Maybe we don't have all the time in the world. A man can die a hundred times, in a hundred different ways, in twenty-four hours.*

CHAPTER 23

She had to finish dinner.

She had to clean up the kitchen afterward, not just tidy but clean down to the bone.

She had to scrub the floor, but she couldn't scrub a dirt floor. But she had to!

She had to scald all the cook pots and search out the last particle of dust. Cobwebs! There might be cobwebs!

What about the slit that opened off her bedroom? What kind of filth lurked in that dark passageway? She had to ferret out every threatening speck so nothing dirty would touch— Her mind veered away from the why. She didn't dare think about the baby on the way.

She became aware that under the urgent need to hurry, she was hearing two different voices guiding her. For the first time in a long time she was separated from herself. The china doll, trying to be perfect, but with a twist because the china doll had been trying to be perfect for Griff. Now, her only standard was for herself, because Red never asked her to be perfect. But in some disjointed way, she knew the drive to have everything sparkling clean and in order was linked to the china doll.

And the other Cassie, the furious, childish Cassie, wanted everything just right, too. But she wanted to holler. She wanted to hit something. She wanted to make Red clean the stupid house himself, for heaven's sake. She shouldn't have to clean in her condition.

Which led her to think of the baby coming, and her mind careened off again. Having a baby was too huge. She was too young. She wasn't ready to give birth to a child, let alone raise one.

Panic roiled in her stomach, blared in her head. The childish Cassie wanted to release all of the tension with violence. . .or at least with a temper tantrum to end all temper tantrums. She yanked tight on the reins of her emotions and kept the angry, terrified Cassie silent.

To cover her turmoil, she forced the china doll to the forefront of her mind and worked. She had to wash and iron her nightgown. It had to be immaculate. She grabbed a bucket and hurried toward the cooler.

Red took it from her.

She nearly jumped out of her skin. "What are you doing in here?"

"I've been here right along, Cass." Red gave her a worried look as he rested his hand on her arm. "I'll get water. You shouldn't be doing heavy lifting."

"Everything has to be clean. Everything has to be absolutely clean." Her ears hurt a little, as though she'd shouted the words, but it hadn't sounded loud, so that couldn't be the source of the pain. Somehow her ears hurting must be Red's fault. She wanted the nightgown washed in boiling water, and he was holding on to the bucket. Everything in the room had to be spotless.

He glanced around the room. "It's fine. You won't even be in the room anyway."

Not be in the room? A vision of her baby being born without her being in the same room with it ricocheted around in her head. What kind of stupid thing was that to say?

He stared at her funny for a few seconds, and Cassie had the sudden sick feeling that maybe she'd spoken her thoughts out loud. She shook her head. Impossible. She'd never call Red stupid, no matter what kind of idiot he acted like.

His eyes widened and he glanced nervously from her, to the bucket, to the cooler, and back to her again. She got the impression he was afraid to leave the room.

She had to wash her nightgown. The baby might take twenty-four hours, but she didn't want to rely on that. She reached for the pail, determined to take care of fetching water if he was too lazy and useless to help her.

His eyebrows shot up all the way to his red hair. He held the pail away from her and practically ran into the cooler.

She wondered what had him acting so weird.

He came back out with a full bucket. They always left one sitting under the trickling spring to fill. Speaking softly, using the same voice she'd heard him use on a spooky, green-broke horse, he said, "I'm not acting weird."

She thought that was an odd comment to make. It was as if he'd read her mind. She shook her head to clear it of such a distracting possibility.

"My nightgown." She raced into her room and came back with the white gown Muriel had given her.

She tried to take the pail from Red.

"Where do you want it?" he asked.

"Fill a basin and hang it over the fire."

He did as she asked with alacrity.

She threw her nightgown in the still-cold water to soak. While she was there, she checked the cook pot, fiercely determined that today of all days the potatoes wouldn't be scorched. She leaned into the fireplace, and using a towel to protect her hand, she lifted the lid on the pot that hung side by side with the stewing nightgown and stirred.

Red took the lid out of her hand and pulled her away from the fire and dealt with the potatoes himself.

Then she elbowed him aside and checked the ham in the cast-iron skillet that sat nestled off to the side of the flames.

"Watch out for the fire." Red pulled her back.

She was just straightening from her task to slug him in the shoulder when the baby made itself known again. She looked down at her stomach in disgust. How was she supposed to get her work done and forget about the coming difficult hours if the child kept pestering her?

"You'll do fine, Cassie. We'll get everything done that needs doin'."

He was reading her mind again and that made her angry, and she had to clamp down on the irate Cassie inside of her all the more. She was aware of Red uncurling her hand, one finger at a time, from his shirt. But she didn't remember how her hand had gotten there to begin with. Then the pain got strong enough that all she was conscious of was Red holding her and sharing his vast strength with her. When it eased, she was sitting in his lap again, and that struck her as completely ridiculous when she had dinner cooking and a house to clean. She leaped off his lap and went back to work.

The noon meal was fine except she didn't eat it and Red ate his so fast she didn't remember his sitting down to the table. And it was all burned because she was forever finding herself hugged up tight against Red. One time she stood up to find the potatoes boiled dry and scorched until they were ruined. Red said he liked them that way and set the pot aside.

The next time the pain eased, the ham had dried out. Cassie didn't mean to cry over something so insignificant as a burned piece of meat, but she heard Red telling her not to cry and so she supposed she had. Red didn't seem to mind the blackened ham. He said he loved ham and potatoes just that way. And when the biscuits burned, Red was the one who pulled them out of the fire, and he blamed himself for not getting them sooner, so that was his own fault.

She thought, *Why does he keep distracting me and holding me when he knows I have work to do?*

"I'm sorry," he said. "I'll never distract you again. I promise."

Which was stupid of him since she hadn't told him what she was thinking.

Then he said, "I agree completely. It *was* stupid of me."

Which confused her all the more, especially since a few minutes later she found herself in his arms again, and after his promise!

He dished himself up a full meal, then she was being held close and the meal was gone. She wondered if he'd enjoyed it.

He said, "It was delicious."

At that point she resigned herself to having a husband who could read her mind and released that worry from her over-crowded collection of worries.

Somewhere the acceptance of Red's mind reading reached through the strange panic that had seized her from the moment of her first pain. She started to feel almost entranced by him. His voice seemed to be the only solid ground as her body acted on its own, hurting her for no reason.

Red crooned to her and stayed by her side while she fussed over her kitchen and the bedroom. He took orders, stirring her gown in the boiling water and rinsing it and wringing it out. Then he even heated the flat iron and pressed the nightgown until it was dry and left it draped over a chair near the fireplace to rid it of its last bit of dampness while he helped her hunt down cobwebs in the cave passageway.

At some point, she quit working altogether and just sat in a chair Red always had at hand and barked orders at him. Then her stomach would begin to tense up and she'd freeze up from her chores, and Red would be right there, a port in the storm that raged around her. He'd hold her and whisper gentle petitions to the Lord for courage and wisdom. The time came when the pains became too persistent, and she had to give up on cleaning the house, although she demanded he mop the kitchen floor.

"It's a dirt floor, Cass. It'll turn to mud."

Then he was wiping tears from her eyes and promising he'd scrub the floor until he was down to bedrock. He held her then and kissed her hair and talked in the casual way he always did to God, bringing a holy presence into the room with them.

He asked her about preparing the bed for the time the baby would come.

She told him of Muriel's instructions on how to boil water and lay out the baby's clothes and sterilize a knife to cut the cord and lay thick sheets on the bed to protect the mattress. Cassie didn't know what the mattress was being protected from, but she was determined to follow Muriel's orders to the letter.

The lantern was lit, which seemed odd to Cassie, because it wasn't noon yet, and Cassie found herself with bare moments between the pains to try and bring order to her thoughts. She thought about demanding time and privacy to put on her nightgown, but then her stomach was grabbed as though a mountain lion sank its teeth into her belly, and somehow she was in bed, wearing her nightgown.

The next clear thought she had was that she must have put her nightgown on very swiftly and gone to bed, because somehow she was in bed but she didn't know how she'd found the strength. Unless she'd found it from Red. He was always there. Always within reach.

The petulant Cassie began to rear her head more fiercely.

She wanted to hurt Red because she was hurting, and it didn't seem fair that she had to hurt alone. She wanted to scream at him and loathe all men through him, because he could never have a child, but he could make a child grow inside a woman and then leave her to die alone.

She even daydreamed of taking a swing at him several times. The china doll controlled all those ugly impulses though, kept them tucked inside, free to rage in her imagination without harming the man who was her only grasp on life.

Suddenly the pains changed. She felt as if she were caught up in the center of a tornado. She saw all the whipping winds whirling around her, but she herself was spared their violence for an instant. Then weight, like the entire mountain over her head, pressed down on her belly, crushing her, crushing her baby. She wanted to cry out because of the unfairness of their home caving in on her after she'd been through so much. Red's voice reached her, warring with the terror in her mind, offering words of calm assurance.

Red sat beside her on the bed. She heard him pray over her as he wiped sweat from her brow. He calmed her as the mountain receded and her bedroom took shape. He moved away from her and she wanted to cling to him.

"It's coming, Cass honey. The baby's coming. I see the head. It's almost time. It's almost over." He kept talking, kept calling on God to be with them, to give them strength sufficient to the task they faced. The words eased the rest of the weight from her, even as she felt the agonizing pressure again. But the mountain didn't cave in again. Red's words kept the roof from falling.

Strength sufficient for the task. That's all she needed. She asked for that herself, speaking the words out loud. She didn't need to take on the whole world. . .or even face the next twenty-four hours that it would take for the baby to be born. She only needed to survive the very instant she was living in. She asked for the baby to live even if she gave up her own life, as seemed inevitable now. The pressure intensified, then relented enough for her to take a breath, then came surging back.

Red shouted just as the strain on her body became un-endurable. And in an instant she went from agony to relief. And Red laughed out loud, and something dark lifted away from Cassie's mind, far enough that she heard a quavering noise. The noise, that tiny cry gripped at her heart and held on so tightly she knew it would never let her go, and she knew she would never want it to.

Her eyes darted toward the noise to see Red standing with a writhing, noisy, messy creature in his hands. She was so exhausted that she couldn't make sense of what she was seeing. Reality tried to force its way past her confused, exhausted mind as a tigress awoke in her at the sound of her unhappy child, but for a long minute she couldn't make that squalling, white and red bundle in Red's arms be the baby she knew she'd just borne.

Then Red pulled a soft blanket around what he held. He sat on the bed beside her on her left and held the baby in the crook of his left arm. He leaned close to her until the noisy baby would have rested across her chest if he'd put it down. He tilted the baby so she could see its face, and the wild confusion that was fogging her mind cleared and the baby was real to her at last.

Red laughed and drew her attention briefly away from the child, the extension of herself. Red was a mess. A joyful mess. His hair was wild as if he'd run his hands through it a thousand times in the few minutes since her pains had started. His brown shirt was wet and tinged pink all across the front. His sleeves were rolled up to his elbows as he liked to wear them when he did his woodwork in the evening.

She forgot about his being a mess when she looked in his eyes. He was looking at the baby, and for a moment, Cassie saw the eyes of a man who had witnessed a miracle. She drank in the wisdom and purity of what she saw in Red and absorbed his joy into her soul.

After a bare second studying him, she looked back at her baby with a renewed strength of her own. All she could see was a tiny, wrinkled face. Red had the blanket she'd knitted wrapped snugly around the squirming infant, even over its hair.

The baby howled with its eyes shut tight and its mouth wide open. The baby's whole body shook from the force of the cries. Suddenly, five tiny fingers poked up from the blanket. Cassie was awestruck by the miniature perfection of her baby. One of Red's big work-callused hands reached between Cassie and the baby, and he touched the wee baby fingers with one of his own, lifting and caressing gently.

The baby's hand suddenly grasped hold of Red's index finger. The tiny hand didn't reach all the way around, but the grip was tight. Each finger bent, grasping firmly. There were nails, so little they were barely visible, tipping each finger.

Everything a human being ever had, the baby brought with it into the world in a package so small it would fit inside a mother's belly, and Cassie knew why Red looked as though he'd seen a miracle. She was witnessing one, too.

She looked away from the baby to Red. He was still smiling; his eyes still blazed with joy. But now a tear streaked its way down his face. Cassie felt her whole world tilt dangerously at the sight of the single tear. She wasn't aware of moving, but she saw her hand touch Red's face and wipe the tear away.

When she touched him, he looked away from the baby. Something solid stretched between them as their eyes locked. More than an emotion, more than a shared memory, it was a connection so tangible that it could have been built from stone.

Cassie believed she could hold it in her hands if she wished. Cassie felt it, whatever it was, wrap around her just as the baby's cry had, entwining with her heart so deeply that it could never be undone.

CHAPTER 24

Red's hand came to rest on Cassie's where it lay on his cheek. He pressed her palm against his skin. The baby screamed louder, and the wriggling presence between them deepened the closeness Red felt between them, if that was possible.

Red's heart turned over to see dark circles under Cassie's heavy-lidded eyes. He knew how tired he was after staying by her side during the endless day and night of her laboring. He couldn't imagine her fatigue. He knew he should insist she rest, but the love that glowed out of her for the baby was too precious to interrupt with something as earthbound as sleep.

Her feather-light touch on his trailing tears moved him so profoundly that he knew he would never be the same. He leaned down to Cassie until their bodies cocooned the baby gently between them, and still holding her hand, he kissed her. He pulled his lips away a scant inch. Her eyes had drifted shut. "Open your eyes, Cass."

She did, but he could see the struggle she put up to keep her heavy lids raised.

He looked at her, but his gaze reached inside and joined

with the ties that were binding them together, until he was part of her and she was part of him. "I love you, Cassie Dawson. I love you and I love our little. . ."

With a sudden start, Red remembered something vital.

A tiny spurt of fear flashed in Cassie's eyes. "What is it?"

Red said, chagrined, "I just realized I don't know if the baby is a boy or a girl."

They looked at each other again, and suddenly they were laughing. All the fear and hard work and wonder erupted from them. Red's deep, warm chuckle and Cassie's gentler laughter mingled, as surely as their hearts had mingled moments ago.

They didn't laugh for long, because the baby gave a particularly furious roar of anger and drew their attention. Red held the infant while Cassie, with hands trembling from exhaustion, unwrapped the blanket.

"A girl," Red whispered. "She'll be as beautiful and ornery as her mama."

Cassie said, "I'm not ornery." Then she said, "Look at her toes." They were as perfect as the rest of her.

Red said, "Check her over good. Then we'd better wrap her back up."

Cassie nodded. "She needs a bath. . .but out by the fireplace where it's warm."

"Should you feed her first?" Red asked.

Cassie looked up at him when he asked. He could see he'd startled her. Then, inexplicably, she was crying. Through her tears she said, "I'm the worst mother who ever lived!"

"I'm sorry, Cass. I didn't mean. . ." He knew she couldn't hear him over her tears, so he quit talking. Her body was battered with the force of her sobs. Red hugged her awkwardly as she lay on her back with the baby still between them in his arms.

The crying eased a bit, and he said, "You don't have to feed her yet if you don't want to."

She snarled at him so savagely he was reminded of a mountain lion he'd come face-to-face with his first year in Montana. "I will, too, feed her. And I'll do it right now!"

The baby jumped wildly when Cassie yelled. She still lay half on Cassie's chest, half in Red's arms. Both arms and legs flew out, her whole, tiny body jerked, and she howled as if someone had stuck her with a pin.

"I scared her." Cassie started crying all the harder.

Wade heard the baby cry.

The child had been born. Something cracked into pieces in his heart to know that the little one had come. Wade didn't know much about birthing a child, but he knew it was a long, hard business for a woman, and he hadn't been there to help or protect his fragile china doll.

He'd crept up to the cabin in the vicious weather early this morning when Red didn't emerge to do his usual chores. He had to know what was going on inside.

He might get caught, coming this close in the daytime, but if he was careful, the storm would cover his tracks and he could have a moment to be close to the china doll.

He crouched by the door to the soddy and ached from the awful cold.

He'd traveled into the high country to keep Red from discovering him. He rarely came down close enough to even spy on his china doll from the high hills. But yesterday the storm had given him enough cover to risk getting close enough to where his spyglass worked. And he'd seen no sign of anyone all afternoon and evening yesterday, nor anyone this morning. With the security of the storm to shield him, and starving for a tiny bit of his woman, he'd crept down close.

The only shelter Wade found big enough for himself and

his horse was a miserable cave that seemed to catch the wind. The gale whipped around inside and moaned until Wade heard voices in the howling current. Sometimes his father's, sometimes the china doll crying for help, sometimes. . .maybe. . .God's.

Wade had taken money from his account in Divide before he'd laid the false trail out of town, but he'd spent almost none of it. He could afford to live better, but he'd have to go to town to spend it. There was warm food and light at his father's ranch. But Wade refused to take another beating in exchange for shelter.

He listened to that baby cry and felt himself transported to another time, another baby born in a lowly place. He remembered the prayers and lessons of his mother and wondered how he'd been brought so low as to crouch in this cold, hurting all the way to his soul for a woman who'd been stolen from him.

He sank to the ground, his head bowed, and he tried to clear the traces of whiskey and hate from his thoughts. Behind that he found fear and hopelessness and terrible, aching loneliness. It was too much to bear, and he pulled his bottle from the pocket of his coat to drown the pain.

One thing did become clear. He loved that new baby as much as he loved his china doll, and he couldn't take them away in this cold. He hated to do it, but there was no way now to rescue them until the cold eased.

The strange, tinny crying stopped, and all that was left was the wind, biting into Wade's coat, laughing in his ear, telling him he'd sunk as low as a man could sink.

Thinking of that badger hole of a cave he slept in, Wade tried to figure out how that was any better than taking his father's fist. His father would laugh to know Wade had been reduced to such lowly straits.

He couldn't be close enough to protect his china doll.

He couldn't work up the guts to kill Red Dawson.

He was worthless.

A poor excuse for a man.

Finally, in desperation, he lurched to his feet and staggered into the woods and up the treacherous slope to where he'd concealed his horse. He'd leave.

His horse seemed eager when Wade swung up onto his back.

"We're gonna find a warm place for a couple of months, boy. But then we'll be back. We'll get the china doll and hightail it to Denver. Live there till the winter weather breaks."

The horse snorted and shook his head, the metal in his bridle clinking. White breath whooshed from the impatient animal.

Wade clapped the horse on the neck. He'd taught the bay to lie down in the cave, and Wade had learned to use the big animal's body for warmth. It had been awhile since Wade had met anyone whom he cared for more than this big, gentle horse.

How had Red managed to turn that cave he lived in into a place so welcoming?

Wade rode his horse down the mountain, far from Red's cave. While he rode, Wade planned. He'd go somewhere and find his backbone. He'd catch a man drunk and he'd learn how to kill.

The thought made him shudder, and Wade believed he heard the soft whisper of his mother's voice, full of gentleness and love. Or maybe it was someone else. Someone who might be near, watching, caring. Wade's mother had taught him about God, but Wade's father had taught him it was foolish to put hope in some fancy.

Wade drank deeply to silence that voice and the pain that came with hearing it. The whiskey separated him from the hurt inside and gave him liquid courage. He'd go to Denver and face down a man who wasn't a danger to him. Once he won a shootout, pulled that trigger for the first time, the next killing would be easier.

The wild air howled at him that he was a coward and a failure.

A poor excuse for a man.

CHAPTER 25

Cassie sobbed as she fumbled with the tiny buttons that ran in a row down the front of her nightgown most of the way to her waist.

Red caught both of her hands in one of his. "Stop, Cassie. Don't cry. Don't be upset. Please, I didn't mean to make you cry, Cass honey. Please."

Red's crooning comfort took awhile to penetrate the maelstrom raging out of her. He prayed silently for patience, afraid praying aloud would make her cry again. Then he said softly, "You're just tired. You didn't hurt the baby. You're fine. The baby's fine."

Slowly the latest outburst of tears eased, and Red, thinking feeding the baby was what had started all of this, propped a folded blanket behind Cassie's shoulders and adjusted it until she was nearly sitting upright. He'd shared such total intimacy with Cassie today that he hoped she wouldn't demand modesty between them. But Cassie wasn't exactly reasonable right now. He hesitated for a split second before he slipped the buttons of her gown free and pushed the fabric aside. Then he laid the still-uncovered baby against Cassie's bare skin until the little girl's face pressed against Cassie's breast.

Cassie didn't protest, but she was still so upset, he wasn't sure her acceptance of his touch meant anything.

He moved Cassie's arms until she held the baby in her own arms. The first time she'd completely supported their little girl. The baby was cuddled securely against her. With a move so sure it was startling, the baby turned its head toward the warmth, latched on, and began nursing vigorously. Cassie jumped and Red noticed with relief she had quit crying.

"Look at the little sweetheart go," Red said with awe. "She knows exactly what to do."

Cassie nodded, but she didn't take her eyes off her baby girl. "She knows how to feed herself. It's impossible. And she knew how to grab your finger."

Red watched as, with aching care, Cassie touched her baby's hand, and the petite hand grabbed hold just as it had with Red. Cassie started crying again.

Red groaned softly, then kissed Cassie's tear-streaked cheeks and held her face cradled in his hands. He lifted Cassie's hand with the baby still clinging to her index finger and kissed both hands together.

Red murmured a prayer against their interwoven fingers. Red asked God to make him good enough to be a father and husband. He asked for patience and wisdom and unshakable faith, and he added silently a request for God to make Cassie stop crying because it was breaking his heart. He also thanked God Seth had warned him about the emotional upheaval a woman goes through during and after the birth of a baby.

Cassie spent the next hour focused totally on her perfect little girl while Red straightened the room, and, lifting Cassie and the baby from one side of the bed to the other, put on clean sheets.

Red brought in warm water and a soft cloth and gave the baby a bath as it lay in Cassie's warm arms. Cassie protested that the room was too cold, but Red told her to keep the baby close to her and she'd stay warm enough. Red carefully exposed one small part of the baby at a time, cleaned it gently, and then covered her again. He even bathed the baby's head while she was still nursing and fumbled around until he'd put on his first diaper.

It was Red's idea to switch the baby to the other breast. He said it was so he could more easily wash her other side, but Cassie said something about feeding her baby on only one side and not thinking to change to the other, and she started crying again.

Red kept up a sweet, meaningless one-sided conversation as he saw to it that Cassie was adequately bathed. She squirmed with embarrassment, but considering the details of birthing a baby, she allowed it. Red even scooted her forward a bit and slid in behind her, unbraiding her hair and combing it. He spent long minutes coaxing the snarls out, intent on sparing her one more instant of pain.

When it was finally a smooth, silken mass in his hands, he tried to braid it, but he made a botched job of it, so he draped it over Cassie's shoulder and said, "I'll hold the little tyke. You braid." Cassie's hair hung down until it was a curtain around the feasting baby. Red circled his arms around Cassie and held the baby to nurse while she did her hair with trembling hands.

Finally, the room was neat. The baby and Cassie were tidy and tucked in warm. The baby fell asleep in the midst of her energetic suckling.

Red eased the baby out of Cassie's grasp, smiling at her reluctance to let go. He had pulled the cradle up to the side of the bed, but before he could lay her down, Cassie said, "Muriel said to hold her against your shoulder and burp her before you lay her down."

Red shifted the baby around, carefully asking just how to

do it. The babe slept limply against his shoulder as he patted her back, and finally she burped to suit Cassie. Then Red laid the baby on her stomach in the crib. The baby curled her knees under her belly until her bottom stuck up in the air. Red covered her with Cassie's thickly knitted coverlet. Cassie groaned as she rolled onto her side to stare at the baby as it slept.

Red sat on the bed beside her. He rested one hand on her shoulder. "Are you all right, Cass honey?"

Cassie glanced at him. "I'm fine, Red. Wonderful. Just tired. Can you believe how beautiful she is?"

The two of them looked at the little miracle that had been added to their lives that day. Red reached through the wooden slats to rub the back of a fist that was curled up near the baby's face. "What are we going to name her?"

Cassie seemed sure about one thing. "I want her name to be Dawson. We haven't talked about it, and I suppose she could be named Griffin, but I want her to be ours, Red. Both of ours. You don't mind, do you?"

Red had thought about it, and he wanted the babe to carry his name so badly that he hurt. But he thought Cassie would want to give this honor to Griff. Now, at her simple request, he felt tears burn in the back of his eyes. "I would be proud for her to carry my name, and it would be good for her to share the name we have."

He looked away from the baby, and the two of them nodded, in complete accord. "What about a first name? Do you want her called for your ma? Or if there was someone in Griff's family who—"

Cassie interrupted him. "I've pictured this baby being a girl from the first. Of course I couldn't really know, but it was just a fancy that took me. I've imagined a girl and I've always thought of her as part of these mountains. This new land. I want her to have a name as strong as the land. I want her to be strong, Red. Stronger than I am."

Red looked at his little daughter, enchanted by the little rosebud mouth that even now suckled as if she dreamed of nourishment.

He smiled at Cassie. "It's hard to see her, so delicate and pretty, and think of a strong name for her."

"I've heard Susannah means 'courage.' My mother told me about an ancient story where Susannah was a woman who defended herself courageously. I'd like a daughter who had courage, Red."

"Susannah is beautiful. We'll call her Susannah Cassandra Dawson," Red said firmly.

"Not Cassandra," Cassie protested. "The poor thing will have a whole alphabet to learn with a name that long."

But Red thought he saw a pink tinge in her cheeks that looked like pleasure, and he brushed aside her objection. "You get Susannah. I should get to pick the middle name."

"You get Dawson," Cassie said pertly.

"I think this little one is goin' to be as beautiful as her mama, which doesn't seem possible. She's goin' to be smart as a whip, so she can learn all the letters there are with no trouble, and she'll be as sweet as my Cass honey ever can be. I'd like her to share your name."

"Red," Cassie breathed his name on a sigh, "I'm not sweet."

Tears began to trickle from Cassie's eyes. She was lying on her side with both hands tucked under her head, watching the baby, so tears pooled in the corner of her right eye and streaked out of the corner of her left eye to drip on the bed.

Red wanted to sigh, but he contained it because he didn't want to sound impatient. He said, "Cassie, you're about the sweetest li'l thing I've ever seen. I tell you all the time to holler at me and call me a polecat, but you just don't have an ounce of mean in you anywhere."

"Oh yes, I do, Red. I. . .I don't think it's fair of you to go on thinking I'm a nice person when I'm not. I have so much anger churning around inside me sometimes that, even if I don't say so out loud, I know God judges me for a sinner. The things I want to say sometimes. . ." Cassie shook her head and swiped at her tears. "The stupid, childish tantrums I want to throw. No, I think we can do better than to hang my name on the innocent baby."

Red thoughtfully rubbed the side of his jaw where Cassie had given him a stiff right cross during one labor pain. She'd have nailed him several times if he hadn't gotten on to ducking. He'd bet his whole ranch she didn't remember doing it, and he had a good idea about exactly what boiled inside her, because he thought he'd heard every word of it the last twenty hours while she delivered the baby. "If you think you're confessing a sin to me, you're wrong. I couldn't be happier to hear you've got strong feelings about things. I've told you before I want to know what you're thinking."

"No, you don't." She shook her head frantically. "Trust me, Red. You wouldn't like the person I am inside."

She was so tired that Red felt guilty about talking with her about this right now. But maybe, while she was so exhausted she barely knew what she was saying and so twisted up inside with her confession, she'd be more open than ever before. Red decided he had to try. "Didn't Griff like the person you were inside?"

"Oh, no. Nobody would," Cassie said vehemently.

"And did he. . .hurt you when he was displeased with you?"

"Only when I was bad."

Red had to control himself from flinching at the calm acceptance in her tone. How could he make her understand that no man had the right to hurt a woman, especially when she claimed all the fault for herself?

Cassie continued, "He had to teach me how to be a woman. I was such a child when he married me, not near good enough to be his wife."

"Griff's way isn't my way. I believe it's wrong to hurt another human being. I'd *never* hit you. I'd *never* treat you like I had to teach you to be good enough for me."

"I want you to." Cassie looked away from Susannah and blinked guilty eyes at Red. "You're already teaching me so many things. I'm not fit, not yet, to be your wife, but I'm trying hard to learn about the cattle and the hogs and Buck. There's so much I have to learn."

Red did teach her all the time. How was that different from Griff? He knew it was, but how did he explain the difference? Then he had an inspiration. "What about all you teach me, Cassie? You know all sorts of things I don't know. That's what makes a marriage. You knew things about having a baby I didn't, and you run the house so much better than I ever did. And you're educated. You read and write."

Red brushed a wispy strand of dark hair off Cassie's forehead. "And you're kind. Griff was never kind. Did Griff ever ask you to teach *him* how to treat people with kindness and respect? He should have, because he was terrible at that, and you are so good at it. All the ladies in town love you, and all the men would die for you. Griff never inspired anyone the way you do. You could have taught him a lot."

"Me teach Griff?" Cassie asked in a bemused voice. "But he knew everything already."

Red reached both hands down to Cassie and gently turned her onto her back.

She looked up at him curiously.

"He didn't know that it was a sin to hit you. He liked the part of the Bible that said a wife should submit to her husband, but he didn't know about the next verse that said a man should care for his wife and love her as Christ loved the church. We talked about this at a Sunday service once. You know how Jesus treated people, don't you? We've been reading the Bible together long enough. He was always kind. He always acted out of love. In the end He died. He sacrificed His own life as a way to save your soul, Cass. Yours and mine. Jesus would have never looked favorably on a man hitting his wife. He'd have told Griff that the way he treated you was a powerful sin."

"A sin? But you only think that because you don't know the real me. You said I'm beautiful but I'm not, not inside where it really counts. I'm full of ugliness. And I'm *not* sweet. My heart is *black* with the anger I feel. And I'm not smart. I can be so stupid. I had to have Griff tell me what to do all the time. And now I need you to tell me."

Red didn't know what to say. He prayed silently for wisdom and listened for a still, small voice telling him where to go next. All he could think of was, "I need you, too. All of us have sin inside us. I know I do."

"Oh no, Red. Not you. You're wonderful."

"Of course I think of bad things and I try to keep my mouth from wrapping around some of the angry thoughts that want to escape from me. But I think what you're worrying about is different. I think so much of what churns around inside of you *should* be said out loud. There's nothing wrong with having an opinion, Cassie. God gave you a fine mind. Not knowing how to milk a cow is not the same as being stupid. Remember the chickens? You're way smarter'n them."

Cassie smiled mildly. "Yes, the chickens. That's right."

"I need you to tell me what you're thinking. You help me so much with the strength of your back, but I need your mind, too. I need two people thinking of all the possibilities to live the best way we know how. Can't you see that holding all of your opinions and ideas inside is a type of selfishness? I know you do it because Griff never wanted your help, but Griff was a failure as a rancher and that's the plain truth. He lost everything he had and he had a lot to begin with. I started with next to nothing and

I managed to build a nice spread. Griff didn't know everything, and he'd have benefited from your help. It sure couldn't have hurt. If anything, I'd say Griff was the stupid one."

Cassie's eyes narrowed as she listened to him. For a second, Red was afraid he'd made her mad saying such harsh things about Griff.

Then Cassie said, "Griff *was* a bad rancher, wasn't he? He didn't check the cattle hardly ever. He said they'd forage on their own, but you check them once or twice a day."

"Well, yeah. You have to check 'em or they wander off or die. Every rancher knows that."

"Griff didn't know it. We had chickens, but they all ran off or got eaten by varmints. He blamed everything on bad luck or dishonest people, but our land was as good as yours. He wouldn't listen to advice from anybody, most especially me. And he couldn't do everything himself, but he wouldn't let me help, so lots of things went undone. Even the fence that he cut himself on was badly repaired because he had done a sloppy job of mending it."

Cassie sat halfway up in bed. Red saw lines of distress deepen around her mouth and eyes, but when he reached out to her to urge her to lie back, she resisted him. He decided her opposition to his wishes was something to be encouraged at the moment.

"I'm not stupid, Red. I was always a good student in school. You're right about that. Why did I let him convince me I was?"

"He was a violent, domineering man, and you were so young that you couldn't stand up to him. Your mother trusted him to care for you, but he betrayed that trust and only cared for himself. He took all of your money by marrying you and squandered it." It made Red furious to think of the way Cassie had been robbed and cheated. "Then he died and left you with a baby on the way, all his bills for a high life he couldn't afford, and no way to care for yourself."

Cassie's eyes had dropped to the middle of Red's chest

while he talked. Red tilted her chin up to see how she was handling his blunt truths. Her eyes blazed into his. She opened her mouth then stopped whatever words were working their way out.

"Say it. Even if you think I won't like it. Even if you think it's a stupid, mean thing to say. I'd love to know what's going on in your head."

She closed her mouth and opened it again as if the words just wouldn't emerge.

Red waited, afraid to push her any further.

Finally the worst of the fiery anger faded from her eyes and she looked over at her sleeping child. "I'm thinking a lot of things, Red. They're all so jumbled I can't seem to get any of them to come out, but the main one is"—she looked back at him—"I'm glad I'm your wife. I'm glad you're Susannah's father. I think. . .I think God knew just what He was doing that day in the cemetery, and I'll thank Him every day of my life for letting me be with you." She launched herself the few inches that separated them and wrapped her arms around his neck.

Red didn't have to think a second before he was holding her snug against him.

Cassie pulled away for just a second. "I'm going to try and say what's on my mind, Red. And God help you when I do because you may not like some of it. But be patient with me, and we'll see if I can. . .start to believe I'm smart and that what I think matters. Maybe the Cassie who's been hiding inside of me all these years isn't such a bad person."

"I like everything about you, Cass honey. I only want to know more."

"Well then, the first thing that's on my mind, now that I've turned over a new leaf is. . .go away and let me get some sleep. I'm exhausted." Cassie leaned back against her pillow with her chin lifted ever so slightly in the air as if she were daring him

276

to tell her to stay awake. She tugged at her covers, and since he was sitting on them, she gave him a disgruntled look.

He stood and helped her smooth them.

"When I wake up, I might demand you make me something to eat. How would you like that, sir?" She sounded very bossy, but a smile escaped her prim lips.

Red smiled right back. "It would be my pleasure to serve you, ma'am. You tell me how your want your eggs, and they'll come out scrambled like they always do."

Cassie nestled herself amid her blankets. "That sounds just fine." She was asleep the instant her eyes closed.

Red looked back as he left the room. He stood for a minute and reveled in the beautiful sight of his family. His two beautiful women, Cassie and Susannah. Sleeping. Trusting him for their care.

It was a moment of crystal-clear clarity. A moment with a value beyond price. They were all bound together with a generous supply of love. And, with God's help, that love would overflow into every corner of their lives. He couldn't bring himself to leave immediately and he almost climbed into bed with Cassie just to hold her close. He would soon.

Fatigue tugged at his sleep-deprived brain, but he had something to do first. He stepped out of the room, a room he'd barely left in the last day, to spend a few moments in communion with God.

He knelt by the fire, his Bible clutched against his chest, and prayed the most sincere prayer of his life.

Thank You. Thank You, heavenly Father, for the gift You've given me. And thank You, thank You, thank You for my life with Cassie, and this joy and perfect peace.

CHAPTER 26

Cassie declared war.

She spent the next three days ranting and raving at him as if he were a slave, and a slow, ignorant slave at that.

He served her perfectly good scrambled eggs and ham for every meal. She told him it was burned, and he was pretty sure, if he hadn't moved quickly, she'd have thrown it at him.

She barked at him when he was slow. She snarled at him if things weren't done to her specification. And if he ever dared to disagree with her, she cried.

Red thought he was losing his mind. Cassie had given birth to more than a baby. She'd given birth to a shrewish temper.

The only time she was cheerful was when she held the baby in her arms, and the little one wasn't cooperating there. Susannah slept all the time, just waking up to demand food or when her diaper needed changing. Red wished fervently she'd keep Cassie a little busier. Red was a little surprised to find out changing diapers was his job. But since it was the only time Cassie would let him touch his babe, he got to liking it.

He also gave Susannah her first real bath. He sneaked her

out of the bedroom late one afternoon when Cassie was napping and spent a cheerful hour washing Susannah in carefully warmed water by the fire and telling her all about the ranch. Susannah went so far as to open her eyes just a slit on one occasion, and Red saw that they were a light blue just like his. He enjoyed that for a moment because Cassie's eyes were a dark, shining brown, before he remembered that none of his blood flowed in little Susannah's veins. Then he decided if he wanted to think she looked one tiny bit like him, he'd just do it and that was that.

He had Susannah back in her bed before Cassie woke up. Red was relieved he hadn't gotten caught. "I've created a monster."

Cassie kept nagging him and finding fault with everything he did for her. When Red confessed about the bath, she had some choice comments about his handling of the situation, even though the little'un had obviously survived and was clean and sweet-smelling in Cassie's arms.

Red kept telling himself that this might be part of those riotous emotions Seth had warned him about. He wanted to talk to Seth about it. He wanted to talk to someone about it before the walls closed in around him. He thought at this very moment he heard the roof creaking under the weight of Cassie's constant emotional turmoil.

Red willed the weather to clear. The sleet that had locked him and Cassie inside together while Susannah was born had changed over to snow. There was no snow like a Montana mountain snow, and this looked like a prime example of nature's worst.

Red struggled out to check his cattle every day. He'd found most of them placidly waiting out the storm in a sheltered canyon just as he'd expected, but there were always a few idiots who wallowed their way into trouble, broke through the frozen creek, or hurt themselves slipping on ice.

He'd found one steer with a broken leg and found one calf born out of season. He was able to rescue the calf and reunite it with its frantic mother. The steer couldn't be saved, so Red shot it and dragged its carcass back to the house, wearing all the ginger out of old Buck in the process. Then he'd had the steer to skin and butcher and the brown and white spotted hide to tan.

That, plus the barnyard chores, kept him busy because he was battling five-foot drifts and whipping winds every step of the way. Then he'd get inside as quickly as he could, even though he wanted to drag his heels, and there would be Cassie, ranting at him for abandoning her.

The blizzard lasted three days. When the snow stopped, the storm seemed to ease inside Cassie, too. Red came inside from watering Rosie one afternoon about sunset and found Cassie dressed and at the fireplace cooking.

He shut the door quickly to keep the heat inside, and she whirled around to greet him with a big smile on her face. Red was struck by the smile. It wasn't the beautiful, serene smile he'd come to expect from his demure little wife, and it sure as certain wasn't the perpetual scowl that he'd learned she was capable of in the last three days. It was a smile full of joy and sass.

Cassie's eyes snapped with pleasure at seeing him. She hurried over to him and started unwrapping the strips of leather that held on his cowhide robe. "You'd better plan on building some kind of entryway so the winter wind doesn't come straight into the house. It gets twenty degrees colder every time that door opens."

"Good idea." Red was struck by how much that would help. Why hadn't he thought of it? "Should you be out of bed? I don't want you to overdo it."

She fussed at him, tugged at the frozen leather, and shooed him toward a chair facing the fire. "Sit down and let me help you with your boots. Your fingers are near frozen. Poor man to be out in such weather. The least I can do is help you warm up."

She had his outer clothes off in a minute, then she studied his face for a long second. "You're going to frostbite your nose if you're not careful. Here, let me warm your face." She laid her open hands over his cheeks, and the warmth of her touch made his skin sting.

Red stirred under her touch. "No sense both of us being cold, Cass. Let me sit by the fire. I'll be fine in a few minutes."

She ignored his protests and touched her thumbs to his nose. "Just sit still and let me help you."

Red almost reached for her hands and pushed her aside, so alarmed was he at the chill she might be catching, but he thought of the change in her from the china doll to the shrew to whoever she was now and decided he'd just mind her for a bit.

It really did make Red's face feel better to have Cassie's hands on him, and on a sudden impulse, he pulled her onto his lap. "There, warm my face from there, darlin'."

Cassie squeaked with surprise, but after a second of forgetting where her hands were as she flapped them at him, she returned them to his cheeks.

"This feels great, Cassie. Thank you. Are you sure it's okay for you to be up?"

Cassie shrugged. "I woke up from my afternoon nap feeling restless, so I took it a step at a time and got up. I'll quit if I get tired and dump everything right back on you." She gave him an impudent grin and raised one hand to lay it on his forehead.

"I'm fine now. I've been thawing out single-handedly for years, you know."

Cassie nodded. "I know." She left her hands right where they were. "But you've got white spots on your cheeks. I noticed them yesterday, too. I've never seen them before. It's a terrible cold day, isn't it?"

"As bad as it gets, I reckon."

"And you've been out with the cattle even in this blizzard."

"The worst is over. And all this snow will fill the creeks and ponds in the spring."

Cassie bobbed her chin silently as she studied his face. She lifted her hands away. "It's better, just red now. I've seen frostbite, Red. It's nothing to fool around with."

"It's worst on fingers and toes, and I'm careful with them."

Cassie smiled. "Good for you. Now let me up so I can get your supper finished." She pressed her hands on his shoulders.

His hands, which had been resting lightly around her waist, tightened. He could have sworn they did it of their own accord because he didn't remember thinking it through. And he definitely didn't plan in advance to kiss her.

Red hadn't done much kissing in his life. But somehow, with Cassie, he found a surprising talent for the activity. At least he thought so if Cassie's response was any indication. Her arms wrapped around his neck and her head tilted just enough so their noses didn't bump, and she settled herself firmly against him, or at least she didn't object when he urged her close. He wasn't sure who was moving first because they were both going exactly the same way. He thought maybe, just maybe, they were both the most talented smoochers who ever lived. He'd have liked to study the question more thoroughly, but Susannah picked that moment to start hollering from in the bedroom.

Cassie leaped off his lap as if a lightning bolt had struck her. She hustled from the room without a backward glance and went to fetch the baby. She came out with the squirming bundle in her arms and a smile big enough to light up a long Montana winter night on her face.

She didn't look at him and he experienced a pang of jealousy, until he decided that she was *not* looking at him too thoroughly and just maybe she was disconcerted by what had passed between them.

Montana Rose

"Take this chair." He stood. "I want you and Susannah to be warm while she eats. I'll get supper, and tomorrow I'm gonna build you a rocking chair."

"Oh, Red." Cassie looked up at him, and the pink flush on her cheeks told him he was right about her embarrassment. She seemed to forget it now that he'd turned her attention. "You're so busy. You don't need to do another thing for me. I'll get supper."

"Sit, woman." Red lifted the chair and set it back down with a firm *crack*.

Cassie reacted by smiling at him. "Yes, sir. If you insist. I was going to make one of the steaks you brought in from the steer."

"I can do steaks," Red said. "Were you going to use the spit in the fireplace?"

Cassie shook her head. "I'd planned to fry them."

"Let me show you how we eat 'em on a cattle drive. It's primitive but it's good. Cattle drive cookin' is about all I know besides eggs and ham."

Cassie sat, dividing her attention between the baby and Red's cooking efforts. He had the sizzling steaks ready by the time Susannah was done and well burped. Cassie changed the baby's diaper while Red moved the crib out near the fire and debated with Cassie about how close it should be. Then the two of them sat and ate with the baby lying nearby, kicking and making an occasional little noise.

Susannah got bored and fell asleep. Red noticed Cassie's eyes growing heavy. He insisted she go back to bed, and although she protested, he won the round and settled her and the baby in the back room.

He cleaned up the kitchen without paying attention to his work. He was busy reliving Cassie warming his face with her hands. And with her lips.

He realized that, with Cassie at his side, he could learn to love the bitter Montana winter.

❧

Belle struggled to her feet after milking the cow. The animal was as round as Belle and would have her calf around the same spring date as Belle got herself her last child. She swore to herself it would be the last.

God, please let it be a girl.

Anthony chose that moment to stroll into the barn from the bitter outside. The man was a living, breathing, walking, talking testament to the general worthlessness of men—Red Dawson notwithstanding. Coming close enough to see how awkward she was, fat with their child, Anthony never so much as offered her a hand, and he certainly didn't say he'd do the milking. The rat didn't even offer to carry the bucket of milk.

Belle didn't snap at him as she would have at one time. Making a serious effort, she kept the scowl off her face. Instead, she smiled. "Let's walk back to the house and talk about what we're going to name the baby. There should be hot coffee and I...uh...*we* could use a cup." She could use the coffee, because she'd been freezing in the bitter cold of the barn and had been outside working all morning. Two hours before breakfast, and now two hours since. She had three more hours to go before time for the noon meal.

Anthony, on the other hand, had gotten out of bed to eat then had gone back to sleep for a while. He claimed his back would fail him completely if he got up and moving around too early in that cold little cabin. And it was too cold to sit under the Husband Tree or atop the house.

She mentioned none of that. She was a changed woman. A woman trying to do her best to be a good wife. As if doing all the work didn't make her good enough.

Sorry, Lord. I didn't mean to let slip with evil, unwifely thoughts.

At least, with the gap snowed shut, Anthony hadn't been able to go to town. Which saved him wheedling a dollar out of her. Of course that meant he was underfoot all the time. His absence was well worth the dollar she gave him twice a week.

She didn't say that either. But oh, how she wanted to. Inhaling slowly to regain her self control, she smiled at Anthony. "Now then, about the baby. . ."

"Her name will be Caterina. It was my ma's name and it'll be my child's if it's a girl. It's likely a useless hope that you can birth a son. I'd prefer it but I hold out little hope. If it's a boy, it will be named after me—Antonio."

"Antonio is your real name?" This was beyond bad that she'd never known. She'd always thought it was Anthony.

"Yes, I adopted an American form of it and my son can, too, but I am named for my father and now my son will be named for me."

God, please let it be a girl. Please, Lord. Please, please, please.

"Those names will be fine." Caterina was no decent name for a child. And if, God forbid, she had a son—*God, please let it be a girl*—she would do her best to train him up to be less useless than the average man and she'd call him Tony. She realized she was assuming Anthony would be dead and would have no say in the child's name. There were, of course, no guarantees. It was most certainly a sin for her to hope against hope.

They reached the house and entered.

Sarah was hard at work on dinner. She had a stew cooking, savory and warm.

Belle smiled at her daughter and handed over the milk.

"Thanks, Ma. Coffee's hot." Sarah poured a cup, giving Anthony a doubtful smile. The child had to work on her false politeness.

Belle hoped her own attempts at being nice were more successful.

"We've just been talking about the baby. Anthony wants the name Caterina if it's a girl and Antonio if it's a boy."

"You think you might have a boy?" Sarah frowned little furrows into her forehead. She pulled the cloth out they used to strain the milk and worked as she talked.

"Most likely not," Anthony sneered. "Your mother doesn't seem able to produce a proper male child."

Sarah's eyes narrowed. "Those are weird names. Can't we call her something normal, like Elizabeth or Ann?"

"It's settled." Anthony took the cup from Sarah as she extended it toward Belle.

Sarah rolled her eyes behind Anthony's back and poured another cup.

It was moments like this that Belle remembered clearly why she'd never wasted much time talking with her husband. It was a useless pastime.

"Thanks." Belle accepted her cup of coffee. "The dinner smells great. You've got it on early enough that it can simmer a long while. It will taste perfect this cold day."

"Sarah, go outside. I need to have a long talk with your ma." Anthony looked at Belle and she shuddered, though she tried to hide it. She knew that look. Where was her skillet?

Sarah glanced at Belle.

"Go on, honey. We just need to. . .talk. . .a bit more." Belle spotted the cast iron, within easy grasp. Anthony was no match for her. They'd been through this before when he was snowed in overly long. Sure she was his wife, but being polite only went so far. Maybe instead of swinging it at his head, she'd aim for his back. As long as he used it for an excuse to avoid chores, he might as well really be hurt there.

Most likely she wouldn't need it at all. Anthony could usually be cowed with a dark look and a cutting remark or two.

As soon as she calmed him down, be it with or without the use of cast iron, she'd go back to being the very soul of kindness.

Anthony smiled and took a step toward her.

Belle decided then and there that she hated winter.

Town didn't hold much attraction for her, but she hated being trapped away from it because it kept Anthony far too close at hand. Two dollars a week was money well spent.

Anthony was soon sitting, disgruntled, in the house by himself. But after she'd properly discouraged the idiot, she'd said good-bye on her way out to work, real friendlylike.

CHAPTER 27

Red loved being forced to stay near Cassie and the baby. He could become a real layabout given time, because he was drawn to the house constantly by an eager wish to check on his girls.

Cassie occasionally wished aloud that she could tell Muriel about the baby. Then she'd burst into tears. But mostly she seemed delighted to be alone with their little family.

The three of them shared a simple Christmas together.

Red got Cassie's rocking chair done in time for it to be her gift.

She knitted him a thick scarf to cover his face and he teased her about liking her warming him better. She told him impertinently that she had enough to do without that troublesome chore, and he chased her around the room. Cassie laughed out loud as they played.

"Your sassy mouth makes me want to kiss you." He caught her by the waist. "You know that, Cass. So you must want a kiss."

"I most certainly do." She giggled as he kissed her soundly.

Susannah's eyes were wide open now, and the sparkling blue

that Red had loved started to turn darker. Red lamented that she didn't have his eyes.

Cassie snorted. "I hope not. Griff would roll over in his grave."

He kissed her every time she teased him, and like any wise wife, she teased him often.

Red shivered as he came inside from evening chores. He saw the flames jump in their fireplace, and Cassie, setting the table for supper while she held Susannah in her arms, turned away from him to shelter the baby from the blast of cold. He knew he had to face the cold, hard job of building on.

"I'm going to start on that entry room tomorrow morning, Cass honey. I've been putting it off because it's so slick, with that layer of ice under everything—figured I'd break a leg trying to chop down trees. But this last snow has covered it deep and I've got some traction. I can get into the woods safely now. What do you think? How big should it be?"

Once the icy wind was blocked away, Cassie turned back with her generous flashing smile. "I'm sure you know best, Red." She held Susannah against her chest, wrapped in a warm blanket. Red could just see his precious daughter's dark hair peeking out of the top of the blanket.

"You're not being submissive again, are you?" Red narrowed his eyes, fighting to keep the grin off his face.

"Most certainly not." Cassie sniffed at him, as if obedience was the furthest thing from her mind. But truth be told, she was a sweet little thing and minded him almost too much of the time. These days though, Red decided being easygoing was just her nature. Since she could be pretty sassy in fun, Red decided he liked her obedience well enough.

They ate a thick stew Cassie had made. She'd been a really

good cook from the first. And now, with Susannah so small, Cassie didn't clamor for her outside chores so much. Red went to the fireplace and thawed while he considered his pretty much perfect life.

Cassie settled the sleeping baby in the crib then moved back and forth between the bedroom and kitchen. She pushed a chair up close to the fire for Red. She grinned down at him. "You need my help warming up."

Smiling, Red let her lay her pretty hands on his cold cheeks without a second of hesitation. As they stood there, so connected, so warm, Red remembered his surety that when he married Cassie he'd been committing a sin.

"You know God put us together, don't you, Cass honey?"

She'd been focusing on resting her hands on his cold skin. Now she raised her eyes to meet his. "He did, didn't He? Who could have figured such a thing in the middle of all that madness at the funeral?" Then Cassie wrinkled her nose. "You did your best to escape your fate, as I remember. Muriel had to practically drag you back to me."

Laying his hands gently over hers, he pulled them away from his face and entwined their fingers, urging her down onto his lap. "I couldn't see God in the choice I made that day."

Cassie's forehead crinkled just a bit, and Red knew that pinched her feelings.

"You want to know the main reason why?"

Doubtful, Cassie said, "Yes. Tell me why. What made you want to run for the hills when every other man in Divide was trying to run off with me?"

"It was because I wanted to marry you so badly." He slid his arms around her waist.

Jumping but not able to escape, Cassie said, "What? Why would that make you run?"

"I told you once I didn't think I should marry you, but I

wanted to something fierce, remember?"

Cassie nodded.

"I'd noticed you from the first time I saw you in town. Which was probably the first day you and Griff moved here." Red slid his hand up Cassie's arm and to her face until he cradled her smooth, pink cheek in one of his rough, calloused hands.

"You did?" Cassie seemed pleased with that, judging from the way she kissed him.

"I set out to avoid you as much as possible because you were so beautiful and you seemed so sweet. I wanted to talk to you and spend time with you and I knew that my feelings were all wrong for a married woman."

"I never knew. You spoke to me a few times."

Smiling, Red said, "That's 'cuz I couldn't resist a few times." He pulled her closer and kissed her more soundly, almost dazed with the full realization that he'd ended up with this almost impossibly beautiful woman in his life.

"Griff wouldn't let me talk to people. He said it was too familiar and not ladylike."

No surprise there that Griff had found a way to hurt her. But Red was in no mood to talk about Lester Griffin right now. "I believe that God has prepared a woman for me from birth to be my life partner. I settled that in my heart that God would provide that woman for me or I'd live my life alone."

"And you didn't think that could be me?" Cassie jabbed him in the chest with a pointy finger and sniffed at him.

That made him happy, that she wasn't going to pout or be hurt. "You know just as well as I do that it was a crazy way to pick a wife. Being the wife in the middle of the picking, you were none too happy about it either, as I recall."

"I'd fully decided that if God really loved me, He'd open up Griff's grave and let me join him." Cassie leaned in and kissed him a quick peck on the lips. "But God had a much better idea."

Red pulled her back and deepened the kiss. "He did indeed." Then he kissed her again, and she melted against him as surely as the spring sun melts the winter snow.

When the kiss ended, he pulled away enough to see her flushed cheeks and shining, slightly swollen lips. Their eyes met and held. "Marry me, Cass honey. I believe God chose you for me and prepared the two of us, from birth, to be together. I love you so much. Will you marry me and be my wife?"

This question wasn't about a promise made to God. Red had made that promise months ago and had from that moment fully honored those vows and intended to for the rest of his life. But right now he was asking for more. He saw Cassie's expression and knew she understood. He knew she'd say the words. He knew from the very beginning she'd have submitted to him. But finally Red knew that she'd be eager, not just obedient. His heart sped up as he waited.

She didn't make him wait long. "I love you, too, Fitzgerald O'Neill Dawson." Wrapping her arms around his neck, she said against his lips, "Yes, I want to marry you with all my heart."

The stew was set aside so it didn't scorch.

Susannah slept peacefully as if she knew her parents were hoping for some time alone.

On that cold winter night, in a dark but warm cave, Red and Cassie Dawson became, at last, fully and beautifully married.

Red built a neat little log shanty to block the wind around their front door.

Cassie stayed inside like a fragile houseplant, when she wanted to be outside helping him. But Susannah demanded her time, and the weather wasn't fit for a baby. Cassie worried that Red was exposing himself to the harsh winter. He held her and reassured her and distracted her from her worry.

She knew he wasn't really being hurt by the bitter temperature, but her heart was so full of love for her husband and her baby and her life that the happiness seemed to overflow in wild emotions with little provocation.

Cassie vowed to him that she'd never ask for anything again.

Red thanked her profusely for giving him a suggestion and told her she was the smartest woman in the state of Montana.

She reminded him with some sass that there weren't that many women in Montana so that wasn't so very much of a compliment. When she talked like that to him, he tended to laugh and chase her around the room and pull her into his arms, so she did her best to talk like that often.

When the tiny new room proved to keep the soddy warmer, Cassie made a point of reminding Red, with a snippy tone, that it had been her idea from the start.

The flashing precious newness of their young love deepened, and they expressed it in all the ways there were.

By the time winter stretched into spring, Red and Cassie had reason to hope that their family might grow larger. When that time came, Red teased her, the baby had every right to resemble him.

When the weather was finally decent for them to go to town, Red had his hands full battling heavy spring rains and a thaw that flooded all the creeks. He spent hours every day checking his spring calf crop. He and Cassie sowed a garden, although Cassie protested that it should be her job alone. He promised she'd do her share when it was warm enough that Susannah could lie on a blanket outside. Now she had to snatch free moments during Susannah's nap time and run inside frequently to check on the growing baby.

It was the end of May when the water finally subsided and they made the time for a trip to town one Sunday morning. Red didn't want to be away from the farm for two days, so they left very early, planning a one-day trip. Cassie fashioned a sling across her chest and she carried Susannah in it while Red carried her. They even galloped, because Buck was feeling his oats after a long, idle winter. The baby slept through the whole trip.

When they arrived in town, the folks were overjoyed to have their preacher back.

Muriel wept over Susannah and presented Cassie and Red with a small mountain of baby clothes she'd sewn over the winter. The Jessups, the Dawsons' neighbors, had ridden to their place and seen that the baby had come safely. Then the bachelors braved the weather and gotten to town and told everyone there was a baby girl at the Dawson place, so the clothes were adorned with lace and ribbon. Muriel declared herself to be Susannah's grandmother so fervently that no one considered for a moment objecting.

The baby was passed from hand to hand among the women. Even the men hovered near to look at her. Red realized that a baby was even more of a rarity than a woman, and he noticed with pride that Cassie generously let the people enjoy Susannah to their hearts' content.

He thought of all the questions he'd had for Seth four months ago and laughed at himself for surviving a childbirth and a baby and a new mother with that minimal advice.

The church service went well, and the whole group made plans to baptize Susannah as soon as Parson Bergstrom rode through town.

Norman York pulled Red and Cassie aside after services. "I have been waiting all winter to tell you that I sold your Bible for a shocking amount of money. Now, I know I told you I'd save it if

I could, but you weren't here and I had to make a decision. I was offered enough for it that it covered everything and left money besides."

Norm told them how much cash they had in the bank, and Cassie's knees gave out. Only Red's quick thinking kept her from sinking all the way to the ground.

"I had already sent a lot of things back East on the same wagon that took the Bible. They sold first because my brother spent a long time finding the best buyer for the Bible. It's extremely rare and it will end up in a museum. So most of your things are gone, Cassie. I'd have saved them back for you if I'd had any idea of the money I could make."

Red's ears were ringing from the windfall of money. He hadn't gathered his thoughts enough to say anything, when Cassie whispered in his ear. All the confusion lifted as he turned to the wonderful woman he'd gotten railroaded into marrying. "Are you sure?"

Cassie nodded. "There'll be enough left to buy the title to the mountain valley you've been grazing."

"More than enough." Red turned to face the milling people in the general store and said loudly, "I think it's time this town had a church."

A flurry of excitement swept through the God-fearing people of Divide. The sedate good-byes turned into a time of praise and worship as they all made plans for Divide's first church.

There was also a letter from Parson Bergstrom that said he was making arrangements for Red to be named to their mission society. It would take awhile to be approved, but soon he'd be allowed to officiate at weddings. If Divide kept growing, there just might be a few of those in the future.

After church, Red arranged for some of his neighbors to trade work with him to drive his steers into town to sell, and Muriel relaxed her rules about Sunday work to allow the Dawsons and several others from out of town to fill orders for supplies. Red also sold all of Harriet's grown piglets and, by doing that, ensured that they'd be having some company in the next few weeks when people came to pick up their hogs.

All in all, they did a winter's worth of worshipping and settled all their affairs in the few hours they were in town.

Or at least they'd settled everything until Wade Sawyer came strutting into the general store.

CHAPTER 28

Y ou're sure pretty now that your belly isn't big with Griff's whelp."

Cassie nearly jumped out of her skin when she heard the familiar voice.

Wade's voice slurred. "I should have had you when you were between men."

He staggered a little as he leaned over Cassie, and she smelled the sharp, stale odor of whiskey on his breath. She stepped away from him, but he snaked out his arm and pulled her hard against him. "I've yet to have my turn with you, china doll. I reckon I'll have at you before we're finished."

Red was there before Cassie could even look around for help. He pulled Wade's arm away from her and tucked her behind his back. "You're drunk, Sawyer. And you're insulting my wife. Go somewhere and sleep it off."

Peeking around Red's stalwart body, Cassie saw that the winter hadn't been kind to Wade. Her winter had been so splendid that she'd gone long stretches without even thinking of the horror of Wade's visit to the ranch. Now it all came rushing back.

His eyes were streaked with veins and red-rimmed from too much drink. A beard grizzled his sunken cheeks, and behind the beard, his teeth were yellowed and stained. She saw in his soulless eyes the knowledge a man gained from long nights spent in debauchery. Cassie shuddered when she thought of what her life might have become if Red hadn't claimed her that day.

She leaned fully against the strength of Red's back and whispered so softly only he could hear her, "I love you."

Red's hand came around her back and rested on her waist for a brief moment, telling her that he'd heard. Then his full attention was back on Wade.

Cassie was taken by surprise by her beloved husband's voice. She'd expected anger. Instead she heard only kindness.

"Wade, you've got to get yourself straightened out. Talk to me. Let's just sit and talk. You're wasting your life. You don't really want Cassie. She's my wife and we love each other. No man wants a woman who doesn't want him. What you think is longing for her is just part of the emptiness that's inside you. God can fill that emptiness. Forget about Cassie and start worrying about your soul."

Red took a step closer to Wade. "You're still a young man. You've got plenty of years to find a wife and have a family. You've got a ranch. You need sons to pass that ranch on to. You need daughters to soften your heart with their smiles. Don't throw your best years away on drink and the Golden Butte women and hate. Please talk to me. I can tell you about how faith in Jesus can help you find your way down the right path."

Red laid his hand on Wade's shoulder.

What she saw in Wade astounded her. Longing. Wade's eyes were riveted on Red's, and in his expression, she saw a longing that ran so deep it bordered on desperation. For the first time she felt something other than fear and revulsion when she looked at Wade Sawyer. She felt love. She understood what the Bible meant when it said, "Love your enemies. . .pray for them which. . .persecute you." She found the compassion to pray for Wade.

"Please," Red said, "you've got intelligence and strength and a good life waiting for you. And if that life isn't on your father's ranch, I'll help you find a life somewhere else." Red's voice dropped so low Cassie could barely hear it. "I know how cruel your father is. You need to get away from him for good. Let's just talk and decide where you can find a new home. I'll do everything I can to help you find a new path."

Wade's eyes shifted from Red to the floor and back to Red, and for a second Cassie could see in Wade's eyes the willingness to search for a better life.

There were still people in the store. The worship had ended but the fellowship had stretched into the early afternoon. No one had wanted it to end.

Wade took an uncertain step forward toward Red. Then suddenly something visceral and cruel slammed down between Wade and all the people who stood before him. Cassie believed she'd seen with her own eyes a battle between the Lord and Satan fought within Wade's soul.

He slapped Red's hand aside. "Save your preachin' for someone who wants it, Dawson. And enjoy your wife for as long as you can keep her. She's a woman who needs pretty things around her and I can give 'em to her. She's for sale and I can outbid you any time I choose."

Wade wheeled drunkenly away from them and left the store.

Cassie was so close behind Red, she heard him whisper, "He needs You so desperately, Lord. Help me to never give up on him."

She wrapped her arms around Red's back and hugged up close against him. "Amen."

Red held her arms tight around his waist and they stood silently as the tension eased from the room.

Finally a squall from Susannah broke the silence. Red retrieved his baby from Leota Pickett.

As Red hoisted Susannah high in the air to make her squeal with pleasure, Cassie heard Maynard Pickett, Leota's husband, say, "He's dangerous, Red. He was gone all winter. After you swore out that complaint against him, no one saw him again till just a few weeks ago. Since he's been back, he's gone pure crazy. He isn't staying at the ranch and I haven't seen him sober. You watch your back and keep close to Cassie."

Red nodded and glanced her way.

She held his eyes to make sure he knew she had heard. She wanted his protection but she didn't want him to keep the truth from her.

Red sighed.

Then Susannah distracted him by kicking him in the stomach a few times and yanking on his hair.

Red settled her on his shoulder and came back across the room. "I'm sorry you had to hear such vile talk from a man, Cassie. No lady should be subjected to that."

"I'll not accept your apology. Wade Sawyer is the only one who can apologize for the way he just acted." Cassie laid her hand on Red's arm. "I thought for just a moment that he was listening to you. I thought maybe you could reach him."

Red nodded. "Muriel asked us to lunch. Then I want to get started back." He looped his arm around her waist and, with his other arm hugging Susannah, moved around the room saying good-bye to his friends.

❧

"They had a girl?" Belle smiled at Muriel. She visited while Seth filled their order.

Belle knew she shouldn't have ridden to town. She was due to give birth any day. But that was also the reason she *had* to come in. The gap had just now melted open and she needed her larders full before the baby came. Getting to town afterward was hard.

"The most beautiful little girl." Muriel's voice softened and her expression made her look twenty years younger.

Belle wondered why Muriel and Seth never had children, but it was too personal of a question to ask.

Seth came back into the store and hoisted another crate. "This is the last of your supplies, Belle."

Normally, Belle would have worked alongside the storekeeper, but Seth had flatly refused to let Belle lift the heavy boxes. Truth be told, when Sarah was born, Belle wouldn't have taken Seth's orders. But she was older now, nearly thirty. Picking up those boxes would have been a strain.

Belle knew she'd started leaving more and more for the girls, too. It wasn't fair to burden them. No more babies, ever. Never ever. *Please, God, let this be a girl.*

She thanked Muriel for the coffee, paid for her supplies, and went out after Seth.

Seth took the two steps down from the board sidewalk that lined Divide's Main Street. Belle stepped out and nearly fell when she saw Anthony. . .coming out of the Golden Butte.

He looked across the hundred or so feet separating them.

The woman on his arm giggled and dashed back inside.

Last fall, Anthony would have slunk away in sullen silence. Now, after a winter of Belle trying to be kinder to him and bringing him into the family, he tipped his hat with narrow, defiant eyes, then turned and followed the woman back inside.

"Belle, why don't you just kick him out?" Seth set the last crate in her wagon bed and fastened the back end with the rattle of metal on wood.

Belle's mind had been a thousand miles away—well, in all honestly, more like a hundred or so feet away—awash in fury and humiliation and contempt. "I spent the winter trying to figure out how to be a better wife to him." She'd never normally have discussed such a thing with anyone, let alone Seth Bates. But what difference did it make? Anthony's cheating was going on with no effort to hide it. "I've been *nice* to that polecat."

"There's divorce." Seth's grim voice with its shocking suggestion drew Belle's gaze away from the still-swinging doorway to the Golden Butte. "You don't have to let him live on your ranch. You don't have to put up with his low-down ways."

"Divorce? How am I supposed to manage that?" Belle thought of the lawyer she'd spoken to before she married Anthony. It had required a grueling trip to Helena because no lawyers were closer. It gave ownership of her ranch to her pa if she died, and her pa had promised to leave it as an inheritance to her daughters. It had been a strange thing to arrange, but a few run-ins with Gerald had scared her enough that she'd decided she needed to protect her children in the event of her death. The lawyer had written up the will and she'd forced Anthony to sign before she'd agreed to marry him.

"I don't know how it works. But I've heard of such a thing."

She knew such things as divorce occurred, but it was a disgrace. Vows were taken before God, and to break those vows was a terrible sin. Plus, Belle knew enough about it that she knew Anthony would have to cooperate, and he'd never give up his two dollars a week. No, divorce wasn't possible.

Her face burning with anger and embarrassment, she swung up onto the buckboard, her stomach making her awkward, and slapped the reins against her horses' backs. She left town far behind before she let herself cry. She could hate Anthony. She could hate Seth even for daring to comment on this shame in front of her. But that was all a waste of time when the real reason she'd ended up like this was because she was a fool.

God, what's missing in me that I keep marrying weaklings? Am I so awful no man with a backbone will have me?

Worse yet, had strong, decent men wanted her, but the missing part of her *needed* a weak man who could be bullied?

Her horses knew the way home, and it was a good thing. The loaded wagon rattled along as tears blinded her. Her head ached with the shame. Her whole body ached as the tears flowed and sobs wracked her.

She'd have never cried like this in front of her girls. And she'd have never let Anthony see her. Pride wouldn't allow it. But she wasn't crying over him. He was lower than a snake's belly, and he had no power to hurt her feelings. She cried over her own stupidity. She cried over what was broken in her to have married so poorly over and over again.

She'd been on the trail nearly two hours, wallowing in her grief, when she realized the ache that seemed to be twisting her body wasn't coming from disappointment in herself.

It was the baby.

The shock of realizing her laboring had started brought Belle out of the self-pity. She rested her hand on her stomach. It was early yet. She'd have time to get home.

What would become of her if she gave birth alone in the wild country? It was a three-hour ride home on a fast horse. She'd be more like six hours driving the wagon. She'd left long before first light to get this trip done in one day. It was closer to ride back to Divide, but not by much. She had to go home. Her girls needed her.

And she needed her girls. Lindsay had helped bring Sarah when Lindsay was only five years old.

Panic nearly took hold. She considered unhitching the wagon and riding one of the horses, but that suited no purpose. She had about three hours to get home, and that was long enough. Why, the baby wouldn't come much before morning if things went as usual. She slapped the reins and made the team step up their pace. With the heavily laden wagon, they couldn't do much better than they were now.

It was a long time before the pangs came again. But they came. Belle prayed for her little unborn daughter, whispered that God would keep them both safe.

The cool spring air gusted around her and the horses kept up their fast walk, the clomp of hoofbeats echoing in the sunset.

The three hours she had estimated shrunk to two. The contractions kept coming, a bit closer each time. Belle saw the rise ahead, the long, treacherous curve of the trail climbing up into the gap that led home. In another hour she'd make it. Not home, but through that gap, on her own land. That was home enough for her. She just might unhitch the wagon at that point, if the pangs hadn't gotten too hard.

As she struggled to move her horses along, she heard something behind her. A rider. She turned back to see Anthony coming at a fast lope. Belle's spirits lifted to know she wouldn't be out here alone any longer. Even Anthony would be better than being alone.

As he drew near, she turned. "Anthony. The baby's coming. Thank goodness you've come. I need help."

Anthony pulled his horse to a walk as he came up beside her. "What can I do?"

"You can just be with me. I'm a long way from home. I'm scared."

"Belle Tanner Svendson O'Rourke Santoni scared of something? I doubt it." He kicked his horse and picked up speed.

"Wait!"

Anthony turned to glare at her, as if she'd asked him to help with chores.

"I need you to stay with me. What if the baby comes before—"

A pain hit, cutting off her speech. This one was stronger than the others. She knew her body. She knew how it felt as the birth came. She still had time, but what if she couldn't drive the team any longer? It would be hard to keep going when the time drew near. She'd need to ride the brake hard all the way down the other side of the gap.

"You've never needed me, Belle. Why should you start now?"

Belle couldn't answer until the pains faded. "Anthony, I have *always* needed you. You're the one who refused to be part of this family. I could use your help every day." She thought of how much he could help. She saw him, sitting straight and strong on his horse. His *back* was fine. But they'd been all through that a hundred times. Repeating it wasn't of any use.

"Oh, you've maybe wanted to make me help on *your* ranch. You've maybe wished for another cowhand you could work like your daughters. But that's not *need*. You don't *need* a husband, Belle. You need a *slave*. I've got too much pride to work as your slave." His voice went beyond contempt and anger. He sounded as if he hated her. His eyes told her that he definitely did. He kicked his horse and tore off at a gallop.

Yes, he'd always been lazy.

Yes, he'd always been a cheat.

But why would he hate her? Would he really be so cruel as to abandon her in pain on the trail?

"At least send one of the girls!"

Anthony laughed, his voice carrying back to her on the wind. "If I see one of your little slaves, I'll send her."

Would he possibly refuse to send help? She'd kept him fed and in spending money for a year now. Belle's spirit felt crushed as if the pains were at work on her soul. She felt the tears come again, the tears that had tormented her on this long ride home. But she didn't let them fall. She had no energy for them.

She clicked to the horses and pushed them on.

God, please have him send the girls.

Her girls would help her.

Did she really work them too hard? Did she treat them like slaves?

She began slow, constant prayer, stopping only when the agony cut her off from her thoughts. When she ran out of prayers, she began reciting all of the Bible verses she knew, and they were many. The Bible was the only book the Tanner family owned. Why, she'd taught her girls to read using it. They took turns memorizing verses during their Sunday services.

The pains came faster. She began the slow uphill climb toward the mountain gap. She remembered Seth's words about divorce. No, never. Surely Anthony would die soon and save her the shame.

Nearly another hour passed as she made the twisting trip to the crest of the hill. The trip back down would be much faster.

The pains came harder. They hadn't yet entered that horrible constant stage she knew to expect near the end. She could make it. She could get home.

She thought of the tortuous trail that descended into her valley. She had to ride the wagon brake hard all the way down to keep from overturning on the sharply winding trail. She wasn't sure she had the strength.

The wagon descended. Belle pulled hard on the wooden brake handle to keep it from running away and harming the horses. Her hands threatened to slip off the brake when a pain was upon her. She went down and down, the trail narrow, snaking. Her hand clutched the brake. She threw her body across it, hoping her weight would do what her normally strong hand couldn't. She made the first turn only a bit too fast. The wagon clattered. The horses snorted, complaining about the dangerous wagon forcing them forward at a pace that scared them.

She passed several more treacherous turns without incident,

but it took all of her strength to keep the buckboard under control. Nearly a third of the way down, a spasm hit so hard she nearly collapsed. She slipped forward. If she fell between the horses and the wagon, the wagon would roll over her and kill her.

She clung to the brake as her body seemed intent on tearing her in half.

Picking up speed as her strength waned, the horses whinnied in fear at the clattering wagon now shoving them at a dangerous pace.

A shout pulled her head up.

Someone came around the sharp curve ahead toward her. Lindsay.

Anthony had sent help.

Belle didn't have the strength to pull the horses to a stop. They rolled on past Lindsay. Too fast.

Lindsay drew off to the trailside as the wagon passed her. "Ma, what's wrong?"

Though she asked, Lindsay didn't pause for an answer. She quickly dismounted, lashed her horse's reins to the back of the moving wagon, and sprinted to jump up on the seat. She grabbed the brake, gently moving Belle aside. With Lindsay's strong hand on the controls, the wagon slowed, but it still moved too fast for safety.

"It's the baby. Didn't Anthony tell you?" The wagon seat had no back. Belle struggled to sit upright.

"No." Lindsay bore down on the brake. The last turn was dead ahead, and it was as tight as a hairpin. The wagon couldn't get around it at this speed.

The horses whinnied in fear. Lindsay fought a quiet desperate fight between herself and the mountain and that brake. The wagon slowed a bit. The tight curve ahead came nearer.

Belle's stomach contracted again. There was hardly time to

breathe between the pains now.

The brakes squealed in protest. The horses began throwing their weight on their back feet under Lindsay's skillful handling on the reins. Lindsay's shout even galvanized her own horse to pull against the wagon from behind.

They turned into the curve, still going too fast.

"Lean up the hill, Ma. We can make this, but I need your help."

Belle obeyed. Years of taking charge, doing what had to be done despite the difficulty, were too ingrained to ignore. Belle leaned away from Lindsay.

The wagon tilted. Two wheels came off the ground.

Lindsay yelled at the nervous horses and threw even more weight against the brake.

They rounded the corner and the trail straightened. The wagon banged down onto four wheels.

Still going too fast, Lindsay now could at least make the horses move a bit more briskly and stay ahead of the wagon. She began winning her fight one second at a time.

Finally, the brake caught firmly ahold of the heavily laden wagon. Seconds later they reached the bottom of the mountain trail.

Belle suspected Lindsay normally would have pulled over and given herself and the lathered horses a chance to calm down, but she was a canny girl and she'd already figured out Belle needed to get home. "What did you mean about Anthony telling me?" Lindsay asked.

Belle gasped as the pain let up. "He came past me on the trail. He wouldn't stay. I asked him to send help. When I saw you—" Belle lost her ability to speak again as another storm swept over her beleaguered body.

"He came in the cabin. He served himself supper in front of all of us without saying a word." Lindsay threw Belle a look of such fury that Belle regretted saying anything about Anthony's part in this. "I just knew it was time for you to be coming, so I rode out to keep you company."

Belle's heart broke at Anthony's cruelty. But she set that aside as another pain threatened to tear her apart. A sudden spate of moisture told her the baby had broken through. It wouldn't be long now.

"What can I do to help you, Ma? Can you ride my horse to get yourself home faster?"

"No, it's too late. I wouldn't be able to sit on the horse."

Lindsay slapped the horses with the reins and yelled. They picked up the pace to a trot.

Belle knew they still had a long way to go. The gap was miles away from the cabin. She didn't think she'd make it, but she held on, her fingers white against the buckboard seat.

Lindsay reached her left arm to support Belle's back, holding the reins in her right hand, now that the brake was no longer needed.

"The horses can't keep up this pace all the way home." Belle wouldn't harm her team to save herself. She'd give birth along the trail first. "Not with the wagon loaded."

"We'll go as long as we can. I'm watching 'em. I won't let them overdo. We'll deliver the baby out here if we have to."

Belle focused on the team, trying to keep her weight off Lindsay, trying not to be any more of a burden to her daughter than necessary.

Slave labor. Was it true?

The pains were nearly constant when the cabin finally came in sight.

"Emma!" Lindsay's shout brought Emma and Sarah out of the cabin at a run. Lindsay pulled within inches of the door.

"What's the matter?" Emma came around the back of the wagon, her eyes on Belle.

"Ma's having the baby. Help me get her down." Lindsay wrapped the reins around the brake with lightning movements. Emma threw herself up beside Belle. Lindsay and Emma eased Belle sideways.

Belle did her best to help. The baby pressed to be born.

The girls, including Sarah, nearly carried her into the house.

The commotion brought Anthony's head up from where he lay on his narrow bed. He smirked at Belle then sauntered outside.

The girls lowered her to her bed, and they were in time. Barely. The baby slipped into the world, into the gentle hands of her big sister. It was a girl.

Belle was home. She'd made it home.

But her marriage made it a sad, pathetic excuse for a home.

CHAPTER 29

For the first time since Susannah's birth, Cassie kept something from Red.

She'd been going whole hog, spouting off her ideas and feelings, and it had seemed to suit Red fine. She surely loved doing it. But now she couldn't forget the threat she'd seen in Wade Sawyer's eyes and the cowardly way she'd acted the last time he'd threatened her. She still had nightmares about that cold, wet crevice where she'd cowered. Cassie was determined to never be so helpless again.

Cassie started practicing with her gun.

Red always left the rifle, loaded and ready, hanging over the door. She didn't fire any bullets. Red never left the ranch yard long enough or went far enough for her to believe she could practice without his notice. And he would have missed the bullets. Griff had always been careless about details like that.

But she'd gotten good before. Now she just practiced grabbing it and aiming quick. The gun started to feel comfortable in her hands. She loaded it while she walked, while she ran, while she lay on her belly in the dirt. She studied the yard for

311

shelter should she be caught out, away from the house.

She knew she should tell Red what she was doing, but she didn't want him to make her quit. And she didn't want to listen to him talk about the right and wrong of shooting a man who hadn't made peace with the Lord. . .because she was ashamed of the cowardice driving her.

She was prepared for trouble when she was alone, but as she scratched in the dirt planting a garden, she knew Red was close by and felt perfectly safe.

Safe turned out to be a luxury she couldn't afford, any more than she could afford black silk dresses.

"Cassie honey, stand up slow," Red said stiffly.

Cassie turned to see what had caused the harsh tone, expecting to find him hurt and bleeding. She froze so solid her heart had to struggle to beat.

Red stood in front of Wade Sawyer. Blood trickled down Red's forehead, and his knees wavered slightly as he walked. Cassie saw a noose snared around Red's neck.

Wade held the end of the rope in one hand and his revolver in the other. He sneered. "It's movin' day, china doll. Go fetch your things and come along with old Wade."

Cassie didn't take her eyes off Red's battered face. She slowly got to her feet. Cassie glanced at the house, and Red blinked his eyes and made a nearly invisible move with his head. He seemed to be asking her for time. Maybe time for his head to clear or time to come up with a plan to get them out of this.

Cassie sent a thousand silent prayers for help in the space of a single breath. Then she spoke with quiet authority. "Wade, untie him and quit this nonsense."

Wade didn't react. He seemed to be processing her words, and Cassie decided he was drunk again. Surely if they could bide their time, he'd sober up enough to know what he was doing was madness. Then Wade jerked on the rope he held, nearly knocking Red off balance.

Red staggered slightly to remain standing.

Wade yanked it again.

Red fumbled for the rope tight around his neck and held it in both hands. Cassie noticed him discreetly try to loosen the rope.

Wade was focused on her and seemed oblivious to Red's efforts. Wade cocked his pistol with a sharp *crack*. "Do it, china doll, or Red dies right now." Wade rested the muzzle of his six gun on Red's temple. "How about it? You in the mood to bury another husband?"

Cassie realized she had a choice. She could go into the house as if to pack her things. Once in there, she could get her hands on her gun. Wade was drunk enough that he wouldn't notice her rifle if she came back out with it hidden behind her coat. She had a better than even chance of beating Wade.

She looked at Wade's cruel, lustful face and at the blood streaming from the cut on her precious husband's head and thought, *"The Lord is my light and my salvation; whom shall I fear?"* In that instant Cassie finally knew the difference between cowardice and courage. She was terrified but she didn't go for the gun. *"Whom shall I fear?"*

She trusted her instincts, believing they were directions coming from God. "The last time we talked, Red told you to let go of your hate, Wade. Think about what you're doing. What brought you to this? When I first came to Montana, you were the rich, powerful son of a cattle baron. You were going to inherit a dynasty. You flirted with me but you never threatened to kill Griff or kidnap me. What has happened? What is eating you up inside that changed you into a man who would threaten murder?"

Wade opened his mouth and closed it again.

She remembered the last time she'd given him time to

respond to her and the vicious tightening of the stranglehold he had on Red. She didn't wait. "Have you ever heard that hate destroys the hater? Who do you hate so much, Wade? It can't be Red. He's never done anything to you. And how can it be me? You've aimed your hate at us like a loaded gun, but this can't be about us. Is it your father?"

"No!" Wade exclaimed loudly. "You leave my pa out of this."

He said it so furiously that Cassie thought she'd found the right direction to proceed.

"What did he do to you, Wade? He's a hard man. I'll bet it's difficult to have such a tyrant for a father. Has he ever let you walk your own path? Has he ever shown you any gentleness or affection?"

Wade laughed bitterly. There was a slightly hysterical note to the laughter. "Gentleness is for women. No one but a fool expects mush and petting from his pa."

Cassie saw Wade's hand tighten on the rope. Red had both hands under the noose now and Cassie could see him hold it so it felt tight to Wade but without it cutting off his breathing. Cassie had the distinct impression that Red's wobbly knees were at least partly an act, too. He just needed a little more time.

"Red fusses over Susannah all the time, Wade. A father should hug his child. He should speak of love. Your father may have treated you harshly because he wanted you to be strong, but instead it broke your spirit. You bully people and they back down because of who your *father* is, not because you're a strong man yourself. Bullies think they're strong, but they're very careful to pick on people who are weaker or sneak up behind rather than face them. But Wade, you've gone too far this time. You've faced a man who is stronger than you in the ways that really count. Red has the strength of God on his side, and so do I. We want to live because God has been so good to us in this life and we love serving Him, but we aren't afraid to die."

Cassie gentled her voice. "I will not go with you. We will not submit ourselves to you. But we will be your friends. We will love you."

"You *do not love me.*" Wade was listening. His shocked reaction to her words was evidence.

"Let go of Red and put down the gun. Come inside and talk to us. We *do* love you, Wade. And God loves you. If you could understand how much God loves you and how it makes His heart break to see one of His beloved children turn away from Him, you'd put down that gun and listen to us. You've tried doing it without God, and look where it's brought you. Let us tell you how to put God in charge of your life. If you do, you'll find out what true strength really is."

"You. . .you. . ." Wade shook his head as if to clear it.

Cassie looked at Red. He was ready. He could have pulled himself free of the noose and grabbed the gun from Wade's unsteady hand, but Red had known the difference between cowardice and courage for a long time. He left the rope where it was and gave Wade the chance to choose God.

The love Cassie felt for Red at that moment was almost violent. She prayed and saw Red's lips move. He was praying, too. They both asked for Wade to open his heart and take the first step back from the terrible path he'd traveled for so long.

"You love me?" Wade said it like it was unfathomable. His throat worked, and Cassie thought she saw a sheen of tears in his eyes. She remembered his longing in the Bates' store when Red had talked to him. She knew Wade wanted help. He wanted something better in his life.

He opened his mouth. Then as if no words could come, he closed it again and threw the rope aside and dropped his gun in the dirt. One hand came up to cover his face and he turned away. He began walking, almost stumbling, his shoulders slumped and shaking.

Red glanced at Cassie and she gave him an encouraging nod. He took the noose off his neck and ran after Wade. "She wasn't just saying that to get you to leave." Red lay his hand across the back of Wade's shoulders, and Wade stopped immediately, as if every step was a huge burden he could hardly bear. "Come into the house with us. We'll make you some coffee and a good meal, and we'll talk about how you can find your way back."

"Find my way back. . ." Wade turned to Red and spoke so softly, Cassie could barely hear it. "Back to where?"

She walked over to Wade and rested her arm on his back so she and Red were surrounding him. He was no danger now. "Back to yourself. You've lost the very best of yourself, Wade. Just like I had. And back to God, because He's the one who created you and loves you just the way you are."

"No, not like I am. Maybe once I was someone God could love." Wade shook his head and a single tear trickled down from the corner of his eye.

"Talk with us, Wade. Come meet our daughter and spend the day with us." Cassie urged him to turn and realized she and Red were nearly holding him up. He'd been drinking, but this was about more than the liquor. It was as if Wade had been knocked almost to his knees by words of love.

For the first time, Wade looked at her in a way that didn't frighten her. She smiled, and Red rested his hand on hers, where they met on Wade's trembling shoulders.

Cassie said, "Every one of us has to choose. I had started down the wrong path with my life just like you have."

"You, china doll? You've always been perfect. A man's dream set down in the middle of the wilderness."

"It may have seemed like that because I always acted the part. But the truth is I had no faith in God. I had no courage. I didn't believe in myself any more than you do. Red helped me see I was worthy of God's love. I didn't believe that when

I came to live here. But now I know my willingness to act like the perfect, obedient wife was just me taking the easy way out and letting someone else make all my decisions for me. You and I have a lot in common. Does your father trust you with any part of the ranch?"

"No, he never has. But who can blame him?"

"And does he make you feel stupid when the truth is you've just never been trained?"

"I am stupid. I never do anything the way it's supposed to be done," Wade said humbly.

"That's exactly how Griff treated me. And I think that you saw that, even though you want to believe I'm perfect. You saw a kindred soul who was going through the same thing and you wanted to save me. That's noble, Wade. That's something I respect and admire in you. We reacted differently to being dominated. I became a submissive little coward and you rebelled, defying your father by leaving the ranch and getting mixed up in every evil vice you could think of just to spite him."

"We're nothing the same," Wade said firmly. "You can't compare yourself to someone like me. I've done so many things, it's impossible for me to ever undo them."

"You're right that you can't undo them, but you can start today living your life differently. Come in with us." She knew Wade still had scars on his heart and he'd still have trouble believing in himself. Look how long it had taken her to trust herself and believe in her own worth. But Wade had taken the first step today. He'd stopped sinking deeper in sin and reached up for God. And God could reach all the way down to meet him and help him the rest of the way.

"China doll. . .I. . .I can't go near your baby." Wade looked her in the eye, and for the first time she realized those green eyes that had frightened her could be vulnerable and soft and even kind. "And you can't want me in your home."

"My name is Cassie. Please call me that. And I *welcome* you to our home." She urged him forward. "I have coffee still warm from this morning, and it's only a little early for lunch."

At her urging, Wade started toward the house. Cassie looked over at Red and she saw him nod at her with deep approval. Some of what she'd said had only really become clear to her as she'd talked. She knew God had guided her words, and she'd spoken them for her own benefit as well as Wade's.

They headed for the tiny soddy with the cave bedroom. A giant step down from the lovely home she'd lived in less than a year ago. She could see now that God could use what she'd been through. He could use her to help someone else. The honor of it made her tremble deep inside.

And as she walked, she felt the china doll shatter inside her. Gone forever. And out of the rubble a new woman emerged. Not perfect. Not even close. She was a sinner who struggled and failed and tried anew each day.

But she was also a new woman in Christ. A woman God loved, but even more, a woman worthy of being loved by God.

What had started as a nightmare on that day of Griff's death had become the fulfillment of all her dreams.

Red's hand, resting on top of hers, moved so their fingers entwined. Together they supported Wade and each other. She smiled at her husband, and they helped bear the burden of their new friend. And as she walked, she realized that her whole life had led her to a plan God had all along.

She'd been following a twisting, turning, sometimes treacherous path that had led her straight home.

ABOUT THE AUTHOR

MARY CONNEALY is a Christie Award Finalist. She is the author of the Lassoed in Texas series which includes *Petticoat Ranch*, *Calico Canyon*, and *Gingham Mountain*. She has also written a romantic cozy mystery trilogy, *Nosy in Nebraska*, and her novel *Golden Days* is part of the *Alaska Brides* anthology. You can find out more about Mary's upcoming books at www.maryconnealy.com and www.mconnealy.blogspot.com.

Mary lives on a Nebraska ranch with her husband, Ivan, and has four grown daughters: Joslyn (married to Matt), Wendy, Shelly (married to Aaron), and Katy. And she is the grandmother of one beautiful granddaughter, Elle. And even though she *begged*, Barbour Publishing would *not* put Elle on the cover of *Montana Rose*.

OTHER BOOKS BY MARY CONNEALY

LASSOED IN TEXAS SERIES:

Petticoat Ranch
Calico Canyon
Gingham Mountain

Alaska Brides (a romance collection)
Nosy in Nebraska (a cozy mystery collection)